THE NEXT VICTIM

Hannah kept wondering why this was happening to her. Two people had been murdered, and somebody was telling her in advance how they would die. But why were they killed?

Someone else stepped into the rest room. Hannah heard footsteps on the tiled floor. For a moment she didn't move. Then she opened her stall door and looked around.

The stall next to hers was empty. There was nobody by the sinks, either. She could have sworn someone was in the bathroom with her a minute ago. She glanced over toward the sinks again and noticed a small black rectangular box on the edge of the counter.

It was a videocassette.

Hannah glanced at the tape. There was no label on it, probably something recorded live or off a TV. From the tape around the spools, she could see the movie had been stopped at a certain scene. She knew when she put that video in the VCR and pressed "Play," she would see another murder sequence.

She knew that her secret admirer was planning to kill again.

And he wanted her to see how he would do it. . . .

BOOKS BY KEVIN O'BRIEN

ONLY SON

THE NEXT TO DIE

MAKE THEM CRY

WATCH THEM DIE

Published by Kensington Publishing Corporation

WATCH THEM DIE

Kevin O'Brien

PINNACLE BOOKS
Kensington Publishing Corp.
http://www.kensingtonbooks.com

PINNACLE BOOKS are published by

Kensington Publishing Corp.
850 Third Avenue
New York, NY 10022

All Kensington Titles, Imprints, and Distributed Lines are available at special quantity discounts for bulk purchases for sales
promotion, premiums, fund-raising, and educational or institutional use. Special book excerpts or customized printings can
also be created to fit specific needs. For details, write or phone
the office of the Kensington special sales manager: Kensington
Publishing Corp., 850 Third Avenue, New York, NY 10022,
attn: Special Sales Department, Phone: 1-800-221-2647.

Pinnacle and the P logo Reg. U.S. Pat. & TM Off.

First Pinnacle Books Printing: May 2003

10 9 8 7 6 5 4 3 2 1

Printed in the United States of America

This book is for my buddy, Dan Monda

ACKNOWLEDGMENTS

Without my editor at Kensington Books, John Scognamiglio, I never would have gotten this book written. My thanks to John for his encouragement, his honesty, and his friendship. I'm also grateful to many of my other friends at Kensington, especially the dynamic Doug Mendini.

Many thanks also to my agents, Mary Alice Kier and Anna Cottle.

For helping me punch up earlier drafts, another great big thank-you goes to my Writer's Group pals, David Massengill and Garth Stein; Dan Monda (again), and my dear friend, Cate Goethals.

Thanks to the gang at Broadway Video, along with several customers there, for being incredibly supportive, especially Paul Dwoskin, Tony Myers, Sheila Rosen, Tina Kim, Larry Blades, Phoebe Swordmaker, Chad Schlund, and Sarah Banach. I'm also beholden to Barbara Bailey, Michael Wells, and the folks at Bailey/Coy.

Thanks to my neighbors at the Bellemoral, especially Brian Johnson, who helped with some medical information.

I'm also grateful to my friends Marlys Bourm, Dan Annear, Dan and Doug Stutesman, Elin Shriver, John Saul and Michael Sack, and Terry and Judine Brooks, for all their support and encouragement. And a very special thank-you to the very terrific Tommy Dreiling.

Finally, thanks to my wonderful family.

Prologue

He was crushing her, but Rae didn't complain. The last thing he probably needed right now was her barking instructions at him. He seemed so nervous and awkward. He acted as if this were their first time. And it wasn't.

She was trapped beneath him on his unmade bed. All around the darkened bedroom, strategically placed votive candles flickered. A couple of incense sticks were smoldering in an ashtray on the nightstand. The smoky, spicy scent had become overpowering. Rae thought about asking him to open a window, but she didn't say anything. All the windows were closed, along with the blinds.

He'd already stripped off his shirt, and now he was on top of her, unbuttoning her blouse. If only he'd climb off for a moment, she could get a breath and maybe wriggle out of her clothes herself. She wanted this to be pleasant for both of them.

He'd been so good to her lately, a godsend. Anyone else would have dismissed her as a crazy, dumb, paranoid blonde. But he took her seriously. And he wanted to protect her.

For the last six weeks, someone had been following her. Rae had even caught the shadowy figure videotaping her on a couple of occasions. Both times, she didn't get a good look at the man. Once, he was in an old burgundy-colored Volvo outside the hotel where she worked as an events coordinator. The sun reflected off the car window, obscuring his face. But she could make out someone holding a video camera. She never saw that Volvo again.

Rae caught him filming her a second time during a date with Joe. It was just a week before Joe died. They were dining at a fancy Italian bistro, where they'd been seated by the front window. She'd heard somewhere that máitre'd's often placed good-looking couples near the front windows because they attracted business. Rae and Joe were discussing this when she noticed the man with the video camera standing in a cafe across the street. By the time she pointed him out to Joe, her "secret admirer" had disappeared.

Joe hadn't taken her very seriously. He never called her paranoid or crazy. He merely humored her, making maddening little remarks like *This stalker character must have good taste to go after you.*

Joe wouldn't have thought it was so cute if he were the one getting those strange calls in the middle of the night. Half the time, Rae was afraid to answer the phone. And whenever she stepped outside her apartment, she was constantly looking over her shoulder.

Though he'd made certain she never really saw him, this stalker obviously wanted her to know she was being followed. He wanted her to be scared. He even let her know in advance that Joe would die. He'd left her a sign, forecasting Joe's death from a rooftop fall.

When Rae tried to warn him that his life might be in danger, Joe had just nodded, smiled, and said he would be careful. If only he'd listened to her and believed her, how different things might have been.

The police said Joe Blankenship had been "under the influence" when he'd toppled from the roof of his apartment building. But Rae knew better. She was the only one who knew.

Whoever said "Knowledge is power" was wrong. Rae had never felt so alone and vulnerable after Joe's death. Yet a man who truly wanted to help her had been there all the time. For a brief period, she'd actually thought he might be the one stalking her. How silly. He wanted to look after her. He took her seriously.

He talked about turning the tables on the man with the video camera. He wanted to catch him on film. Had she thought about going to Joe's apartment building and asking if anyone had spotted a maroon Volvo parked nearby on the night Joe fell from the roof? Maybe they could recall part of a license-plate number.

He said he wouldn't let her out of his sight. No one would harass or threaten her as long as he was around.

This was Rae's third night in a row at his place. She wasn't in love with him; she even told him so. Still, he made her feel safe, and that was good enough right now.

He opened her blouse, then kissed her breasts. Smiling, Rae ran her fingers through his hair. With his tongue, he drew a warm wet line up to the base of her neck. Rae shuddered gratefully. Maybe he wasn't so clumsy after all.

Still, he was squashing her.

"Babe, could you move for just a sec?" she finally piped up. "Honey?"

With a grunt, he shifted to one side, but he just felt heavier. Pinned beneath him, Rae was sinking into the mattress. "Sweetie?" she said, hardly able to talk. He was crushing the breath out of her.

He reached toward the nightstand and flicked a switch on a cord. A strobe light sputtered on, like a series of camera flashes. It was too bright, almost blinding.

He reached for something else, something hidden between the mattress and box spring, but Rae couldn't see it. His every movement seemed fractured by the strobe light. Rae thought he might have grabbed a condom. Whatever it was, he quickly slipped it into his back pocket.

He still had on his jeans. As he ground his pelvis against hers, she felt his erection through the layers of clothes.

Rae squirmed beneath him. "Wait," she protested. "I'm not comfortable—"

"It's okay to scream if you want," he whispered. "That's why I closed the windows."

"I don't want to scream," she said, with a weak laugh. "Why would you say that? What are you talking about?"

In the staccato light, she saw his face contorted in a grimace as he writhed on top of her, A vein bulged in his neck.

Something's wrong here, she thought. A panic swept through her. Rae began to shake uncontrollably. She felt trapped beneath his weight.

"Please," she said, trying to push him away. "I just need you to climb off me for a second. Really . . ."

He kissed the side of her neck. He didn't seem to be listening. He kept slamming his pelvis against hers. It hurt.

"Please, stop," she cried, struggling now. "I—I just need to . . . to change positions. You're crushing me. . . ."

"Can't move," he muttered, his breath swirling in her ear. "You'll ruin it."

"Ruin it? What do you mean?"

He reached into his back pocket. His movements seemed jerky in the flickering light. Rae saw something shiny in his hand.

It looked like a knife.

Oh, dear God, no, this isn't happening. Desperately, Rae fought to get out from under him. She wanted to scream, but she couldn't even breathe. Hard as she tried, Rae couldn't budge an inch.

But then he shifted around, and all at once, his knees were pinning down her arms.

In the fractured light, she saw him drawing back the knife. Sweat glistened on his face. His eyes looked so cold.

Suddenly Rae realized those cold eyes had been studying her for the last few months.

And she realized she was going to die.

Terrified, she struggled beneath him, but it was useless.

"Don't move. Don't ruin it, baby," he whispered, raising the knife over his head. He smiled a little. "I need you in camera range."

* * *

The death of Rae Palmer was documented by two concealed video cameras that night.

Rae's self-appointed director and leading man had over two hours of footage shot in the bedroom that night. Only thirty-five seconds of videotape showed the actual stabbing.

The strobe light made for a murky image at times, and the abundance of blood wasn't quite as evident on tape. He also had to tinker with the sound to raise the volume of her screams. But all in all, he was happy with the results.

He edited the raw footage down to eleven exciting, harrowing minutes. Careful not to take anything away from Rae's final performance, he left his likeness on the cutting-room floor. He became a mere shadowy figure in the foreground, wielding the knife. Watching the final product, he didn't recognize himself at all.

Seeing the video was exhilarating. But he should have remembered. It had happened before. Once he'd done all the work and admired the fruits of his labor, he became overwhelmed with an emptiness, a sort of postpartem depression. There was only one way to remedy that. He knew what he had to do.

He had to find a new leading lady.

One

Hannah glanced at the videocassette in the plain plastic box. There wasn't much tape on the spools, certainly no more than a half hour's worth of viewing. The mystery video had been sitting in the "Return Tape Limbo" drawer behind the counter at Emerald City Video for over two weeks now. In that bottom drawer they stashed defective tapes and DVDs, lost-and-found items, and cassettes dropped off at the store by mistake.

Hannah Doyle had been working at Emerald City Video for eighteen months. In her opinion, every hour at the place had taken its toll on her appearance. Hannah thought she looked pale and tired most of the time. But the customers who saw the pretty, blond clerk with the trim figure wouldn't have agreed with her. Though she was thirty-two years old with a toddler son at home, Hannah's youthful looks had many people assuming she was fresh out of college. A prominent scar on her chin lent some character to her lovely face. People in the store had asked, but Hannah didn't talk about how she got the scar.

Crouched behind the counter, she stared at the mystery cassette. She was always curious about these "wrong return" videos. Customers often asked if she'd ever found any homemade sex tapes among those mistaken returns. Hannah hadn't. After a couple of weeks, she'd always take them home and review the tapes before throwing them out or recycling them.

If the store employees wanted to see sex tapes, they had over two thousand adult titles to choose from.

Emerald City Video was a neighborhood video store, and the neighborhood was one of Seattle's most eclectic. Street urchins who looked as if they'd wandered in to shoplift might be renting an Audrey Hepburn movie on their parents' account. An old lady might be patiently standing in line with *Upstairs, Downstairs* clutched in her liver-spotted hands, while the man in front of her checked out four adult videos.

The shop was ideally located across the street from a mini-mall that housed an Old Navy, Starbucks, and a dozen smaller stores. Emerald City Video's storefront was all windows, allowing Hannah and her coworkers a good look at the bustling street scene. People-watching helped pass the time when business was slow. The employees didn't have to wear uniforms either, and for that, Hannah was grateful.

There were stories painting Emerald City Video's back room as a hot spot of furtive gay sexual activity. But Hannah had never noticed any funny business in the small alcove where they kept the adult titles. The only real trouble she'd encountered in the adult section was a few months back. A nicely dressed, pale man of forty had ducked into the alcove one afternoon, then spent two hours browsing. He finally emerged from the back room and stomped up to the counter, glaring at Hannah. "I was getting sick to my stomach back there, looking at all that filth," he hissed.

Hannah fought the urge to roll her eyes at him. She managed to smile. "Well, all you need to start a membership here is a photo ID, credit card, and a ten-dollar downpayment that applies to your first three rentals."

He'd stormed out of the store, but returned a week later. Now he was one of their regular customers, renting up to ten adult titles a week. He was also one of Emerald City Video's rudest, most obnoxious customers. There was a note on his account whenever they pulled his name up: *This guy's a creep. Argues late fees. Don't take it personally. He's rude to everyone. Be nice.*

He was one of the exceptions. Most customers at Emerald City Video were friendly. Hannah knew many of them by name now. She had a window into their lives too. She'd heard it all:

"I need to take my boyfriend off my account. We broke up. . . ."

"I have a friend who's going to be renting for me for the next few weeks. I have to go in for surgery on Wednesday; then I'll be on chemo. . . ."

"Sorry about the late fee. My mom died, and I had to go to back to Nebraska. . . ."

"I believe my husband has an account with you, and I'd like to know if he's been renting any adult videos, specifically gay videos. . . ."

"We never got a chance to watch it. We both fell asleep. The baby has kept us up so late the last couple of nights. . . ."

Hannah became sympathetic ear, nursemaid, confidante, beard, and cheerleader to scores of people. She'd even learned some sign language to communicate with their deaf customers. But she still hadn't mastered Korean, Japanese, Chinese, or Spanish.

At the moment, only a handful of customers were in the store. Hannah's pick, *Strictly Ballroom*, played on the three strategically located TVs. Her coworker, Scott, stood at his register, staring down at her. "Hannah, for God's sake, take the damn tape home and look at it. You know you're dying to, which, by the way, is kind of pathetic. You really need a life."

The phone rang, and he answered it. Twenty-six, tall, and thin, Scott Eckland was almost too handsome. He had spiky, gelled black hair, deep-set blue eyes, a male model's cheekbones, and a strong jawline. With his video store salary, he dressed in Salvation Army finds that never quite came together. Today he wore a pair of green plaid slacks and a yellow shirt that was missing all its buttons. So he'd stapled up the front. The look was a cross between cutting-edge trendsetter and total nerd.

"God help us all," he muttered, hanging up the phone. "If I have to reserve one more of the new-season *Sopranos*, I'll kill someone." He logged the reservation into his register, then glanced at Hannah again.

Shutting the drawer, she started to slip the tape into her purse, but hesitated.

"So take it home already," Scott groaned. "The stupid video has been here—what—two weeks? You're not violating anyone's privacy. And if there's a cute naked guy on the tape, you're giving it to me."

Hannah dropped the cassette in her purse.

Suddenly, and in steady succession, one person after another began filing into the store, many of them dropping tapes in the return bin. "Oh, crap," Hannah whispered. "It's going to get crazy."

She was right. It got crazy. The phones started ringing, too. About a dozen customers descended on the front counter at the same time. Hannah and Scott were swamped, but they managed to handle the rush without a problem— for a while at least.

Only two people were waiting in line behind the smartly dressed brunette who stepped up to Hannah's register. With her hair pulled back in a tight bun, the thirty-something woman's tanned face had a pinched look. She set her video on the counter. "Finkelston is the account," she mumbled, reaching into her purse.

"Did you say 'Hinkleston'?" Hannah asked. "H-I-N-K-L—"

"There's no 'H' in Finkelston." She spoke in a loud, patronizing tone. "There's never been an 'H' in Finkelston. F-I-N-K-E-L-S-T-O-N."

"Cindy Finkelston?" Hannah said.

Nodding, the brunette woman pulled out a twenty-dollar bill.

Hannah decided she didn't like Cindy Finkelston very much. Now that she pulled up the account, she disliked her even more. She remembered writing the note on her account: *REWIND!!! And tell this slob that she returned Of-fice Space with ketchup all over the cassette. Took forever to clean it off—Erase when done—Hannah.*

Hannah started to delete the note. "Well, there's a couple of things here," she said gently. "Um, it says 'please rewind.' And you returned *Office Space* to us with ketchup on the tape and the box."

"Okay, whatever." The woman rolled her eyes. "I happen to be in a hurry."

"Yeah, well, sorry to take up your time," Hannah muttered. "You also have a late fee of twelve dollars."

"I can't pay that now," she replied. "I don't have the money."

Hannah stared at the twenty-dollar bill in Cindy Finkelston's hand. "I'm sorry, but we have to settle late charges before we can rent to you."

"You know, I can just walk down the street to Block-buster," she retorted, her voice growing louder. "I don't have to take this crap. What's the late charge for anyway? It can't be right."

Hannah pulled the date from her account. *"Panic Room* came back—"

"I returned that the very next day," Cindy Finkelston interrupted.

Hannah saw the line of people behind Cindy getting longer. "Actually, it was rented on August eighth, due back the ninth, and returned on August twelfth. Three days late at four dollars a day, that makes twelve dollars."

"I thought that was a three-day rental."

Hannah stared at her. "Which is it? Did you return it 'the very next day,' as you just said, or did you think it was a three-day rental?"

Cindy seemed stumped for a moment; then she became indignant. "What's your name?" she demanded. "I want to talk to your supervisor."

"My name's Hannah. And the manager went home at

five. She'll be back in tomorrow when the store opens at ten."

"Well, you just lost me as a customer," Cindy announced—for half the store to hear. "You can close my account."

Hannah shrugged. "I'm sorry. I can't close your account until your late charges are paid off."

One of the store regulars was in line behind Cindy. "Lady, just pay the stupid fee and stop giving her a hard time!"

"It's none of your goddamn business," Cindy growled, shooting him a look. She turned her glare at Hannah. "I don't have to take this shit from some nobody clerk." She shoved the cassette across the counter, and it fell on the floor by Hannah's feet. "I'll be talking with your superior. If I want to close my account here, I certainly can. Do you want a lawsuit? I'm a paralegal for a very prestigious firm. I'll take legal action."

Cindy flounced toward the door.

"See you in *People's Court*!" Scott called.

"I can help the next potential witness," Hannah announced. She still had Cindy's account on the computer screen, and quickly typed in a note: *Accept no substitutes or imitations. This woman is a genuine asshole.*

She hated letting people like Cindy Finkelston bother her. She could go for days with one nice customer after another; then someone like Cindy Finkelston could bring her down in a minute. The truth be told, she was indeed "some nobody clerk," stuck in a go-nowhere job and barely making ends meet for herself and her four-year-old son. Free video rentals were poor compensation for the time she had to spend away from her little boy.

Hannah had to remind herself that, despite everything, she and her son were far better off than they'd been two years ago. They were safe now. No one knew where they were. All things considered, she was lucky to have this go-nowhere job and her little two-bedroom apartment. Maybe she didn't get to spend much time with her son, but at least they were together. These were precious days. She was indeed lucky.

The past hadn't caught up with her yet.

Her name was Cindy Finkelston. Anyone who had been in Emerald City Video forty-five minutes before certainly knew that. She'd even spelled out the name for all to hear, loudly enunciating each letter. Her grand exit had been quite an attention-getter as well.

She probably had no idea that someone was videotaping her.

It was no stroke of fate that he'd had his camera with him. He always carried it around. Today his video camera was concealed in a shoulder-strap carryall that looked like a laptop computer bag. He often filmed people on the sly that way. It just so happened he'd been keeping surveillance of the video store when Hannah Doyle had her run-in with Ms. Finkelston. He hadn't expected to find someone like Cindy today. It was almost as if Cindy had chosen him rather than the other way around.

Now he was following her, videotaping her every move. After leaving Emerald City Video, Cindy walked two blocks to the Thriftway. On tape, he caught her slipping an expensive bottle of shampoo into her coat pocket.

Her BMW was parked in a three-minute loading and unloading zone in front of an apartment building. She'd been in that space for at least an hour now. It had grown dark, and the streetlights were on.

Obviously, Cindy Finkelston lived her life getting away with as much as she could, not caring about anyone else. If she ever became the victim of some freak accident, no one would really miss her.

He was on foot, and thought he'd lose her once she drove off. But three stop signs—and one particularly irate pedestrian whom Cindy almost mowed down at a crosswalk—helped him keep a tail on her for six blocks. Still, he was winded by the time he filmed her pulling into a gated lot beside the sterile, slate-colored, five-story apartment building. He wondered about the picture quality for this impromptu night shoot, but decided to take his chances and keep filming.

Cindy climbed out of her BMW, took the stolen shampoo from her pocket, and transferred it to the bag of groceries. Once she stepped inside the lobby, he zoomed in with the camera, catching her in close-up through the glass doors as she rang for the elevator.

The camera panned and scanned across the ugly building for a couple of minutes. Then a light went on in one of the fifth-floor windows. He zoomed in again, and taped Cindy as she came to the window and opened it a crack. She stepped away, out of camera range.

He turned off the video camera. He'd taped enough of Cindy Finkelston—for now. She wasn't really that important. He didn't want to waste any more time with a supporting player.

His new leading lady required some looking after.

Two

Hannah had walked this way home from work hundreds of nights. It was only six blocks from the store to the front door of her building. The route she took was well traveled and well lit. Not a bad night for a walk, either. Trees swayed and leaves rustled in the chilly October breeze. The stars were out, too.

Approaching a narrow alleyway between two apartment buildings, Hannah suddenly stopped in her tracks. A passing car's headlights swept across the dark alcove, briefly illuminating a man who stood by the dumpsters. He wore a bulky jacket and a hunter's hat.

A chill ran through Hannah. Her heart seemed to stop for a moment. Picking up her pace, she hurried past the alley and glanced at him out of the corner of her eye.

He stood in the shadows. Hannah thought he was drinking something from a bottle. But then she realized that he was holding a video camera.

Just a minute ago, she'd been thinking about her tired feet, and getting home in time to tuck in her son before he fell asleep. She'd been thinking about a shower and the leftover pasta for dinner. But now, none of that mattered. She just needed to get away from this strange man in the hunting cap who was videotaping her.

Hannah started to run. Her apartment building was another three blocks away. She glanced over her shoulder.

He hadn't emerged from the alley yet. Was he really

recording her? Maybe he'd just found a broken video camera in the dumpster. Maybe it wasn't even a video camera. Her eyes were tired; she could have been mistaken. After staring at the register's computer screen all day at work, it was a wonder she could focus on anything.

Hannah slowed down for the last block. She kept peeking over her shoulder. No one was following her. She felt silly, frightened by a harmless dumpster-diver lurking in an alley. What did she expect, living in the city?

Hannah was still chiding herself and catching her breath as she stepped into the lobby. Her apartment building was called the Del Vista, one of many former hotels built for the Seattle World's Fair in 1962. A three-story, tan-brick structure, it offered Space Needle views in many of the units, including Hannah's two-bedroom apartment. Hannah had gotten it cheap because the previous tenant had committed suicide in the living room. Seattle housing regulations required that landlords pass along such information to potential renters. Hannah didn't know how the poor guy did himself in. Revealing those details wasn't part of the housing rule's requirements. All she knew was that word of the suicide drove away prospective tenants and drove down the unit's rental price. She never could have afforded the place otherwise.

She had nothing but junk mail. *"Why be Single?"* was written on one envelope. As Hannah tucked the letters in her bag, she saw the mystery video in there. She'd almost forgotten about it. Probably some customer taped a Seahawks game—or an episode of *ER*. Maybe it was somebody's wedding or a baby's first steps. If she recognized anyone in the video, she could return it to them, do a good deed.

She climbed three flights in the cinderblock stairwell that lead to an outside balcony. Approaching her door, Hannah noticed the flickering light from the TV set in the living-room window. She passed the window and waved at her baby-sitter, Joyce. A husky woman in her early sixties, Joyce sat on the sofa with a bag of Chips Ahoy at her side. She had dyed-red hair and cat-eye glasses. Joyce waved back to Hannah and started to pull herself off the couch.

Hannah beat her to the door. Joyce waddled around the coffee table. "You're going to hate me," she announced. "I polished off the chocolate-chip cookies. If you want dessert tonight, all I left you was Melba toast."

"No sweat," Hannah said. She set her purse and coat on a straight-back chair by the front door. "How's Guy?" she asked. "Is he asleep?"

Joyce switched off the TV. "He's waiting up for you. At least, when I checked on him a couple of minutes ago he was still hanging in there."

Joyce retreated to the kitchen, separated from the living room by a counter. Three tall barstools were lined up by that counter, the closest thing Hannah had to a dining-room table. Her apartment had been furnished entirely with finds from Ikea and secondhand stores. It all blended together nicely. An Edward Hopper print hung on the wall—along with framed movie posters of *The Philadelphia Story* and *Double Indemnity*.

Family photos were also on display: her deceased parents; her favorite aunt, with whom she'd lost touch since moving to Seattle; and, of course, several pictures of Guy.

But there were no pictures of Guy's father.

Hannah didn't talk about him. *He died in a car accident before Guy was born.* That was the story she gave whenever anybody asked; it was the story she'd given Joyce.

Joyce Bremner lived in an apartment building two doors down the block. While walking with Guy, Hannah always used to see her in front of the building, working on the garden. A widow, Joyce had three children and seven grandchildren, none of whom lived in Seattle. She'd made it clear that if Hannah ever needed a baby-sitter, she was available.

Four nights a week Joyce picked up Guy from Alphabet Soup Day Care; then she took him home, cooked dinner, and got him ready for bed. Guy was crazy about her, and so was Hannah.

After being pleasant to people all day, Hannah had very little social energy on tap at night. All she wanted to do was see her son and spend a few minutes with him before he fell asleep. Joyce always seemed to understand that. Once Hannah plodded through the front door, Joyce stayed just long enough to welcome her home and give her an update on Guy. She also told Hannah what they'd had for dinner—usually something canned or processed; Joyce wasn't much of a cook.

As she threw on her raincoat, Joyce revealed that SpaghettiOs had been tonight's fare. Also, they were running low on milk, Parmesan cheese, and, of course, Chips Ahoy.

She opened the door, but hesitated and turned to Hannah. Behind her, the Space Needle was illuminated in the distance. "Before I forget, honey," she said, her brow furrowed, "you had two more hang-ups tonight. I think it's the same person who kept calling and hanging up yesterday. I tried star-six-nine, but both times, it told me the number was blocked."

Hannah sighed. "Like I said last night, I wouldn't worry about it. Probably some telemarketer."

Joyce grimaced a bit. "Well, I thought there was someone on the other end of the line, listening to me. But—I don't know, I've been wrong before, once or twice in my life." She shrugged and blew Hannah a kiss. "Oh, well. Take care, hon. See you tomorrow."

Hannah nodded. "G'night, Joyce." She watched the older woman retreat along the walkway to the stairwell. The night wind kicked up.

A chill passed through Hannah. She stepped back inside and closed the door. Her son was waiting up for her. The thought of him made her smile. How did he know that she really needed to spend some time with him tonight?

Hannah padded down the hallway to his room. Guy's nightstand lamp was still on, but he'd fallen asleep. A picture book of trucks was slipping from his grasp. Studying him, Hannah ached inside. She hadn't gotten a chance to say good night to her little guy.

He was a handsome kid: straight blond hair, beautiful green eyes, and impossibly long lashes. Last week, she'd had him in the cart seat at the supermarket when another woman approached her, asking if she'd ever considered having her son model. "A couple of commercials, and it'll pay for his college education," the woman had said. She'd given Hannah a business card. She'd seemed on the level.

Hannah knew she didn't stand a snowball's chance in hell at putting Guy through college on her video-store salary. Yet she'd thrown out that business card. No matter how much money they offered her, Hannah wouldn't let them put Guy on TV or in a magazine—not the briefest appearance, not the tiniest ad. After all, what if someone recognized him?

She gingerly pulled the book out from under his hand, then set it on the bookcase. Trucks were his latest thing. Just a few months ago, he'd been crazy about rockets and outer space. He still had a mobile of the planets hanging from the ceiling, but Hannah knew that was old hat to him by now. Various Tinkertoy trucks occupied the bookcase where model rockets, star charts, and plastic replicas of the planets had once resided.

Hannah switched off his bed-table lamp. A Bugs Bunny night-light glowed in the corner of the room. Tucking the blanket under Guy's chin, she kissed his forehead. She'd missed him tonight, but they'd have tomorrow morning together.

Hannah's feet started aching again as she retreated to her bedroom. She peeled off her outer clothes, then wandered into the bathroom.

Under the shower's warm, wet current, she began to relax. She let the gushing water wash away all the stress and bitterness.

Once she'd dried off, Hannah changed into a sweatshirt and flannel pajama bottoms. She poured a glass of wine, then set some leftover pasta on the stove.

While dinner cooked, Hannah fished the mystery video

from her bag and turned on the TV. She ejected a tape from the VCR: her daily recording of *The Young and the Restless*. All those free videos to choose from, and here she was taping silly soap operas and sneaking a peek at someone's home video.

Hannah popped the cassette into her machine, then sat on the sofa arm and sipped her wine. "Oh, my God," she murmured, suddenly mesmerized.

She'd gotten someone's homemade sex tape. On the screen, a woman Hannah didn't recognize squirmed beneath a man in bed. The picture quality was very professional, even with the dim lighting. But the shirtless man was out of focus. He seemed like a mere shadow hovering over the attractive, slim, thirtyish blonde. Hannah couldn't tell if the woman was in ecstasy—or just uncomfortable. While writhing beneath her partner, she winced and rolled her eyes. He opened her blouse and began kissing her breasts.

Hannah watched with fascination as they kissed and fondled each other on the bed. Somehow, the man seemed to elude the camera the entire time. Hannah could see his actions, but she couldn't see him, couldn't even make out his hair color. He was Caucasian; that was the only thing she could tell about him. Otherwise, he was just a blur in the foreground. The woman was the star of this little movie. And Hannah got the impression that she didn't know she was being videotaped.

The movie must have been shot with two steady, mounted cameras, then edited, because the angles changed at different times, yet all the movements matched. Whoever made this video certainly knew what he was doing.

For a moment, the woman's face was obscured by the man as he reached toward the nightstand. He must have switched on a strobe lamp, because the scene became illuminated by pulsating flashes of light. The woman seemed disoriented.

Hannah thought she saw him pull a knife out from under the mattress. She wanted to stop the video; play it back and see if she was mistaken. She glanced around for the remote, but didn't see it. Her living room was bathed in the stark, flickering light from the TV screen.

On the video, the man's lovemaking had now become frenzied. Almost in sync with the frantic, pulsating strobe, he pounded against her with his pelvis. The woman seemed to be pleading with him to stop. Hannah saw him raise the knife. "Oh, my God," she murmured. "What is this?"

She watched in horror as he plunged the knife down into the woman's chest. He did it again, and again. The pretty blonde started to scream, but then she appeared to go into shock. She stopped struggling.

He kept stabbing her. Yet the wide-eyed, dazed expression on her face didn't change. Her body took each savage, bloodletting blow without so much as a twitch. The woman was dead.

Numbly, Hannah stared at the TV screen—and at that poor woman. The blurry form of a man finally pulled away from his victim. The blonde lay amid the bloody bed sheets, naked and perfectly still, illuminated by the staccato light flashes. Her eyes were open, unblinking.

"Jesus," Hannah whispered. "This looks real."

From the sidewalk, he had a view of the third-floor balcony walkway—and her living-room window. She was watching the tape, he could tell. He could see the rapid, flickering light from her TV, like a lightning storm going on inside her apartment. It was the strobe lamp in the video.

Hannah was watching the murder right now.

He wished he could see her reaction. Was she terrified? If only he were watching the movie with her: That would have been something. Like a great director, he manipulated his audience. He pulled the strings, and Hannah Doyle responded.

He wanted to be there while she responded.

Soon enough, he told himself. He would get closer to her—much, much closer.

The video was rewinding in Hannah's VCR.

She took her dinner off the stove and threw it away. The videotape had made her sick. She couldn't stop shaking. She kept telling herself that it couldn't have been real.

In fact, the home video seemed eerily familiar. That death scene had already been played out by Tom Berenger and Diane Keaton at the end of *Looking for Mr. Goodbar*. It was the climax of Richard Brooks's 1977 film: the strobe light, the couple in the throes of violent sex, him pulling out a knife, then repeatedly stabbing her in the chest. The video's blond victim even had the same death stare as Diane Keaton in the original movie.

Hannah refilled her wineglass and stared at her blank TV screen. She needed to prove to herself that the tape was just a reenactment, a fake.

She took another gulp of wine, then edged up close to her TV screen. She pressed "Play." With a hand over her mouth, she forced herself to watch.

Hannah thought she'd catch a false note. But the more she saw, the sicker she felt. It was like studying the Zapruder film. Every frame was real. Wincing, she played the stabbing in slow motion, and it didn't look fake. She studied the dead woman, and didn't see her draw a breath or blink.

At the end of the video, Hannah was shaking again.

It didn't make sense. How could this reenactment of *Looking for Mr. Goodbar* look so real? More important, who had made the movie, and why?

Whoever had dropped off the video at the store must have been a customer. But Hannah didn't recognize the woman in the film, and despite her constant scrutiny, she couldn't make out the killer. He must have edited himself out.

Hannah ejected the tape. She thought about calling the

police. Instead, she called Tish, the store manager, at her home.

"Tish, it's Hannah. Did I wake you?"

"No, I'm up. What's going on?"

"Well, I took home a video that's been sitting in the limbo drawer for two weeks. I just looked at it, Tish. I think it's some kind of snuff film."

"You're kidding," Tish murmured.

"I wish I was," Hannah said. "In it, this poor woman is stabbed over and over again. And it looks very real. Maybe you could take a look at it, Tish. I think it's some kind of reenactment of Diane Keaton's murder in *Looking for Mr. Goodbar*. Maybe it's just a hoax and I'm too freaked out right now to see it. You might recognize the woman in the video; I didn't."

"Oh, I'm sure it's nothing, Hannah," her boss said. "Take it from me, I've been working in video stores for over ten years. Snuff films are something you read or hear about, urban legend stuff."

"Well, I wish you'd at least look at this."

"Okay, I'll take a gander," Tish said. "Bring it in tomorrow. I bet it's somebody's project for a film class or something. Don't let it scare you, Hannah. Mellow out. Pour yourself a glass of wine."

She managed to chuckle. "I'm way ahead of you."

After Hannah hung up the phone, she studied the unmarked cassette again. Perhaps she'd see it was fake if she looked at the tape just one more time. But she couldn't. Hell, she didn't even want the damn thing in her apartment overnight.

Hannah stuffed the cassette in a bag and set it on the kitchen counter. Then she topped off her glass of wine and opened the Melba toast.

Hannah flipped her pillow over, gave it a punch, and turned to look at the luminous digital clock on her night-

stand: 2:53 A.M. What had made her think she would fall
asleep tonight?

Every time she closed her eyes, she kept seeing that dead
woman lying amid the rumpled, bloodstained sheets. Hannah had been tossing and turning for the last two hours.

She finally flung back the covers and climbed out of bed.
She wore a T-shirt and flannel pajama bottoms. Rubbing her
forehead, she staggered toward the bathroom next door. She
glanced down the hallway.

And gasped.

A shadowy figure moved at the end of the hallway. For a
second, all she saw was a blur, like that faceless killer in the
video. It darted away so quickly it might have been a
ghost—maybe that young man who had killed himself in
this apartment.

Hannah stood paralyzed for a moment. Goose bumps
crept over her arms. Her feet grew cold, and she realized the
front door must be open. Had someone broken into the
apartment? Was he still there?

She stepped in front of Guy's doorway, instinctively
blocking anyone from getting in. The door was closed, but
she heard Guy breathing as he slept. Hannah told herself
that he was all right.

Another shadow swept across the hallway wall. She was
dead certain someone was in her living room.

"I have a gun!" Hannah heard herself say in a loud, shrill
voice. Her whole body tingled.

Not a sound. After a minute, Hannah caught her breath,
then crept toward the living room. She switched on the light.
No one.

The curtains on the window were open a few inches. She
noticed the headlights of a car coming down the street, three
stories below. Were those the shadows she'd seen?

Hannah checked the front closet. Then she peeked into
Guy's room.

He was sitting up in bed, looking utterly terrified.
"Mommy?"

"It's okay, honey," she said, still trying to catch her breath. "Just stay there, sweetie. Everything's all right."

She poked her head in the bathroom, then returned to the living room. She checked the door. "Oh, shit," she whispered.

It wasn't locked. She could have sworn she'd double-locked it earlier in the evening.

But that had been at least three glasses of wine ago. Just last night, she'd resolved to cut back on the chardonnay consumption.

Her heart still racing, Hannah double-locked the door. She glanced around the apartment. Nothing was missing. Nothing had been disturbed. Was she drunk? Maybe she was just a little paranoid after watching that creepy video.

She checked her purse—just where she'd left it, on one of the barstools at the kitchen counter. Inside, her wallet, cash, and credit cards were still there.

"Mom!" Guy cried out. "Mommy, where are you?"

Hannah hurried back to Guy's room. He was still was sitting up in bed, clutching the bedsheets to his chin. "There was a scream," he murmured.

Hannah smoothed his disheveled blond hair. Her hand was shaking. "I, um, I just had a nightmare, honey," she whispered, trying to smile. "I'm sorry I woke you."

Guy squinted at her. "What did you dream?"

Hannah shrugged. "I can't remember now. Isn't that silly?"

Sighing, she sat down on the edge of his bed. She kept having to tell herself that they were all right. Safe.

"Think you can go back to sleep now?" she asked.

Guy yawned, then tugged at the bedsheets. "Could you stay a little longer, and make the choo-choo sound?"

Hannah kissed his cheek. "Okay, just pretend the train is carrying you off to Dreamland."

She swayed back and forth, rocking the bed ever so slightly. "Listen to the train," she whispered. Softly she began lulling him to sleep with her rendition of a locomotive. "Choo-choo-choo-choo-choo-choo . . ."

"Are you still scared?" he muttered sleepily.

"No, I'm okay, honey," she said, with a nervous laugh.

"It was just a bad dream, Mom."

"Sure it was," she agreed, patting his shoulder. "Now get some sleep. It'll be morning soon."

Three

For the last five minutes, they had been looking at static on the TV screen.

Hannah and the store manager, Tish, were in the cluttered closet that was the employee break room. There were a desk and chair, and several shelves crammed with old receipts, defective tapes, office supplies, and one tiny television with a built-in VCR. Tish screened allegedly flawed videos on this TV to make sure complaining customers weren't just trying to score a free comp rental.

But this morning, Hannah and Tish were crammed in that little room, watching the *Goodbar* copycat video. It was a continual gray blizzard. Standing behind Tish in the chair, Hannah reached past her and tried the fast-forward button. Nothing. More static.

"Sure doesn't look like Diane Keaton," Tish cracked.

"I don't know what happened," Hannah murmured.

"Do you think you brought the wrong tape back?" Tish offered.

Hannah shook her head. "I couldn't have. I remember last night taking it out of the VCR and putting it on the kitchen counter."

"Well, maybe you taped over it by accident," Tish said.

Bewildered, Hannah stared at the static on the TV screen. Had she erased the tape? She couldn't have been that drunk last night, though she certainly had a hangover this morning.

"Well, fine," Tish sighed, getting to her feet. "My one shot at seeing a snuff film, and you bring me fifteen minutes of snow."

A buxom black woman in her mid-forties, Tish had a beautiful face and long, straight hair she always pulled back with a barrette. She wore a pair of jeans, boots, and an oversized purple V-neck sweater. Tish, along with her girlfriend, Sandra, had been the owner and manager of Emerald City Video for almost eleven years.

She squeezed past Hannah and started out of the break room. "C'mon, let's get these returns checked in before the store opens."

Hannah ejected the tape from the VCR, then wandered toward the front counter.

Tish was at the register, stacking up the returned videos and DVDs.

"You know, I woke up early, early this morning," Hannah said. "And I thought someone was in the apartment. Maybe somebody switched the tapes."

Tish stared at her. "You had a break-in? And you didn't call the cops?"

"I said I *thought* someone was there." She shrugged. "When I checked, I didn't see anyone, and nothing was missing. I figured I was wrong. Only now, I don't know."

Tish looked at her as if she were crazy.

Hannah started filing away DVDs. She couldn't explain it. Hell, she didn't know what to believe. She'd had a run-in with a bitchy customer last night, gone home, skipped dinner, and downed a glass of wine. Then she'd started to look at a video, and it scared the hell out of her. Two and a half glasses of Chardonnay later, she had thought someone was in the apartment. She didn't want to share any of this with Tish. She didn't want her to know that she sometimes drank too much.

"I don't get it." One hand on the counter and the other on her hip, Tish frowned at her. "I mean, if you really think someone broke into your place last night to rip off what looked like a snuff film, maybe it really was a snuff film. You might want to contact the police."

Hannah tried to keep busy with the DVDs. She sighed. "They'll just say it was a hoax. It's what you thought last night. You were trying to convince me it was someone's project for a film class. You said so yourself; there's no such thing as a genuine snuff film. They're all fake."

"Well, maybe you found a real McCoy. What's the harm in putting in a call to the cops, huh? Let them know what happened—"

"No," Hannah said. "It's too late to call them now. There's nothing to back up my story. The video's just static now. I'll come across as some nutcase. Please, let's just drop it. No need to call the police, really. I don't want you to."

"You sure?" Tish asked.

"Of course," she replied. Hannah finished filing DVDs and started in on the tapes. She could feel Tish studying her. After a minute, Hannah glanced at the clock on the wall, then at the door. "Time to open up," she said. "And Howard's waiting. He'll want to know *What's new in new releases?*"

"Yeah, goddamn pain in the ass," Tish muttered, sauntering toward the door. "Always wants me to recommend something, puts me through the wringer, and never rents a damn thing I tell him to." She unlocked the door and opened it. "Well, Howard, how's my favorite customer?"

"What's new in new releases?" the older man asked.

"Come on over here," Hannah heard Tish say. "Let's take a look. . . ."

Hannah continued to file away the DVDs. She hoped she'd gotten through to Tish about not calling the police. If the video had still been intact, and they'd determined it was real, she would have asked Tish to handle everything. She'd have asked to be left out of it.

Only a week ago, she'd confirmed once again that it still wasn't safe for her to become involved with the authorities in any way.

In the store, they'd been showing a new comedy called *Way Out There*. Hannah had recognized one of the actors as a fellow student from her days in Chicago's Second City troupe. They used to hang out together.

Way Out There was still playing when Hannah took her break. She dropped ten dollars in the change box, pulled out a roll of quarters, then went across the street to the mall. From a pay phone, she called an old friend in Chicago, Ann Gilmore. Ann had also been at Second City.

Hannah caught her at home.

"Hannah? Well, hi. Are you okay?"

"Yeah, I'm doing all right. It's so good to hear your voice, Ann. Makes me homesick." She meant it, too. She wished she didn't have to call her from some public pay phone with all these people around. She covered one ear to block out the music from Old Navy next door.

"Is Guy all right?" Ann asked, concern in her tone.

"Oh, yes, he's fine, cute as ever. I just haven't talked with you in so long, I wanted to catch up. You know, I thought I saw Rick Swanson in this movie, um, *Way Out There*."

"Yeah, that's him. He's doing really well. We talked just about a month ago. Your ears were probably burning. Rick was going on and on about how you were the prettiest and most talented of our group."

"Oh, please," Hannah groaned.

"No, he's right. I can't help thinking, you might have gotten the same kind of break as Rick—if only things hadn't turned out the way they had." Ann paused. "I guess you don't need to reminded of that. I'm sorry."

"It's okay, really," Hannah said with a pitiful laugh.

"Rick asked if I ever heard from you at all. I—um, I told him 'no.' I hope that's okay."

"You did the right thing," Hannah murmured. "Thanks, Ann."

"A few weeks ago, I had another visit from a private investigator, a new one this time. Apparently he talked to a bunch of people from our old group. Of course, none of us could tell him anything."

"Well, thanks for letting me know, Ann."

"Are you really doing okay, Hannah? I mean, are you settled wherever you are? Do you have friends and a decent place to live?"

"I'm all right," Hannah replied. "I have friends, too, only none of them know me the way you do, Ann. None of them know."

After she'd hung up, Hannah realized that Ann no longer really knew her either. She'd stood near the phone station in the crowded, noisy mall, and she'd felt so alone.

At the same time, she couldn't let anybody get too close. And she was always looking over her shoulder, always wary of the police.

She couldn't admit that to Tish. There would be too much to explain, too much at risk.

"Excuse me?"

Hannah put aside the DVDs, then turned to smile at the tall young man on the other side of the counter. "Where's *Gandhi?*" he asked.

"He's dead," Hannah quipped. Then she quickly shook her head. "Sorry. Actually that's in Ben Kingsley's section. I'll show you."

Hannah tracked down the tape for the customer. He thanked her, then went off searching for a second movie. On the shelf above Ben Kingsley's section were Diane Keaton movies. But Hannah didn't see *Looking for Mr. Goodbar* among them. She went back to her register and looked up the movie on the computer. It was supposed to be in the store—just where she'd been looking. The video had last been checked out five months ago.

Someone must have lifted the video from the store. Perhaps they had needed to study the original for a while—in order to get everything right for the reenactment. But was it just an act?

She rang up *Gandhi* for the young man, probably a college student. He was also renting an adult movie called *Good Will Humping*, with a chesty blond bimbo by a blackboard on the cover. *Nice combination,* Gandhi *and porn,* Hannah thought as she rang up the sale.

The tall young man looked her up and down, then gave her a playful smile. Hannah pretended not to notice. She remained polite, professional, and distant. Yet, throughout the transaction, she wondered if he could have been the man in that video last night. After all, it could have been anyone.

Her very next customer was Ned Reemar, a slightly strange man of forty who came in the store every day. He always wore the same clothes: a brown shirt with a Snoopy emblem sewn over the pocket, jeans, and sneakers. He had ugly haircuts, but he wasn't a bad-looking man. In fact, Scott once admitted he'd sleep with Ned if someone gave him a makeover. Now he regretted making the statement, and Hannah still teased him about it. Ned always talked their ears off, mostly about the technical aspects of every film ever made. That wasn't so bad. What was unsettling was Ned's way of picking up personal information about each one of the employees. "Is Hannah married?" he'd asked Scott months ago. "Is Scott gay? Does he have a boyfriend?" he'd asked Hannah.

"I think Nutty Ned wants to be your main man," Hannah had later told Scott. "Maybe he'll get a makeover—just for you."

"Not even with a blindfold and a case of Stoli's would I let him touch me," Scott had replied.

Hannah had always thought Ned was a bit peculiar, but harmless. Yet as she waited on him now, and he complained about the sound on their DVD version of *A Clockwork Orange*, Hannah studied him with a sudden wariness.

For the rest of the day, she regarded practically every male customer with the same apprehension: the strangers, the regulars, the ones she knew and liked, and the few who were jerks. With each man, she couldn't help wondering if there was something more behind the simplest smile, the off-hand polite comment, or even a blank stare. Any one of those men could have been the killer in that video.

Any one of them.

"Do you know what the movie is tonight?"

The man sitting next to Hannah in film class was ruggedly handsome in a Gary Cooper kind of way. He had wavy blond hair, and blue eyes that matched his pale denim shirt. Hannah guessed he was in his mid-thirties. He'd just joined the class a couple of weeks ago. She'd noticed him looking at her several times during the last two sessions. Tonight he'd sat down next to her.

Ordinarily, she might have been flattered. But not tonight. Slouched in his chair-desk, he grinned sheepishly at her. "Hope it's something good," he said. "I'm really bushed. I'm afraid I'll fall asleep."

Hannah gave him a cool smile. "It's *All Fall Down*, with Warren Beatty and Eva Marie Saint. I've seen it before. It's very good."

He planted his elbow on the desk panel. His sleeves were rolled up. Hannah noticed his muscular arms, covered with blond hair. "By the way, my name's Ben," he said, reaching out his hand.

"Hannah." She quickly shook his hand. Then she opened her spiral notebook and tried to look interested in it.

"If I start snoring during the movie, promise you'll give me a nudge."

She didn't look up from her notebook. "If you're so tired, maybe you should have sat in the back, where no one would notice you sleeping."

"But I wanted to sit next to you."

Hannah glanced up at him.

He smiled. "I've been trying to figure out a way of introducing myself to you for a couple of weeks now."

"Well, that's very flattering," Hannah replied. Then she went back to her notebook. "Thanks anyway."

"Ouch," he whispered. "Shot through the heart."

Hannah looked at him again. "Pardon?"

He shook his head. "Nothing. Never mind."

The instructor stepped up to the front of the room. "Tonight we'll be checking out an overlooked classic from John Frankenheimer," he announced.

Hannah tried to concentrate on what he was saying. But all the while, she felt this Ben character in the next chair looking at her. She finally turned to glare at him, but he was staring at their instructor. He actually seemed interested in the lecture.

"Frankenheimer assembled a terrific cast here," the instructor was saying. Perched on the edge of his desk, he was the embodiment of a relaxed, confident authority figure. "They're all at the top of their form: Beatty, Eva Marie Saint, Angela Lansbury, Karl Malden. . . ."

His name was Paul Gulletti. He had a swarthy complexion, dark eyes, and receding black hair. He was a nice dresser, too: expensive sweaters, silk shirts, Italian footwear.

In addition to teaching a film class at the community college, Paul reviewed movies for a popular Seattle weekly newspaper. He also rented at Emerald City Video. Hannah used to think he was kind of a cocky, womanizing creep. His wife was on his account at the video store, but that didn't stop Paul Gulletti from coming on to Hannah, her coworker Britt, and even Tish.

Hannah had been immune to his charm—until he asked her about her mini-reviews. She typed the critiques on index cards, then posted them alongside her Employee Picks for the month. Paul liked Hannah's writing style—and her taste in movies.

"Ever think about reviewing films for a newspaper?" he asked one afternoon in the store. "The money isn't bad. . . ."

Paul said he received 130 dollars for every review. But he wouldn't be reviewing movies much longer. He was preparing to direct his own independent film—as soon as the financing came through. They'd need someone to replace him at the newspaper. He said there was even more money if her reviews got syndicated in other newspapers. Was she interested?

Hannah imagined cutting back on her hours at the store and spending more time with Guy. She figured she could write under a pseudonym to keep her name out of the papers. And she loved creating those mini-reviews. It suddenly seemed possible that she could make a semi-decent dollar with her writing. Womanizing sleazeball or not, Paul Gulletti was offering her a wonderful opportunity.

Paul also suggested she take his film class at the college. "It'll fine-tune your skills," he said. "I think you'll benefit from it. And I'd feel better recommending one of my students as my successor at the paper."

Though Hannah hated giving up precious time with Guy for this class one night a week, it seemed worth her while.

She'd been in the film class for five weeks now. Clearly, she was Paul's favorite student, and all the special attention embarrassed her. She kept Paul at arm's length. She needed his help, but didn't want to become another notch on his bedpost.

Paul's assistant, an arty, edgy young man named Seth Stroud, confirmed for Hannah that his boss did indeed want to get her in the sack. "Professor G. usually picks one female student every year," Seth had confided to her one evening after class a while back. "He leads her around, tells her she's brilliant and he's gonna leave his old lady for her. Then he drops her at the end of the semester. You seem nice. I don't want Paul doing that to you."

"Well, thanks for the warning," Hannah had replied. "But I'm not interested in Professor Gulletti that way." Then she'd added, "You must not think very highly of your boss."

"Actually, he's okay," Seth had admitted, with a shrug. "He's just a shit to women. Hey, do me a favor and don't tell him I said anything, okay?"

Now, whenever Paul asked her to stay after class for something, or picked her to explain the workings of a certain film director, Hannah would steal a look at Seth. Standing at the side of the room, he'd grin and roll his eyes a little. He was an oddly attractive man in his late twenties, with rectangular designer glasses, and brown hair that he'd gelled to stand in a dozen different directions. They'd had only a few brief conversations in the past few months. But Hannah had come to like him.

"Seth, if you could get the lights," Paul announced, clapping his hands together and rubbing them. "From 1962, John Frankenheimer's *All Fall Down.*"

Seth switched off the lights, then stepped over to the projector and started the film. The MGM lion was roaring as Paul made his way down the aisle. He took the seat on Hannah's left.

She caught Seth giving her one of his looks.

Paul leaned toward her. "I called you this week," he whispered. "Didn't you get my message?"

Hannah nodded. "Yes. Sorry I haven't gotten back to you. It's been kind of crazy at work. I was hoping we could talk during the break tonight."

"I thought you could help me with some research," Paul explained, while the music swelled on the film's soundtrack. "It'll get your foot in the door with my managing editor. I'm doing an article for the newspaper on movies that broke the blacklist. Maybe we can discuss it over dinner this week?"

Hannah hesitated.

"Excuse me, Professor," Ben piped up. "I can't hear the movie."

Paul frowned at him, then reached over and touched Hannah's arm. "We'll talk later," he whispered.

Squirming, Hannah sat between the two men. She gazed at the screen.

At the break, Paul said he'd talk with her after class.

Hannah nodded. "Okay. But I promised the sitter I'd be back by ten."

She wandered out to the hallway, where the other students gathered by the vending machines and rest-room doors. Ben

Whats-his-name seemed to be waiting for her. "You were right," he said. "It was a good movie. I didn't nod off. Warren Beatty's character was sure a jerk, though, wasn't he? I thought Eva Marie Saint would be too smart to fall for him."

Hannah gave him a polite smile, then stepped over to the vending machine. "Maybe you ought to bring it up when the class reconvenes for the discussion period."

"I don't think I'll stick around for that." He leaned against the vending machine. "I wasn't exactly gaga for his theories on *Casablanca* last week."

Hannah slipped some coins in the slot, pressed a couple of buttons, then fished her candy from the vending machine's drawer. "Would you like a Good & Plenty?" she asked.

"No," he said, frowning. "Listen, I'm sorry about earlier."

"What do you mean?" she asked.

"I didn't realize you and the teacher . . ." He trailed off. "Well, I heard people in class say you two were together. But I thought you were too smart to fall for a guy like him. Guess I was wrong about you *and* Eva Marie, huh?"

"What?" Hannah said.

"Like I said, I'm sorry." He turned and started down the hall.

Hannah wondered how he'd gotten this misinformation about her and Paul. Had he been asking people about her?

She watched him walk away. Then he ducked into the stairwell.

Hannah decided she would take a cab home from the community college. She could hardly afford a taxi, but it was raining. Besides, she was still feeling a little leery after last night; first seeing that video, then thinking someone was in the apartment. And now, this Ben character. He unnerved her.

Paul was very curious about him. "How well do you know that guy?" he asked, pausing with Hannah outside the empty classroom. Everyone else had already left, including

Seth. "I noticed him talking to you," Paul went on. "He's very good-looking, isn't he? Is he a customer from the store?"

"I don't know him from Adam," Hannah said. "He just sat next to me in class tonight. Up until two hours ago, I never even said 'boo' to the guy. Do you know his last name? You must have it somewhere on a class list."

According to the registration list, his name was Ben Sturges; phone number, 555-3291. Hannah wondered if the number was blocked. She thought about all those hang-ups she'd received lately. Could the calls be traced to his number?

Paul started telling her about his current project. "Some night this week we ought to get together for dinner or drinks and discuss it further."

Hannah sighed. "Well, this week is kind of crazy," she said. "But I really want to work for you, Paul. I can squeeze in the research on my own time, and then e-mail you."

Paul frowned a bit. "Well, then I guess we'll chat on-line later in the week. Listen, why don't you let me drive you home?"

"Oh, well, thanks," Hannah replied. "I don't want you going to any trouble. I was going to take a cab—"

"Okay, suit yourself," Paul grumbled; then he marched down the corridor to his office.

Hannah sighed. Obviously, he was ticked off at her. Otherwise, he'd have insisted on driving her home—just to be polite. After all, it was raining, for God's sake.

She called the cab service from a pay phone by the community college's main entrance.

Eleven blocks, and it cost her six dollars with tip. She'd have to skip lunch tomorrow. Still, the taxi ride kept her out of the rain.

Hannah stepped inside the apartment and pried off her shoes. She woke up Joyce, who had been dozing in front of the TV.

"Guy's fast asleep, the little angel," she told Hannah while collecting her purse and raincoat. "I put a big dent in that bag of Pepperidge Farm cookies. You really shouldn't have bought those. Oh, and no one called tonight, not a single hang-up either. How about that?"

Hannah loaned Joyce an umbrella for the walk home. She locked the door after her, then checked in on Guy, who was asleep. After a shower, Hannah climbed into her T-shirt and flannel pajama bottoms, and threw on a robe. Pouring herself a glass of wine, she plopped down on the sofa and grabbed the remote. She hoped her soap opera would take her mind off everything. She pressed "Play" to make sure the tape hadn't run out early on her program.

What came over the screen wasn't *The Young and the Restless*—or the soap after it. Hannah stared at a young couple, walking down the street. He wore a seersucker suit with a narrow tie, and she had a light coat over her minidress. It took Hannah a few moments to recognize John Cassavetes and Mia Farrow outside the Dakota apartment building in a scene from *Rosemary's Baby*. They walked into a nest of police and onlookers gathered in front of the building. Amid the flashing lights and chaos, Mia got a glimpse of something on the sidewalk.

Hannah knew the movie. Still, she gasped when the camera cut to the bloodied corpse of Mia's neighbor and friend sprawled on the pavement. One of the cops said that the girl had jumped from the building's seventh-floor window.

"What is this?" Hannah muttered. Grabbing the remote, she ejected the movie. She went to the VCR and looked at the videocassette. It wasn't the blank tape she'd slipped into the recorder this morning. It was a store-bought copy of *Rosemary's Baby*. "Where the hell did this come from?" she whispered.

"Well, it's not mine," Joyce told her on the phone, three minutes later. "I've never even seen *Rosemary's Baby*. I don't go in for those scary movies."

"Did you take Guy out tonight?" Hannah asked, thinking they might have had a break-in, a real one this time. Maybe the last one was real, too. "Did you leave the apartment at all?" she pressed.

"No, honey. It started raining shortly after you left. We stayed put."

"Okay, Joyce. Thanks. Sorry to bother you."

Hannah hung up the phone, then went back to the VCR. The carpet was damp in spots, and she figured she must have tracked in some rain earlier. On top of a stack of videocassettes, Hannah found the tape she'd slipped into the machine this morning. She played it in the VCR. It was her soap opera; a new episode she hadn't seen yet, today's episode.

Hannah stepped back from the TV. Again, she felt the cold, wet patches on the carpet beneath her feet. Frowning, she turned and gazed back at her shoes by the front door, just where she'd kicked them off when she had stepped inside. She looked out the window at the continuous downpour.

Someone else had tracked in the rain—and not very long ago, either.

Swallowing hard, Hannah moved toward the door, along the damp trail on the carpet. She'd locked up before taking her shower. Now, with a shaky hand, she reached for the knob and pulled open the door.

"My God," she whispered. How did it get unlocked? Was he still inside the apartment?

She hurried down the hall to Guy's room. A hand over her pounding heart, she listened at the door for a moment, then quietly stepped inside. He was asleep, still breathing. She peeked into his closet.

Hannah checked every closet and every damn corner of the apartment. She made sure all the windows were locked, too. Along the way, she turned on several lights. She and Guy were alone in the apartment, but she still didn't feel safe.

Hannah inspected the door. Whoever had broken in must have jimmied open the long, sliding window, then reached inside and manipulated the door locks.

Hannah wanted to call the police, but she couldn't. They

were probably looking for her, like that private detective in Chicago. She couldn't afford to go to the police.

Instead, she finished her glass of wine and poured another. By half-past midnight, she had a tiny buzz and figured she was the worst mother in the world for getting drunk at a time like this—with her little boy asleep down the hall.

She pulled a broom and saw from the kitchen closet. After measuring the front window and the broom, she set the broom across her two barstools, then sawed off part of the handle. Maybe she wasn't so drunk after all, because the broom handle fit perfectly in the window groove. If anyone wanted to get into the apartment through that window now, he'd have to break the glass.

He would probably be coming back for the tape—as he had last night. She was now convinced that someone had indeed broken into the apartment and switched videotapes on her.

She didn't want to give him a reason to break in again. And she didn't want the damn tape in her apartment tonight. After peeking out the window, Hannah grabbed the cassette, hurried outside, and moved down the walkway a few feet until she was standing directly over the dumpster—three stories below. Someone had left the lid open again.

Whoever had delivered the *Rosemary's Baby* tape was probably watching her right now. She almost hoped he was. She wanted him to know that the tape wouldn't be in her apartment tonight. She wanted him to see her pitching his video over the railing into the dumpster.

The cassette landed on top of a green trash bag in the large bin.

Hannah quickly ducked back in the apartment, and double-locked the door behind her. Then she tugged together the front window drapes, but they still had an inch-wide gap between them.

She grabbed her blanket out of the bedroom, and a hammer from the tool drawer in her kitchen. Hannah curled up on the sofa, with the hammer on the floor beside her. She listened to every little sound in the night. Whenever she opened her eyes, she glanced at the sliver of darkness and moonlight between the drapes.

Hannah didn't really fall asleep until traces of dawn showed through those curtains.

Four

"Mom, are you awake?"

Hannah managed to get her eyes half open. It took her a moment to realize she was lying on the living room sofa. Guy stood in front of her in his underwear. He gave her shoulder a shake. "Mom?"

She cleared her throat. "Hi, honey," she muttered. "What time is it?"

"The big hand is on the eight, and the little hand is on the seven."

"Okay. Go brush your teeth."

Throwing back the blanket, she climbed off the sofa. She couldn't have gotten more than a couple of hours of sleep. She tried to focus on the door and the front window. Everything was locked up. The broom handle was still in the window.

Putting on her robe, Hannah rubbed the sleep from her eyes. With a bit of trepidation, she unlocked the door and opened it. She padded down the walkway a few feet and stared down at the dumpster, still open. She noticed the green trash bag in there, but no video. He'd picked it up.

He'd seen her throw it away last night. How long had he stayed out there? Was he still watching her?

Shuddering, Hannah hurried back inside and locked the door again. She told herself that anyone could have taken the tape. The building's maintenance man, the newspaper deliverer, or maybe a neighbor had absconded with it.

After walking Guy to Alphabet Soup Day Care, she returned home and called the video store. She told Scott she needed a mental health day. "I think it's sleep deprivation," she explained. "Can someone cover for me?"

"Yeah, there's Cheryl," Scott said. "I hate her with the white-hot intensity of a thousand suns, but I'll call her for you. Hope you feel better."

"Thanks. Listen, can you do me another favor? Do we still have our copy of *Rosemary's Baby* in the store?"

"Yeah, hold on a sec."

Hannah waited. She wanted to know if the tape had been stolen. She hadn't noticed an Emerald City Video label on it, but someone could have peeled it off.

Scott got back on the line: "Hannah? It's here. Do you want me to hold onto it for you?"

"No, but can you do me one last favor? Could you go into the computer and see if it was rented recently, maybe returned early this morning? Sorry to be such a pain."

"Want me to donate a lung to you while I'm at it? Ha, just kidding. I'm here to serve. Okay, *Rosemary's Baby* was last rented two weeks ago by Laheart, Christopher. Returned on time. Anything else?"

Hannah sighed. "No, thanks. You're a doll, Scott. I'll be back to work tomorrow. See you then."

After Hannah hung up with Scott, she called Joyce and gave her the night off. Then she phoned her apartment building manager. After some haggling, she persuaded him to let her change the locks on her front door, and add a second dead bolt. Then Hannah called a locksmith and made an appointment for that afternoon.

"I'm sorry." The twenty-something Asian man with the Seattle Mariners sweatshirt shook his head at him. "I can't give out anyone's phone number."

Ben stood at the counter, in front of an open sliding glass

window. The man refusing to help him was alone in the community college's administration office.

"I understand," Ben said, drumming his fingers on the countertop. "But this woman and I are in the same film class, and last night she accidentally left her Palm Pilot on her desk. I want to get it back to her. Her name's Hannah, but I'm not sure about the last name—"

"Tell you what, leave the Palm Pilot with us," the clerk said. "We'll call her."

Ben shook his head. "I don't have it with me right now. I—"

"Then leave us your name and a number where she can reach you." The man slid a pen and a pad of paper across the counter at him. "We'll phone her for you."

Running a hand through his blond hair, Ben sighed. "Listen, I'll be honest. I'm in the same film class with this woman, and I really want to ask her out. I was hoping you might give me her phone number—or at least her last name. Could you throw me a bone here? I mean, I look like a decent enough guy, right?"

The clerk frowned at him. "No, not really. What's your name, anyway? Whose film class are you in?"

Ben took a step back. "Forget about it. Sorry I bothered you."

He turned away from the counter and almost bumped into a tall, thin black woman with tangerine hair. "Excuse me," he muttered, continuing down the hallway.

"Well, hello, Ben!" the woman called. Her tone was singsong, teasing.

He stopped and stared at her. "Oh, hi. How are you doing?" He recognized her from the class. She sat in the back row.

The woman sauntered toward him. She wore jeans, a white peasant blouse, and gobs of silver jewelry. The orange-colored hair was done in a pageboy flip with bangs. It looked like a wig. Her eyelashes were false, too. In fact, Ben had always figured she was really a man. This close, he could see her Adam's apple.

"You don't know my name, do you, Ben?" she asked, one hand on her hip. "Are you embarrassed at the social faux pas?"

He stole a glance at his watch. He didn't feel like chatting, but didn't want to be impolite, either. And there was the whole gender-bender thing that made him slightly uncomfortable, but eager not to offend. Ben tried to smile. "Well, um, I know we're in the same film class, but I don't think we've been introduced."

"You're Ben Sturges. I made it a point to find that out three weeks ago when you started the class. I said to myself, Dede, you are going to get the name of that gorgeous man with the blue eyes and the wavy blond hair." She snapped her fingers. "And, child, I knew your name by the end of the break that first day."

"Well, that's very flattering, thanks, um, Dede." Ben looked back over his shoulder at the door.

"Dede Liscious," she said, patting his shoulder with her man-sized hand. "But what do you care, Ben? You only have eyes for Miss Hannah, the ice-queen blonde. Am I right?"

Ben gave her a wary grin.

"Oh, I saw you try, try, and try again with Miss Thing last night. And I couldn't help overhearing just now. Why do you want that girl's digits? She's not buying or selling, honey. The market is closed. Hannah is the teacher's property."

Eyes narrowed, Ben stared at her.

She nodded, then placed her hand on her chest. "It's been going on for a few weeks now, ever since she started class."

"Well, you certainly know a lot," Ben said, with a forced laugh. "Um, you don't happen to know Hannah's phone number, do you?"

She smiled. "No, Ben, but I can tell you where she works. If you want your heart stomped on by an ice queen, that's your business. You can call Hannah at Emerald City Video. You can call her, Ben. But she won't call you back."

* * *

"Is Hannah working today?" Ben asked.

There were only a couple of customers in the video store. Behind the counter was a petite young woman with long, curly blond hair. She gave Ben a little flirtatious pout. "Hannah called in sick today."

"Sorry to hear that," he said. "Do you know if she'll be in tomorrow?"

The woman shrugged, and flicked her hair. "Not until Monday."

"Oh, she's that sick, huh?"

"No, she has weekends off. She's probably okay. Often when Hannah calls in sick, it's actually because her little boy isn't feeling well or something."

Ben nodded. "Oh, yeah. It's been a while. How old is he now?"

"Four, I think. She brings him in the store every once in a while."

"Have you ever met the father?" Ben asked.

"No," she whispered. "Hannah never talks about him. Did you know him?"

Ben shook his head.

"I think he died a couple of years ago," the young woman said.

"Oh," Ben said. "Well, I guess Paul comes in here quite a lot."

She frowned. "Paul?"

"Paul Gulletti. Isn't he kind of seeing her?"

The clerk laughed. "That's news to me. I don't think Hannah's dating anybody."

"Really? Huh," Ben said, raising his eyebrows. Then he smiled at her and casually leaned on the counter. "Listen, it's been forever since I've seen her. You don't happen to have Hannah's phone number, do you?"

"My coworker probably has it. Want to hold on for a sec?"

"Thanks." Ben watched her retreat to the back room.

The young woman glanced over her shoulder and gave him a big smile. She opened the door to the break room, where Scott sat at the desk, labeling a new shipment of videos.

He looked up from his work and squinted at her. "Cheryl, who were you talking to out there?" he whispered.

"I think he might be an old boyfriend of Hannah's or something. He was asking about her—"

"Yeah, I heard. I was about to come out there. Listen, Cheryl, I don't think Hannah would be especially thrilled that you're telling strangers all about her personal life. Is he a customer? Did you get his name?"

Cheryl frowned. "God, do I have to get, like, a security check on somebody just because he asks a couple of questions? He's cute, and I'm just trying to help. All he wanted was Hannah's phone number."

Shaking his head, Scott got to his feet. He brushed past her and stepped out of the back room. "Um, can I help you—" he started to say, making his way toward the counter. Scott stopped in his tracks.

No one was there.

She was deciding whose Sunday newspaper she'd steal this morning. Dressed in a lavender jogging suit, and with her black hair pulled back in a short ponytail, Cindy Finkelston stood at the mail table in the lobby of her apartment building. She hadn't been jogging. Cindy had power-walked to the coffee shop three blocks away for her usual Sunday morning latte to go.

Some asshole in line at the coffee place had given her flack, because she'd cut in front of him while he was glancing out the window. She'd dished it right back to him, claiming she hadn't known he was in line. He'd called her "rude" and "obnoxious." But, ha-ha, she'd gotten her coffee before him.

Cindy set the hot, heavy-duty paper container on the mail table, and studied the pile of newspapers. She ignored the note that had been taped by the mailboxes about three weeks ago:

*SOMEONE HAS BEEN STEALING MY VANITY
FAIR MAGAZINES. THIS WAS A GIFT SUBSCRIP-
TION FROM MY BROTHER, AND WHOEVER HAS
BEEN HELPING HIS-OR-HERSELF TO MY MAG-
AZINES ISN'T VERY NEIGHBORLY. IF THIS
CONTINUES, I'M TAKING IT BEFORE THE
CONDO BOARD.*
                               —*RACHEL PORTER #401*

A couple of other residents at the Broadmore Apartments
had scribbled comments on the typed notice: *"I have the
same problem. Someone keeps taking my Sunday paper . . .
M. Donovan #313,"* and *"Ditto - J. Vollmer, #407."*

Cindy took *The Seattle Times*, with #313 written on the
clear plastic wrapping. The way she figured, if they really
wanted their Sunday paper, they should have gotten up earlier. *You snooze, you lose.* After all, it was past eight o'clock.
This was her newspaper now, and there wasn't a single, solitary thing they could do about it.

She picked up her coffee and rang for the elevator. Cindy
rode up to the fifth floor. Tucking the newspaper under her
arm, she pulled out her keys and unlocked her door.

Cindy stepped into her apartment, then stopped. It was
too cold. She automatically glanced over at the sliding door
that led to a small balcony off her living room. But the door
was closed. Along the other wall, she noticed the sliding
window—wide open. The screen was open too.

Suddenly, something flew down at her from above, flut-
tering past her shoulder. Cindy dropped her coffee—and her
neighbor's newspaper. Her heart seemed to stop for a moment. She realized it was a pigeon. The damn thing must
have been perched up on her bookcase. Now it settled on the
back of one of her dining room chairs.

"Goddamn it!" Cindy hissed, once she got her breath
back. Coffee had spilled on her pale blue carpet.

She hadn't opened that window earlier. What was going
on?

"Filthy thing," she muttered. "Shoo, get out!" she said, waving at the bird.

But the pigeon only flapped its wings as if it were about to take off at her. Cindy got scared and backed away. "Shit!" she muttered. She decided to let the caretaker get rid of the damn thing.

Then it suddenly dawned on her that she might not be safe in the apartment. Someone else had opened that window, and he could still be there—hiding, waiting for her.

Cindy turned toward the door and gasped.

A man stood in her path. He wore an army jacket and black jeans. A nylon stocking was pulled over his face, distorting his features. Cindy couldn't tell what he looked like. But she could see he was smiling.

She started to scream.

All at once he was on her. He slapped his hand over her mouth. Cindy couldn't breathe. She struggled and kicked. She tried to bite his hand, but his grip was so tight, she couldn't even move her jaw. Cindy thought he might break her neck.

He maneuvered his way behind her. He was twisting her arm.

The pigeon took off, flying out the open window.

"Shhh," he whispered, the nylon material over his face brushing against her ear. "This won't work if you scream. I don't want to hurt you."

He lowered his hand a little from her mouth, and Cindy was able to breathe through her nose. She stopped struggling. She knew she was trapped.

"It was pretty funny with the bird flying in like that, wasn't it?" he said, chuckling. "But you know what's not so funny? The way you treated my Hannah at the video store the other night. You might think she's some nobody clerk, but she's *my* Hannah, you stupid, silly bitch."

Cindy tried to speak, but again, his hand was clasped firmly over her mouth. She merely whimpered in protest. She couldn't break free of him.

"We need to make sure you don't scream," he said.

Cindy noticed a second man, coming from her kitchen. His face was deformed with the same nylon disguise. They both looked like monsters, something out of a nightmare. But they were real. The pain in her arm was real. That warm, moist nylon mask scraping against her face was real.

"If I take my hand away, will you promise not to scream?" he asked.

His partner was coming toward her. Eyeing him, Cindy nodded anxiously. But as soon as she gasped some air through her mouth, Cindy started to yell.

Certainly, one of the neighbors would hear and come help.

"Shut her up," grunted the man holding her.

All at once, his partner punched Cindy in the stomach. All at once, she couldn't breathe, much less scream. She automatically dropped toward the floor, and curled up— fetal-like—from the overwhelming pain in her gut.

But the man still had ahold of her. "Get her feet," she heard him tell his friend.

Suddenly, they were dragging her toward the open window. She was still breathless, paralyzed by the pain in her stomach. They had her by the arms and feet. She tried to struggle, but it was useless.

She felt the chilly wind sweep across her as they hoisted her up on the windowsill. She still couldn't breath—or scream. Her head was swimming.

Cindy Finkelston knew she was going to die. And there wasn't a single, solitary thing she could do about it.

"Well, what exactly did you tell him about me?" Hannah asked, keeping her voice low. There were customers in the store that Monday afternoon. She had to stifle the inclination to scream at Cheryl. The two of them stood behind the counter.

"I hardly told the guy anything. God!" Cheryl rolled her eyes. "He came in on Friday and asked if you were working.

I said you were out sick, and might be back today. That's all. Scott's blowing it all out of proportion."

Hannah glared at her. No one liked Cheryl very much. At twenty-one, she was younger than everybody else on the Emerald City Video payroll, yet she treated her coworkers in a fake-pleasant, condescending manner. She was a theater major, and always seemed "on." Hannah found her obnoxiously perky and phony.

"Well, what did this guy look like, anyway?" Hannah asked, one hand on the countertop. "Can you describe him? Age? Hair color?"

Cheryl rolled her eyes and sighed.

"Okay, tell me this much. Have you seen him in the store before?"

"God, Hannah," she said, with a stunned little laugh. "Why are you making such a big deal out of this?" She flicked back her long blond hair. "I really don't remember much about him. He was here for, like, two seconds. You know, Hannah, I have guys in here every day asking for my phone number. It might not happen to you so much, because you're older. But if I were you, I'd be flattered."

Hannah slowly shook her head. "Cheryl—"

"Hannah, could you come in here?" Scott called from the back room.

She shot Cheryl one last, venomous look. "Give me a yell if it gets busy," she said evenly.

Retreating to the cramped back room, Hannah found Scott at the desk with a newspaper in front of him. He was on his break. Hannah closed the door. "I want to kill her," she whispered.

"Yeah, well, get in line," Scott replied. He folded back the newspaper page. "I thought you'd want to see this. Did you know about it?"

"About what?" Hannah asked, taking the newspaper from him. She glanced at the headline near the bottom of the local news page, and read it aloud: *" 'SEATTLE WOMAN PLUNGES FIVE STORIES TO HER DEATH.' "*

"Keep reading," Scott said.

" 'Authorities are investigating the circumstances behind the death of a Seattle woman, Cindy Finkelston, 34, who fell from her fifth-floor living-room window at the Broadmoore apartment building on Sunday morning. . . .' "

"There is no 'H' in Finkelston," Scott said. "Remember her from the other day? Miss I'll-take-legal-action? Looks like she took a half gainer instead."

"My God," Hannah whispered, stunned. "How weird. I— I don't know how to react."

"Well, please don't act sad, or I'll throw up," Scott said.

Hannah frowned at him.

"Call me a coldhearted SOB, but she was kind of a jerk. Remember how she treated you?"

Hannah anxiously scanned the article. "They don't say if it was suicide or not."

Scott leaned back in the chair. "No, they don't give you much to go on. You look pale. Are you okay?"

"I don't know about this," Hannah murmured. "There's something wrong. I have the strangest feeling—"

A knock on the door interrupted her. "I need help up front!" Cheryl called in a shrill voice.

"That's really bizarre," Hannah said, stealing one last glance at the article. She sighed, gave him back the newspaper, then reached for the doorknob. "Aren't you coming?"

"Sorry, sweetheart. I still have ten minutes left on my break."

Hannah emerged from the back room to find about a dozen customers waiting for service. A couple of men were arguing who had been in line first, while another woman moved up to the counter, asking loudly if there was a section for the Beatles.

"I can help whoever is next," Hannah announced, stepping up to her register. "The Beatles are on the top shelf in the far-right corner of the store."

Three other people started yelling questions at her—all at once. Hannah weathered the onslaught of customers. In about five minutes, the line had dwindled down to one person: a very handsome black man in his early thirties. He set his video on the counter and smiled at Hannah. "I was watching you," he said. "You got through that rush pretty well. Talk about grace under fire."

"Thanks," Hannah said. "I juggle, too. Can I have your name, please?"

"I just opened up an account here yesterday," he said. "Tollman is the last name. Craig."

With his chiseled features, Tollman, Craig looked like a model out of *GQ*. Tall, broad-shouldered, and wiry, he wore his hair so short he was nearly bald. He wore a deep blue shirt, tie, and black pants.

Hannah pulled up his account, then punched in the code for his video.

"I just moved up here from Phoenix last week," he said, taking out his money. ""Maybe you can help me. Could you recommend a nice restaurant around here?"

Shrugging, Hannah gave him his change. "I don't get out much, but I know the Pink Door is nice."

"Well, would you care to go with me sometime?" he asked. "For dinner?"

"You mean, like on a date?"

He chuckled. "Yeah. I'd like to treat you to dinner."

Hannah felt herself blushing. "Oh, well, thank you." She glanced down at the counter. "But I'm afraid I can't."

"We can make it for lunch—if dinner's too much too soon. Or if you're totally date-a-phobic, I'd love to meet you for coffee sometime."

Hannah shoved his video in a bag. Her face still felt hot. She managed to smile at him. "Thanks anyway," she said. "I'm very flattered, but no."

"Maybe some other time?"

She shrugged. "I can't make any promises. But it was a very nice offer." She handed him the bag.

He glanced at his receipt. "Are you working Thursday?"

"Yes. Why?"

"Well, I might see you when I bring the movie back. Hey, you know, I never got your name."

"I'm Hannah," she said.

"You've got a terrific smile, Hannah. You know that?"

As he strolled out of the store, Craig Tollman glanced over his shoulder at her. Hannah met his gaze, and he grinned.

Through the front window, Hannah watched him walk away.

She took her break at three o'clock on Mondays. Alphabet Soup Day Care was a short walk from the video store, and at three-fifteen, they had snack-time. Parents were welcome to join in. Hannah was there every Monday afternoon for Guy—usually with some kind of special treat.

At five minutes to three, Hannah went to the store's break room, where she fetched her coat and purse. She noticed Scott's newspaper on the desk.

Nearly an hour had passed since Scott had shown her the article about Cindy Finkelston's death. Hannah hadn't given her any thought since then. She'd been too busy with customers. Now she felt a little guilty for not caring more. Of course, Scott had a point: Cindy wasn't a very nice person. Had she really taken her own life, or was it an accident?

Hannah tried to shrug it off. Maybe there would be an update about it in tomorrow's paper.

She stopped by the mall's food court and bought a couple of fruit shakes to go. The banana shake was Guy's favorite.

As she walked the five blocks to Alphabet Soup Day Care, Hannah gazed up at some of the taller apartment buildings along the way. She stopped in front of one, figuring it was as tall as Cindy Finkelston's building. She could almost see Cindy falling from one of those windows near the top story. Then, like a dream, the images in her mind took a strange turn. She pictured Mia Farrow and John Cassevetes walking along the street below to discover a throng of onlookers and police. Hannah remembered how Mia reacted when she saw the bloody corpse on the pavement.

The bag with the fruit shakes slipped from her grasp, and hit the sidewalk with a splat. A dark stain bloomed on the brown paper bag.

It dawned on Hannah that the videotape of *Rosemary's Baby* was someone's way of telling her what would happen to Cindy Finkelston.

This person had gone to a lot of trouble to make sure she saw the tape. It had even been cued to that scene. Hannah tried to make some sense out of it all. She'd found the video in her apartment on Thursday night. Cindy Finkelston had taken that fateful fall yesterday morning, Sunday. Why would someone choose to forecast Cindy's death for her? She barely knew the woman.

There had to be some connection to the *Goodbar* video. But what? She didn't really know the victim in that one, either. Someone was singling her out to preview these "movie" deaths. But why?

Ever since the second break-in three nights before, Hannah had been sleeping on the sofa—with a hammer on the floor beside her. Even after changing the locks, she didn't feel safe.

She couldn't shake the feeling that someone was watching her every move. She was constantly looking over her shoulder. She didn't let Guy out of her sight, and they'd spent most of the weekend inside—with the door locked.

This morning, she'd told Joyce that someone had tried to break in, and warned her to be on her guard.

"It's those darn crack-heads ruining the neighborhood," Joyce had lamented. "Well, don't worry about Guy while he's with me. I keep pepper spray and one of those electric-shock zap'm things in my purse. I'm armed and dangerous, hon. No one's gonna tangle with this grandma."

Just the same, on her way to work, Hannah had a hard time convincing herself that Guy was safe. After a few hours in the store, she'd almost felt as if things were back to normal. But then she'd learned that over the weekend, someone had been there asking questions about her. And now this incident right out of *Rosemary's Baby*.

Frowning, Hannah bent down and picked up the soggy bag. She tossed it in a dumpster beside of one the apartment buildings, then took a Kleenex from her purse and wiped off her hands.

The sudden screech of car tires made Hannah swivel around. A white Taurus was stopped halfway down the street. Hannah felt her heart skip a beat, and she started moving away.

"Hannah?" someone called.

She glanced over her shoulder. It took her a moment to recognize the handsome black man behind the wheel. "Hannah?" Craig Tollman said, climbing out of the car. He left his emergency blinkers on and started across the street to her. "Hey, I was just driving down to see you again. I hope I didn't startle you."

Hannah quickly shook her head. "No, not at all." She was hugging her purse to her chest.

"Glad I caught you," he said. "I wanted to apologize if I came on a little too strong earlier. I hope it wasn't inappropriate for me to ask you out."

"No, not at all," she repeated.

"Anyway," Craig said. "If you change your mind about getting together, you have my cell-phone number on file at the store. You can call me anytime. Um, listen, can I give you a lift wherever you're going?"

She shook her head again. "I'm fine. But thanks anyway."

Craig backed away. "Okay, well, see you in the store."

He turned around and almost walked into an oncoming car. The driver honked at him. Craig jumped back. He waved an apology at the car, then glanced at Hannah. "Nice, huh?" he called. "I have a lot of finesse."

She managed to smile, and she watched him climb back inside his car. The one thing she could discern about the man in the video was his skin color. He was white. So why

was she so apprehensive around this handsome black man?
On the surface, Craig Tollman was just being friendly.

Still, she waited until Craig drove off in his white Taurus.
Hannah wanted to make sure he wasn't following her before
she moved on.

"Mom, can I play with Trevor?" Guy asked. "I already
had my snack."

Hannah nodded. "Sure, honey, go ahead. I'll stay here and
have my lunch."

Her lunch was a container of yogurt that she'd bought at
a 7-Eleven near the day care center. She'd picked up a peach
yogurt for Guy as well. But three people had been in front
of her in line, with a clerk as "slow as molasses in January,"
as Hannah's father used to say. By the time she'd gotten to
the play field near Alphabet Soup Day Care, the children
had already finished their snacks.

The kids were playing on the swings, jungle gyms, and
slides. There were three park benches, where some of the
other mothers sat. But not Hannah. At the moment, she
didn't have the will or the energy to socialize.

Neighboring the playground was a baseball diamond.
From her seat on the bleachers, Hannah watched Guy carefully maneuver his way down each plank. Then he made a
beeline toward the jungle gym.

He didn't look very much like his father, thank God. That
would have been pretty awful, having this sweet little boy
running around with that man's face. Guy's father wasn't
homely. In fact, he had a rather goofy-cute look to him: a
long, narrow face with a prominent nose, and curly brown
hair. His sleepy, dark brown eyes were very sexy. Hannah
had fallen in love with his offbeat looks. He didn't become
ugly to her until later.

His name was Kenneth Muir Woodley, Jr.

When she'd first met him, five years ago, Hannah had
been taking classes at Chicago's Second City, and waitress-

ing at a bar and grill called McNulty's, near Wrigley Field. Her father had been a bartender there. He'd recently lost his battle with cancer. Her mom had fought the same fight and lost years ago, back when Hannah was a girl. She had no siblings, no one too close—except her friends from college and Second City. She was very much alone with a very small inheritance when she met Kenneth Muir Woodley, Jr.

That was the name on the Visa card she'd found on the floor by the corner of the bar. "Is Kenneth Woodley here?" Hannah called out over the noisy crowd. She was also competing with Bobby Darin's rendition of "Mack the Knife," and several customers who had decided to sing along with him. "Kenneth Woodley? Kenny? Ken?"

She saw him waving at her from near the jukebox. "Present!" he replied loudly. He sat at a small table, nursing a martini and reading a paperback version of *To Kill a Mockingbird*. He wore an airy yellow silk shirt. He looked very sexy with his curly hair and deep, dark tan. He grinned at Hannah as she approached his table.

She fanned the credit card in front of her. "I think you lost this," she said. "That is, if you're Kenneth Woodley."

He pulled out his wallet, opened it up, and frowned. "Jesus Christ," he muttered.

Hannah smiled. "No, Kenneth Woodley."

"God, you saved my ass, thanks." He held out his hand.

Hannah hesitated. "Not so fast. I want to make sure you're Kenneth Woodley. What's your middle name?"

"Muir. And please don't tell anyone."

She gave him the credit card. While he tucked it in his wallet, she glanced at his book on the table. "You're reading *To Kill a Mockingbird*?"

"I've already read it—a couple of times." He stashed his wallet in his back pocket, then raised the martini glass. "It's a chick magnet. I come across as extremely sensitive and intellectual when seen reading this. It really reels in the babes."

"That's amazing," Hannah remarked. "Pretty sleazy, too."

"Thank you," he said, sipping his drink. "And thank you for finding my Visa card."

"No sweat, Kenneth. Listen, can I get you another martini?"

"I'm fine. But I'll tell you what I'd like."

"What's that?" she asked, one hand on her hip.

"I'd like to see your good deed rewarded. My credit card and I want to take you out to dinner some night this week."

She sighed. "Well, I have no problem stepping out with your credit card. But I'm concerned about some potential trouble with you."

He laughed. "Me? I'm a terrific guy. What do you take me for?"

Hannah tilted her head to one side and studied him for a moment. "I'd say you were a spoiled, rich party boy who deep down suffers from a lack of self-esteem and subsequently drinks too much. And I'd be making a big mistake if I went out with you."

He took her to a fancy dinner at the Drake Hotel the following week. He was a perfect gentleman throughout the date. In fact, Ken didn't even kiss her until their third date. They had sex that same night. Waiting for him to finally kiss her had been excruciating, and Hannah had a low resistance.

Within six months, Ken moved into her little studio apartment. They might have gotten a bigger place together. He certainly could have afforded it. That Visa card of his seemed like a bottomless source of cash. The closest thing he had to a job was charging people for chartered cruises on his small yacht. He spent most of his days on that boat; some nights too.

Ken fit in well with her friends—especially since he was always the first to grab a check at a group gathering. He *was* a party boy. He showered her with gifts, jewelry, clothes, and dinners at three-star restaurants. She kept wondering when his money would run out.

Hannah continued to work at McNulty's, and her reputation was growing at Second City. She even filmed a couple of TV commercials for a local bank. It was one of the happiest times of her life, and when Ken asked her to marry him, she immediately said yes. An impromptu ceremony was held aboard a big yacht that Kenneth had chartered. About twenty friends were in attendance, and the reception went on all night.

His money ran out about five months later. He even started going through *her* money. Their rent check bounced twice. Hannah hocked all the jewelry he'd given her, and dropped out of Second City to take on extra shifts at McNulty's.

They got the eviction notice the day after she came up positive on a home pregnancy test. They had no place to go—except to his parents'.

Kenneth came from one of the richest families in Green Bay, Wisconsin. It was old money, too, which made Woodley one of the most respected names among the rich country-club set. In fact, Kenneth's parents lived in a huge, pristine-white stucco house with a view of Green Bay on one side and the country club's golf course on the other.

Kenneth's father had married into money. He also held the patent for some kind of machinery that all the airlines used to refrigerate and heat food. They had a factory just outside town. Kenneth Senior wasn't a warm man. They could have used what ran in his veins to cool those refrigerating machines. The mother wasn't much of an improvement: a skinny, graceful matriarch with stiff-looking, mink-colored hair. Every time she smiled at Hannah, the strain showed on her face.

Hannah couldn't really blame them for resenting her. Kenneth hadn't told his parents he was married. Introducing them to his new wife was more an act of defiance than anything else. He seemed to relish telling them she was a waitress, rubbing their noses in that fact.

His parents wanted the marriage annulled. Hannah had become so fed up with Ken that she might have agreed to it, but she was pregnant. Kenneth Senior privately offered to pay her twenty-five thousand dollars to have an abortion.

When she told Ken about it, his response was: "Hey, we could live off that money for years. Want to do it?"

"Are you serious?" Hannah whispered. She kept her voice down because they were in the guest room. Never mind that they were half a football field away from Kenneth's parents' room. She still felt compelled to whisper. "What the hell is wrong with you? I can't believe what you're saying."

"I'm just not ready to have a kid. What makes you want one all of a sudden?"

"Because it gives me hope for something," she said. "I have to tell you, Ken, in the last few months, I haven't had much hope for us." She sighed. "In fact, if you want to call it quits, I won't give you an argument. I won't even expect you to support the baby."

His dark eyes narrowed at her. "What the fuck makes you think you can take my kid away from me? I'll never let that happen."

Hannah shook her head. "Two seconds ago, you were all ready to take your father's money and have it aborted. You just said—"

"Listen." He stabbed his finger at the center of her chest, punctuating each word. "If . . . you . . . have . . . this . . . kid . . . you'll . . . never . . . take . . . him . . . away . . . from . . . me. Understand?"

She pushed his hand away. "You're hurting me."

He frowned at her. "Sorry. Just so you understand."

Hannah stared at him. She had no way of knowing that it was the last time Kenneth would ever apologize for hurting her.

Like their son, Mr. and Mrs. Woodley did a total about-face once they realized that Hannah intended to keep the baby. As long as she was providing them with a grandson, Hannah was welcomed into the family. In fact, the Woodleys didn't let her out of their sight. They bought her and Ken a beautiful, three-bedroom ranch house, then furnished it. Mrs. Woodley introduced Hannah to the country-club set. Ken went to work for his father.

She and Ken were miserable. One evening, she pointed out to him that it had been nearly three months since they'd made love. His response was, "Yeah? So?"

"Well, don't you think it might make things better between us if we at least tried?"

Frowning, he gazed at her swollen belly. "If I wanted to fuck a cow, I'd go over to Nellinger's Dairy and hump one of their heifers."

Hannah probably should have run away then. But she didn't want to have her baby at a free clinic. She moved into the guest room. Ken found himself some diversions. He had his yacht moved up to Green Bay. He'd go sailing off without her for entire weekends. She welcomed his absence. When he was home, he sometimes took his frustrations out on her. At first, the abuse was verbal: she couldn't cook; he'd married way beneath him; she was a pig. When she became numb to his occasional tirades, he started throwing things: a plate of pasta that ended up on the dining-room wall; a clock radio, which just missed her head. Once, he hurled a cup of hot coffee at her. Hannah managed to avoid direct contact with the mug, but it smashed on the floor at her feet and scalded her legs. She had to drive herself to the hospital, where they treated the burns.

She was back there two weeks later to give birth to their son. The Woodleys were unbearably meddlesome over the baby, even picking out his name: Kenneth Muir Woodley III. Hannah called him Guy-Guy, or just Guy. She used to like the name Ken, but didn't anymore.

She discovered that Ken had actually been exercising some restraint during those tirades before Guy was born. Now that she was no longer pregnant, Ken didn't have to be so careful with her. He didn't have to hold back. His outbursts were just infrequent enough that she couldn't predict them. Kenneth took it out on her if the baby was crying too much, or if the house was messy or smelled of baby poop. Such offenses were grounds for a black eye or a swollen lip. *Want another?* he'd ask, after the first blow. That question always seemed to precede a beating. Hannah only made things worse for herself by fighting back, but she fought back anyway.

She begged him: "For God's sake, Ken, don't you think this Ike and Tina routine has run its course? We're both miserable. You were a pretty nice guy back in Chicago. You were no prince, but at least you weren't mean. I know you feel trapped here. So do I. If we broke up, things would be easier for you. I'll give you the best visitation rights in the world if you let Guy and me go."

She was trying to reason with a total cokehead. Apparently he got the stuff from someone at work. Ken must have been hooked on it back in Chicago, too. Maybe that was why he'd gone through her money so quickly.

One of the most stupid moves of her life—right up there with first going on a date with the son of a bitch—was confiding in his mother that they should consider intervention. Of course, Mrs. Woodley fell into denial about her son's drug problem—the same way she'd failed to notice all the bruises on her daughter-in-law. Just to make sure her boy was on the straight and narrow, Mrs. Woodley asked Ken if there was any truth to what Hannah had told her.

Hannah ended up in the hospital that night. He'd blackened both her eyes and fractured her jaw. She took seven stitches in her chin where she'd hit the edge of a glass-top coffee table during the scuffle. She also had a broken arm. Ken told everyone that Hannah had been in a car accident. He even went so far as to total her car, so he could back up his story. Ken visited her at the hospital, pampering her with flowers, an expensive nightgown, all the comforts. A nanny was hired to look after Guy.

During her stay in the hospital, Hannah decided that she had to leave him. She told her doctor that the car accident story was a cover-up. "Ken did this to me," she whispered to him, her mouth nearly immobile due to the wire around her jaw. "You know that, don't you?"

Her doctor didn't look surprised; merely annoyed. "I

didn't hear that," he replied, shaking his head. "I can't do anything about it."

The Woodleys were major contributors to the hospital, and Ken's mother was chairwoman of the Cantor Ball, an annual fundraiser for the Children's Ward. Hannah couldn't expect anyone in that hospital to help her. All legal avenues were blocked by the family as well. No local lawyer would represent her in a divorce. And no way was the family going to let her walk away with their grandson.

She began to hatch her escape plan while in the hospital, looking out the window of her private room. She would gaze down at the water, the bayside park with all the trees, and the happy families walking along those winding paths.

The doctor had her on soft foods because she couldn't chew well. She remembered eating a lot of yogurt—too much. At the time, Hannah thought she'd never want to see another container of Yoplait. She could only imagine eating solid foods—and being free of Kenneth Muir Woodley, Junior.

Sitting on the bleachers, Hannah watched Guy play on the jungle gym. She set aside the peach yogurt and glanced at her wristwatch; only about ten minutes more before she had to hurry back to work.

In many ways, she still wasn't free of Ken. He still haunted her. It wasn't intentional, but she hadn't been with another man since him. She was afraid of getting too close to anyone, afraid of getting hurt again.

Pam, the head of the day care center, blew a whistle. All the children started to gather together to file back into the building. Hannah smiled and waved at Guy, who jumped up and down excitedly and waved back. She watched him walk away with the other children. He was the only man in her life right now.

Hannah suddenly shuddered. She realized Guy wasn't the only man in her life at the moment. There was another man, imposing on her, playing some sort of strange, deadly game. And Hannah had a feeling that he was just getting started.

Five

He stared at the piece of wood that she'd lodged in the groove of the sliding window. It looked like the sawed-off handle to a broom or a rake. He smiled. His leading lady was very clever. She'd caught on to how he'd been breaking into her place. She'd changed the locks on him, too.

It was kind of sweet, really—her thinking she could keep him out with that puny piece of wood and a new dead bolt.

He stood on the walkway at her front door. He had a good view of the Space Needle from here, but the Needle's lights were off right now. It was five-fifteen in the morning.

He'd last been inside her apartment five nights ago. There was something very romantic about that walk in the rain when he'd dropped off the tape of *Rosemary's Baby*. He'd missed her these last few days.

He'd spent far more time than he'd intended figuring out how to break into the Broadmoore Apartments and planning his date with Cindy Finkelston. Of course, she hadn't known about it.

She hadn't been expecting him at all.

She hadn't expected to die Sunday morning.

Smiling again, he touched Hannah's front door and brushed his fingertips against the doorknob. The newspaper carrier would be around soon. And in about ninety minutes, Hannah Doyle would be waking up. She would drop off her kid at the day care place, then go to the video store. On Tuesdays, she worked nine to five.

He liked watching her at work. He had hours and hours of videotape footage of Hannah at the video store.

She might not notice him today. She wouldn't be expecting him. But he would be watching her every move.

Guy's class was taking a field trip to the Woodland Park Zoo. When Hannah dropped him off at Alphabet Soup Day Care that Tuesday morning, she pulled the teacher aside and asked her to be extra-vigilant with Guy. "I've got this—stalker situation," Hannah explained. "I don't think he'd go after Guy, but—well, I'll feel better knowing you've got your guard up, Pam."

Pam was a tall, athletic woman in her mid-twenties with short-trimmed blond hair. "Well, I'll keep an eye out, Hannah," she assured her. "Do you know what this creep-o looks like?"

"Um, no. It's, um, a telephone talker thing."

"Have you contacted the police about it yet? Maybe they can put a trace on your line."

Hannah nodded. "Yes, they're doing that," she lied.

"Good. Can't be too careful," Pam said. "We have extra people for this trip. And I'll keep close tabs on Guy. Don't you worry about him."

"Thanks, Pam."

Hannah spent her break time that afternoon at the Broadmoore Apartments, six blocks from the store.

She gazed up at the row of windows along the top floor of the five-story slate-colored structure. She wondered which window Cindy Finkelston had fallen from. Did her body land in the shrubs on the east side of the building, or in the parking area along the front and west sides?

Hannah took a pad and pen from her bag as she approached the lobby doors. She studied the list of residents' names on the keypad of buzzer codes. There were close to fifty names. Hannah recognized some of them as customers at Emerald City Video. She started scribbling down the names of Cindy Finkelston's neighbors.

She was down to the last few when someone snuck up behind her and cleared his throat. Hannah swiveled around. Staring back at her was a tall, gaunt man in his fifties. He had a dirty-gray mustache and very thin, long hair that he'd pulled back in a ponytail. He was nearly bald on top. He wore a denim shirt and jeans, and leaned on his broom. "Can I help you with something?" he asked.

"Oh, hi," Hannah replied, caught off guard.

"Are you one of those insurance people again?"

She nodded. "Yes, um, I'm—Rosemary Farrow with Northwest Fidelity Life. The—ah, late Cindy Finkelston had an account with us. I'm a claims adjuster, here doing a little preliminary poking around. It's very sad what happened. Are you the building manager?"

For a moment, he gave her a cool, sidelong stare. Hannah had to wonder if he'd bought any of it. Finally, the tall man puffed out his skinny chest a bit and nodded. "I'm Glenn, the caretaker here," he said. "You'll probably want to talk to me."

"Oh, yes. I imagine not much gets past you, huh?" Hannah said.

"Not much at all. I knew the deceased as well as anyone else around here, which isn't much. I don't think too many people liked her. But I don't believe in speaking ill of the dead, so that's all I'm saying about that."

"Do you know how it happened?" Hannah asked.

He glanced up at the west corner of the building's roof. "You know, I'm the one who heard her scream. I was working around back. I heard this shriek, and then something went thump. That was her body hitting the car. There's a gate back there, so I had to go all the way around the other side of the building. Otherwise, I would have been the first one to get to her. But a couple of neighbors beat me to it."

Hannah gazed over at the parking area on the west side of the building. "She landed on a car?" Hannah asked; then she remembered her cover story. "Um, they didn't mention that in the report," she added.

Glenn nodded and reached back to scratch under his gray ponytail. "A brand-new silver Mazda. She hit the edge, then rolled off. Smashed the roof and windshield. You should have seen all the blood and glass." He shook his head. "A goddamn mess. They finally took down the police tape and towed away the car yesterday morning."

"What about the people next door to her?" Hannah asked. "Did they hear anything? Maybe someone was in the apartment with her."

Glenn shook his head again. "Neighbors didn't hear diddly. And from what I caught the police saying, it looked like she was alone in the apartment when she went out the window."

"So they don't think she was pushed out?" Hannah asked.

He let out a little chuckle, then pointed to the roof. "Take a look up there," he said. "Top floor, second window from the end. See it?"

Hannah squinted up at the long, narrow window along the fifth floor. "Yes, I see it."

"That's where she fell from. Now, go over one window, and you see her balcony. Check out the sliding glass door, the low railing. If I was gonna give somebody the heave-ho from up there, that balcony would have been a much better place. Why go to all the trouble of opening up that window and tossing her out when you got a whole balcony to work with? You wouldn't even have to leave the living room. It's a short balcony. One good shove and she's gone."

"You should be a detective," Hannah said, buttering him up. "Listen, I'm not supposed to ask this, but what do you think happened? Do you think it was an accident?"

Scratching his chin, he gazed up toward the building's top floor. "Like I say, if it was anything intentional—suicide or homicide—why not use the balcony and make it easier? Why the window?"

Hannah thanked Glenn, saying that she and Northwest Fidelity Life were both grateful to him for providing his expertise. As she walked back to work, the caretaker's remark haunted her. *Why not use the balcony and make it easier? Why the window?*

Hannah suddenly knew the answer, and with that realization, a shudder passed through her. Cindy Finkelston's death sentence had been carried out to the letter.

The girl who died in *Rosemary's Baby* didn't plunge from any balcony. She fell from a window.

Sixteen residents from the Broadmoore Apartments were customers at Emerald City Video. Hannah looked up the histories on all of their accounts. Two of them had rented *Rosemary's Baby*: Smith, Collyer & Jeanne had checked out the movie eighteen months ago; and Webber, Rosanne had watched it back in February. *Looking for Mr. Goodbar* had never been rented on either account.

It wasn't much to go on. Hannah wondered if cross-referencing all these names was just a waste of time.

She'd been at her register, tapping into the files for the last half hour. She'd gracefully weathered interruptions from customers. But Hannah didn't see this one coming.

"I have a DVD on hold," the middle-aged man announced—without so much as an "Excuse me."

Hannah glanced up at him. With his silver hair and tan, he had a certain kind of cold handsomeness. A Ralph Lauren logo was embossed on his lightweight, navy blue jacket. He must have been drinking, because he smelled like a distillery. "The name's Hall, Lester. The movie is *Sorority Sluts II: Anal Adventures*."

Nodding, Hannah kept a straight face. "All right, let me see if we have it back here for you."

"Well, you should," he replied, his tone a bit ominous. He drummed his fingers on the countertop. "I called earlier, and they told me it was in."

Hannah turned to the back counter.

"Hate that guy," her coworker, Britt, murmured as she passed Hannah with a stack of videos. "He's such an asshole."

All Hannah could do was nod her head, and think to herself *Well, you'd know. You're living with the poster boy of assholes.* Britt's boyfriend, Webb, was scum, a drug dealer who often beat her. Hannah liked Britt a lot, but knew she was kind of a screwup. As their coworker, Scott, once said about Britt, *One minute, you want to hug her and protect her from the world, and the next you want to slap some common sense into the poor, sorry bitch.*

Twenty-nine and pencil-thin, Britt had short, maroon-dyed hair, a pale complexion, and—at last count—thirteen piercings. She also had a certain gentle, vulnerable quality that was endearing. Nearly every week, she gave Hannah some little gizmo for Guy that she'd saved from a cereal box.

"Last week, he called me an idiot, right to my face," Britt whispered. She snuck a wary glance over her shoulder at Lester Hall. "He phoned earlier about a DVD porno. It's right there."

It wasn't there. Hannah checked the reservation pile. Britt must have transposed a couple of digits on the DVD's code. An adult DVD was there for him, but it was the wrong one. Hannah looked in the drawer, and the DVD that Lester Hall wanted was checked out. "Oh, shit," Hannah muttered.

She put on her best contrite look and turned to him. "I'm really sorry, Mr. Hall," she said. "They put the wrong movie back here for you. The DVD you wanted is checked out." Hannah looked it up in her computer. "We have *Sorority Sluts II* in VHS format, and I can—"

"I don't want it on VHS," he said firmly. "They told me the DVD was here. Why would they tell me it's here when it isn't?"

Beside her, Scott looked up from his register.

"They goofed," Hannah explained. "The DVD back here is two numbers off. I'm sorry. If you'd like another DVD, we'll rent it to you for free."

"I don't want another DVD! I wanted *Sorority Sluts II*. It's not there?"

Hannah shook her head. "No, the movie back here is something called *Debutante Whores*."

Scott piped up. "You know, those Debutante Whores are just like Sorority Sluts, only classier." He paused. "Because—they're debutantes."

Hannah shot him a You're-Not-Helping look.

Lester Hall glared at Scott, then at Hannah. "I don't understand how this happened. You said my DVD was here, and it isn't. This is fucked. How stupid are you people?"

"It was just human error," Hannah said patiently. "I'm very sorry. We'll credit your account—"

"I don't want a credit. I want my movie, you stupid bitch. And I'm sick of you saying you're sorry—"

"Hey, you know," Scott interrupted. "Take it easy—"

"I'm not talking to you, faggot," Lester Hall retorted.

People in the store were stopping to stare. Britt came up to the register. "I think I'm the one who screwed up your reservation," she said meekly. "I'm really sorry—"

"I don't want apologies. I want my fucking movie!"

"All right, this is getting out of hand," Hannah announced. "We can't help you, Mr. Hall. And you're being abusive. You need to leave the store."

"Oh, really? Are you going to make me, bitch?"

"That's it," Scott said. "I'm calling the cops on you."

"No need. I'll show him out."

Craig Tollman stepped up to the counter beside Lester Hall. He smiled at the silver-haired man. "Let's go."

Dumbfounded, Hannah stared at them. She hadn't seen Craig in a few days. She had to admire his timing.

Lester Hall was mad and drunk, but he wasn't about to tangle with Craig. He turned to Hannah. "I want a credit on my account!" he demanded. "I should get a free movie!"

She nodded. "I'll tell the manager exactly what happened."

Craig nudged at him. "Now say good-bye."

Lester Hall didn't say anything. He stomped out of the store—with Craig right behind him.

"Thanks for shopping with us!" Scott called out, for the benefit of the other customers in the store. Some of them laughed. One person applauded.

But Hannah was staring out the window. Lester Hall retreated down the street, while Craig seemed to stand guard outside the door. He glanced in the store window, and gave Hannah a little salute.

She nodded at Craig and managed to smile.

"Do you know that black guy?" Scott whispered. "He's a major babe. I didn't even see him come into the store. Did you?"

Hannah just shook her head. She looked back outside, but Craig was gone. She wondered how long he'd been in the store before stepping up to the counter. How long had he been there watching her?

"You're shaking a little, Hannah," Scott said. "You okay?"

Britt patted her on the back. "God, you really stood up to that creep. It was all my fault. I'm sorry, Hannah. I'm the one who screwed up—"

"Don't sweat the small stuff," Hannah said, with a nervous laugh. She started collecting returns from the drop-off bin.

"Sure you don't want to take five in the back room or something?" Scott asked.

Hannah began checking in the return videos. "I'll be fine; nothing to worry about." She said it again, hoping she might actually believe it. "Nothing to worry about at all."

He watched Lester Hall climb into a black Mercedes. Then he hurried back to his own car so he could follow Lester home. Small wonder the son of a bitch was peeved about not getting his porn DVD. He lived about eight miles away—in a sprawling, white stucco ranch house on a big, secluded lot near Lake Washington.

He videotaped Lester stepping inside his house. The results

on these night shots always left a lot to be desired, but the picture quality didn't have to be perfect for Lester the Letch.

The camera panned across the house, then tracked down a slope and past a gate to a side garden. Through various windows, snippets of videotape caught Peeping Tom shots of Lester moving about the house. He took off his jacket, shirt, and some kind of corset to hold in his girth. Then he walked around in his slacks and V-neck T-shirt.

In the back, a row of bushes against the house provided some camouflage, while sliding glass doors offered a view into Lester's recreation room—with a state-of-the-art entertainment center, a fireplace, and bar. No family pictures. The guy was probably divorced. His place looked too much like a bachelor pad for any woman to be living there.

Lester made a couple of phone calls, poured himself a drink at the bar, and finally settled down in front of an adult movie on his flat, wide-screen TV. The camera zoomed in on the girl-on-girl action. It must have been from his private DVD collection. Through the glass doors, the audio caught muffled purrs and moans from the two porn actresses pleasuring each other.

The camera's audio also captured the sound of a car pulling up the front drive. Lester Hall must have heard it, too. He switched off his movie.

The next image caught on video was a tall brunette taking a duffel bag and a large folded-up case from the backseat of a cab. She wore tight jeans, a stylishly torn sweatshirt, and heels. The camera zoomed in for a close-up. Her hair was pulled back in a small ponytail. She'd overdone the mascara, and her maroon lips appeared swollen by collagen. She paid the cab driver and carried the bag and bulky case to Lester's front door. The audio picked up the curious click-click of her high heels on the pavement.

Lester greeted her at the door, then ushered her inside. A series of shots into the windows along the side of the house yielded nothing but images of empty rooms. It was back in the large recreation room that Lester and his guest settled.

He didn't bother helping her with her case or the bag. But he did fix her a drink at the bar.

The woman opened the oblong case, which turned out to be a massage table. "I almost thought you weren't gonna call," she said, the words barely audible through the glass doors.

"It's every Tuesday night," he said, handing her a drink. "Shouldn't be too tough to remember."

"I remembered. I thought *you'd* forgotten." She pulled out a folded sheet from the duffel bag and spread it over the table. Lester Hall grabbed the remote and clicked on some jazz music; then he began to undress.

So did the girl. Lester stopped to watch her shed the torn jersey top, then peel down her jeans. For a moment, she posed for him, running her hands up and down her tanned body, stopping to caress her breasts. All she wore was a red thong. She pointed to the table, whispered something, then sauntered away—most likely to the bathroom.

While she was gone, Lester finished undressing. With his barrel chest, protruding gut, and spindly legs, he didn't look good naked. Despite the porn earlier and the girl stripping for him just now, Lester's penis looked small and flaccid. He sipped his drink before laying facedown on the table.

A minute passed before the tall brunette returned. She pulled down the flimsy thong, then reached for a bottle of oil. She started massaging his back.

The camera zoomed in on her face. It caught a flicker of sadness in those heavily made-up eyes.

As was now his custom, Paul Gulletti took the empty seat beside Hannah in class that Thursday night. Hannah furtively glanced at his assistant, Seth, who rolled his eyes and smirked at her. He was standing in his usual spot by the windows. He strolled over to the projector and switched on the movie, *Chinatown*.

Ben Sturges sat in the back of the room tonight. At the beginning of class, Hannah had peeked over her shoulder at

him, but he didn't seem to notice her. The tall, black trans-
vestite, Dede or Dodo or whatever her name was, had been
bending his ear about something.

During the movie, Paul leaned over and asked if she was
free for dinner one night during the upcoming week. "I was
thinking of the Hotel Monaco," he whispered. "They have a
wonderful restaurant there. You'll love it."

Hannah tried to smile. "Well, Paul, I'd like go over my
notes with you on movies that broke the blacklist. But I
think the Hotel Monaco is a bit too fancy for something like
that." She shrugged. "I'll have my notebook and a couple of
library books with me. Maybe we can meet someplace for
coffee instead, a Starbucks or—"

"Hannah, I'm trying to ask you out for a lovely dinner," he
whispered. "We can discuss the blacklist project some other
time. I think we both owe ourselves a nice evening out."

Hannah glanced up at the movie for a moment; then she
turned to Paul again and leaned closer to him. "Um, Paul, I
want to help you with your project, and I'll gladly meet you
for coffee or something. But if you're asking me out on a
date, I don't date married men."

He frowned a little. "Funny, I thought you were serious
about wanting that job at my newspaper."

"I'm very serious about it," Hannah replied.

"Well, you sure fooled me," Paul grumbled. Then he settled back to watch the film.

Hannah turned toward the screen. She yearned to tell him,
*You're the one who's not serious about this job possibility.
You just want to get me into bed, you sleaze-bucket.* But she
didn't risk saying it. What if he really did intend to help her
out? Maybe socializing a bit with him was a part of that.

When the movie ended and the lights came on, Paul said
to her under his breath, "Listen, stick around after class,
okay? We should talk."

With a sigh, Hannah nodded, then retreated to the hallway.
She bought a box of Milk Duds from the vending machine.

"How are you doing?"

She turned to see Ben Sturges smiling at her.

"I'm fine, thanks," Hannah coolly replied, taking a little step back.

He leaned against the vending machine. "I want to apologize for acting like such a horse's ass last week. It's really none of my business whether or not you're—ah, involved with the teacher. I was way out of line. I'm sorry."

Hannah glanced down at the box of Milk Duds in her hand. "Well, for the record, I'm not involved with Paul Gulletti. He's married, and I don't date married men." She shrugged. "So, would you like a Milk Dud?"

He held out his hand. "Yeah, thanks."

Hannah shook a couple of Milk Duds into his palm. She had a hard time looking directly at him. His apology was endearing, and she found him very attractive. Maybe that was why she couldn't really trust him. It was part of her history that she had lousy taste in guys.

"Great movie, huh?" he said. "Have you seen any other Roman Polanski movies?"

"*Knife in the Water, Tess,* and *Rosemary's Baby.*" She popped a Milk Dud in her mouth. "In fact, someone just loaned me a video of *Rosemary's Baby* last week."

"That's weird. You have people loaning you videos? I figured you could rent them for free."

Hannah stared at him, eyes narrowed. "What do you mean?"

"Well, you work in a video store, don't you?"

"Yes, but how do you know that? I didn't tell you."

"I asked around."

Hannah frowned. "Were you at the video store last week, *asking around* about me and my son?"

He shrugged. "I—I came by looking for you. I wanted to apologize—"

"And you asked about me and my little boy?" she pressed, a sharp edge in her tone. "Do you know how creepy that is? Are you following me around?"

His back against the vending machine, Ben glanced at the

other students in the hallway. Hannah now noticed a few of them staring.

Ben shook his head at her. "No, I'm not following you around."

She didn't believe him. She stared into those cold blue eyes of his. "You're lying," she whispered. "I can tell. Listen, I don't know what you want or what kind of game you're playing. But you need to leave me alone."

He let out a little laugh, and kept shaking his head.

"Understand?" she said loudly. "Leave me alone!"

She ran back into the classroom, and grabbed her coat.

Sitting on the edge of his desk, Paul glanced up from the *Film Comment* magazine he was reading. "Hannah? What's wrong?"

Ignoring him, she hurried out to the corridor, then down the stairwell. She didn't look back at Ben Sturges—or at the others who were staring at her. She just kept running.

He didn't follow Hannah home from the community college. But he came by her apartment building around ten-thirty that night. From the parking lot of a neighboring building, he had a good view of her door and the living-room window. For nearly an hour, he watched. It was a beautiful, unseasonably warm night, with a smell in the air of impending rain. Her windows were open. From the flickering light inside, he could tell she was watching TV.

Her door opened. He hadn't expected her to be stepping out at this time of night. Hannah came out to the balcony walkway for a minute. She retreated back inside, then reemerged with a straight-back chair and a glass of wine. She wasn't going anywhere after all. She sat down, gazed out at the Space Needle, and sipped her wine. He saw her wipe her eyes several times, and he realized she was crying.

It began to rain, yet he remained, hiding behind a mini-van in the lot. For a moment he thought she'd noticed him, but it was a false alarm. Around midnight, she finally went back inside, taking her chair and wineglass.

Ben stayed until he saw the light go out in her window.

He caught the bus back to his studio apartment in one of the seedier neighborhoods of town. His place was on the first floor. The iron bars somewhat defeated the purpose of his large picture window, but it didn't matter. He had a view of a dumpster, an abandoned car, and the dirty street.

Ben didn't bother turning on the light. He flopped down on the daybed sofa, which wasn't so bad. The place came furnished—early fire-sale stuff. Kicking off his shoes, he glanced over at his answering machine on the beat-up old desk. The message light was blinking.

With a sigh, Ben pulled himself up and pressed the message button. *"Ben? Ben, it's Jennifer. . . ."* She sounded as if she'd been crying.

"Are you there? Please pick up. Please? Listen, I'm really worried about you. . . ."

Frowning, he shuffled over to the refrigerator and took out a beer.

"Please, call me, okay? I miss you, honey. I want you to come home. I want to take care of you. We'll make everything right. I think we should see somebody, don't you? Get some help? Wouldn't that be good?"

In the dark, dingy apartment, Ben sat back down on the bed and sipped his beer.

"I have a feeling you're there, listening to me," she went on. *"Please pick up. Ben? Are you there?"*

Six

Hannah knew Paul Gulletti taught another film class at the community college on Friday afternoons. But she hadn't come to the college during her break to see Paul. In fact, she hoped they wouldn't run into each other.

Sometimes, when she arrived for class early, she'd spot Paul's assistant, Seth Stroud, in the cafeteria, sitting alone at a table with a cup of coffee and some film book.

That was where she hoped to find him today. She needed Seth's help with something. And she didn't dare ask Paul.

The cafeteria, with its two dozen cafe tables, a counter along the wall, and a painted mural of the Seattle skyline, wasn't too crowded at twenty to three that Friday afternoon. Hannah could see right away Seth wasn't there.

She slumped against the cafeteria's arched entrance. As long as she was on her break, she decided to grab a late lunch. Seth could still show up before Paul's class.

Hannah got a tray and went to the food counter. She was assessing the entrees on display when someone nudged her arm. Hannah turned to see the young man with spiked brown hair and designer glasses. He had a cup of coffee, a donut, and a copy of *Movieline* magazine on his tray.

"Hey, Seth," Hannah said. "I was hoping I'd run into you here."

"Yeah? Well, steer clear of the hot dogs. Might as well eat a time bomb."

"Is the salad safe?"

He shrugged. "They can't screw that up too much."

She nodded at the food on his tray. "Is that all you're having?"

"Yeah, just a snack to get me through the next couple of hours. How are you doing? You left class in such a hurry last night, I thought you might be sick or something."

"Oh, I'm fine," Hannah said, taking a small plastic container of salad. "Let me pay for yours, okay? I want to hit you up for a favor."

"Sounds mysterious." He grinned. "Okay. I'll get us a table."

The cafeteria started to fill up while Hannah was paying for the food. She met Seth at a small table in the corner.

"So, what's going on?" he asked.

"It's just a little favor," Hannah said, settling back and opening her salad container. "I was hoping you could save me from going through a lot of red tape. You know Ben Sturges, the tall, blond-haired guy in class?"

"The dude who looks like the Marlboro Man?" Seth nodded over his coffee cup. "Yeah, I know him."

"Well, I guess he found out I work at a video store. He asked if I knew anyone who deals in out-of-print videos. I found a local dealer who has this video Ben wants, only the guy's leaving town tomorrow. Anyway, I can't get a hold of Ben on the phone. I have the information all written down. So I thought I'd go by his place—"

Seth chuckled. "And you'd like me to get his address for you."

Bewildered, Hannah nodded. "Yeah. What's so funny?"

"Nothing. It's just smart you came to me with this instead of Professor G, because he absolutely hates that guy."

Hannah nibbled at her salad. "Why is that?"

"Because Paul thinks Ben's making the moves on you. And the Prof has a thing for you. In fact, he's really kind of obsessed."

Hannah shrugged. "Well, I've never done anything to encourage him. And I'm not interested in Ben Sturges, either.

I'm just trying to do him a favor." She managed to smile. "So—think you could get his address for me?"

Seth nodded. "No sweat, Hannah. What movie?"

"Hmmm?"

"What hard-to-find movie is Ben Sturges looking for?"

"Oh. *Bonjour Tristesse*." In the store this morning, Hannah had waited on a customer who wanted to buy the out-of-print video. It was how she came up with the excuse for wanting Ben Sturges's address.

"Bonjour Tristesse." Seth nodded with approval. "Good one. Otto Preminger directed, 1958. I saw an interview with Deborah Kerr about making that. She was talking about how Preminger picked on and screamed at Jean Seberg all during the filming. The critics had roasted him the year before for casting her in *Saint Joan*. She was his discovery, and he was going to show them they were wrong about Jean Seberg—even if it killed her."

"Interesting," Hannah said, picking at her salad.

"A lot of great directors put their leading ladies through the wringer, especially when they've 'discovered' them. You know, the old Svengali and Trilby story. Maybe it's an artist's control thing, all part of realizing a vision."

"Or maybe sometimes the director is just a son of a bitch."

Seth leaned back and grinned at her. "Still, it was a pretty good movie, wasn't it?"

Hannah nodded. "Actually, I'm a big fan of Otto Preminger's movies." She pushed her food tray aside and glanced at her wristwatch. "Anyway, do you think there's time before class to give me that address?"

"Yeah, come on," he said, getting to his feet. He grabbed his tray. "Just don't tell Paul that I gave you Marlboro Man's address, or he'll have my ass in a sling."

Hannah bused her tray after him. "So Paul really has it out for Ben Sturges, huh?"

"Oh, he'd hate any man who got close to you. Hell, he'd put a contract out on me if he knew I was sitting with you just now. Why do you think I picked that corner table? So do me a favor and don't let on to the Prof that we broke bread together."

Hannah frowned at him. "Paul really isn't that bad, is he?"

As they strolled out of the cafeteria together, Seth seemed to ponder her question. He tapped his rolled-up magazine against his leg, and smiled cryptically. "Hmmm, just don't tell Paul about us talking together today, okay? I don't want to get into trouble with him." He pointed to a stairwell entrance. "Why don't you wait for me over there? I'll be back in a couple of shakes with that address."

Hannah retreated toward the stairwell. She watched Seth amble down the crowded hallway, and she realized he truly didn't want to be seen with her. He was dead serious about Paul.

The Prof has a thing for you, Seth had said. *In fact, he's really kind of obsessed.*

Hannah stepped back, ducking into the stairwell. She suddenly had a feeling someone was watching.

She got off the bus on Yakima Way, then glanced again at the address Seth had scribbled down for her. He'd said it was a *dicey neighborhood,* and he wasn't kidding. She'd ridden the El through worse areas of Chicago. Still, it was hardly the place to be alone on foot at nine o'clock at night.

She'd gotten Joyce to stay later with Guy, and taken the bus from work. On the bus, she'd tried to ignore the foul-mouthed ranting of a crazy man in the back. She wondered if this attempt to investigate Ben Sturges wasn't a little misguided. Paul Gulletti, with his movie knowledge and his *obsession* for her, seemed a far more likely suspect. Hannah had to wonder if she'd get mugged tonight, investigating the wrong man.

As the bus pulled away, she felt as if her last chance for safety had just driven off. The lone corner store at the end of the block provided no refuge. Four teenagers, who looked like gang members, loitered by the entrance of the run-down establishment. One of them was tormenting a derelict who had passed out against the side of the store. A pawnshop was located across the street from the grocery, but it looked closed.

Hannah started down the block of dilapidated houses and boarded-up buildings until she found the address for Ben Sturges. The apartment building looked like a big, neglected house and had bad aluminum siding that might have been painted yellow at one time—but now Hannah couldn't tell. The front door had a faded, handwritten "No Trespassing" sign. On the second floor, two windows had stained sheets hanging up in lieu of curtains. Hannah checked the mailbox for Apartment 1, and saw a new label on it: *B. Podowski*.

Frowning, Hannah checked the address and apartment number that Seth had written down. She opened the front door and stepped inside. The dark foyer smelled of cat urine, and there was a stairway with a tattered, thin carpet. On either side of Hannah were Apartments 1 and 2.

The front door opened, and Hannah backed away. A husky young black man ambled in. He wore a sleeveless sweatshirt. He scowled at her, but said nothing. He pulled out a set of keys and started to unlock the door to Apartment 2.

"Hi, excuse me," Hannah said.

He turned to glare at her. "Yeah?"

"Does a tall, blond-haired man live here?" she asked, nodding to Apartment 1. "He's about thirty years old."

He nodded. "Yeah. Moved in about month ago." The young man started to duck into the apartment.

"Excuse me again," Hannah said. "Is his name Ben? Ben Sturges?"

The man frowned. "No, it's Ben Something-else. Some Polock name. I don't remember, okay? Any other questions?"

Hannah quickly shook her head. "No. Thank you very much."

He stepped inside his apartment and shut the door. Hannah heard two locks click.

She glanced at the door to Apartment 1. She wondered why Ben Sturges, who always came very nicely dressed to film class, was living in a tenement. And why did he live there under another name? He'd moved in a month ago, the neighbor had said.

A month ago. Give or take a few days, that was when the *Goodbar* video had been dropped off at the store. That was when all this began.

Hannah wandered outside again, then turned to stare at the large picture window on the first floor. It was where he lived. There were bars over the window, and within the apartment, only darkness.

"So what kind of cookies do you think Joyce would like?" Hannah asked Guy. She had him in the shopping cart seat.

"Those! Joyce likes those!" he said, pointing to the Oreos.

"What an amazing coincidence," Hannah said, grabbing a package of the cookies. "You happen to like Oreos, too, don't you?"

"Yeah, I sure do." Guy nodded, very matter-of-fact.

"Well, here, guard these," Hannah said, setting the Oreos in the cart. "And don't touch." She paused to glance at her shopping list.

It was Saturday, her day off. She'd spent it with Guy, buying him a haircut and new shoes, Burger King for lunch, a trip to the park, and now the supermarket.

All the while she was outside with her son, Hannah knew she was vulnerable. She didn't let Guy out of her sight for a minute. She always felt someone watching. It was bad enough walking to and from work by herself, constantly glancing around for someone lurking in the shadows or behind every corner. But the idea that he might be studying her—with Guy—terrified her.

Even in the supermarket, Hannah didn't feel entirely safe. Still, she tried not to think about the *Goodbar* and *Rosemary's Baby* videos and Cindy Finkelston's death. She tried not to think about Ben Sturges or Ben Podowski—or whatever he was calling himself. And she tried not to think about Paul Gulletti. Either one of them could have been her stalker, playing this deadly game with her. Either one—or neither—could have been the intruder who had broken into her apartment twice. Perhaps it was a customer at the store or a total stranger.

She felt so helpless and frustrated. All she could do for now was make sure Guy was safe, keep Joyce on alert, and hope whoever had been behind all this was finished with her.

She'd rented *Aladdin* for Guy tonight, and they were going to eat in—with the door and windows locked.

"Mom, push me again, okay?" Guy said, kicking his feet back and forth.

"All right, hold your horses, kiddo," she replied, checking her coupons. "I'm trying to score us some bargains here."

"Well, hello."

Hannah looked up to see Craig Tollman, carrying a shopping basket. He wore a sweatshirt and jeans, but still managed to look like a *GQ* model.

Hannah smiled nervously. "Oh, hi. How are you?"

"Great." He nodded at Guy, then smiled at her. "Looks like you picked up a hitchhiker."

She laughed. "Guy, say hello to Craig."

"Hello, Craig," he said politely. "How are you?" Then he turned to look at the Oreos in the cart.

"Well, I'm fine, thanks, Guy. And what have you been up to today?"

Guy didn't seem to hear him. He touched the package of cookies.

"I think the 'hello' is all you'll get out of him for now," Hannah said. "He's kind of shy around new people."

Craig grinned at her. "Like mother, like son," he said. "He has to be yours, he's a great-looking kid."

"Well, thanks," Hannah said. "Listen, I've been meaning to thank you for handling that rude customer the other night. After saving my life, you just disappeared."

"I wanted to make sure he didn't try to go back in the store."

"Well, anyway, thanks. I owe you big time."

"Really? Then maybe you'll let me take you out to dinner—or lunch?"

Hannah gave him a wry smile. "That was very sneaky."

"Yeah, do you like how I just slipped it in there?"

She nodded. "Very smooth."

"Mom, can I get out of here?" Guy asked.

"Here, let me," Craig said. He quickly set down his shopping basket, then hoisted Guy out of the cart seat.

Hannah automatically reached out to take her son from him. She thought Guy might protest, but he seemed comfortable in Craig's arms.

"So—you didn't answer my question," Craig said, rocking Guy a little. "How about dinner? If you need Guy to chaperon, the three of us could go to a family place, my treat."

She laughed, then took Guy from him. "How about *lunch?* Wednesday?" Guy wiggled in her arms, and she tried to keep him still. "Um, I get a forty-five minute break at one o'clock, but I can stretch it to an hour. Meet me at the store, and we'll go from there, okay? And it's *my* treat."

Craig nodded. "We've got a date."

Lunch with Craig Tollman; it would be her first date in over five years.

Hannah didn't linger in the supermarket. She kept thinking she'd run into Craig again in one of the aisles, and she didn't want to. She didn't want to make small talk again, and she couldn't stand the silences—even when they were fueled by an unspoken attraction. If she'd ever had any talent for flirting, she'd lost it long ago. Craig made her nervous. Now they had a date. Well, she'd deal with it on Wednesday, when the time came.

Walking home, Hannah carried two well-laden bags by the paper handles—certain to break at any minute. Guy struggled with his little plastic bag containing two rolls of paper towels. He was huffing and puffing as if he were lugging a bowling ball. "You sure that's not too much for you, honey?" Hannah asked.

"I got it," he said, his blond head tilted down.

"Let me know if you get tired," she said.

Finally, he slung the bag over his shoulder, which seemed less awkward for him. After a moment, he asked, "Did Craig know my dad?"

Hannah hesitated. "Um, no, sweetie. Craig's a friend of mine from the video store."

"How did my dad die?"

"I've told you before, honey," Hannah said. "He died in a car accident a couple of months before you were born."

Guy nodded. "Oh, yeah." He was quiet for a while.

Hannah walked a step behind, studying him.

She'd decided while in the hospital, recuperating from the beating Kenneth had given her, that in her new life she'd tell everyone that Guy's father had died in a car accident. After all, a car crash was the excuse Kenneth had given for how she'd landed in Our Lady of the Sacred Heart Hospital.

The worst part of her hospital stay was the separation from her little boy. Guy was eighteen months old at the time, starting to talk and trying to get around on two feet. Every day was a new adventure for him, and she missed out on that. Hannah whiled away the days in that hospital bed making decisions about a whole new life for Guy and herself.

She had to run away with her son and start fresh someplace else. Seattle came to mind. The TV show *Frasier* was set there, and she watched the reruns every night she was in the hospital. It seemed a good choice, and she didn't know a soul in Seattle. Total anonymity.

She would need money, of course. Her plan was to make gradual, intermittent withdrawals from their joint account and tuck the cash away. She figured it would take about eight months to save five thousand dollars.

She'd have to change her name, erase her past, and sever

all connections. Kenneth and his family weren't going to let her steal Guy away—not without an extensive search.

The more she planned her escape, the more obstacles she saw. Sometimes it seemed utterly pointless. And there was no one she could confide in. She had people visiting her in the hospital every day: Kenneth (on his best behavior), her in-laws, and Mrs. Woodley's country-club friends. Nearly everyone on the hospital's staff seemed to like Hannah, and they were always dropping by her room. People kept sending flowers and cards. She'd never felt so popular—or so alone.

No one wanted to hear what had really happened to land her in that hospital, bruised and broken.

During her last week there, she was starting to eat solid foods again. One afternoon, the Woodleys came with Guy and his nanny, and some of their country-club friends. They made a big deal of wheeling her to the second-floor lounge, where an outside terrace overlooked the park and the lake. Several hospital staff members joined in what turned out to be an unveiling.

From the terrace, they all watched Kenneth, looking very dapper in his blue suit. He waved to them from the street. Then, in a showy gesture, he pulled the parachute-like draping off a new-model red Jetta. Tied around the car was one of those ridiculous large gold bows—the type rich people put around gift cars in TV commercials.

Everyone applauded. Hannah tried to smile. But she was embarrassed. A couple of the nurses with them on the terrace were struggling to support families. Here she was, getting wheeled back and forth from her private room. And her in-laws were giving her an expensive new car to replace the one she was supposed to have smashed up.

Standing beside Hannah—and wheeling her around that afternoon—was a husky, brooding, Latino orderly named Juan. He didn't applaud with the others. Of all the hospital staff, he was the only one who didn't seem to like her very much. He was terse and sullen around her. Juan became more talkative when someone speaking Spanish was in their vicinity. Then he'd go on and on in his native tongue, and Hannah figured he was deriding her half the time. She wondered what "rich bitch" sounded like in Spanish.

Kenneth joined them on the terrace. He gave Juan a bottle of champagne to open, then started passing out paper cups. One of the doctors pointed out that it was against hospital regulations to drink on hospital property, but he cited this as a special occasion. Everyone except Juan toasted to Hannah's remarkable recovery.

The celebration didn't last long. The doctors and nurses were on duty, and Kenneth and his father had to return to work. Kenneth took her new car. Guy's nanny announced that it was time for his nap. For a few minutes, Hannah was stuck on the terrace with Juan, her mother-in-law, and a couple of the country-club ladies. They were still talking about the new Jetta.

"Well, hindsight is twenty-twenty vision," Mrs. Woodley said. "But I wish we'd have given her a nice new car last year, instead of that horrible old hand-me-down.

"I feel partly responsible for Hannah ending up in here," she went on. "That piece of junk used to be my car. Well, you girls remember. I always had the worst time driving it. Poor Hannah, it's really not her fault."

Kenneth's mother was still going on about it after she and her friends pecked Hannah on the cheek and said good-bye. Hannah sat in her wheelchair and gazed out at the choppy gray water. The sky was turning dark. She listened to Mrs. Woodley talking to her colleagues as they headed inside for the elevator: "I never should have given the old car to Hannah. That automobile had terrible brakes. . . ."

"That automobile also had a mean right hook," Juan muttered.

Hannah glanced up at him. "Pardon me?"

"It wasn't the car that put you in here," Juan growled. "I know, Mrs. Woodley. I know. I don't blind myself like everyone else around here. I know the truth. Is there anything I can do to help you?"

Hannah started to cry. Maybe it was suddenly realizing she wasn't so alone after all. Juan put his hand on her shoulder. After a minute, he handed her a Kleenex.

"A man who beats his wife doesn't deserve to live," he said.

Hannah wiped her eyes and blew her nose.

"There was a girl he was seeing about five or six years ago, nice girl, very pretty. He put her in here, too; worked her over with a golf club. The family hushed it up. He's a son of a bitch, Mrs. Woodley."

Sniffling, Hannah shrugged. "I can't leave, not without my son. And my husband and his family aren't going let me take him."

"Listen," Juan whispered. He squatted a little, so he was face-to-face with her. "Working in this place, I've gotten to know a lot of people. We have all types coming through the emergency room. I have friends in high—and low—places. I know some guys who will handle it for you. They'll work cheap, too. That son of a bitch will have a real hard time beating you when he's in a wheelchair himself."

"No, I don't want that. But thanks anyway, Juan. God bless you." Wiping her eyes one last time, she noticed a flash of lightning over the lake. "Maybe you should take me inside now, okay? I think it's going to rain."

Juan let out an audible sigh; then he patted her shoulder again. "Forget I said anything," he whispered.

He wheeled Hannah back to her room. Neither of them uttered a word. He took her by the arm to help her into bed. Once Hannah settled back and pulled up the sheets, she broke the silence. "Maybe you could help me with something else," she said. "Maybe you know—from the emergency room or wherever—someone who can make me a few pieces of fake ID?"

A brand-new driver's license, a Social Security card, and Guy's new birth certificate would cost twelve hundred dollars. Hannah managed to save the money from three separate savings withdrawals that month after her release from the hospital.

Kenneth didn't notice. He was hardly around. He spent nearly every weekend sailing, and nearly every night with a young woman named Holly who worked at a florist in town. He wasn't very discreet about it, either. Kenneth had set up a little love nest for Holly and himself. Hannah had found the canceled rent checks amid their bank statements. She didn't really care. Holly was welcome to him.

Kenneth was dead to her. It would say as much on Guy's new birth certificate. *Father: deceased.* Guy's new name would be James Christopher Doyle. New birthplace: Evanston Hospital in Evanston, Illinois. Same birthday. Hannah's new name would be Hannah Dean Doyle—after James Dean, and Barney Doyle, a good friend of her dad's.

Those fake documents were like visas out of some sort of prison state. She was terrified that something would go wrong. She didn't really know Juan that well. Maybe his contact would leave with her money. Maybe Juan would disappear, and she'd never get out of Green Bay. When he called to say the documents were ready, she wouldn't allow herself to believe it until they were actually in her hand. She arranged to meet him in the east stairwell of the hospital during one of her follow-up visits to Our Lady of the Sacred Heart.

On the landing between the third and fourth floors, Juan slipped her an envelope. It had Guy's new birth certificate, an Illinois state driver's license for Hannah Dean Doyle, and a Social Security card.

Everything looked genuine. Hannah was impressed with the job they'd done. She hugged Juan and started to give him an extra hundred dollars.

"Save it," Juan said, his voice echoing in the stairwell. "Put it in your escape fund. You can leave a little sooner. I don't want to see you again, Mrs. Woodley, especially not in here."

"I'm not that worried. He's found himself a distraction in town. I hardly ever see him anymore."

"That could change very soon," Juan said. "Her name is Holly Speers. She was in here this week, all banged up. They put five stitches in her forehead. She was wired up on cocaine when they admitted her. She claimed she fell against a coffee table."

Hannah numbly stared at him.

"I think for Holly, the honeymoon's almost over. Besides, too many people know about them now. The Woodleys will be stepping in pretty soon. Your husband might be coming back to you. So—you keep that extra hundred for travel money, Mrs. Woodley. And get yourself and your little boy out of here as soon as you can."

Juan's prediction came true about ten days later. Kenneth started spending his nights at home again. He was on another "good behavior" streak. Hannah figured that his father must have given him a talking-to.

She slept in the guest room, which had more or less become her bedroom. Hannah had no intention of letting him touch her. She wondered how long Kenneth would go before he forced himself on her—or beat her up.

Though she saw it coming, Hannah was still caught off guard when he finally exploded. She was washing the dinner dishes on a Tuesday night. As long as Kenneth was playing the dutiful husband, she'd done the dutiful wife bit and fixed his favorite supper that evening, a special recipe for grilled halibut and baby potatoes. He'd stuffed himself. Now he was in the den, watching TV and looking after Guy. All was quiet, except for the slightly muted television. Then Hannah heard him.

"Goddamn it!" he shouted.

She heard a smack; then Guy shrieking. Hannah dropped a wineglass, and it smashed in the sink. She didn't even turn off the water. She just ran toward the den.

"You want another?" Kenneth was yelling. Hannah had heard that question too often at the start of a beating.

She stopped in the doorway to his den for a second, long enough to see what was happening. Her son was on the floor, crying. Standing over him, Kenneth had one hand raised. In the other hand, he held an expensive miniature model of his yacht. Kenneth cherished the stupid thing. Guy must have started playing with it, which was a no-no.

"Did you hit him?" Hannah asked, her voice shrill.

She didn't wait for an answer. She lunged at Kenneth and started beating him in the face. She was like a crazy woman. She didn't let up until he hauled back and knocked her to the floor. All the while, Guy was screaming.

"Fucking bitch!" Kenneth growled.

Blinking, she stared up at him. He had his hand to his face. Blood streamed from his nose down the front of his shirt. Hannah didn't even realize she'd done that to him. His prized model yacht had fallen out of his grasp and now lay broken by his feet.

"You're dead," Kenneth muttered. Then he stomped out of the room.

Hannah quickly gathered Guy in her arms, grabbed her purse, then hurried out the front door. Taking her new Jetta, she drove to a Holiday Inn Express on the edge of town. She parked the car in back so no one could see it from the highway. At the 7-Eleven next door, she bought a box of Huggies and some toiletries.

And so Guy spent his first night in a motel. Hannah hardly slept. She was so certain that she'd wake up to the phone ringing—or Kenneth pounding on the door.

In the morning, she drove back to the house. Not seeing his car in the driveway, she figured it was safe to go inside. She started collecting the essentials: everything from the fake documents, to a stuffed giraffe that Guy couldn't live without.

It took her ninety minutes to pack four suitcases and load up the car. All the while, she worried that Kenneth would come home and find them. She hated leaving behind certain items: an old clock and a few other knickknacks that had been in her family forever, certain books and CDs, a couple of photo albums. She had to say good-bye forever to these mementos, and move on.

Her heart sank when she stepped into the Savings and Loan. There was a line; about a dozen people. Guy began to fuss and cry, attracting the attention of everyone in the place—including a friend of her mother-in-law's. Of course, the woman came up to her and chatted on for a few minutes. Hannah could only pretend to listen. Every second was grueling.

At the teller window, Hannah filled out a savings withdrawal slip for eight thousand dollars. By the time she left the bank, Guy was screaming in her arms, and she was soaked with perspiration.

They drove to Milwaukee, where she sold the Jetta at an upscale used-car lot for twelve thousand dollars. She and Guy took a bus to Minneapolis. He cried most of the way. In her effort to keep a low profile, Guy wasn't helping. No doubt all the other passengers utterly despised the two of them.

From the Twin Cities, they took the train to Seattle. Guy liked the train. For the first time in forty-eight hours he actually seemed content, and slept well. Hannah could almost convince herself everything would be all right.

In Seattle, she found a cheap hotel with kitchenettes in the rooms. Every day, she and Guy went apartment hunting. She always picked up a *Milwaukee Journal* at the magazine store, and searched for any articles about the disappearance of Mrs. Kenneth Woodley II and her son. She didn't find anything.

She phoned Juan at Our Lady of the Sacred Heart.

"It's not a good idea to call me," he warned her. "They're looking for you. A private detective has been asking questions around here."

Hannah talked with an old friend from McNulty's Tavern, a coworker named Arlette Ivey. "Some guy came by two nights ago, asking about you," Arlette told her. "He was really obnoxious. He said you're in some kind of trouble, and we're all accessories to kidnapping and grand theft if we hold back any information. What's going on, Hannah?"

"Nothing. It's all just—a big misunderstanding. I'm all right. But please, Arlette. Don't tell anyone I called, okay?"

Once Hannah found her two-bedroom apartment at the Del Vista, she and Guy lived like hermits. Except for trips to the park, the supermarket, and video store, she didn't go anywhere. The only person who even knew her by name was Tish at Emerald City Video. When Hannah's money started to run out, she went to Tish for a job.

Guy wouldn't have to worry about money once he was an adult. Among the essentials she'd taken from the house in Green Bay was his real birth certificate. Her son was heir to the Woodleys' fortune. She'd tell him the truth when he was college age. Until then, he was hers.

As they walked up the steps to the apartment, Hannah watched him struggling with the small bag of paper towels. "You're doing a great job there, sweetie," she said. "You're really helping me out. Such a gentleman."

"I have to tinkle," Guy replied.

"Okay, hold on." Hannah unlocked the door and let him run inside first. He dropped the small bag, then made a beeline to the bathroom.

Hannah hoisted the groceries onto the kitchen counter and began to unload them. Underneath the Oreo cookies, she found a videotape.

"What's this?" she whispered.

The tape didn't come in a box or container. It was just a cassette: Tape B of *The Godfather*.

With a glance toward the bathroom, Hannah went to the VCR and slipped the tape inside. She switched on the TV and turned down the volume.

On the TV screen, Al Pacino and Diane Keaton were acting as godparents at the christening of their nephew. Hannah knew the movie. But she hadn't anticipated the very next cut: Alex Rocco, playing "Mo Green," lay seminude on a massage table. Someone approached him. He reached for his glasses to look up at the intruder. Hannah knew the scene now. Cringing, she watched the faceless visitor shoot Mo Green in the eye.

"Mom?"

With a shaky hand, she switched off the TV. Hannah glanced over her shoulder at Guy. She quickly ejected the tape. "Did you flush, and wash your hands?" she asked.

Guy nodded.

Hannah sat down on the floor and motioned him to come to her. She put her arm around Guy, then showed him the tape cassette. "Honey, did you see someone put this in our shopping cart?"

He shrugged and shook his head.

"Did you see it in the cart? Was it in there?"

Guy picked at his nose. "Yeah. But I didn't touch it."

She tried to smile, but a tremor crept into her voice. "Was this tape in the cart before Craig came up to talk to us? Think real hard, sweetie. It's important."

He winced. "I don't remember. Are you mad?"

"No, no," she assured him, kissing his forehead. "It's all right. Everything's fine."

Guy pointed to the cassette in her hand, then touched it. "What is this, Mom?"

"I don't know, honey," she whispered. She held him closer. "I don't know what it is."

Seven

The young woman stepped out of the taxicab. She wore tight black leather pants and a fuzzy, baby-blue angora sweater. Her chestnut-brown hair was in pigtails tonight. She pulled her folded-up massage table and duffel bag from the backseat. "Think your fucking arm would fall off if you helped me?" she muttered to the cab driver.

The audio probably didn't pick it up. But he caught the woman on videotape as she threw her money at the driver, then kicked the door shut with her spiked boot. She carried her table and bag to the front door, then rang the bell.

It was Tuesday night at Lester Hall's house.

He'd been watching Lester—and videotaping him—on and off for the last week. He'd already figured out how to break into Lester's house. There were several times he could have snuck into the place and quite easily murdered Lester in his sleep. But he needed to wait until tonight.

His video camera captured Lester coming to the door and letting the girl inside. The camera shut off for a minute. The next image was rickety. His hands were a bit shaky from running to the backyard, where he now photographed them through the sliding glass doors of Lester's recreation room. The woman was setting up her massage table. Lester stood at the bar, fixing them drinks.

One of the neighbors was throwing a party. The music and laughter drowned out what little conversation went on inside between Lester and his masseuse. He handed her a drink, then started to undress. The camera panned to her. She sipped her drink, then pulled the sweater over her head, pried off her boots, and wriggled out of her pants. She'd peeled down to just her thong before Lester even got his pants unzipped. The woman took another hit of her drink, then excused herself and padded toward the bathroom.

Lester Hall started to step out of his pants.

The camera went off.

Tarin Siegel sat naked on the toilet in Lester Hall's bathroom. For the next ninety minutes, Lester would demand her undivided attention, and that meant no bathroom breaks.

If she had the cash, Tarin would have gladly given Lester her one-hundred-and-twenty-buck fee just so she wouldn't have to touch his paunchy old body tonight. Lester was Tarin Siegel's best and worst customer. Every Tuesday night she could count on him. No other client was as steady. He had a nice place, and always fixed her a drink. The fact that he was out of shape and had a couple of weird moles on his back didn't actually matter to her. She barely noticed the bodies any more—unless the guys were cute and really fit.

But there was nothing cute about Lester. Tarin had learned early on that he didn't like her talking during the massage part. But when it came time for the big finish, she couldn't read his mood. Often he wanted verbal encouragement; sometimes not. Nine times out of ten, she'd make the wrong call. *"Well, don't just jerk me off, stupid, say something!"* he'd complain one week. Then, during the next session, he'd grouse *"How do you expect me to concentrate when you won't shut up?"*

One thing predictable about him was the way he acted afterward: sullen and mean. Once he was finished, he was finished—with her. It was like he couldn't wait for her to leave. He was such lousy company, she preferred to wait outside for the cab to pick her up. Of course, Lester didn't want her standing on the curb in front of his house, so she always had to hide behind a stupid hedge near his front door. Those nights when the cab was late, she absolutely dreaded having to ring his damn bell and use his phone again. Some nights, it just wasn't worth the one hundred and twenty bucks.

The son of a bitch was out of toilet paper. Tarin sighed. Still crouching a bit, she moved over to the cabinet beneath the sink. It was a tiny, windowless powder room—no tub or shower. She found a roll of Charmin under the sink, sat back on the toilet, and loaded up the dispenser.

Tarin wiped herself, and was about to flush the toilet. That was when she heard Lester raise his voice: "Who the fuck are you?"

"You shouldn't have called her a bitch," someone whispered.

Though he spoke softly, Tarin could still hear him. In fact, the words sliced right through her.

"No, God, no!"

A loud shot rang out.

Tarin gasped. Her heart seemed to stop for a second.

Paralyzed with fear, she didn't dare utter a word. Her whole body start to shake. Tarin thought she might be sick, and she swallowed hard. Tears filled her eyes, but she couldn't cry. She had to keep very still.

She heard his footsteps. He was getting closer. Did he know she was in here?

Slowly, Tarin stood up. All of a sudden she felt naked, and she covered her breasts. She glanced over at the door, then cringed. She hadn't locked it.

The footsteps got louder, then stopped.

Waiting for the next sound became unbearable. Her eyes riveted to the door, Tarin watched the knob slowly turn to one side.

All at once, the bathroom light went out, and she was engulfed in total darkness. She'd forgotten that the light switch for the bathroom was outside the door. At the threshold, a line of light cut through the blackness. She could see the shadows of his feet skimming across that line.

She heard him laugh, a strange cackling.

Tarin couldn't breathe. Blindly groping in the dark, she tried to find the towel rack or something she could hold on to, something with which she could defend herself.

The door burst open, and slammed against the wall.

Tarin screamed.

The last thing she saw was a man's silhouette coming at her. His face was swallowed up in the shadows, and he held a shiny object in his hand.

"Chicago," Hannah said, over her glass of Diet Coke. "I'm originally from Chicago."

Craig was asking way too many questions. It had been years since she'd dated. But she didn't recall ever having to weather through so many inquiries about her background.

They were eating lunch across the street from the video store, at a place called Bagels & Choosers. It was an upscale sandwich shop with high ceilings, metal tables, and regional artwork hanging on brick walls. Craig looked handsome in his gray turtleneck and jeans. But that didn't matter, because Hannah's guard was up. At this point, she didn't trust anyone. Still, it was a date, and she'd dressed a notch above her usual store-clerk knockabouts. Her hair was pinned up, and she wore khakis with a pink oxford shirt.

"When did you move to Seattle?" Craig asked, picking at his Cobb salad.

"About three years ago," Hannah lied.

"Are you—um, still in touch with Guy's father?"

She shook her head. "He died in a car accident before Guy was born." Hannah put down her spoon. The chicken noodle soup was a bit too salty. "Listen, do you mind if we change the subject?"

"I'm sorry."

Forcing a smile, Hannah shrugged. "It's okay. The marriage was pretty much kaput by the time I got pregnant. I just don't feel like discussing it. Let's talk about you. What exactly does a Web content director do anyway?"

Craig started explaining it to her. Hannah nodded and pretended to listen. All the while, she wondered about that *Godfather* cassette in her shopping cart. She'd been wondering for days. It was why she couldn't really trust Craig Tollman. Was he the one who had slipped that tape in her cart? She hadn't had a chance to ask him yet. So far, he'd been the one asking all the questions.

"Anyway, it's not what I thought I'd end up doing," he was saying. "How about you? What line of work were you in before you got married?"

"Um, retail," she lied. "I worked at Marshall Field's."

Hannah sat back. "Hey, speaking of shopping," she said. "I've been meaning to ask you about that tape you slipped into my shopping cart at the store the other afternoon."

He squinted at her. "What tape?"

"The videotape of *The Godfather*—or at least its second half. It was in my shopping cart at the checkout line. Didn't you put it in there?"

Craig shook his head. "I don't know what you're talking about."

Hannah studied him for a moment. Craig seemed genuinely confused.

She sighed. "Never mind. I guess someone was playing a joke on me or something." She glanced at her wristwatch. "Listen, I should head back to the store."

Craig got to his feet. "I just need to use the men's room for a minute. Then I'll walk back with you. Okay?"

While he headed toward the rest rooms, Hannah flagged down their waiter. She got the check, then stepped over to the cashier to cover it. By the register was a stack of discarded newspapers. The one on top caught Hannah's eye. She saw a photograph, and a headline near the bottom of the front page:

RETIRED SEATTLE BUSINESSMAN
SLAIN IN HOME
'A Night of Terror,' for Surviving Witness
Madronna Neighborhood on Alert as
Police Continue Their Investigation

Hannah picked up the newspaper and moved away from the register. She studied the grainy photo of the victim, then read the caption beneath it: *L. Hollis Hall, 58, former Executive Vice President of Savitch, Inc., is survived by a daughter, 25.*

She recognized the cold, crudely handsome older man in the picture. How could she forget the belligerent Mr. *Sorority Sluts* who had caused such a scene in the store last week?

Hannah glanced over at the rest-room area. She didn't see Craig, so she started reading the article:

A retired businessman, L. Hollis Hall, 58, was shot to death, execution-style, by an intruder in his Madronna home Tuesday night.

Investigating officers are relying heavily on the testimony of a witness, Tarin Siegel, 31, who was also attacked in Hall's house at the time of his death. Siegel sustained a mild concussion after being knocked over the head in Hall's bathroom. Hall, who suffered from chronic back problems, had employed Siegel, a massage therapist, for the evening.

What Siegel called "a night of terror," began at 9:30 P.M. with her arrival at Hall's home in the quiet, affluent Seattle neighborhood. . . .

Still standing near the restaurant door, Hannah skimmed over the rest of the newspaper story.

Apparently, the woman had been in the bathroom when she'd heard Hall talking to an intruder, then the gunshot.

Someone had broken into the john and knocked her unconscious with the butt of a revolver.

Hannah slowed down to read Tarin Siegel's account of
what she found when she regained consciousness and staggered out of the bathroom: "*I stepped back into the room
where we were. I saw him lying on the massage table, and I
saw all the blood. . . .*"

"My God," Hannah murmured. "It's *The Godfather*
scene." The newspaper began to shake in her grasp.

"There you are," Craig said, touching her shoulder. "I was
looking for you."

Hannah recoiled.

He laughed. "Are you okay?"

She quickly folded up the newspaper, almost crumpling it.
"I'm fine," she answered. "I need to get back to the store."

"Let me just take care of the check—"

"I got it already," she said impatiently. "Let's just go."
Tucking the newspaper under her arm, Hannah headed for
the door.

As she walked back to the video store with him, Hannah's
mind was going in a dozen different directions. The last
time she'd seen Lester Hall, Craig was throwing him out of
the store and threatening him. Craig had been in the supermarket with her when that *Godfather* tape had made its way
into her shopping cart. She didn't care what he'd told her a
few minutes ago. She didn't trust him.

He took hold of her arm as they crossed the street. Hannah wrenched away from him. "I'm all right, thanks," she
said over the traffic noise. She started toward the door to
Emerald City Video.

Craig stepped in her path, blocking the way. "Listen,
Hannah, did I do anything to upset you?"

"No, I'm just—awfully late for work. I'll call you. All
right?" She moved around him and grabbed the door handle.

He braced a hand against the door. "Wait a second—"

"Please," she said, losing her composure. "I need you to
leave me alone. Just go! Okay?"

With a wounded look, Craig stared at her. Hannah hurried inside.

Scott manned the register nearest the door. He'd obviously heard the last part of her exchange with Craig. "Ouch," he said. "That has to be one of the worst wrap-ups to a first date I've ever witnessed. What the hell happened? Are you all right?"

Through the front window, Hannah watched Craig slink away down the street. She moved behind the counter to her register. She was trembling. She set down the newspaper, and opened it for Scott to see. "Take a look at this. Isn't this the *Sorority Sluts* guy from last week?"

Hannah logged into the customer account records: Hall, Lester.

"Holy shit," Scott muttered.

Hannah had seen the photograph. But she needed to make certain L. Hollis Hall was indeed Lester Hall.

On the register's computer screen, the account for Hall, Lester H. came up. Same first and middle initial, and his address was in the Madronna area. Hannah noticed the icon blinking on an "N" in the corner of the screen. It meant there was a note on his account. She pulled up the note: *THIS CREEP MUST DIE!*

Hannah gasped. "Oh, my God, look what somebody wrote."

Scott came to her side. "Relax, Hannah," he said, a hand on her shoulder. "I wrote that last week—right after he had his hissy fit in here." Scott let out a stunned laugh. "Christ, I didn't know it would come true."

Hannah backed away from the register. "First that rude Cindy woman who fell out of her apartment window a couple of weeks back," she whispered. "And now this Lester Hall is shot. Don't you see what's happening?"

Scott nodded. "Yeah, it means I better be nice to you from now on, otherwise I'm dead meat."

"That's not funny," Hannah said. She grabbed the newspaper. "Cover for me, okay? I'll be right back."

Hannah hurried out of the store, then started to cross the street toward the mall. Suddenly, a car horn blared, and tires were screeching. "You moron!" someone screamed from his car. "Watch where you're going!"

Hannah stepped back to the curb. She hadn't realized she was crossing against the traffic signal. She caught her breath and waited for the "Walk" signal. Her face felt hot. People were staring at her.

The traffic light changed, and Hannah hurried across to the mall. At the phone stations, she dug some change out of her purse, then checked the newspaper again. At the bottom of the article was a blurb about the reporter: *David Serum can be reached at DSerum@seattlenews.net or 206/555-0405.*

Hannah dialed the number, then counted two ring tones.

"This is David Serum," he answered. Rock music from the Old Navy next door competed with him. Hannah had to cover her other ear.

"Yes, I have a question about your article today, about that murder in Madronna."

"Can I get your name, please?"

"I just have a question," she said. "I need to know if he was shot in the eye."

"Um, I have to get your name, ma'am."

"Answer my question, and I'll tell you my name. Please, it's important."

She didn't hear anything on the other end of the line.

"Are you still there?" Hannah asked.

"Yes, ma'am, but that information is not—"

"Please, tell me. Was he shot in the eye?"

"Yes, Mr. Hall was shot through the left eye. Now, if you could—"

Hannah quickly hung up.

She thought she was going to be sick. She wove through the crowd of shoppers in the mall, and hurried into the women's rest room.

It was empty. Hannah ducked into the last stall. Bracing

herself against the divider wall, she took several deep breaths until her stomach felt a little better.

She kept wondering why this was happening to her. These two people were murdered, and someone was telling her in advance how they would die. But why were they killed? Because they'd been rude to her?

Hannah felt another wave of nausea. Tears welled in her eyes.

Someone else stepped into the rest room. Hannah reached over and closed her stall door. She heard footsteps on the tiled floor. For a moment, she didn't move. Hannah wiped her eyes with some toilet paper, and took a few more deep breaths. She flushed the toilet paper down the john, then opened the stall door.

The stall next to hers was empty. There was nobody by the sinks, either. She could have sworn someone was in the bathroom with her a minute ago.

Hannah glanced over toward the sinks again and noticed a small black rectangular box on the edge of the counter.

It was a videocassette.

Eight

Hannah hurried out of the women's room with the video in her hand. Slowing down, she passed several shoppers in the mall: a pack of teenage girls, some women with their children, an elderly couple. She was searching for a man alone; maybe someone from the store or her film class, maybe a total stranger.

She knew he couldn't be far. He'd been in the bathroom less than a minute ago. He was probably still watching her right now. She kept wondering why he was doing this to her. Did he somehow know that she couldn't go to the police?

Hannah spotted a man with a sweatshirt, jeans, and curly gray hair. He stood near the food court entrance and stared back at her. He smirked a little, then shoved his hands in his pockets.

She froze. The familiar, almost lecherous way he grinned seemed to invite some kind of encounter—or confrontation. Hannah felt a chill pass through her.

A woman brushed by Hannah, then went to the man and gave him a hug. He kissed her. Arm in arm, they went into the food court together.

Sighing, Hannah resumed her search, scanning the crowd for the person who was playing this lethal game with her. She thought she saw a man staring at her from inside the entrance of Old Navy. But then she realized it was a mannequin. She felt so stupid. She knew her tormenter was watching her right now, amused at her silly mistakes.

She glanced at the videocassette in her hand. There was no label on the tape, probably something recorded live or off a TV. From the tape around the spools, she could see the movie had been stopped at a certain scene. Hannah knew when she put that video in a VRC and pressed "Play," she would see another murder sequence.

She knew that her secret admirer was planning to kill again. And he wanted her to see how he would do it.

As soon as Hannah returned to the store, she ducked into the break room. She slipped the mystery video in the VCR and switched on the little television.

Audrey Hepburn came up on the screen. She was sitting in a rocking chair, with a walking cane across her lap. She wore a pink sweater. The room was awfully dark, and the poor quality of the video didn't help matters.

As soon as Hannah saw Audrey talking to Richard Crenna, she figured out that the movie was the thriller *Wait Until Dark*. She hadn't seen the film in years, and she didn't know what came next.

Someone knocked on the break-room door; then Scott poked his head in. "You okay back here?" he asked.

Hannah quickly switched off the video. "Yeah, I was just checking this movie for a glitch," she said. "Do you need me up front?"

"No, Britt's handling it," Scott replied. He stepped inside, then closed the door behind him. "Hannah, are you all right? You seem to be taking it pretty hard about this Lester guy getting shot."

She wanted to tell him about the videos, but couldn't. She shrugged uneasily. "It's just—he was in the store only last week. And pretty much the same thing happened to Cindy Finkelston after she was in the store."

"Well, it's just a coincidence. I don't mean to sound heartless, but I'm not shedding any tears for either of them." Folding his arms, he leaned against the doorway frame. "So what happened over your lunch date with the dreamboat? Or shouldn't I ask?"

"Oh, he's just really pushy. He got on my nerves." Hannah sighed. "I'll be a couple of more minutes back here, then I'll come help up front. Okay?"

He nodded. "Sure thing. Take your time."

Scott stepped out and closed the door behind him.

Biting her lip, Hannah pressed the control on the VCR again, and *Wait Until Dark* came back on the screen. Audrey Hepburn was still talking to Richard Crenna in that dark room; then the scene cut to a parking lot at night. A man in an overcoat was walking across the shiny, wet pavement. They didn't show his face. Suddenly, a car's headlights glared into the camera, and tires screeched. It was a big, sleek, metal monster of an automobile from the mid-sixties. The car peeled out of a parking spot and came careening at the man.

Hannah watched in shock as he started to run. The car hit him full force, throwing his body against a chain-link fence. Its engine grinding, the car backed up, then slammed into him once more. His prone, lifeless body bounced against the fence. Its tires squealing, the car slammed into the man again and again.

Just as suddenly as the movie had cut to that harrowing murder in the parking lot, it switched back to Audrey Hepburn in the dimly lit room. Hannah remembered now. It was Richard Crenna's accomplice, Jack Weston, killed in that parking lot—by the main heavy, played by Alan Arkin.

But Hannah didn't know who would be killed that way in real life. And she didn't know the killer.

Hannah ejected the video from the VCR. She kept thinking that she should call the police. But what could she tell them? *Someone will be mowed down by car in a parking lot. I don't know when. I don't know who it will be. But I've been getting videos predicting all these deaths. And oh, yeah, there's a warrant out for my arrest. I'm wanted for kidnapping and theft.*

She pulled the video out of the VRC and stared at it.

Someone knocked on the door again. This time, Britt peeked into the room. "Scott sent me back here to make sure you aren't slashing your wrists or anything."

Hannah let out a weak laugh. "I'm fine."

"Honest?" Britt asked.

"No, I'm not," Hannah admitted, shaking her head. "Something weird has been going on, and I—I haven't been able to talk to anyone about it." Hannah sighed. She felt herself tearing up. "Listen, Britt, can you keep a secret? I mean, you really can't tell anyone about this. . . ."

His head on the pillow, Guy gazed up at her with sleepy eyes.

Hannah stroked his blond hair. "If you hear somebody at the door a little later, it's Britt. She's spending the night."

Guy squinted at her.

"You remember my friend Britt from work, don't you?"

"She has a pierced ear here and here, doesn't she?" He pointed to his eyebrow and then his nostril.

Cracking a smile, Hannah nodded. "That's right. Now, get some sleep."

She tucked the covers under his chin, and made the choo-choo sound. He nodded off after a few minutes. Hannah left his night-light on, then tiptoed out of his bedroom.

She took some sheets from the linen closet so she could make up the sofa for Britt.

It had been such a relief to finally unload on someone today. At least, she didn't have to feel so alone in this nightmare. Unfortunately, Britt didn't entirely understand the situation.

"So—somebody's leaving these movies where you can find them?" she'd asked a couple of hours ago in the break room. "And it's like clues to these murders you're supposed to solve?"

"Well, not exactly," Hannah tried to explain. "You see—"

"Why is this happening to you?"

"I wish I knew," Hannah said.

"Well, why don't you go to the cops?"

"That's just it. I can't. Swear you won't tell anyone, Britt. But I've had some trouble with the police, and I can't go to them without sinking into deeper trouble. It's something totally unrelated to what's happening now."

"What did you do?" Britt whispered.

Frowning, Hannah shook her head. "I can't say any more about it."

Britt stared at her for a moment; then she shrugged. "Well, I've had a few run-ins with the law too, Han. You're in good company." She nudged her. "Hey, speaking of company, how about if I stay over tonight?"

Hannah managed a smile. "Oh, that's not necessary, Britt. I appreciate the offer—"

"To tell you the truth," Britt interrupted, wincing a bit. Her voice dropped to a whisper. "You'd be doing me a favor, Han. Y'know, like the last time when Webb was being a shitheel, and you let me stay over? I really don't want to go back home to him tonight. Do you mind?"

Actually, Hannah didn't mind at all. She'd sheltered Britt a few times in the past when Webb was on the warpath. She sympathized. She'd been down that road herself. Tonight, she welcomed the company. Britt didn't offer a lot of protection, but there was safety in numbers. Hannah had warned her friend to be careful on the way over.

She was changing a pillowcase from one of her bed pillows, when someone knocked on the front door. She wondered how Britt had gotten past the lobby's security entrance downstairs.

Hannah checked the peephole before opening the door. She saw a man, tall with broad shoulders. She couldn't quite make out who he was until he stepped back under the outside light.

"Scott?" She pulled the door open. "What are you doing here?"

"Britt sent me," he said. He was holding a backpack. "Something came up with her loser-of-a-boyfriend. They were fighting, but now they've kissed and made up or something. She said you might need someone to spend the night. Are you going to ask me in, or what?"

Dumbfounded, Hannah stepped aside and opened the door wider. "I really don't need anyone staying with me—"

"Oh, relax, I'm here," Scott said. "I can crash on the sofa. I brought along *Sixteen Candles*. We'll do each other's hair and try on each other's makeup. It'll be a blast." He glanced around. "Hey, I like your place."

He set his backpack on her counter. "Britt said you have a stalker, some kind of weirdo sending you videotapes."

"She told you?" Hannah asked,

He nodded. "She said you were in trouble with the cops, too."

"What?" Hannah murmured incredulous. "I swore her to secrecy."

Scott rolled his eyes. "Oh, Britt's the worst. I thought you knew that. Telephone, telegraph, tell-a-Britt. She sang to me the minute you left work tonight. Anyway, don't worry about me. I can keep a secret."

Hannah gave him a wary look. "Aren't you going to ask why I'm in trouble with the police?"

"Do you want to tell me?" he asked pointedly.

Hannah frowned. "No, not really."

"Fine. It's none of my goddamn business. I won't ask. But if you—"

There was a knock at the door. Hannah and Scott looked at each other. "Were you expecting someone else?" he whispered.

Hannah shook her head. She went to the door and checked the peek hole. It was Craig. She was suddenly very grateful for Scott's company. She opened the door.

Craig stared past her shoulder at Scott; then he looked at her again. "Hi. I know it's late," he said, smiling awkwardly. "I would've called first, but you never gave me your number."

"How did you get past the lobby door?" Hannah asked.

"It was open," Craig said.

"It was open when I came in, too," Scott volunteered. "But I closed it." He extended his hand to Craig. "Hi, I'm Scott. I work with Hannah."

Craig shook his hand. "Hi, yeah. I recognize you from the store."

Hannah cleared her throat. "I'm sorry I can't invite you in. Scott and I are in the middle of something."

"Well, could I talk to you for just a couple of minutes?" Craig asked. "Maybe out here on the balcony?"

Hannah gave Scott a look over her shoulder. She put the door on the latch and stepped outside.

"I didn't mean to intrude," Craig said, leaning against the walkway balcony's railing. "It's just, I had to see you and talk to you; otherwise I couldn't hope for any kind of sleep tonight. I keep thinking about our lunch date today. Did I do anything to upset you?"

"Actually, I was upset about something else."

"And it had nothing to do with me?"

Hannah rubbed her arms from the chill. "It may have," she admitted. "That man you threw out of the store, he was murdered yesterday."

Craig appeared genuinely stunned. "What?"

Hannah nodded. "Somebody shot him. I read about it in the newspaper at lunch today, while you were using the rest room."

Craig frowned at her. "Do you think I had something to do with it?"

"I'm not sure."

"Hannah, I didn't even know the guy. The last time I saw him was when I tossed him out of the store. You say somebody shot him?"

"Yes. He was shot in the eye." She shivered a bit, and rubbed her arms harder. "Craig, how did you find out where I live?"

He seemed stumped for a moment. He stared back at her,

then shrugged. "Hannah, I—I'm just trying to help you, for chrissakes."

"You've been following me around, *watching me,* haven't you?"

"God, no. It's not like that at all—"

"How did you get past the door downstairs?" she asked. "Have you done it before?"

"What kind of question is that? Hannah—"

Staring at him, she backed toward the door. "I think you'd better go now." She opened the door.

"Oh, c'mon, please. Don't be this way."

Scott came up behind Hannah. "Everything okay here?" he asked.

"Craig's just leaving," she said.

"Hannah, you're wrong about me," Craig said, frowning. He shook his head, then turned and stomped toward the stairwell.

"Funny, he's not so good-looking to me anymore," Scott said, putting an arm around her shoulder. "Plus, he's wearing sandals with black stretch socks. What was he thinking?"

Hannah stepped toward the railing and glanced down at the sidewalk and the parking lot below.

"Think he's your stalker?" Scott asked.

Hannah shrugged. "I don't know. I'm not sure of anything anymore." She watched Craig, three stories below, walking away from her building.

"I'll bet he saw me coming up here," she heard Scott say. "He probably wanted to check out the competition."

"Maybe," Hannah muttered. She saw Craig head into the parking lot, which was reserved for tenants only. She noticed an old white car that she'd never seen in the lot before: a big, sleek, metal monster of an automobile from the mid-sixties.

"Oh, my God," she whispered.

Craig walked in front of the car. Its headlights suddenly went on; high beams. Craig seemed to freeze.

"No!" Hannah cried, grabbing Scott's arm.

Helplessly, she watched the big car lunge forward. With tires screeching, it plowed into Craig. He seemed to fold over the hood. The car didn't slow down at all. Carrying Craig's prone body on its nose, the old automobile barreled into the back of a minivan parked in the lot. Hannah turned away and buried her head in Scott's shoulder.

"Holy Jesus," she heard Scott murmur, over the smashing glass and twisting steel. A car alarm went off, blaring in the night. Tires squealed, and the old car's motor roared once more. There was another loud crash.

Hannah pulled herself away, but still held on to her friend as she peered down at the parking lot. She could see Craig Tollman's crumpled, broken body on the pavement. He was lying in a pool of blood that looked black in the night.

She knew the automobile would hit him again. Poor Craig was obviously already dead. But the automobile had to hit him three times because that was how it happened in *Wait Until Dark*.

Its engine grinding, the car lurched toward Craig's corpse one more time. Hannah automatically turned her head away. Then she heard another crash. When she looked down at the lot again, the car was heading for the street. Its smashed, crumpled front hood was covered with Craig's blood.

She and Scott were no longer alone on the balcony. Several residents from her building had come out of their apartments, drawn by all the noise. Within a couple of minutes, about a dozen people had gone down to the parking lot. They slowed down to a stop as they approached Craig's corpse. They seemed reluctant to get too close to him.

Hannah was numb. She wanted to do something, but she couldn't even move. It was too late to help him. Craig was dead. She just stood there, her hands gripping the railing.

Scott tried to talk, but he couldn't seem to get any words out. His face was the color of chalk. He kept shaking his head.

"Mom?"

She turned and saw Guy, in his Spider-Man pajamas,

coming toward the door. He rubbed his eyes. "What's all that noise?" he asked.

Hannah rushed toward him before he could reach the door. She scooped him up in her arms. His body felt warm. "It's only a car alarm, honey," she said, a tremor in her voice. "Nothing for you to see. C'mon, let's get you back to bed. Say good night to Scott."

"G'night, Scott," he said, his arms and legs wrapped around Hannah.

Scott just nodded and gave Guy a pale smile.

Tears in her eyes, Hannah carried Guy down the hall.

"Mom, are you crying?" he asked.

"No, I'm fine, honey," she lied.

He needed to go to the bathroom, then asked for a glass of water. By the time Hannah got him settled back in bed, she heard the police and ambulance sirens. Through Guy's bedroom windows, she could see a red whirling light from the emergency vehicles outside, three stories below.

To her amazement, Guy started to drift off within a couple minutes, despite all the noise. Her legs a little unsteady, Hannah wandered out of his bedroom and up the hallway. She wiped her eyes and tried to focus on Scott.

He stood in the doorway, nervously smoking a cigarette. "So—aren't we going to talk to the police?" he said.

"I can't get involved," Hannah said. She felt so ashamed and scared. All she wanted to do was run away—from this murderer, from the police, from everything.

"Your trouble with the cops," Scott said. "It's really serious, isn't it?"

Hannah sighed. "You said you weren't going to ask."

"That was before," Scott replied. He rubbed his forehead. "Jesus, I can't believe it. He was just standing here talking to us a few minutes ago. Listen, Hannah. I'm not asking about your problem with the cops to be nosey. I'm concerned for you, Han. They're sure to go through Craig's pockets, and search his car. He might have your address on him."

Hannah numbly gazed down at all the people, police, and flashing emergency vehicles in the parking lot below.

Scott took a drag from his cigarette. "Hannah, you're involved—whether you want to be or not."

Nine

The parking lot was still a mob scene.

They'd managed to silence the car alarms, but there were still engines idling and people talking over one another. Static-garbled announcements came on patrol car radios, and one loud, very angry cop was yelling at everyone to step back.

About fifty people had gathered at the parking lot entrance. Hannah made her way through the crowd while paramedics loaded Craig's shrouded body into the back of an ambulance.

Only ten minutes ago, Craig had been talking with her. And now he was a corpse. Hannah still couldn't quite comprehend it. Who had been driving that old-model white car?

Maybe the police knew. It was a long shot, but Hannah tried to listen to their conversations with one another. So far, she wasn't having much luck finding out anything.

She thought about what Scott had said earlier. Craig must have had her name and address written down somewhere—in his wallet, his pocket, or in his car. Had the police found it yet?

She'd left Scott in the apartment. Someone had to stay there in case Guy woke up again. If that happened, Scott was supposed to flick the living room light on and off a few times.

Hannah kept looking back up at her building. She heard some people talking, and apparently, the police were looking for a white Impala that had been reported stolen late last night.

Then Hannah overheard one officer tell another that the car had been found two miles away. "Somebody torched it," he said. "Lots of luck getting reliable prints or DNA samples there. Smart SOB. Y'know, I think—"

"THERE'S NOTHING MORE TO SEE!" yelled the cop in charge of crowd control, drowning out his coworkers. "COME ON, PEOPLE, GO HOME. . . ."

Hannah stepped back, and bumped into someone. "Excuse me," she muttered. Then she looked up at the man and gasped.

"Hi," Ben said.

Hannah numbly stared at him. "What are you doing here?"

He glanced at the other people around them, then winced a bit. "You won't like this, but I've been looking out after you. Did you know this Craig guy?"

"What do you mean, you've been 'looking out after' me?" Hannah asked.

"It's hard to explain. I just wanted to make sure nothing bad happened to you."

The siren began wailing as the ambulance pulled out of the lot. Ben stopped to look at the vehicle speeding down the street. Then he turned to her again. "Did you know him very well?"

"Not very," Hannah replied, her guard up. She glanced over at the puddle of blood on the parking lot pavement.

"Do you know what he was here investigating?" Ben asked.

"What are you talking about?" Hannah murmured.

"Ronald Craig, the guy who just got killed. Do you know why he was here?"

Hannah frowned. "His name is—*was*—Craig Tollman."

Ben shook his head. "I was one of the first people here, Hannah. I saw the police take out his wallet and identification. I heard them. His name was Ronald Craig, and he was a private investigator from Milwaukee."

"He's from Wisconsin?" Hannah whispered.

Ben nodded.

She wanted to grab Guy, pack their bags, and catch the first bus or train out of Seattle. No doubt, Kenneth and his family knew where she was now. Their private detective, Craig—or rather *Ronald* Craig—had probably been sending daily progress reports back to Wisconsin.

"I noticed you and him talking outside your apartment," Ben said.

Hannah stared at him, eyes narrowed. "Where were you standing that you could see us on the balcony?"

He nodded toward an alley across the street. "Over there."

"Then you must have seen the car that hit him," she whispered. "Did you get a glimpse of the driver?"

He shook his head, then pointed to a van parked nearby. "That blocked my view of the lot. I heard it happening, but didn't see a thing. I only caught a glimpse of the white car as it sped away." He sighed. "Listen, I think this Ronald Craig must have uncovered something, and that's why he was killed."

Hannah edged away from him. "What are you talking about?"

"He was following you. And I think he might have seen someone else who was following you."

"Someone else?" Hannah said, with a stunned laughed. "You mean, besides you? What? Is half the city of Seattle following me?"

Ben frowned. "I've seen two men. One was Ronald Craig. I haven't gotten a good look at the second guy. But I think he's videotaping you."

Hannah shook her head, but she knew Ben was right. There had to be a third person, and he was Craig's killer. Ben couldn't have been driving that white car. He'd have had to move awfully fast, coming back to the scene of his crime just minutes after ditching and burning the old white Impala. He didn't smell of gasoline.

"Who are you?" she whispered, eyes narrowed at him. "Your name isn't Sturges."

"No. My last name's Podowski. I came out here from New York last month, I—" He sighed. "It's a long story, and I can't go into it now. Just trust me, Hannah. I'm trying to help you."

"Craig said he was trying to help me, too."

Ben shrugged. "Well, do you want to talk with the police?" He glanced at one of the officers by the parking lot gate. The policeman seemed to be staring back at them.

"No, I don't want to go to the police," Hannah admitted quietly.

She still didn't know who Ben *Podowski* was, or what he wanted. But she figured she had no choice but to let him "help" her, whatever that meant. At least, she'd go through the motions and pretend to trust him. "How exactly do you plan to help me?" she asked.

Ben looked over at the lot for a moment. "When the police went through Ronald Craig's pockets, they found a hotel room key. I heard them talking. He was staying at the Seafarer Inn on Aurora Boulevard. I'll go check this place out, do some snooping around. Maybe I can find out who Craig was working for, and how much he knew about this guy with the video camera. It's a long shot, but might be worth it."

He sighed, then smiled at her. "Could you do me a favor? Could you phone a taxi for me when you get back up to your place? I'll be waiting out here. I have no other way of getting to this hotel."

Nodding, Hannah backed toward her lobby door. "I'll call a cab for you."

"Thanks," Ben said. "I'll phone you later tonight. What's your number?"

"555-1007. Don't you need to write it down?"

"I'll remember it," he said. "Thanks, Hannah."

She unlocked the door, then ducked inside. As Hannah wandered up the stairs, her footsteps echoed in the cinderblock stairwell. She could hardly comprehend any of the events in the last hour. She tried to put all the pieces together.

Hannah could only guess what led *Ronald Craig* halfway across the country to her. Kenneth and his family probably had detectives tapping her friends' telephones. Maybe they'd traced one of her rare calls to Chicago and come up with the number of a Seattle pay phone.

However he'd pulled it off, this detective calling himself Craig Tollman had found her.

And now he was dead.

A police car occupied the Seafarer Inn's "Reservations Only" spot near the front door.

Ben had thought the place would be swarming with cops, maybe even a few reporters. He'd figured he could get lost in the crowd; listen to what people were saying and pick up some secondhand information. That was how he'd learned about Ronald Craig—by hanging around the parking lot of Hannah's building.

But aside from the solitary patrol car, things looked pretty quiet at the Seafarer Inn. Ben hoped at least the desk clerk might tell him something.

After giving the taxi driver a five-dollar tip, Ben asked him to wait near the edge of the lot. He stopped to check his wallet. He still had Paul Gulletti's business card from a few weeks ago when he'd first joined the film class. The card had the newspaper's logo on it, and identified Paul as a "Reporter-Contributor." Ben slipped the card inside his shirt pocket, then hurried into the small lobby.

Sitting on a brown sofa by the door was a thin, long-legged redhead with dark eye makeup. She looked Ben up and down, then smiled.

Ben nodded politely and stepped up to the front desk.

The lobby was done up in a nautical theme, with old fishing nets draping the walls. Ensnared in the nets were dusty shells, balls of colored glass, starfish, and sea horses. Even the desk clerk looked like an old sea cook. He was stocky, with a weatherworn face and gray mustache. He wore glasses, along with a white shirt and a red vest with anchor emblems all over it.

"What can I do ya for?" he asked with a friendly growl.

Ben took the business card from his shirt pocket. "Hi. I'm Paul Gulletti, and I'm a reporter with the *Weekly*. I was hoping you could tell me something about one of your guests. He had a—an unscheduled early checkout. His name was Ronald Craig."

The old desk clerk frowned at him. "Gulletti, that's Italian, isn't it? You don't look Italian."

"I take after my mother's side," Ben replied. "Now, about this guest."

"Yeah, about that," he said. "I think your 'early checkout' crack was in bad taste. I hope you don't write that kind of smart-ass stuff in your newspaper. The man's dead."

"Oh, for Christ's sake," the woman piped up. "Give him a break, Walter. He's cute."

The old man shot her a look over his spectacles. "Down, girl," he muttered. Then he glanced at Ben. "What is it you want, Mr. Gulletti?"

"I thought you might tell me something about this Ronald Craig. For starters, I was wondering how long he's been staying here."

The gruff old man didn't respond.

Ben shrugged. "And, of course, you'd know if he made any long-distance phone calls. And maybe you've seen him with someone."

"The police already asked me all that." The desk clerk cocked his head to one side. "They're down the hall right now, poking around in Room 29. Why don't you go talk to them?"

Ben tried to smile. "Well, it's always tough getting a straight answer from those guys. You look like a smart man. I thought you might know something more than what the police could tell me."

Stone-faced, the old desk clerk stared at him. Ben could tell that he wasn't going to get anything from him. He'd thought the slick-reporter angle might give him an in, but no such luck.

"Looks like I'm barking up the wrong tree," Ben said finally.

"And you're digging around the wrong yard," the old clerk grunted.

"Well, good night." Starting for the door, Ben caught the woman's eye again. "Thanks for trying to put in a good word. You're pretty cute, too."

She grinned and let out a startled little laugh.

Ben retreated outside. He didn't know what he'd expected to learn from the desk clerk. It wasn't like the old buzzard would know anything about the Ronald Craig investigation.

Ben glanced around the gloomy parking lot. No sign of the taxi. It had driven off.

"Son of a bitch," he muttered. He trudged toward the highway and stopped at the curb. The traffic on Aurora was sailing by at about forty-five miles an hour. He tried in vain to wave down one cab, and then another.

"Need a lift?"

Ben turned to see the long-legged redhead from the hotel lobby. Standing, she was nearly as tall as he was. Her black dress hit her at mid-thigh. She held a big purse with a red garment draped over it. She smiled. "You can't just tell a girl she's cute, then walk out the door, honey. Where are you going?"

"I thought I'd head home."

She nudged him. "I'll give you a ride if you buy me a drink."

Ben hesitated. A semi truck whooshed by, and he stepped back a bit.

"Well, don't leave me dangling too long, honey. It's not very flattering. Plus, I'm cold." She took the red garment from around her purse strap, then shook it out. She donned a red vest with little anchors all over it. Her name tag was on the lapel: *Wendy.*

"You work at the hotel?" he asked.

She nodded. "I'm Wendy. You were talking to the wrong clerk in there, hon. Grandpa Walter started about fifteen minutes ago. He missed all the excitement. But I've been stuck in this dump since two o'clock this afternoon. There's been a lot of weird stuff going on today, too. I let the cops into Room 29 about a half hour ago."

"Why didn't you mention anything back there?" Ben asked.

Wendy shrugged. "Well, that was before you said I was cute." She turned and strolled to her car, an old red Ford Probe.

Ben followed her. "So—can you tell me anything about Ronald Craig?"

"Hmmm, I have some stuff you might use in your newspaper, as long as you don't mention my name." She unlocked her car door. "And as long as you buy me that drink."

He nodded. "I'll buy you a whole bottle of champagne if you want."

Wendy stared at him over the roof of her car. She smiled coyly. "Ha! All of a sudden I'm not so sure I should get into this car with you. Maybe you're some kind of serial killer or something."

Ben managed to laugh. "Well, I'm some kind of something."

Wendy giggled. "Yeah, you've got a killer smile, all right. C'mon. . . ."

She ducked into the car, leaned over, and unlocked the passenger door for him.

"I don't get it," Scott said. He was sitting at the kitchen counter with a glass of wine in front of him. "What terrible crime did you commit that you can't get involved with the cops now?"

"You said you weren't going to ask." Hannah stood across the counter from him. She was too wired to sit down.

"It's just that I can't see you ever doing anything really bad. How can it be so awful that you'd let these murders go unreported?"

"Scott, please," she whispered. "I think you'd better go."

He sighed. "All right, all right, I'm sorry. I'll stop asking about your deep, dark past."

"I still need to be alone," Hannah said. "It has nothing to do with you."

"Are you kidding? After what just happened you want to be left alone? I mean, God, look at me. I'm still shaking. We've both just experienced something really horrible, Hannah. If you don't want to go to the police, I think we have to approach this in the only other sensible way. We should both get incredibly drunk."

Hannah let out a little laugh, but she started to cry at the same time. She held back her tears. "You're sweet, but I drink too much already. Anyway, you really need to leave. I'm kicking you out."

Climbing off the barstool, he gave her a wary smile. "You sure that's what you want?"

Hannah nodded. She walked Scott to the door, opened it, then impulsively hugged him. "Thank you for being a good friend," she managed to say. "Call me when you get home. Let—let me know you made it back safe."

She watched Scott retreat toward the stairwell. He turned to glance back her. She waved, knowing that she would never see him again. She would miss him. She'd even miss the stupid video store.

Hannah ducked back inside. She took a napkin from the counter on the way to her bedroom. She wiped her eyes and nose. Opening the closet, she pulled her suitcase from the top shelf. She tried to be quiet about it. She didn't want to wake Guy—not until she was finished packing.

For now, he needed his sleep. In a couple of hours, they would be leaving Seattle, probably by bus. Hannah didn't know yet where they were going. But they had a long journey ahead.

* * *

"Those tits are fake," Wendy said, gazing up at the stripper on stage. "Pure silicone."

Wendy slipped out of her anchor-logo vest, unfastened a couple of shirt buttons, then leaned back in the corner booth.

Ben started to sit down across from her, but she patted the spot next to her and winked at him. "C'mon a little closer. I won't bite you. That's for later. Ha!"

Wendy had driven him to a strip joint with the name "CLUB FOXY" in pink neon script above the door. "NIGHTLY SHOWS," it said on the illuminated yellow sign by the parking lot. "12 BEAUTIFUL PUSSYS & NO DOGS!"

Wendy seemed to know the doorman, and he'd let them in without the ten-dollar cover charge. Apparently, she also knew the stripper, who at the moment wore only a silver G-string. She wrapped herself around a pole at the end of the stage's catwalk. Despite her sexy gyrations, she appeared bored. She was a trim blonde with a hard edge, and breasts that seemed a bit too perky.

"If you came in this dump about three years ago," Wendy said, lighting a cigarette, "you'd have seen her as a brunette, and flat as a pancake. Two peas on a breadboard. She says it's because she had a baby two years ago that suddenly she's got a rack. But I know a boob job when I see one—or two, rather. Hell, I've had a couple of kids, and it didn't give me a pair of headlights like that. The kids are in high school now, living with their dad." She cleared her throat, then said in a loud voice. "So, who do we have to fuck to get a drink around here?"

She had chatted nonstop ever since they'd pulled out of the Seafarer Inn parking lot. Ben had tried to ask her about Ronald Craig, but she'd insisted, *I'm not talking about him until you buy me that drink, handsome.*

A thin, blond waitress sauntered up to their booth. She

wore a pink tube top and silver shorts. "Hey, Wendy," she said, with a tired smile. "What are you having tonight?"

"You mean, besides this tall drink of water?" she asked, nudging Ben. "Ha! I'll take an Absolut, hon."

"A light beer, please," Ben said.

The waitress rolled her eyes, then sighed. "I'm supposed to find out who the hell you are, and what's going on."

"Well, tell Rick to mind his own goddamn business," Wendy piped up. "If it's okay for him to bang Miss Silicone Tits up there, I can certainly step out for a drink with whomever I please." She turned to Ben. "Is it whomever or whoever? I can never remember."

"I think you're right: whomever," Ben muttered.

"He's a *journalist*," Wendy pointed out. "You can tell that to Rick. And tell him not to water down my goddamn drink. Thanks, Charmaine."

Once the waitress stepped away, Ben turned to Wendy. "So I'm here to make your boyfriend jealous. Is that it?"

"Soon to be ex-boyfriend."

Ben nodded. "Okay. Well, I just bought you a drink a minute ago, so it's payback time. What can you tell me about Ronald Craig?"

"Put your arm around me," Wendy said.

Ben complied. "How long was Mr. Craig a guest at the hotel?"

She snuggled up to him. "A little over a week."

"In all that time, did you ever see him with anyone?"

"Nope. A lone wolf that one was."

"Did he get any faxes at the hotel?"

Wendy shook her head. "No phone records, either. I saw him walking in and out of the lobby a couple of times, talking on a cell phone."

"Did you take any messages for him?" Ben asked.

"Nope."

"Until today, did anything—unusual happen with him?"

"Until today?" She shook her head again. "Not really."

"Back at the hotel, before we even got in the car, you said

there was a lot of 'weird stuff' going on today. What did you mean by that?"

"Well, the maid reported that when she went in to clean his room at eleven o'clock this morning, it looked like somebody had broken into the place. The window was open. Someone had screwed with the lock."

Ben frowned. "Could she tell if anything was missing?"

"There was a laptop carrying case, and a cord, but no computer and no computer discs. He also had a briefcase, but it had been emptied out." She suddenly kissed Ben on the cheek. "Heads up. Charmaine's back."

The waitress set the drinks down. "Rick said these are on him. And he asks you to *please* come talk to him. He wanted me to be sure to say *please*."

"Well, tell him 'thanks,' and I'll think about it," Wendy replied.

The waitress nodded, then walked away. Ben took a sip of his beer. On stage, the silicone blonde was lying on the floor with her legs in the air, forming a "V."

Ben put down his beer. "Sounds like Rick wants to make up."

"Well, let him suffer a bit longer." She reached for her drink.

"Did you report the break-in to the police?"

She sighed. "Yeah, but all they did was send over some rookie to make a report. When three of them came back tonight, I figured it was about the break-in. But then one of the cops said this Craig fella was killed in a hit-and-run."

"Did they tell you anything else?" Ben asked.

"No, but I stood in the doorway for a couple of minutes while they went through the room, so I heard a few things."

"Like what?"

"Like he was a private detective, working out of some agency in—um . . ."

"Milwaukee?" he said.

"Yeah, that's right. How did you know?"

"I spent some time listening to the cops, too. Did you get the name of the detective agency, by any chance?"

"Huh." She frowned. "Great Something. It was written on the tag on his computer case . . . *Great Lakes Investigations,* that's it."

She took another sip from her drink. "Y'know, they must have forgotten about me, because they just started talking like I wasn't there. One of them said that whoever this Ronald Craig was tailing—or is it *whomever?*"

Ben quickly shook his head. "Doesn't matter. I get it. Go on. Whoever he was tailing . . ."

"Yeah, well, apparently this guy's pretty damn crafty. The cop said everything this Ronald Craig fella had written down—on his laptop, in his briefcase—it all just vanished, went up in smoke. They said where this hit-and-run happened, Craig's car was broken into and cleaned out."

"Did you hear anything else?" Ben asked.

"Nothing worth remembering," Wendy replied. She sipped her drink, then studied her glass for a moment. "Think I should go talk with him?"

"You mean Rick?" Ben asked. "Sure. I need to scram anyway. You can tell him we had a lovers' quarrel."

"Ha! I like that," Wendy said. "You're good!"

"Thanks," Ben said. "You sure you don't remember anything else the cops might have said? Anything?"

She shook her head.

"Did they mention any names? For example, Hannah Doyle?"

Wendy shook her head again. "Sorry."

"What about the name Rae Palmer?"

"Nope, never heard of him."

"Rae's a woman. R-A-E. She was a friend of mine. She's been missing for about five weeks now."

Wendy shrugged. "Wish I could help ya, hon."

"It's okay, you already have." Ben stood up, pulled out his wallet, then set a ten-dollar bill on the table. "Next round is on me, okay? Thanks for your help. Hope you and Rick work things out."

She raised her glass to toast him. "You're sweet."

Ben headed out of the strip club. Outside, the cool night air felt good. There was a pay phone at the edge of the parking lot. He called Hannah's number. After three rings, he wondered if maybe she'd given him a fake number.

Then her machine came on. *"This is 555-1007,"* Hannah announced on the recording. The voice didn't sound quite like her. *"No one can come to the phone right now. Please leave a message after the beep."*

"Hannah?" he said, after the tone. "Are you there? Okay, well, listen, whoever this stalker is, he covered all his tracks. He broke into Ronald Craig's hotel room and his car, cleaning out all evidence of the investigation. I don't think the cops have anything yet. My guess is it'll take another day before they can—"

He heard an abrupt click on the line. "Hello?" she said.

"Hannah?"

"Yes. I was just down the hall."

"I'm glad," he said, leaning against the pay phone enclosure. "I was worried something had happened to you. Are you okay?"

"I'm fine. You said there's no evidence of Craig's investigation—at all?"

"That's right. I'm guessing it'll take at least another day for the police to get any information from Ronald Craig's detective agency. Even then, I'm not sure how much help they'll be. The agency might not even know anything. Craig could have been freelancing. Anyway, I really need to talk with you. Can I come over there?"

"Now?"

"Yeah, I can be there in a few minutes," Ben said. "I won't stay long."

"No, I'm sorry. It—it's late. I'll see you tomorrow in class, okay? We can talk then. We'll go out afterward. All right?"

Ben hesitated. "Okay, I guess. Are you sure you'll be okay?"

"I'll be fine," she said. "See you tomorrow."

"Hannah?"

There was a click on the other end of the line. She'd hung up.

Ten

The phone rang, and Hannah felt her insides tighten up like a fist.

For the last several hours, she'd been expecting—and dreading—a call from the police. Perhaps they wouldn't phone; they'd just show up at her door. Either way, she knew they'd be coming for her eventually. She was living on borrowed time.

The telephone hadn't rung since Ben's call around midnight last night. That had been nearly twelve hours ago. At the time, Hannah had thought she'd be long gone by now—on a bus with Guy, on their way to another city.

For every minute she stayed, Hannah knew she was pushing her luck. She risked exposure, arrest, and having her son taken away from her. But the police weren't her only concern. That maniac was still out there, stalking her, and last night she'd seen what he was capable of.

She stood by the kitchen counter, staring at the phone. Her stomach was in knots.

Joyce was unloading a small bag of groceries. "Aren't you going to answer that?" she asked, a bottle of Children's Tylenol in her hand.

Hannah shook her head. "I'm screening."

The answering machine picked up. Hannah anxiously waited for the beep.

"Hello, Hannah? It's Britt, calling from work. Are you there?"

Despite her relief, Hannah still couldn't move. She tried to get her breathing right again.

"I'm wondering how much longer you'll be, because I'm supposed to get together with Webb today. I really don't mind filling in, but if you won't be coming in for another hour or so, I just need to call him. . . ."

Finally, she grabbed the phone. "Britt?"

"Oh, hi. I'm sorry. I don't mean to pressure you—"

"No. It's okay. You're a doll to fill in for a couple of hours. I should be there in about fifteen minutes."

"Okay, Hannah. See you soon."

Hannah hung up the phone. She crept back to Guy's room, and poked her head in the doorway. The shades were drawn, and in the darkness Hannah couldn't see the rash on his face and hands. He was asleep. She longed to hug him good-bye, but couldn't. She kept thinking this might be the last time she'd see her little boy before the authorities came to take him away.

The knots tightened in her stomach, and she wandered back toward the living room.

"You look like you're about to face a firing squad." Joyce handed Hannah her coat and purse. "Would you relax? He'll be fine. I've seen all my kids through the chicken pox—and a lot worse. He's in good hands."

Hannah hesitated in the doorway. "You'll call if anything happens?"

"Yes." Joyce nodded. "Now, get out of here. You're driving me crazy with all your worrying."

"Don't answer the phone unless it's me. And don't answer the door, either. I'll call you in an hour."

"I'm sure you will," Joyce said, giving her a gentle shove. "Now scram!"

Hannah turned and hugged her. Then she started off to work.

She wore a black pullover, black jeans, and her hair was swept back in a loose ponytail. She didn't have on any makeup, and knew she looked terrible. Plus, her back ached. She'd gotten only three hours of sleep last night, curled up on the beanbag chair in the corner of Guy's room.

It had started around two-thirty in the morning. She'd just finished packing when she heard Guy coughing. She went to him.

"Mom, I feel kind of cruddy," he whimpered.

Guy had a fever of 100.9, as well as a rash all over his face and hands. Hannah unbuttoned his Spider-Man pajama top, and gasped at the sight of the little red welts on his stomach and chest.

"Sounds like chicken pox," Joyce told her over the phone at six in the morning. Hannah had known she'd be up. "I have a dental appointment at nine, but I can be over there by eleven if you need me to baby-sit. In the meantime, you'd better call the doctor."

An hour later, Hannah got Dr. Donnellan at his home. "If it's chicken pox, I'd rather you not bring him in. Chicken pox is awfully contagious. I'm on my way to the office; I'll swing by. What's your address again, Hannah?"

Dr. Donnellan always struck Hannah as one of those guys who was considered a nerd throughout high school and college—and maybe even medical school. But there was something very cute about him, too. Tall and skinny, he had glasses and curly, receding brown hair. Hannah guessed he was in his early thirties. Having him in the apartment, making a good old-fashioned house call, gave Hannah a sense of relief.

Then came the bad news: Guy did indeed have the chicken pox. He'd have to remain in bed for at least ten days. Dr. Donnellan asked Hannah if she'd had chicken pox as a child.

Hannah remembered that she had.

"Um, listen, my aunt wants Guy and me to visit," she lied, wringing her hands. She and Dr. Donnellan were standing in the hallway. "My aunt has an extra room. She'd be a lot of help with Guy. I was wondering if it would be okay to move him. Her place is just a couple of hours away by bus. I'd keep him warm—"

Dr. Donnellan was shaking his head. "You might as well take a bomb aboard that bus, Hannah. Chicken pox is highly contagious. Exposure to adults is serious. It can lead to hepatitis, encephalitis, and pneumonitis. Exposure to pregnant women often causes birth defects." He shook his head again. "You don't want to take Guy on any bus rides. Just keep him in bed. There's a risk he could develop scarlet fever if you're not careful. Guy needs to take it easy. No trips or outings, Hannah."

Nodding, Hannah tried to smile. So much for her great escape.

She phoned Britt and got her to fill in at work for a couple of hours.

When Joyce arrived, Hannah asked if she and Guy could possibly stay at her place. It was a stupid idea—right up there with wanting her doctor's permission to infect a busload of people. But Hannah didn't feel safe at home. How soon before the police or her stalker or some goon the Woodleys had hired showed up at her door? Hiding out at Joyce's apartment seemed like the only option. No one would be looking for her and Guy there.

"Guy could sleep on your sofa," Hannah heard herself babbling. "I'd be fine on the floor. It would just be a couple of days—until I feel okay about everything. I know it sounds silly, but—"

"It sounds nuttier than a fruitcake is how it sounds, hon," Joyce broke in. "He's better off in his own bed. You really shouldn't move him. If anybody sleeps on a sofa, it's me. I'll stay here as long as you want."

Hannah gave Joyce her purse and sent her to the supermarket for some calamine lotion, coloring books, and other last-minute essentials. "I don't have any cash," Hannah said, handing her the shopping list. "The ATM card is the silver one in my wallet, and the code is 1963. Just remember the year Kennedy was assassinated. And get yourself some cookies."

While Joyce was out, Hannah quickly showered and changed her clothes.

In a strange way, work was probably the best thing for her right now. She could carry on as if nothing was wrong—total denial.

As Hannah stepped into the store, the anti-theft alarm went off.

The loud beeping gave her such a start, she almost lost what little composure she had. Scott and Britt looked up from their registers, and several customers stared at her. Hannah hurried past the sensors. "What was that about?" she managed to ask.

"Probably that metal plate in your head again," Scott replied. Then he went back to waiting on his customer.

Hannah moved behind the counter. Scott glanced back over his shoulder at her. "How's Guy doing?"

"I think he'll be okay," Hannah muttered. "It's me I'm not so sure about."

Britt ducked into the break room, then came out again with her sweater and purse. Sometime within the last couple of days, she must have changed her maroon hair color. It was black again, but she'd added two blue streaks on one side. The ring in her eyebrow now had a blue stone that matched the hair dye.

"This was in my cereal," Britt said, pulling a cellophane packet from her bag. She handed it to Hannah. "They're Cap'n Crunch decals and stamps. I saved them for Guy. I figured he could play with them in bed."

Hannah thanked her. Once Britt hurried out of the store, Scott leaned against the back counter. He plucked the cereal prize from Hannah's hand, then studied it. "Wish *I* had something to play with in bed." He tossed the packet on the back counter, and sighed. "Well, I don't know about you, but I'm still a little freaked out over last night. I looked for a story about it in the morning newspaper, but I didn't see anything. Did you?"

"No," she said. "I didn't even have a chance to look." Hannah stashed her purse in the drawer below her register.

"Did that good-looking blond guy from last night ever call you? What's his name again?"

"Ben," she said, nodding. "Yeah, he called. Apparently, someone broke into Craig's hotel room and car. They cleaned out everything. So the police don't know much about Craig or what he was after here—at least, they didn't late last night."

"What do you think?" Scott asked. "How does this Ben character fit in? What's his angle?"

"I really don't know," she murmured. She stepped up to the register to wait on a customer.

Scott took a couple of videos from the return bin and checked them in. He waited until Hannah's customer left; then he leaned against the back counter again. "I was tossing and turning all night," he said. "I think I figured it out. You're in your own kind of witness protection program, aren't you? You're running away from something."

She sighed. "Scott, I really don't want to talk about it."

"Does it have something to do with your husband's death? You never talk about him. Please tell me you didn't bump him off."

"That's a pretty tactless statement," Hannah muttered. She turned away and noticed some movies in the return bin. Without even a glance at Scott, she started checking them in. She felt herself trembling inside.

"He's alive," Scott said. "Isn't he?"

Hannah tried to appear interested in her work.

"Did your husband—smack you around?" Scott asked with concern. "I've often wondered why you're so tight-lipped about him. I once asked how you got that scar on your chin, and you quickly changed the subject. Did he give it to you?"

Hannah finished keying in the video codes. She still couldn't look at him. She swallowed hard. "You're the one who should have been a detective," she finally said. "He's from a very rich and powerful family in a small Midwestern town. There was no way I could have divorced him and kept my son. And there was no way I could have stayed."

"What makes you so sure the police are looking for you?"

"Since I ran away, I've talked to a couple of old friends. They've been hounded from time to time by a private detective."

"You mean, this 'Craig' fella'?"

"Maybe. I'm not sure. When I left town with Guy, I also took some money from the joint checking account. Anyway, this detective told my friends that I'm wanted for grand larceny and kidnapping."

"Did any cops actually talk to your pals?"

"I don't think so."

"Well, how do you know the police are really looking for you?" Scott asked. "I mean, maybe this private dick—if you'll excuse the expression—maybe he was just jerking your friends around. If your husband's family is so rich and powerful, wouldn't they want to keep the whole runaway thing under wraps—especially if he was beating you up? That's probably the reason for the private detective—to avoid involving the cops. Hell, the police might not even know anything about you, Hannah."

"Maybe," she granted. Scott's theory gave her a little bit of hope. Perhaps the authorities weren't really after her. Still, her name was bound to come up when the police asked the detective agency what Ronald Craig had been investigating in Seattle.

"God," Hannah whispered. "They'll think I had something to do with it."

"Something to do with what?"

"Ronald Craig was here investigating me," she said, glancing around to make sure no customers were nearby. "He was murdered. All evidence of his investigation was stolen. They'll blame me."

"No, no, they can't," he said, patting her shoulder. "Han-

nah, I was with you when it happened. You have a witness—
me. Craig came over uninvited. You asked him to leave. We
saw him get killed together. They can't pin his death on
you—not as long as I'm around—"

Scott seemed to choke on the last word. The reassuring
smile faded away from his face. "Oh, shit," he muttered.
"I'm toast. I'm a fucking dead man."

"What do you mean?" Hannah asked.

"I know too much," Scott said, running a hand through his
moussed hair. "And I'm the only one who can testify you had
nothing to do with killing that guy. This weirdo who's been
following you around, he'll go after me next. I know it."

Wincing, Hannah shook her head. "Don't say that."

He let out an exasperated laugh. "But it's true! Hell, who's
always one of the first to go in slasher movies? The funny gay
best friend, that's who! It's a wonder I'm not dead already."

Despite everything, Hannah rolled her eyes. "Oh, Scott,
I wouldn't worry. You're not really that funny."

"Yeah, but I make up for it by being super-gay."

She actually laughed, then hugged him. "Thanks for making me smile—at least for a second or two."

"I'm semi-serious, you know," he said, patting her back.
"What are you going to do?"

"I haven't a damn clue," she replied, her head on his
shoulder. "I'd planned on leaving town this morning. Then
Guy got sick. I can't move him. Chicken pox is serious stuff.
We're stuck. I'm going crazy, just sitting here."

She clung to a shred of hope that what Scott said was
true. Perhaps the police weren't looking for her. And maybe,
just maybe, Ronald Craig hadn't yet reported anything
about *Hannah Doyle* to the Woodleys.

It was a good scenario, but not very likely. She was sec-
ond-guessing everything. In the meantime, all she could
do was maintain this awful, idle holding pattern for the next
ten days until Guy recovered.

She held Scott at arm's length. "Listen, please don't tell
anyone else about Guy's father or any of this."

He smiled. "Hannah, I didn't come out to a soul until I was twenty-three. And as long as can I remember, I knew I was a great, big homo. So I know how to keep things under my hat. Your secret's safe with me."

Hannah hugged him again. She held him tightly—until she heard someone on the other side of the counter, chuckling *"Hey, you two, either cut it out or get a room!"*

"Oh, Ted, you're such a pain in the ass," Scott groaned. "I was just about to get to second base with her, too. Hold on, I'll take care of you." Scott went to his register to wait on one of their regulars. He glanced over his shoulder at Hannah. "Don't forget Britt's toy for Guy."

Nodding, Hannah grabbed the cereal toy off the counter, then opened the drawer below the register and reached for her purse. She started to put the toy in her bag, but suddenly froze up. "Oh, no," she murmured. "No, no, no . . ."

For a moment, she just stared at the video stashed in her purse. She wondered how and when it had gotten in there. Had someone been following Joyce around at the supermarket this morning when she'd had Hannah's purse?

After a minute, Hannah felt Scott hovering behind her. "What is that?"

"It's another 'special delivery,'" she heard herself say. She took the video out of her bag.

"It's one of ours," Scott pointed out. "The store sensor tag is still on it. That's why you set off the alarm when you walked in here."

Hannah straightened up, then closed the drawer with her foot. She looked at the label on the cassette. It was Tape B of *Casino*.

"He didn't give you the box," Scott muttered. "And only one tape. Just a sec . . ." Scott hurried around the counter and started toward the back of the store.

Hannah could see that the tape was wound to a certain spot near the end of the spool.

Scott came back with the box for *Casino*. "It was on the shelf like this," he said, showing her the double-cassette box with only one tape. "I don't understand how he got the video out of here undetected. You'd think he would have ripped off the sensor tape and made it easier to steal. But he left it on. I wonder why."

"To show me how clever he is," Hannah replied numbly. She studied the videocassette. "I haven't seen *Casino*. What happens near the end?"

Frowning, Scott shrugged uneasily. "It's really violent, Hannah," he said. "A lot of people die."

"Everything's fine here," Joyce told her over the phone. "I just put some calamine lotion on Guy's rash, and he's playing with the puzzle book we got him this morning. Do you want to talk to him?"

"Yes, put him on, please," Hannah said. She stood behind the counter at the store. Scott was helping a customer; otherwise they weren't too busy. Hannah waited for to Guy come on the line.

"Hi, Mom," he said.

"Hi, honey. How are you? How are your chicken pox?"

"The chicken pox are fine," he answered. "Joyce put pink stuff on them. It looks like Pencil Bismal."

"Pepto-Bismol. That's calamine lotion. It'll stop the itching. Are you being a good boy?"

"Yes. Here's Joyce."

"Well, bye—" Hannah barely got the words out before Joyce was back on the line.

"Not one for long conversations, is he?" Joyce said. "Listen, you got a call a while ago. I let the machine take it. Ben Somebody. He left a number."

"Do you have that number handy?"

"It's right in front of me. Ready? 555-3649."

Hannah scribbled down the number. "Got it. There haven't been any other calls or hang-ups?"

"He's the only one."

"Listen, Joyce, have you noticed anyone hanging around outside or anything?"

"No, honey."

"You're on the cordless, right? Could you check outside for a second? And be careful. I just need you to see if there's anyone out on the balcony—or down in the parking lot."

"Sure, Hannah. But what the heck is all this about?"

In the background, Hannah could hear the door opening. She bit her lip and waited. Some static came on the line. "Joyce? Are you still there?"

"Yeah, honey. No one on the balcony, and nobody down in the lot either."

"Okay, don't forget to lock the door when you step back inside. And that front window needs to be closed and locked."

"Hannah, what is going on?"

"Um, I'm—still worried about that break-in from a couple of weeks ago. Plus—well, did you notice anyone following you around the store this morning? Did someone bump into you or brush against you by accident?"

"I don't think so."

"Did you have my purse with you in the store?"

"No, I took your wallet and left the purse in my car. But I put a sweater over it and locked the car doors. Why? Was something missing from your bag?"

Hannah cracked an ironic smile. "No, nothing was missing, Joyce." She sighed. "Anyway, thanks. Listen, give me a call if anything—"

"Call you if anything happens, yeah, honey, I'll call," Joyce cut in. "We're fine. What's that expression? Take a chill pill? Relax. We're all locked up, and I have the pepper spray in my bag. We'll be fine. First sign of trouble, you'll hear from me."

"Thanks, Joyce."

Hannah hung up the phone. She glanced at Scott, who met her gaze, then eyed the *Casino* tape on the back counter. "Are you going to look at it?" he asked.

She nodded.

"I pulled up the last rental record," he said. "It was checked out and returned three days ago. So he must have ripped it off within the last couple of days."

For all she knew, Hannah might have been in the store when her "secret admirer" stole the tape.

She took the cassette and went into the break room. Scott followed her. She switched on the TV and inserted the cassette. Scott stood behind her, at the break room door.

The sound and picture came up on the little TV screen. "The House of the Rising Sun" churned over the soundtrack while a drugged, zombie-like Sharon Stone stumbled down the hallway of some seedy motel. Every few steps, she stopped and rested her blond head against the wall. Hannah recognized Robert De Niro in the grim voice-over, explaining that Stone's character, Ginger, had been given a "hot dose." He said they never found out who gave Ginger the drugs that killed her.

"So explain to me again," she heard Scott say. He sounded a bit scared. "Why would this guy want you to see this particular scene?"

"He's telling me that he's ready to kill again." Hannah nodded at the screen, at the dazed, depleted Sharon Stone, staggering though that barren corridor. "And this is how the next one will die."

"Hannah, can I call you right back?" Britt asked, on the other end of the line. "I'm in the middle of something. I'll call in two minutes, I promise."

"All right," Hannah said.

"Okay, bye." Britt replied; then she hung up.

Sitting at the desk in the break room, Hannah replaced the receiver on its cradle.

Scott was behind the counter, minding the store. He and Hannah had tried to figure out whose death the *Casino* scene forecast. If the pattern stayed consistent, the next victim would be a woman—like the victim in the video.

"It sounds crazy," Scott had said. "But I keep thinking of Britt. She's a sweetie pie, and I love her dearly. But Britt has a drug problem, and she's just dumb enough to end up dead from an overdose in some fleabag hotel."

Hannah could almost picture Britt repeating Sharon Stone's *Casino* death scene in a hotel corridor. She suddenly realized how her stalker worked.

He had to be watching her constantly. No doubt, he saw or heard those confrontations with Cindy Finkelston and Lester Hall. As much as he stalked her, he must have kept surveillance on his intended victims, too. He must have decided to push Cindy Finkelston out of that fifth-floor window when he saw she lived in a tall apartment building. The killer was a film buff. He sent Hannah a sneak preview of Cindy's murder with the *Rosemary's Baby* tape cued on the scene with the fallen corpse splattered on the pavement. He had to know about Lester Hall's massages before he furnished her with that murder-on-the-massage-table scene from *The Godfather*. And how long had he been following around Ronald Craig before deciding to mow him down with a stolen car in the fashion of that scene in *Wait Until Dark*?

His next victim would be a woman with a drug habit, most likely someone from the store, someone *just dumb enough to end up dead from an overdose in some fleabag hotel.*

When the phone rang, Hannah grabbed it. "Hello?" Then she realized it could be a customer. "Um, Emerald City Video. Thanks for calling."

"Hannah? It's me, Britt. Sorry I couldn't talk earlier. I was in the middle of something. What's going on?"

"Well, remember I told you how someone was giving me these videos?" Hannah said. "They were cued to just the spot when a murder takes place."

"Oh, yeah. Did you ever find out who was doing that?"

"No," Hannah said. "But the thing is, after I got each video, someone was killed a couple of days later in the same way the characters in each of the movies died."

"I don't get it," Britt admitted.

Hannah tried to explain it again, but she could tell Britt wasn't grasping the seriousness of the situation. She sounded a bit foggy in her responses. Hannah figured Britt must have been getting high when she'd called her a few minutes ago.

"Anyway, the video I just got was *Casino*," Hannah continued, a bit exasperated. "It was set to a scene with Sharon Stone in this crummy hotel, and she's dying of a drug overdose, or a 'hot dose.'"

"Oh, Sharon Stone was so good in that movie," Britt said.

"That's not the point, Britt," Hannah replied, an edge creeping into her tone. "I'm worried about you. I'm worried you'll end up dead from a bad dose of some drug. It might not be your fault. You might not know."

"Oh, Hannah," Britt said with a little laugh. "You act like I'm this major addict or something. I just get high once in a while. God, stop worrying about me. I'm fine. In fact, I'm great. I have the next two days off. I'll be with Webb practically the whole time, so I'll be safe. We're just gonna kick back. So don't sweat it."

"Listen, Britt. Will you promise me something? Will you call me if you find yourself alone for a while? I don't want you to be alone."

"Sure, but like I said, Webb will be with me," she replied.

"And promise to be careful, okay? I know you'll probably want to get high, but please don't take any chances. I don't want you to end up with a bad dose. Do you understand?"

Britt laughed. "Sure, whatever you say, Hannah. Listen, I gotta go. Webb's here, and we're headed out."

"Okay," Hannah said. "But promise me you won't take any chances."

"All right already," Britt replied, giggling again. "God. Hannah, I'm not Sharon Stone in *Casino*. I wished I looked like her, but I'm not her. Listen, I need to motor. I'll call you later, okay? And hey, mellow out. Remember, it's only a movie."

Hannah heard the click on the other end of the line.

* * *

She figured her coworkers hated her right about now. After coming to the store nearly four hours late this morning, she'd spent most of the afternoon in the break room. She'd been tapping into the computer for rental histories on *Wait Until Dark* and *Casino*. But she wasn't coming up with any names that matched.

Hannah began looking for patterns elsewhere. She charted out a timetable of the events since all of this started:

3rd Week September (approx)—Video dropped off at store.

Wed-10/9—Run-in w/Cindy F. Took GOODBAR video Home. Break-in.

Thurs-10/10—2nd break-in. ROSEMARY'S BABY tape left in VCR.

Sun-10/13—Cindy Finkelston killed.

Tues-10/15 (or Mon?) Run-in w/Lester Hall.

Sat-10/19—GODFATHER video left in shopping cart.

Tues-10/22—Lester Hall is killed.

Wed-10/23—Found WAIT UNTIL DARK tape in public restroom. Craig killed.

Today-10/24—CASINO video in purse.

There was no consistency in the time lapse between her receiving a video and the subsequent murder. The first two victims were each killed three days after she got the videos forecasting their deaths. But Craig had been mowed down within hours of her finding the *Wait Until Dark* video in that lavatory. She couldn't hope to predict when the *Casino*-style murder would take place.

Hannah felt like she was banging her head against a wall. The only pattern she saw was the obvious one: someone was making her a reluctant, silent accomplice in a series of murders. He slipped her videos of Hollywood death scenes as a preview of his lethal handiwork.

The homemade *Goodbar* tape was the exception. That was no preview. It was a real murder, caught on tape; she had no doubt about it now. Had the other deaths been captured on videotape as well? Did he have an accomplice filming Cindy Finkelston's fall? Was someone else lurking in the parking lot last night, and did he have a video camera to shoot the *Wait Until Dark* reenactment? How had they filmed Lester Hall's death?

On that first night, October 9th, she'd thought she saw someone videotaping her from an alley.

She kept coming back to Paul Gulletti, with his knowledge of film and his unhealthy interest in her. When she'd first met him, he'd claimed he was planning to direct his own movie. Was it the *Goodbar* homage?

She'd been selected to see that video. The cassette hadn't been dropped off at the store by accident. Someone knew she would take it home and look at it.

Hannah remembered her first day in Paul's class last semester. Each student had to stand up, introduce themselves, and talk about their interest in film. Hannah mentioned working in a video store. Paul got a laugh when he jokingly asked if anyone ever dropped off their homemade sex tapes at the store by accident.

"Well, I haven't seen any," Hannah had replied. "And I'm the only one who ever takes home the wrong-returns and looks at them. No one else cares. Guess I'm just curious."

The *Goodbar* cassette had been in the store for over two weeks before Hannah had brought it home. How she must have stretched his patience while he waited for curiosity to get the best of her.

He must have been watching her that whole time. Somehow, he must have been listening, too.

Three different men had been following her, so Ben Podowski claimed. If she were looking for patterns, there were a few common denominators with two of those three men. Both Ben Podowski and Ronald Craig had lied to her about their true identities. Yet each man professed a desire to help her. She wondered if Ben—like Ronald Craig—had been hired to spy on her by her estranged husband. Ronald

Craig had been murdered because he'd seen too much. Ben could die for the same reason. Maybe he would be the next victim, dying from a "hot dose" in some hotel. Her stalker could have taken liberties with the locale in *Casino*. If Ben Podowski died from an overdose in that tenement, no one would blink an eye.

Hannah stared at his phone number—among all the notes and lists she'd been making. She picked up the phone and dialed. While it rang, she wondered if her husband, Kenneth, was somehow behind all these killings. Thanks to Ronald—and perhaps, Ben—he might have tracked her down. Maybe he was playing some sort of sadistic game with her for revenge.

There was a click on the other end of the line, then a recording: *"Hello, this is Ben. I'm not home right now, but—"*

Hannah hung up. She wanted to warn Ben. But for all she knew, he could be the killer or an accomplice.

"Shit," she muttered, staring at the phone. She didn't know what to think or whom to trust. If she was compelled to make a phone call, it should be to the police.

Someone knocked on the door, and she jumped a bit. "Um, yeah? Do you need me up front?"

Scott poked his head in. "No, in fact, it's dead as Planet Hollywood out there. C'mon, step outside with me while I grab a smoke. Cheryl can take over for a few minutes. You need some fresh air. It's really pretty out."

Scott was right. Orange and pink streaks slashed across the twilight sky. Along the sidewalk, leaves scattered in the cool, autumn breeze. Hannah and Scott leaned against a bicycle rack outside the store. He lit up a generic-brand cigarette.

"Scott, you understand my situation," she said. "I have no business asking you to do this. But could you—maybe contact the police for me? You can say all this has been happening to you. Tell them about the videos, and the deaths that followed."

He exhaled a puff of smoke and gave her a deadpan stare.

"So—I'm supposed to tell them I found this latest video in my purse?"

"Okay, say it was in your backpack," Hannah retorted. "The important thing is someone—maybe Britt—could be in trouble. Maybe the police can do something. Maybe they can catch this guy before he does any more harm."

"You want them to follow Britt around? Hello? Hannah, they'll pick her up for possession. And hell, I'll bet good ol' Webb is dealing. They'll throw his sorry ass in jail, too. I don't give a crap about him, but I couldn't do that to Britt."

"Would you rather see her dead?"

"Of course not. But I won't get her—and myself—in trouble because you want me to tell this story to the cops for you. Hannah, you need to do it yourself." He took another drag off his cigarette and shook his head. "The cops would have all sorts of questions for me that I couldn't answer. I'll back you up, but I can't be your beard here."

"You're right." She sighed. "I shouldn't have asked."

If she hoped to prevent another murder, she would have to go to the police with her story. But once they found out who she really was, she'd be as good as dead.

"What are you thinking?" Scott asked quietly.

"I'm thinking I'm screwed," Hannah replied.

They got swamped with customers in the store. Hannah worked an extra hour to make up for all her time in the back room. She didn't clock out until six-fifty. On a regular Thursday evening, that would have given her ten minutes to get to film class, but she wasn't going tonight. She felt bad enough that work took her away from Guy while he was sick. She needed to be with him tonight.

But she had an errand to run on her way home. She'd bought two rolls of quarters at the store. It made her purse a bit heavier as she started to take a roundabout way home.

There was a phone booth outside a little mom-and-pop grocery store four blocks from her house. It was on a quiet street; in fact, so quiet the little grocery store had recently closed from lack of business. Of course, maybe their charging $1.59 for a can of Coke had something to do with it.

Tonight, Hannah was sorry they were closed. There was something sad and creepy about the boarded-up store. The light from its RC Cola sign used to illuminate that section of the sidewalk. Hannah had made calls to Chicago friends from this phone booth, but never when it had been this dark. The light above the phone was dim and flickering.

She took out her rolls of quarters and dialed directory assistance for Green Bay, Wisconsin. She asked for the non-emergency number for the Green Bay police. Hannah dropped fourteen quarters into the slot, and was automatically connected to her party.

"Green Bay Police, City Precinct," the operator answered.

"Um, yes," Hannah said. "I have a question about a potential missing person."

"One minute while I connect you with a detective."

While she waited, Hannah glanced around. The sidewalk was deserted except for a cat lurking around a dumpster halfway down the block. Most of the trees had lost their leaves. It was so dark it seemed more like midnight than seven P.M.

"This is Detective Dreiling," a gravel-voiced man piped up on the other end of the line. "Can I have your name, please?"

"Yes, I'm Deborah Eastman," Hannah said, using the name of a favorite customer from the store. "I'm on vacation here on the West Coast. And yesterday, I ran into someone in San Francisco who I think might be a missing person from Green Bay. Her name is Hannah Woodley. I think she was supposed to have disappeared a while back or something."

"One minute, please," he said.

Hunched inside the phone booth, Hannah could hear a keyboard clacking faintly on the other end.

"Can I have your phone number, please?" he asked.

"Where I am now, or my home phone?" Hannah asked. "Because I'm in the middle of moving, a divorce really. I can give you a number where I'll be tonight. I'm staying with some friends—"

"Ma'am," he interrupted. "I need a number where we can contact you—"

"Well, I can give you one," Hannah replied, talking fast and trying to sound a bit agitated. "But I really don't want to waste any more of your time or mine if they aren't looking for Hannah Woodley. This is a long-distance call, you know. I heard something about her disappearing a while back, and I'm just trying to help out."

"Ma'am, yes, she and her son are listed here as missing persons. Mrs. Woodley is also wanted for questioning in connection with reported kidnapping and larceny charges. Any information as to her whereabouts would be appreciated. Now, can I get your phone number?"

Hannah felt as if someone had just punched her in the stomach. For a second, she couldn't breathe. She knew the Woodleys had probably brought up charges against her, but Scott had convinced her there was a chance they hadn't. Now, as she listened to the police detective read off those charges, she felt so doomed.

"Ms. Eastman?" the detective said. "Are you there?"

Hannah quickly hung up the phone.

She hoped she hadn't been on the line long enough for them to trace the call. She sagged against the inside of the booth. A couple of moths flew around the flickering overhead light. Hannah had to remind herself that she wasn't really any worse off than she'd always figured. She just didn't like hearing it.

Sighing, Hannah grabbed what was left of the torn-up roll of quarters on the little shelf under the phone. She started to step out of the booth, and gasped. The coins fell out of her hand.

He stood halfway down the block, by the dumpsters. He was filming her with a video camera. She couldn't see his face, just a tall, shadowy figure silhouetted by a streetlight in the distance behind him.

Hannah backed into the booth and hit her shoulder against the edge. Desperately, she glanced around to see if anyone else was nearby. No one. She was alone. She quickly dug into her purse for her little canister of pepper spray. Then she looked toward the dumpsters again.

He was gone.

A car drove by. Hannah raised a hand to flag it down, but it kept going. Its headlights swept against the dumpsters and an alley behind them. She didn't see him, but she had a feeling he was still there, watching.

Hannah found the pepper spray. Clutching it in her fist, she dared to take a couple of steps down the sidewalk—toward the dumpsters and the mouth of that gloomy alleyway. She hoped he didn't notice she was trembling.

She got to a point and suddenly couldn't move any further. Her legs froze up on her. She stood in the middle of the block.

Wide-eyed, she gazed down the line of cars parked along the curb. He didn't seem to be hiding behind any of them. There was no sign of him by the dumpsters. Even the cat from a few minutes before had disappeared.

Hannah kept absolutely still. She could hear a very faint mechanical humming. Was it his video camera?

"Who's there?" Hannah finally called in a shaky voice. "What do you want from me? Why are you doing this?"

No response. Then, as muted as that mechanical hum, she thought she heard a man chuckling.

A chill passed through her. She took a step back.

A woman screamed in the distance behind her. Hannah swiveled around to see a young couple weaving down the sidewalk across the street. They were coming toward her. The woman's scream turned to high-pitched laughter. She leaned against her boyfriend and kissed him.

Hannah moved to the middle of the street. She ran in the direction of the young twosome. Passing them, she raced another two blocks toward home.

She kept running, and didn't look back.

Eleven

Paul Gulletti strolled into the classroom. He sat back on the edge of his desk and glanced at the clock on the wall. "I don't think all of us are here yet," he announced. "But let's get started anyway. . . ."

Ben was seated behind Hannah's empty desk. Since phoning her this morning, he'd left another message offering to walk her to class. She hadn't returned either call.

Yesterday evening, Hannah had said she would see him during class tonight. Was that her way of brushing him off? He wasn't sure if he should be worried, or annoyed, by her absence.

Still, he kept hoping that she'd show up. Paul Gulletti must have felt the same way. Ben noticed that as he spoke about tonight's movie, Michelangelo Antonioni's *L'Avventura*, Paul kept looking at the classroom door. He also seemed preoccupied with the vacant chair in front of Ben. Paul even locked eyes with him, then frowned and looked away.

"I lost track of what I was saying," Paul admitted, rubbing his chin.

His assistant, Seth, cleared his throat. "You were talking about the missing girl," he said, with a half-smile. "In the movie, Monica Vitti's friend, who disappears . . ."

Paul nodded. "Yes, that's right," he said, visibly annoyed. After stealing another glance at the door, he lectured for a few more minutes; then he cued Seth to start the film.

While Seth dimmed the lights, Paul gathered up his notes

and folder. He came down the aisle toward Ben. He turned and sat at the desk next to Hannah's vacant spot.

About ten minutes into the movie, Ben gave up hope that Hannah might arrive late. He decided he'd leave during intermission, then walk over to Hannah's place and check in on her.

"Do you know where she is?"

Paul Gulletti caught him off guard. Ben blinked and stared at the teacher. Turning in his desk chair, Gulletti was leaning toward him—almost in a private huddle. "I'm sorry, what?" Ben asked in a hushed tone.

"Do you know where Hannah is tonight?" Paul whispered.

Ben shook his head. "Why are you asking me?"

"I thought you two were friends or something. Last couple of classes, I saw you talking with her."

Ben frowned at him. "Well, we might have been talking with each other. But that doesn't mean anything."

"Really? Seemed to me the two of you were getting along pretty well."

"I wasn't aware that we had an audience," Ben replied. "In any event, I'm sorry. I can't help you. I don't know where Ms. Doyle is."

"Well, thank you, Mr.—um, I'm sorry. I forgot your last name."

"Sturges," Ben said.

Paul nodded. "Thank you, Mr. Sturges," he said coolly. Then he turned forward to watch the movie.

At the break, Ben grabbed his notebook and jacket, and started out of the classroom. He passed by Seth, who was leaning against the doorway.

"Man, he sure hates your guts," Seth remarked, with a lopsided grin.

"What's that?" Ben asked.

"The Prof," Seth said, peering over the top of his glasses toward the front of the classroom. Paul was once again seated on the edge of his desk. "He thinks you're horning in on his girlfriend," Seth said.

"You mean Hannah? I didn't know she was his girl-friend."

"Neither does she. But Paul is working on it. And in most situations, what the Prof wants, the Prof gets. What's with you? Are you taking off?"

"Yeah, I've got a headache."

"Well, take care," Seth said. He glimpsed over his shoulder at Paul once more. Ben followed his gaze.

Paul Gulletti was glaring back at him.

"Huh, 'if looks could kill,' right?" Seth whispered, smirking.

Ben just nodded, then moved on down the corridor.

"Read it again, Mom," Guy said. He was sitting up in bed with a pillow behind his back. He took the Dr. Seuss book from Hannah's hands and opened it to the first page. "Here, Mom. Do it again. . . ."

"Oh, sweetie, I'm so tired," she groaned, pushing the book away. Seated on the edge of the bed, she slouched against the headboard. "I can hardly keep my eyes open. You read to me for a change. Tell me what's in the pictures, and see how fast I fall asleep. We'll pull the old switcheroo."

"Okay," he said. His brow wrinkled as he studied the book in front of him. With his rash and the remnants of calamine lotion, Guy's complexion was a bright pink against his blond hair. "The first pitcher is of this yellow guy in a big balloon, and he's singing. . . ."

"Hmmm, that's nice," Hannah murmured.

She was so tired. Yet as Hannah closed her eyes, she could once again see that man from earlier tonight, standing by the dumpsters, videotaping her. She tried to convince herself that she was safe now—with Guy at her side. The door and the windows were all locked. There would be no intruders tonight—unless, of course, the police paid her an unexpected visit.

She was on borrowed time with them, and considered hiding out in some cheesy little hotel until Guy recovered.

The thought of a cheesy hotel reminded her again of that scene from *Casino*. She was still worried about Britt ending up dead in some such place. Hannah had called her an hour ago. Britt had reported that she was fine: "I told you before, I'm spending the weekend with Webb. Jeez, quit worrying about me!"

But Hannah couldn't trust Britt to look out for herself. She didn't trust Webb, either.

Any notion of going to the police had been shot down by that detective on the phone three hours ago. That was just the tip of the iceberg, too. In addition to kidnapping and larceny charges, she'd forged documents and committed fraud. She was also implicated in three murders that she'd failed to report.

All she wanted to do was run away. Maybe then the killings would stop. The police and the Woodleys' private detective wouldn't know where to look for her. But she had a sick little boy who had to stay at home in his own bed. Doctor's orders.

Besides, someone was out there, watching her every move. How did she expect to slip past him? Even if she moved to a tiny little desert town or a major city on the California coast, how could she be sure he wouldn't follow her there?

What in God's name made her think she could nod off while her mind was going in a dozen different directions? She'd never felt so tired and on edge at the same time.

Guy's storytelling had diminished to some snoring.

When Hannah opened her eyes, he was asleep with the book in his lap. She carefully climbed off the bed, stole the book from under his hands, then tucked him in. Just as she was switching off his nightstand lamp, someone buzzed from the lobby.

Hannah flinched. Immediately, she thought of her stalker, and then, the police. For a moment, she couldn't move.

Guy stirred a little, but he didn't awaken.

The buzzer sounded again. Hannah hurried to the intercom. She glanced at her wristwatch: 9:40. This was no casual call. She pressed the intercom switch. "Hello?"

"Hannah? It's Ben Sturges."

Hannah let out a little sigh. At least it wasn't the police. Still, she was perturbed. "Don't you mean Ben *Podowski?*" she said into the intercom.

"I can explain that—if you'll let me come up."

She hesitated. The last person to drop by unannounced was Ronald Craig on the night he was murdered.

"I don't think that's such a good idea," she said.

"Couldn't I see you for just a few minutes?" he asked.

Hannah bit her lip. She didn't feel safe letting him in while she was alone with Guy—and at night. "Listen," she said. "I'm sorry. It's late. I've already gotten ready for bed. If you need to see me, drop by the video store tomorrow. I take my break at two."

"Are you okay?" he asked. "I didn't see you in class. I was worried."

"I'm fine," she said. "I just didn't feel like going tonight, that's all." Then she remembered something. "Um, Ben? Was everyone else there—at class? Paul didn't come late, did he?"

"No, he was there on time. Why?"

"I'm just curious. Was anyone else absent—or late?"

"Well, I didn't notice anybody else. I was mostly concerned about you. Are you sure you're all right?"

"Yes, I'm okay, thanks," she said vaguely. She was thinking about that man videotaping her tonight. It had happened just around the time class was starting. If that figure in the shadows wasn't Paul Gulletti or someone from the class, who was he?

"Hannah? Are you still there?"

"Listen, Ben, why don't you come by the store tomorrow? I want you to."

"I'd like that," he replied. "In the meantime, take care, okay?"

"Good night." She switched off the intercom. After a moment, she unlocked the door, opened it, and stepped out on the balcony. She folded her arms against the chill. The wind whipped through her hair. She gazed down at the lone figure heading down the street, away from her building.

Ben didn't look back over his shoulder.

Hannah wondered if she'd done the right thing, sending him away. The lives of everyone around her suddenly seemed so tentative. She watched him walking in the distance, and she couldn't help thinking he might be dead by tomorrow.

"I hate to bug you on your day off, Tish," Hannah said into the phone. "But I'm here alone." She stood behind the counter at Emerald City Video. It was almost one o'clock in the afternoon.

"Where's Scott?" the store manager asked on the other end of the line. "Wasn't he supposed to start at eleven today?"

"Yeah. I've tried calling his place. I can't even leave a message. I keep getting this stupid recording on his answering machine that says *'Memory is full.'*" Hannah tried to control the little tremor creeping into her voice—without much success. "Anyway, Tish, I think something's happened. I'm really worried. Do you have another number we can call for him?"

"No. We better get someone else to fill in."

"I tried Britt, but she's spending most of this weekend with Webb. So I'm not surprised she isn't answering. Cheryl and Victor are both due in at two." Hannah sighed. "I'm okay here by myself for now, but I'm really worried about Scott."

She kept thinking about what he'd said the day before:

I'm toast. I'm a fucking dead man . . . He'll go after me next, I know it.

"Well, we can't be short a person today," Tish said. "Not on a Friday. It'll be N-U-T-Z, nuts. I'll drag my ass over there. In the meantime, don't worry about our Scott. He's a big boy. Bet you a latte you'll hear from him or he'll show up before I make it to the store."

"I'll take that bet," Hannah replied. "And hope I lose."

Two hours later, they got the word from a friend of Scott's that he was in the hospital.

Tish gave Hannah the rest of the afternoon off so she could visit him at Group Health Hospital. The doctors estimated that Scott would be in isolation there for ten days.

In the hospital gift shop, Hannah bought him some flowers and magazines. Before entering the corridor to Scott's private room, she had to check in with a nurse stationed at the desk. The woman made her sign a form, then gave her a disposable smock and surgical mask to wear.

When Hannah stepped into the small, dimly lit, beige room, Scott was curled up on top of the unmade bed. He wore one of those hospital gowns, the kind that make even the healthiest person appear sickly.

Hannah cleared her throat. "Scott?"

He lifted his head up, then squinted at her. His handsome face was flushed and covered with tiny red welts.

"Oh, Jesus," Hannah whispered. "I'm so sorry. It's my fault you're in here. I should have been more careful washing up after being with Guy—"

"Oh, relax," he groaned. "Neither you nor Guy gave me the damn chicken pox. The doctor told me chicken pox has like a twenty-day incubation period. I was exposed a while back." He sat up. "Speaking of exposed, can you see up my gown?"

"My eyes are avoiding that area," Hannah admitted. She set the magazines and flowers on a side table. Her mask seemed to be slipping, and she adjusted it. "I got you *Vanity Fair, GQ,* and *People.*"

"Thanks," he grunted, with a tired smile. "You're sweet.

I'm going out of my mind here. I can't believe I have to stay in this place for another ten days. I guess it's serious stuff when an adult gets the chicken pox."

Hannah glanced down at her hospital smock and pointed to her mask. "Tell me about it. Do you know how you might have been exposed?"

As Scott moved over to the window, Hannah noticed the small abrasions on his arms and legs. The blinds were drawn, and he fiddled with the cord. "I think Guy and I caught them at the same time," he said. "Remember about three weeks ago, that Saturday afternoon you brought him to the store? That lady with the Eeyore voice had her brat with her, and he was wearing pajamas. She said he was sick, and she wanted to get him some videos. . . ."

Hannah nodded. She recalled the little boy throwing several videos on the floor. Scott was picking up after him, and Guy tried to help. At the time, Hannah hadn't been too alarmed about Guy being exposed to anything serious. People were always coming into the store to rent videos when they were sick. She didn't think a mother would be stupid enough to bring in a kid with chicken pox. Of course, she was one to criticize. She'd been ready to take Guy on board a bus until her doctor put the kibosh on it.

"Anyway, I think Guy and I got chicken pox from that little creep," Scott went on. "So if you see that lady and her kid again, give them both a swift kick in the ass for me. The only good thing about all this is there's a real cute intern here, and I think he plays on my team. Soon as this rash clears up, I'll see if I can get him to give me a sponge bath."

"Too much information," Hannah said. "Besides, that's something a nurse or an orderly would do, not an intern. I know—from a couple of lengthy hospital stays."

"Did it freak you out when I didn't show up at work today?" he asked.

She nodded soberly. "A little."

"You thought I'd pulled a Sharon Stone in *Casino,* didn't you? So what's the plan? Are you going to the police?"

Hannah shrugged and adjusted her mask again. "I can't. I checked last night. It's official. I'm wanted 'for questioning' in connection with kidnapping and larceny charges. They're ready to throw the book at me. Anyway, no police. I'm on my own in this—especially now that you've been sidelined."

"Yeah, guess I'm not much use to you in here. Sorry to let you down."

"Oh, skip it. Just get well, sweetie."

"Would you do me a favor, Han?" Scott asked. "Could you check on Britt for me? My buddy has left her a bunch of messages since early this morning, and he hasn't heard back from her."

"Well, I talked with her around nine o'clock last night, and she was all right. She's supposed to be with Webb, the Wonder Creep. I might have his number. I'll check, and keep you posted. I'm pretty concerned about her myself."

"Thanks, Hannah." He scratched his arm and frowned. "Listen. There's something you should know. After you left last night, a woman came into the store, wanting to rent *Psycho*. When I went to get it for her, the case was there, but the tape was missing. Someone ripped it off, just like *Casino*."

Gazing at him, Hannah slowly shook her head.

"It could be nothing," Scott said. "But I figured you'd want to know. Be on your guard, okay? Your um, secret admirer might soon be sending you another video valentine."

Outside Scott's room, Hannah shed the smock and the surgical mask, then dumped them in a waste bin labeled "Biohazard." Starting down the hall, she saw someone by the nurse's desk, and she stopped dead.

Ben put up his hand in a sort of half wave.

Hannah took a deep breath and walked up to him.

"Yeah," he said, nodding glumly. "I followed you here from the store."

"Do you have any idea how creepy that is?" Hannah asked pointedly.

"I know," he said. "I'm sorry. Can we please talk?" He pulled out a folder he had tucked under his arm. "I have something I want to show you."

Hannah just sighed and started toward the elevator.

Ben came up beside her. "I'll go away and not bother you again if I'm wrong," he said. "When that man was murdered the other night, did you know in advance something like that was going to happen?"

Hannah stopped. Her eyes searched his.

"Did you see it happen beforehand—in a video?"

Hannah kept staring at him. She swallowed hard. "Where do you want to talk?" she asked.

The woman in the picture was blond and pretty, with a round face and large blue eyes. Hannah guessed she was in her late twenties. Ben Podowski had his arm around her in the photo. They stood in front of a reservoir. Ben hadn't aged much since the snapshot was taken. His golden hair was now a shade darker and not quite as curly.

The girl in the photo was Rae Palmer. Ben said the picture was six years old. He'd taken it with a self-timer in Central Park one afternoon. It had been the last time he and Rae had seen each other.

"I think I've seen her somewhere before, but I'll be damned if I can figure out where." Hannah handed the photograph back to Ben.

They sat at a window table in an upscale bohemian coffeehouse called Victrola, down the block from Group Health Hospital. Ben had the folder open on the little cafe table between them.

"Rae and I were together for eight years," he explained, gazing at the photo with a trace of sadness in his eyes. He tucked the picture under the papers in his folder. "We started dating in college. She was a good person, very conscientious—socially and politically. She was arrested at least a dozen times while we were together—always some protest march or demonstration to help the downtrodden. She was a champion for the underdog. And *underdog, underachiever* describes me during my first few years out of college. Then I became an overachiever, and we didn't really need each other so much anymore. Anyway, in a hundred words or less, that explains Rae's and my relationship. We stayed friends after the breakup. In fact, since then, she never really got serious with anyone else."

Hannah stirred her latte. "Are you trying to tell me you're irresistible?"

With a strained smile, Ben shook his head. "No. I just want you to understand that we stayed friends. I felt responsible for her, and I know Rae pretty much considered me one of the most important people in her life—even after I got married, and she moved away."

Hannah shifted in her chair. "Are you still married?"

"That's a whole other story," he replied, frowning. "Anyway, Rae and I kept in touch, mostly phone calls and e-mails."

"How did your wife feel about that?" Hannah asked.

"Well, she didn't feel threatened or anything," Ben said, fingering the straw to his Italian soda. "It wasn't as if Rae and I were corresponding every day. It was more like every few weeks. Rae had her own life in Seattle, working as a hotel events coordinator." He took some of the papers from his folder. "Before I came here last month, I pulled some of her e-mails from my computer records and printed them out. I think you should see them."

Ben handed her a printout. He'd circled the date on top: *1/27/02*. He'd also drawn brackets around the paragraph he wanted her to read:

I met someone & I know you won't approve, Ben, because he's married & totally unavailable. I decided to take a film class last fall, & he's the professor. His name is Paul Gulletti. I think every woman in the class has a crush on him. He's very sexy & charismatic. We

*started dating in December. It was really sweet. He
helped me pick out my Xmas tree & for my present, he
gave me roses & we spent the night at a ski lodge. Very
romantic. I'm trying not to get too serious, but I think
I'm falling in love with him. Don't be mad, Ben ...*

Frowning, Hannah handed the piece of paper back to him.
"Why did you think I'd be interested in this?" she asked. "I
told you already that I'm not in any way involved with Paul
Gulletti."

Ben gave her another printout. "Just keep reading, okay?"

The date on the next e-mail was *4/16/02*. Again, he'd
marked the section he wanted her to see:

*You'll be proud of me, because I told Paul I don't want
to see him anymore. In fact, I dropped out of his film
class. It was kind of embarrassing. Everybody in the
class knew we were seeing each other. Paul doesn't
want to let go, and we've had some fights. It's weird.
He keeps saying he's going to leave his wife for me,
but I've never asked him to. Anyway, you were right
about him. It's been rough, Ben. I hate the idea that
I'll be alone again ...*

Hannah could tell this woman was still in love with Ben,
from the way she kept seeking his approval.

"I'm sorry." Shrugging, Hannah set down the sheet of
paper. "I still don't see what any of this has to do with me."

Wordlessly, Ben gave her another e-mail to read. This one
was dated *6/7/02*:

*Someone keeps calling me & hanging up. I'm con-
vinced it's Paul. The breakup was so dragged out & I
know he's bitter. Then again, perhaps he has moved on.
It's been a while since we actually talked, so maybe it's
not him. Don't think I'm paranoid, but someone has
also been following me & watching me. I even caught*

*a glimpse of this person videotaping me last week.
That's right, I have a stalker. For the last few years,
ever since we broke up, Ben, I've always thought nobody cared enough about me. Now I have someone
who cares too much. It's very weird. I can't prove it,
but I have a feeling he's been in my apartment . . .*

Neither Ben nor Hannah said a word. He just handed her
the next e-mail, dated *6/19/02:*

*I took your advice and changed my phone number. It's
been a major pain. I had to tell practically everyone
I know about the new number, which, of course, de-
feats the purpose, especially if this stalker is someone
I know. Anyway, the good news is that the calls and
hang-ups have stopped.*

*Now for the bad news. The strangest thing has hap-
pened & it has me very scared. I almost called you
about it, but I feel funny calling, especially when I get
Jennifer on the phone. She's perfectly sweet, but I just
feel strange.*

*Anyway, last week someone broke into my car—in the
parking garage at work. They didn't take anything.
They left something. It was a video of that old Hitchcock movie,* Strangers on a Train. *Have you seen it? I
took the video home. It was set to start on this scene
that takes place at an amusement park. There's this
boat ride to a little island. Robert Walker follows this
pretty woman with glasses to this place & he strangles
her. Her glasses fall off & we see her being murdered
in the reflection of her glasses.*

*I didn't know what to think. I suspected Paul again, but
now I'm not sure. I reported the break-in to the police.
Since nothing was stolen & no damage was done to the*

*car, they didn't think much of it. Of course, it's no help
that they checked on me when I reported this. They
mentioned that I'd been arrested four times in the last
five years, twice for participating in antipolice demon-
strations. I was like, "Well, duh!" Anyway, I guess I'm
labeled a troublemaker and a kook. After a few days,
nothing else happened & I managed to put it behind
me. I'd nearly forgotten about it.*

*Then, two days ago, a coworker at the hotel, Lily
Abrams, didn't show up for work. I didn't give her absence much thought. I've never been too fond of her.
She's always been kind of snotty to me. But that
doesn't matter. I found out yesterday that she was
murdered. Someone strangled her. They found her
body floating in Lake Washington, right by a little
patch of land called Foster Island. It's part of a nature
trail near the university district. Lily wore glasses.
They found them right near the water's edge.*

*Do you see what happened? Lily got strangled on a
little island, just like the woman in the movie. I tried
to tell this to the police, and they're acting like I'm
crazy . . .*

Hannah set down the e-mail printout.

Ben dug another sheet of paper from his folder. "One of
the first things I did when I got to Seattle was go to the library and look up a few things. My wife kept saying Rae
was making all this up so I would come out here, but Rae's
not that scheming. Still, I needed to make sure about what
she was telling me."

Across the table, he slid a copy of a newspaper article,
dated June 18. The headline read: *"WOMAN FOUND
STRANGLED IN ARBORETUM AREA."* There was a map
of the nature trail near Seattle's Arboretum, with an X mark-
ing off the tip of Foster Island. Beside it, a casual, blurry

photo of Lily Abrams, a thin-faced brunette with glasses and a slightly impish smile.

Hannah scanned the article, which revealed a bit of inside information that must have embarrassed the police. Among the baffled authorities, Lily Abrams had become known as "the Floating Flower." The name, Lily, had something to do with that epithet, as did, apparently, the position of her body when it was discovered. Lily's bracelet had gotten caught on some pilings in the shallow water off Foster Island, and she remained there, floating within a few feet of the shore, a floating flower.

The article also revealed that Lily's glasses were discovered on Foster Island, not far from the water. The police also found Lily's purse inside her unlocked car, parked a block away from her apartment building in Seattle's Eastlake neighborhood. They were examining the possibility that she'd been abducted there and taken to the Arboretum area, where she was strangled.

"Did you hear about this case?" Ben asked.

Hannah shook her head. "You'd think I would have."

"I looked at the articles. The press made a big thing out of that Floating Flower business. For a week, they made it out like another Black Dahlia case. Rae mentioned in one of her e-mails that the police must have written her off as one of the many nuts that were calling them with *inside information* about the Floating Flower. They basically blew her off. Anyway, they never solved the case."

Hannah set down the newspaper article, then sat back. "What happened to Rae?" she asked.

"That's what I'm still trying to find out," Ben replied. He gave her another document from his folder.

Hannah stared at the e-mail printout, this one dated *8/3/02*:

Thanks again for calling me back the other night. I'm really sorry I woke up Jennifer. I totally forgot about the time difference. Anyway, thanks for caring, Ben.

I took your advice & went out with Joe Blankenship again. So we're kind of dating now. He's a nice guy & so what if his kisses don't send me to the moon? He really seems to care for me. Besides, I don't want to be alone right now. This stalker person is back. I've seen him videotaping me again. I haven't seen his face. He's always too far away. I think I figured out what kind of car he drives—a wine-colored Volvo. He paid me a visit last night.

The TV woke me up around one A.M. I got scared & grabbed this baseball bat I've been keeping near my bed lately. (OK, I know you're thinking I'm a major loon, but having it there makes me feel safer.) Anyway, I recognized what was on TV before I even reached the living room. It's one of your favorites, On the Waterfront. *As soon as I realized no one was in the apartment, I figured out that the movie was cued at a scene near the beginning when the mobsters throw Eva Marie Saint's brother off the roof & he's killed. The character's name was Joey.*

My Joe lives in a eleven-story apartment building, and I'm certain the same thing will happen to him. He thinks I'm imagining things or vying for more of his attention. He's almost as bad as the police. He just won't take me seriously.

I went to Paul Gulletti, because I figure someone with a film background is behind all this. I confronted him, Ben. He tried to pretend he didn't know what I was talking about. But I could tell he was covering something up, or lying. Unfortunately, I can't prove anything.

Ben, I feel so helpless & scared . . .

"She called me a few days later," Ben said, sliding a copy of yet another newspaper article in front of Hannah. It was dated August 8. She glanced at the headline:

SEATTLE MAN PLUMMETS TO HIS DEATH
FROM HIGH-RISE
Police Probe Rooftop Fall:
Freak Accident or Suicide?

Hannah skimmed over the article, which suggested that the victim, Joe Blankenship, had been indulging in some illegal substances at the time of his demise.

"Did she try talking to the police again?" Hannah asked.

"Yeah," Ben said, frowning. "It was pointless."

Hannah imagined how the police must have reacted when Rae Palmer once again approached them saying this drug-induced freak accident had been forecast to her in a video.

"This is the last e-mail," Ben said, handing her another printout. It was dated *8/29/02:*

You haven't returned my message from a couple of days ago. I hope I haven't become a total pain, Ben. It's just that I have no one else to turn to.

I found another video, this one in my desk drawer at work. I don't know how he got in there. This time the movie is Looking for Mr. Goodbar, *and it was cued to start up near the very end, the scene where Tom Berenger is having sex with Diane Keaton & suddenly he pulls out a knife and stabs her to death.*

I know a woman named Diane who's in payroll. But I don't know her that well. Yet I feel I should warn her. It's crazy. I don't know why this is happening. I wonder who could be doing this & I keep coming back to my ex, Paul. But I can't prove anything.

*Meanwhile, I know sometime soon some woman I
know will be stabbed to death in bed.*

*I wish I could just run away someplace. I know it's a
lot to ask, but could I come out there & stay with you
for a while? Or maybe, better still, you could come
out here? I could even put you & Jennifer up at the
hotel, give you two a suite at a ridiculously low rate.
In fact, I'd pay for you guys. I feel so alone, Ben.*

Anyway, please, think about it & get back to me.

Hannah set down the e-mail sheet. Her eyes met Ben's.
"Did you find out the identity of this *Goodbar* victim?" she
asked.

He slowly shook his head. "I tried calling Rae afterward,
but there was no answer. I kept trying—on and off—for
over a week. Then I came out here." He straightened the pile
of papers and tucked them back inside the folder.

"Can I see Rae's picture again, please?" Hannah asked.

Ben found the photo, then handed it to her.

She studied Rae's eyes. Weren't they the same blue eyes
with the dead stare in the *Goodbar* homage? It had been
over two weeks since Hannah had seen the grisly video. She
didn't think she'd ever forget that woman's face. Obviously,
she had—for a while. But looking at Rae Palmer's picture
helped her remember.

She handed the photo back to Ben. "Do you mind if we
get out of here?" she asked quietly.

"Not at all," he said, leaving a tip on the table. "Are you
okay?"

"I just need some air," she said, getting to her feet.

Hannah headed for the door, with Ben right behind her.

She'd been right earlier. She had indeed seen Rae Palmer
before.

She'd seen her die.

Twelve

He videotaped them sitting at the window table of the coffeeshop. Due to a reflection on the glass, he caught only a few, fleeting, usable close-ups of her with his zoom lens. Still, he knew he had some beautiful shots of Hannah in that twenty-five minutes of footage.

He put his video camera away as he followed them out of the coffeeshop. He watched them through the trees. Walking side by side, the two of them looked like a couple of lovers. Even from across the street, he could see Hannah was smitten with Ben. The son of a bitch.

Of course, he knew it would happen. Hell, he'd *made* it happen, orchestrating their every move. He was pulling the strings.

Still, he'd expected more from his leading lady. He'd thought she would hold out a bit longer before succumbing to Ben's charms. He was disappointed in her. Hannah still fascinated and aroused him, but she'd lost his respect.

He'd been through this before with the others. Once a leading lady fell out of favor with him, he became all the more anxious to realize her death scene.

Hannah's demise had already been planned—down to the last detail. Now it was time to put the plan in motion.

He stopped, and watched Ben and Hannah move on together.

He smiled, even laughed a little to himself.

Poor Hannah: so beautiful, so stupid.

And doomed.

* * *

"You never heard from Rae again after that last e-mail?" Hannah asked.

"No," Ben replied, walking alongside her. "Like I said, I wasn't able to get ahold of her. I wish I'd come to Seattle earlier, but I was having problems at work—and at home." He sighed. "Anyway, I came out here the second week in September. But I think I may have been too late."

Hannah didn't say anything.

They were strolling down the sidewalk by a busy residential street across from Volunteer Park. Through the trees they could catch a peek at the park's water tower, the art museum, conservatory, and a playground.

Ben said that when he arrived in Seattle, one of the first things he did was go to the hotel where Rae worked. They hadn't seen or heard from her in over a week. It was more of the same at Rae's apartment building, where Ben interviewed her neighbor and the building manager. Rae seemed to have just disappeared.

Ben knew Paul Gulletti reviewed movies for the local weekly. He tore Paul's picture out of the paper and showed the photo to Rae's coworkers and neighbors. Nearly all of them recognized Rae's married boyfriend, but no one had seen him for months.

Ben went to the police and reported Rae as a missing person. "It was incredibly unspectacular," he told Hannah. "You'd think I was applying for a fishing license or something. I tried to tell this cop at the desk what had been happening to Rae the past few months, and he didn't seem to give a crap. So I filled out a form, and gave them a photo of Rae which I really kind of cherished. The cop said they'd contact me if they came up with anything. In other words, *Don't call us, we'll call you.* And guess what? Big surprise, they haven't called."

He ran a hand through his wavy blond hair. "To be fair, the cop pointed out that they have hundreds of new missing persons on file every week." Ben squinted across the street at the entrance to Lakeview Cemetery. "I didn't know there's a cemetery here."

Hannah nodded. "Bruce Lee is buried there. His son Brandon's grave is right beside his."

They reached a curve in the road, and a small, scenic overlook park with a view of Lake Washington, the University's Husky Stadium, the floating bridge, and the Cascade Mountains. They sat down on a wooden bench built around a tree at the edge of a huge ravine. With dusk creeping over the horizon, many of the cars on the bridge had their headlights on. The little sailboats glided on darkening silver-blue water.

As Ben gazed out at the view, Hannah allowed herself to study his handsome profile and the sadness in his beautiful eyes. She still felt a bit cautious around him, and had to fight her attraction for this lonely man who was away from home.

And she had to tell him that his onetime girlfriend was dead.

He turned to her, and Hannah quickly looked away— toward the lights across the lake. "So," she said, "what kind of job do you have that allows you to pick up and go to Seattle for a month?"

"A *former* job, I think," he said. "I'm not sure I still have it. I'm in advertising. Do you know Gustov bottled water?"

" 'The champagne of seltzer waters'?"

He nodded. "I came up with that—and the advertisements about it being easier to open than champagne. If you hate those commercials, blame me."

"Actually, I think those ads are very funny."

"Thanks." He shrugged. "Anyway, I took a leave of absence without pay. They hadn't really approved it yet when I left. So I'm not sure the job will be waiting for me when I get back."

"Your wife doesn't mind that you went to Seattle for a month? And you're chasing after an ex-girlfriend, no less. Jennifer—isn't that her name? She must be very understanding."

Frowning, Ben gazed out toward the bridge. "I'm not sure if she'll be waiting for me when I get back, either." He sighed. "It's a long story. Maybe I'll bend your ear about it sometime, but not now."

Hannah nodded. Neither of them said anything for a moment. Hannah thought about his former girlfriend, Rae Palmer. Every concern Rae expressed in those e-mails was familiar to Hannah. In the last e-mail, when Rae mentioned wanting to run away, it scared Hannah that she'd had exactly the same reaction. Rae had admitted that she slept with a baseball bat at her bedside. Hannah had kept a hammer by her nightstand ever since the break-in. She remembered the *Goodbar* video, with the bloodied bed sheets and Rae's dead gaze.

"What happened to Rae is happening to me now," Hannah whispered.

"I know," he said. "It took a while to figure out. I hadn't planned on staying here in Seattle this long. But once I realized Rae might be lost to me, I couldn't go back to New York. So I rented this cheap, dumpy studio apartment and signed up for Paul Gulletti's film class. I registered under the name Ben Sturges in case Rae had ever told him about me. Sturgis, Michigan is where I'm from originally. I just changed the spelling a little. Anyway, I asked around in class, very casually of course, but nobody had heard of Rae Palmer. Apparently, no one in this current class has been taking Paul's course for more than three semesters."

"You didn't ask me," Hannah said.

"Well, I figured out pretty quickly you were Paul's favorite. People said you two were an item. I kept thinking you must be Rae's successor. When I heard you worked at a video store, I thought you might know something. But I couldn't approach you about it; at least, not directly."

"So you started following me around?" Hannah said, not smiling.

"Yeah," he whispered, nodding. "I know that gives you a major case of the heebie-jeebies, and I don't blame you. But

I'm glad I did start following you, because I noticed someone else was watching you, too. That's when I realized that this . . . this video stalker must have moved on from Rae to you."

"Do you think it could be Paul?" she asked.

He shrugged. "I've never really gotten a good look at the man following you. I thought Ronald Craig might have. That's why I went to his hotel the other night. I was hoping Craig had left behind some information about this man. I thought Craig might be tailing you for the same reason I was. He was a private detective out of Milwaukee. I don't think Rae knew anyone from Milwaukee. She had no family left. So I don't know who hired him, or why. I can't figure that out."

Hannah said nothing.

"Gulletti's married. Maybe his wife is from Milwaukee. Maybe she hired Craig to investigate you."

Hannah gave an awkward shrug. "You know, I spotted a man videotaping me last night," she said steadily. "It was around the time film class started. You said Paul was there, so he couldn't be the man following me."

"Well, maybe it's someone working for Paul. He's involved in this somehow. I feel it in my gut. Maybe it's his assistant."

"Seth? Why? Wasn't he in class last night?"

Ben rolled his eyes and nodded. "Of course, yeah. He was there. I don't know what I'm thinking."

"He might be a good one to talk with about Rae," Hannah suggested.

"Well, I didn't approach him because I thought he was pretty tight with Paul. But Seth talked with me last night, and I guess he's not Paul Gulletti's biggest fan. If he's been working with Paul since last December, he'll remember Rae. I'm sure he can tell us something."

Hannah gently took the folder from his lap, then opened it up. She studied Rae Palmer's photo again.

"If only I had one definite lead about her," she heard Ben say. "Someone doesn't just disappear."

"Did Rae ever mention to you getting a homemade video?" Hannah asked carefully.

"What do you mean?"

"The same way she was getting those other videos, only this one would have been homemade—with someone being murdered on it."

Squinting at her, Ben shook his head. "I'm sure Rae would have mentioned it."

"Such a video was dropped off at the store about a month ago. I think it was meant for me. It was a homemade, copycat version of the ending to *Looking for Mr. Goodbar*. It was the scene Rae described in her e-mail. A woman was being stabbed in bed. I couldn't see the man who was stabbing her. But I saw the woman." Hannah reached over and took hold of his hand. "Ben, I think the woman was Rae. I—I'm so sorry."

His eyes searched hers for a moment, as if he didn't believe her. Then he got to his feet. Hannah stared at his back. "Are you sure?" he asked, his voice raspy.

"I'm not absolutely positive," Hannah admitted. "But I'm pretty sure. I don't have the video anymore. It was stolen."

Hannah noticed his head bobbing a little along with the tremors in his slightly hunched shoulders. She realized he was crying. She wanted to reach out to him, console him. But she held back and stayed seated on the little wooden bench.

Ben finally turned to face her. His blue eyes were bloodshot and a bit puffy. He took a deep breath. "Do you know Seth's last name?" he asked.

"Um, Stroud," she said. "Seth Stroud."

"Well, let's go find him and talk to him," Ben said.

There was a "1/2" behind the number address on Aloha Street for Stroud, Seth. Hannah and Ben had returned to the coffeeshop and borrowed the phone book to look him up. Hannah thought it might be a basement apartment, and Ben guessed he lived over someone's garage.

It was within walking distance. They didn't say much on

their way to the Aloha Street address. Hannah could tell Ben was still numb over the news of his friend's death. She slid her arm around his. At the end of a couple of blocks, Hannah gently pulled away.

"That was nice," he murmured. Then he didn't say another word until they reached Seth's block.

Ben had been right. It was a garage apartment at the end of the driveway to a large, slightly neglected Tudor estate. Though the lawn was mowed and the leaves were raked, the place still had a seedy grandeur. Water stains marred the yellowing wall to the Tudor-style garage. The stairs to the second-floor apartment were on the side.

Hannah and Ben climbed up the rickety steps and knocked on the door. Through the window in the door, Hannah could see someone coming. She saw his tall, lean build and the wild, wavy dark hair. It took her a moment to realize he wasn't Seth.

A stranger opened the door. He was about Seth's age, with olive-colored eyes, a large nose, and a goatee. He wore a black T-shirt and jeans. Those eyes shifted back and forth from Ben to Hannah. "Yeah? Can I help you?"

"Does Seth Stroud live here?" Ben asked.

"Seth?" the young man said. "What did you want to see him about?"

"We're in his film class," Ben replied. "I'm Ben Sturges."

"Hi." Hannah reached out her hand to the young man. "I'm Hannah."

"Oh, well, hi." He smiled and shook her hand. "I'm Richard Kidd, Seth's roommate. Um, he's not around right now. You want to leave a message?"

Hannah nodded. "Yeah, we really need to talk with him."

"Wow, sounds urgent. PDQ. Is it an emergency?"

"Let's just say it's important," Ben chimed in.

"Then, hell, man, we'd better write it down. Hold on."

While Richard Kidd retreated to another part of the apartment, Hannah and Ben remained on the outside landing at the top of the stairs. She caught a glimpse of their living room: brick-and-wood bookshelves, furniture from garage sales and Pier 1 Imports, a big poster for *La Dolce Vita* on the wall, and clothes and newspapers strewn about. The two of them could have used a maid.

Richard returned to the doorway with a notepad and a pen. He handed them to Hannah. "Why don't you write down the message yourself? I might be stepping out. I'll leave it where he'll be sure to see it."

Hannah scribbled on the pad:

> *Seth:*
> *Could you call me tonight (Friday) at 555-1007, or stop by the video store some time before 7 P.M. tomorrow? It's important I speak with you.*
> *Thanks, Hannah Doyle*

As they left Seth's place together, Ben stopped at the end of the driveway. "Well, that was kind of a bust," he said.

Hannah patted Ben's arm. "We'll just have to wait," she said. "I think he'll call. Seth likes me. If he knows something, he'll tell us."

Ben nodded glumly. "Listen, can I walk you home?"

She smiled. "I'd like that."

Aloha was a dark, winding, tree-shaded street. Fallen leaves blanketed patches of sidewalk. A few houses already had Halloween decorations out. Hannah was glad for Ben's company. She thought about taking hold of his arm again, but decided against it.

"Did you recognize him?" Ben asked. "Did he look familiar to you?"

"Who? The roommate?"

"Yeah, Richard Kidd."

"No, I didn't recognize him. Did you?"

He shrugged. "Not really."

She brushed her arm against his. "You're like I was when this whole thing started. I suspected everyone."

"Including me?" he asked lightly.

"Especially you," she admitted.

"And now?"

"Now, I know you better," she carefully replied. "And I like you, Ben."

"I like you, too. But you didn't really answer my question."

"You noticed that, huh?"

Patting her shoulder, he nodded. "It's all right if you still suspect me a little. You'd be crazy not to."

When they reached her apartment building, Ben asked if he could come up. "I'd like to be there if Seth calls tonight," he said. "I could also use a drink. If you could spare a glass of wine, I'll buy you a pizza dinner—or Chinese."

Hannah hesitated.

"It's okay if you say no. I won't be offended."

She worked up a smile. "Quit giving me permission to not trust you. It makes me—not trust you."

He chuckled. "All right. To tell you the truth, I'll be hurt if you turn me away."

Hannah sighed. "My little boy's sick, and I want to spend some time with him. I also need to track down a coworker friend who could be in trouble. If Seth calls me, I'll get in touch with you right away, Ben. I'm filling in for a coworker tomorrow. Why don't you stop by the video store? I take my break at two."

"Okay," he muttered, looking crestfallen. "See you tomorrow, Hannah." He seemed ready to hug her for a second, then drew back and awkwardly shook her hand. "Well, um, good night."

Hannah opened the lobby door.

She wanted so much to let down her guard and invite him in. But she turned and started up the cold, cinder-block stairwell by herself.

"What a miserable fuckhead," Britt muttered, as she stormed out of a dance club called The Urinal. The loud, pulsating, pounding music still echoed in her ears.

Everything had been terrific when she and Webb first went into the place. They'd both been a little high. He had a couple of deals he needed to make there, so she'd expected to be ditched for a few minutes. She could handle that. She looked pretty damn good tonight in her favorite black jeans and a black sleeveless T-shirt with a blue thunderbolt on the front. The blue matched exactly with the streaks in her hair and the stone in her eyebrow ring. She caught several guys checking her out as she stood alone at the bar. She didn't mind waiting for Webb.

But he was gone forty-five minutes, for God's sake. She finally discovered him by the rest rooms. He had his tongue halfway down the throat of this skanky bitch with orange hair and a black bra for a top.

That was when Britt ran out of The Urinal.

Halfway down the block, she started crying. She began to think of all the awful things Webb had done. The most recent was earlier in the week, when she'd gotten a phone bill for three hundred bucks and change because he'd made a bunch of 1-900 sex-line calls on her phone. They'd fought. He punched her in the stomach and knocked the wind out of her. By the time she could breathe normally again, Webb was crying. So she forgave him.

Now she was the one crying. She was through forgiving him. The miserable prick wasn't worth all this aggravation.

Britt was freezing as she hobbled down the sidewalk. Mascara streaked down her face. She didn't see any cabs. She was wondering how the hell she'd get home when, just ahead, a burgundy Volvo pulled over to the curb.

Britt stopped. She watched a man step out of the car. He leaned on the roof of his car, his chin in his hand. It took a moment for Britt to recognize him from The Urinal. He'd been one of the guys checking her out.

"Do you need a ride, sad lady?" he called softly.

She took a few steps toward the car. "I know you," she said.

"Yeah, I'm a friend of Hannah's," he said. His face was almost completely swallowed up by shadow.

"Hannah?" she repeated. Britt was about to tell him that she'd seen him in The Urinal. "You know Hannah?"

"Yeah, get in the car. I'll take you home."

"Thanks," Britt said, reaching for the door.

"You look real, real sad," he remarked as she climbed into the car. "I have something that will make you feel a lot better."

Britt leaned back in the passenger seat. "Sounds good," she muttered, wiping her eyes.

He got behind the wheel, then shut his door.

The burgundy Volvo drove off.

Hannah had to wait through one verse and the chorus of The Beatles' *Good Day, Sunshine* before Britt's recorded voice finally came on: *"Hey, this is Britt. Guess what? I can't come to the phone. You know what to do!"*

Beep.

"Hi again, Britt. It's Hannah. I was hoping the third time tonight would be the charm. Call me. And you've got to change that message. If I never hear *Good Day Sunshine* again, it'll be too soon. Anyway, call me at home. It doesn't matter how late. I have Guy's door closed. Talk to you soon—I hope. Bye."

Sara Middleton threw back the covers, switched on the nightstand lamp, then squinted at the digital clock: 2:43 A.M.

If she nodded off within ten minutes, she would still catch about four and a half hours of sleep. She would still be able to function and look halfway decent for her big presentation in the morning.

She'd been trying to fall asleep for the past ninety minutes. What she needed was a shot or two of bourbon to take the edge off. She'd packed a pint of Jack Daniel's in her luggage for that very purpose. Lately, she'd been under a lot of pressure with her job. At thirty-one, she was the youngest executive manager at her company—and one of only three women in upper administration. With all her responsibilities came insomnia. She was becoming a slave to the bourbon-at-bedtime habit. Tonight she'd been determined to go without.

Well, screw that. Right now she was desperate for sleep—however she could get it.

Sara liked her bourbon on the rocks.

If she were staying at the Westin with the upper-upper management boys, she could have just picked up the phone and had room service bring her a bucket of ice. But the Best Western Maritime Inn was all her expense account could afford. She had to get her own ice.

Sara slept in panties and a white tank top. She'd be damned if she got completely dressed again for a trip down the hall in the middle of the night. She stepped into a pair of sweatpants, grabbed her room key and the ice bucket, then started down the dimly lit corridor.

She was so tired and frayed she didn't care if someone saw her—barefoot, with her nipples practically poking through the flimsy tank top. The damn hallway was cold—and a bit creepy too.

Then Sara suddenly realized how vulnerable she was. When she'd booked the hotel two weeks ago, a friend back home in Santa Rosa had said this place was in an "iffy neighborhood." Anybody could wander in from the street and hide in one of the shadowy doorways or alcoves.

Just a minute ago, Sara had been fearless. Now she couldn't wait to go back inside her room and lock the door behind her.

She hurried toward the ice room. Sara figured once she got some ice in the bucket, at least she'd have something to throw at an attacker. She could scream and wake up half the hotel.

A few steps from the ice room door, Sara stopped in her

tracks. Straight ahead, a man came around a corner and
started down the hallway toward her. The light was in back
of him, and for a moment all she could see was this tall,
shadowy thing coming at her.

"Burning the midnight oil, huh?" she heard him say.

He stepped under a dim overhead light, and Sara noticed
his tie and the hotel badge with his name on it. She also
noticed him shyly checking out her breasts. She crossed her
arms in front of her and almost dropped her ice bucket.

"Have a nice night," he said, passing her.

"Thanks, you too," she whispered.

Sara watched him continue down the hallway. She had
to laugh a little. She put her hand over her heart and felt it
pounding away. No doubt about it now, she really needed
her Jack Daniel's tonight. She'd catch four hours of sleep
and take some aspirin in the morning.

Sara pushed open the ice room door. She gasped, and
dropped the ice bucket.

The thing splayed on the tiled floor seemed to be staring
back at her. The dead girl was so white her skin appeared
chalky and translucent. Dark red blood was smeared around
her nose and open mouth. The blue jewel in a ring that
pierced her eyebrow was the same color as the streaks in her
black hair; the same color as those unblinking eyes.

Sara screamed and screamed. She would wake up half the
hotel.

That night—or what was left of it—Sara Middleton
wouldn't sleep at all.

Thirteen

The uniformed driver stood near the American Airlines terminal's security checkpoint, holding a sign: *KENNETH WOODLEY.* Arriving Seattle passengers filed past the husky, middle-aged Arabic man on their way to baggage claim. Ari held the placard a bit higher. There were a half dozen other chauffeurs waiting around with signs. One by one, they met up with their fares. Ari was beginning to think Kenneth Woodley hadn't made his plane from Chicago.

He didn't see him coming. The lean man in his mid-thirties wore a Polo sportshirt and carried a duffel bag. His dark eyes seemed very intense, and there were traces of gray in his wavy brown hair. He was talking on a cell phone. Without a word or a nod of recognition, he unloaded his bag on Ari, then kept moving toward the escalator. Startled, Ari chased after him with the duffel and the sign.

"No, listen," Kenneth Woodley was saying into his cell phone. "Just keep doing what you're doing. You don't think she's caught on to you yet, do you?"

Ari hovered behind him as the escalator carried them down to baggage claim.

"Well, she might not be letting on that she's wise to you. Watch out for her. She's a crafty bitch. Have you seen the kid yet? What? Well, what the fuck is wrong with you? How long have you been on the job?"

He stepped off the escalator and headed toward the baggage carousel. Ari was a step in back of him.

"Well, if we can, I want to pin Craig's murder on her. I don't care what you say. You stick with her long enough, and we'll come up with something. One way or another, I'll see she gets what's coming to her. So—keep doing what you're doing. I gotta go. You're breaking up here."

With a flick of the wrist, he folded up the tiny phone and shoved it in his pants pocket.

"Excuse me?" Ari piped up finally. "You're Mr. Woodley?"

Kenneth Woodley turned and laughed. "No, I'm fucking Santa Claus. Who do you think I am?" He handed Ari his ticket envelope. "A black suitcase with a royal blue stripe down the center. Think you can remember that?"

"Yessir," Ari replied. "We're going to the Four Seasons Hotel, sir?"

Kenneth chuckled again. *"I'm going* to the Four Seasons. I don't give a shit where you end up. Only, along the way, I want you drive me to someplace where I can lease a yacht. I might be here a few days. I may as well get some sailing in."

"The fishing here is excellent, too, Mr. Woodley," Ari offered.

"I don't give a damn about that," he replied. "I'm not fishing here. I'm on a hunting expedition. Now, get the suitcase, okay? I gotta take a leak."

Neither of them had finished their lunch. Hannah's chicken was gnarly and hard. All she could do was pick at her rice.

Tiptop Teriyaki was new to the mall's food court, and not likely to last very long. Hannah and Ben were the only customers seated at the counter bar that curved around Tiptop's nearly vacant eating area.

Over their inedible meal, Hannah told Ben about the other murders, and the videos forecasting them. She didn't have to explain much. He was already familiar with the pattern. She told him about finding *Casino* in her purse, and her concern for her coworker.

Britt hadn't shown up for work today, and she hadn't answered any of Hannah's phone messages since the night before last.

"Anyway," Hannah sighed, pushing her plate away. "I'm worried she might be next."

"What do the police think?" Ben asked.

"Well, I—I haven't talked to them," Hannah answered. "I haven't contacted them about any of this."

"What?" Ben squinted at her. "Why not?"

She glanced at her wristwatch. "Listen, I need to get back to work. You want to walk with me?"

They headed back toward the store.

"I can't believe you haven't talked to the police," Ben said, as they crossed the street. "You know, after that deliberate hit-and-run the other night, it struck me as weird you never approached the police about Craig. I mean, he'd been there to see *you*. Why didn't you say something?"

Hannah hurried toward Emerald City Video. She shook her head. "I'm not sure. I was scared, confused."

"Well, why don't you talk to the police now? Between the two of us, we have enough information—"

"Ben, I'm going to be late for work," she cut in, pausing in front of the door. "Maybe we can talk tonight. Okay?"

"Well, wait a minute—"

Hannah opened the door, stepped inside, and stopped dead.

Two uniformed policemen and a third man—heavyset with a tie, and badge on his windbreaker—stood by the front counter. At the register, Cheryl seemed confused. Tish stared back at Hannah with tears in her eyes. A slapstick comedy was showing on the store's TVs.

"Ms. Doyle?" the plainclothes cop said.

Hannah took a step back, and almost bumped into Ben. She'd known this was coming, yet they'd still caught her off guard. They were here to arrest her. "Where's my son?" she heard herself ask.

Tish approached her. "Honey, it's not Guy. It's Britt. Something happened."

Wide-eyed, Hannah shook her head.

Tish hugged her, then whispered in her ear, "Oh, Han, they found her this morning in some hotel. . . ."

"She was seeing this man named Roy Webster," Hannah explained while shelving videos and DVDs. She moved from aisle to aisle with a stack of movies. The husky detective was following her around the store. He held a little recorder in his hand.

"He goes by the nickname 'Webb,'" Hannah went on. "Britt was spending the weekend with him. As I said, I just talked with her the night before last, and she was fine."

Hannah stayed as busy as she could around the plain-clothes cop. That way, she could avoid looking him in the eye.

As she ran around the store, Hannah caught an occasional glimpse of Ben, browsing in New Releases. She could tell he was studying her, probably waiting for her to say something to the detective about the video murders. But she couldn't. She could barely get through this casual interrogation without almost giving herself away. Fortunately, Ben had kept his mouth shut—so far.

He'd been in the store for about twenty minutes now. Ben had waited, along with the three policemen, while Tish and Hannah had ducked into the break room.

"Listen, honey," Tish said, once they'd had a good cry in the little closet of a room. "I could send you home, but it would kill us here. I hate to ask, but could you hang in there and finish off your shift? You can take tomorrow off. I'll fill in for Britt."

Hannah hunted for a Kleenex in her purse. Her heart ached as she pulled out the packet of Capt'n Crunch decals Britt had saved for Guy. She began to cry all over again.

Tish handed her some tissues from her own bag, and suggested maybe she should go home after all.

"No, I'll stick it out here," she'd managed to say. "It's best I keep busy for the next few hours."

The two uniformed policemen left. Tish took to the register with Cheryl, while Hannah darted around the store, filing away returns.

"Were you aware that your friend had a drug habit?" the detective asked her, in the Documentaries section.

"That's a side of her I don't know much about," Hannah answered steadily. "The person you should really ask is Webb. He's the one you ought to talk to."

"Britt had a couple of priors for possession," the detective said, following her to the Sci-Fi section. "Do you know any of the people she might have—um, partied with?"

"No. As I said, that was a part of her life she didn't share with me." Hannah's voice began to quaver. "She was really a sweet person, with a kind heart." She paused and took a couple of deep breaths. Standing there among the Sci-Fi videos, she didn't want to cry in front of this man. She just wanted him to go.

"I don't know what else I can tell you," she finally said, her voice raspy. "I wish I knew more, but I don't. I'm very sorry."

When the detective finished questioning her, Hannah had to give him her home phone number and address. She felt sick to her stomach, telling a policeman how to reach her.

The cop asked Tish if there were any other employees who knew Britt very well. Tish turned to Hannah. "Do you think Scott could tell them anything, Han?"

She quickly shook her head. "Not really. He didn't know any of her friends. Plus he's been in the hospital since yesterday morning."

Tish turned to the detective. "His name is Scott Eckland," she said, "In case you want to talk with him, he's at Group Health Hospital—"

"I don't think we need to bother him," the detective said, slipping his little recorder in the pocket of his windbreaker. "But thank you anyway."

After watching him step outside, Hannah wanted to retreat to the back room and have another breakdown. Instead, she stepped behind the counter. Tish came up to her and rested a hand on her shoulder.

"It just dawned on me," she whispered. "Scott doesn't know about Britt yet. Who's going to tell him?"

"I can do it," Hannah murmured, gathering up another stack of videos. "I'll put these away first, then call him from the back room."

As she came around the counter, Ben started following her.

"Hannah, what's going on?" he whispered. "You told me over lunch you thought your friend was going to die like that—and she did! Why didn't you say anything to that cop?"

Hannah couldn't respond. She filed some movies in the Classics section.

"Listen, don't pull the same shit with me you pulled with that detective," Ben hissed. "I want you to stop and look at me and explain why you won't go to the police about any of this."

"It has nothing to do with you," was all Hannah could say. She hurried down the aisle. "Can we please talk about this later?"

In the Children's section, Tish stepped up to them and cleared her throat. "Sir? Can I help you with anything?"

Ben shook his head. "No thanks. I'm just talking to Hannah."

"Well, we're awfully busy right now," Tish said, very cool and businesslike. "Hannah has work to do. I'm sure you understand."

Ben turned and frowned at Hannah.

"I'll talk to you tonight, Ben," she said.

"Will you call me if you hear from Seth?" he asked.

She sighed. "Of course. I'll talk to you later either way."

Tish waited until Ben walked out of the store. "I hope I did the right thing chasing him away. Was he a friend of yours? He's kind of cute."

"He's also married," Hannah said.

"Then I say avoid him like the plague."

Hannah shook her head. "It's not like that."

"Well, here." Tish collected the stack of videos from her. "I'll put these away. Why don't you go in the back and call Scott? Get it over with."

Hannah nodded and reluctantly started for the break room.

"Jesus, no," Scott whispered. "It was like in the movie, wasn't it?"

"Yes. The police were here." Hannah was on the phone, hunched over the desk in the tiny room. She had a Kleenex in her hand.

"I don't think they've talked with Webb yet," she continued. "I doubt if he could tell them anything. I mean, you and I know what really happened." She wiped her eyes and sighed. "Scott, I didn't tell the police anything. I saw them here when I came back from my break, and I got so scared. All I could think about was saving my own skin. If I tell the police what's happening, they only have to run a check on my name to know I'm a fraud. . . ."

Hannah paused. She heard a strange, strangled rasping on the other end of the line. "Scott?"

"Yeah, I'm here," he replied, his voice strained. He coughed a little.

She realized he was crying. "Oh, sweetie, I'm so sorry," she said.

"Well, at least you don't have to worry," he said finally, a tremor in his voice. "Once they talk to a couple of Britt's burnout friends, they'll just chalk it up as an overdose. You're safe for now. The cops won't be bothering you anymore." He sighed. "I'm sorry. Did that sound snotty? I didn't mean it that way. What are you planning to do, Hannah? How's this gonna work itself out?"

She didn't have an answer for him. Her only "plan" had been to run away. And for the time being, she couldn't even do that.

"Hannah, I'm really worried about you," he continued. "I hate knowing you're alone in all this. I wish you had somebody to help you out."

She thought of Ben. "There may be someone, a guy from my film class. But I'm not sure yet if I can completely trust him."

"Yeah?"

"Yes," Hannah said. "Only now, I think I'd better take a chance on him—before it's too late."

"Hannah?"

She was just leaving the store. She turned to see Seth Stroud coming up the block. It had been dark for a couple of hours and the streetlights were on, but Seth still wore sunglasses. He also had on a black jacket, black jeans, and a gray T-shirt. He always looked very cutting-edge.

"Hey, another minute and I'd have missed you," he said. "I heard you and some dude stopped by yesterday. Was it Marlboro Man?"

Hannah didn't understand at first, then she nodded. "Oh, yeah. I was with Ben."

"I didn't get the message until this morning. Anyway, I'm glad I caught you. In fact, it's funny you stopped by last night, because I wanted to get ahold of you."

"Really?"

"Yeah, I was wondering if they have any openings for a part-timer here at your store." He nodded toward the storefront, then took off his sunglasses and replaced them with the designer glasses he usually wore in class. "Money's a little tight lately, and I was just wondering. . . ."

Hannah let out a sad, ironic laugh. "Well, yeah, we—we'll be hiring for sure. Why don't you stop in tomorrow morning? The manager will be there. Her name's Tish."

"Cool. Thanks. Could you put in a good word for me?"

She nodded. "Sure thing. Listen, do you have a couple of minutes?"

"Sure. There's a bar in the Mexican joint down the block. You look like you could use a drink. Can I buy you one?"

"Actually, I need to get home. Would you mind walking with me? We could talk along the way."

He shrugged. "Sounds cool."

Hannah moved away from the storefront and its lights. Seth strolled beside her, his hands in his pockets. "By the way," he said. "Please don't tell Paul that you're helping me get a job here. Otherwise, you'll find my body parts in Puget Sound." He laughed—until he glanced at Hannah.

She squinted at him. "Is it really as bad as that?" she asked. "Because that's what I wanted to ask you about. The other day, you said Paul was 'obsessed' with me—or words to that effect. Does he talk to you about me?"

"God, no," Seth replied, shaking his head. "Paul doesn't confide in me about his personal life. But I know him. I've seen how he is when he wants a woman. Believe me, he's got it bad for you. And Paul's used to having his way. He gets pissed when that doesn't happen. And FYI, he ain't a very happy camper lately."

They crossed the street together, toward a block where two new condominiums were being built. Hannah never walked down this block alone at night. It was too dark and creepy—with the tall, skeletonlike frames to the buildings, the piles of wood and steel rods, and the portable outhouses. Hannah should have felt safe with Seth at her side, but what he was saying frightened her.

"You're right not to get involved with him," he continued. "He's bad news. I've seen how he treats the women he's with—and the ones he's had."

"So there have been a lot of women, huh?" she asked. "Students like me?"

"No one like you," he said, a strange warmth in his voice. "But yeah, they were students. He must have a thing for blondes. The last was a blonde named Rae Palmer."

Hannah stopped walking for a moment. Seth stopped with her. "What? Do you know her?"

"I've heard the name," Hannah said, walking again. "What can you tell me about her?"

"Well, let's see," Seth said, pulling a pack of cigarettes from his jacket pocket. He lit one up with a disposable lighter. "Rae was in the class for two semesters. If I remember right, she started in September of last year, and dropped out in April. Hands down, she was the prettiest one in the class, and I could tell ol' Paul was interested in her from the get-go. Anyone could see it. I can't say exactly when they started up, but they seemed pretty hot and heavy by Christmastime. It had definitely cooled down when she dropped the class. It might have gone on a little longer after that, I'm not sure."

"Did you ever see her again? Did Paul ever talk about her?"

He took a long drag of his cigarette. "No on both counts."

The wind kicked up, and Hannah adjusted the collar to her jacket. She crossed her arms in front of her. "So—you don't know what became of her?"

"Haven't a clue." Seth exhaled a cloud of smoke; then he paused. "I was surprised Paul waited so long after Rae to set his sights on you. Hell, it took him only a few weeks between Rae and the one before her. Can you believe that? You'd think Paul would have been freaked out enough to swear off sleeping with his students for a while."

"What are you talking about?"

"The girl before Rae was Angela Bramford, and she was murdered."

Hannah stopped under a streetlight on the corner at the end of her block. "When was this?" she whispered.

Seth took a last drag from his cigarette and tossed it away. "She was a summer semester fling, this very beautiful redhead, like a young Piper Laurie. She was an artist, very earthy. It only lasted a few weeks, from early June until—well, she'd dumped him before the end of the month. He was really bitter. She kept coming to class after, and it just drove Paul up the wall. Finally, she dropped out. About three weeks later—it was mid-August, she was killed."

"How did it happen?" Hannah asked.

"They found her early in the morning, on the second-floor patio area of the Convention Center downtown. She was over by some steps. Somebody had strangled her. I remember reading about it in the newspaper. What a shame. She was so pretty."

"Did they ever find out who killed her?"

Seth shook his head. "I always thought the cops should have had a nice, long talk with Professor G., but they never even approached him." He glanced up and down the dark side streets. "Which way? Down there?"

Hannah nodded. As they crossed toward her block, Seth glanced over his shoulder.

"Do you really think Paul had something to do with this Angela Bramford's murder?"

"Oh, I don't know," Seth said. "He just pisses me off sometimes. He's probably too much of a wimp to bump someone off. Still, I think the police should have at least talked with him. Like the weasel he is, he got out of that one unscathed. Then, a month later, he started chasing after Rae."

Hannah stopped in front of her building. "This is me," she said, pulling her keys from her purse. Again, she noticed the Capt'n Crunch decals Britt had saved for Guy.

"You okay?" she heard Seth ask.

She nodded. "Yes, I—I'm fine. Listen, does Paul have any male friends? I mean, have you seen him hanging out with anyone in particular?"

"Not really," Seth said. "Then again, he might have a buddy or two at the newspaper where he writes his crummy reviews. I don't really know." Seth gave her a sidelong glance. "Why all the questions about Professor G.? I mean, if you don't mind my asking."

Hannah shrugged. "Oh, I was just curious. You said he likes me."

Seth grinned. "And Ben? What did he want?"

Hannah was stumped for a moment. "Oh, he—he was just coming along with me. There's nothing going on with us. Anyway, thanks for the talk. I'll call Tish at the store to-morrow. She's the manager. With your knowledge of film, you're a shoo-in. She'll probably want you to start right away."

Hands in his pockets, he rocked on his heels. "Thanks, Hannah."

He glanced over his shoulder. "You know, I don't mean to freak you out or anything, but I'm pretty sure someone has been following us since we left the store."

"What?" Hannah stepped back and bumped against the door.

"I didn't get a good look at him," Seth explained. "I think he's gone now. Just the same, I'll wait here until I know you're inside."

Hannah glanced down the darkened street for a moment: at the shadowy trees and the unlit recesses between the houses and buildings. She didn't see anyone.

She turned to Seth. "I don't feel good, leaving you to walk all the way home alone. Let me phone a taxi for you. I'll treat."

He shook his head. "No, thanks. I'm cool. It's only—what—seven-thirty? Besides, I have some errands to run back up on the main drag. I'll be okay."

Hannah unlocked the door, then impulsively kissed him on the cheek. "Thanks, Seth. Be careful, okay?"

"You bet. Good night, Hannah."

She hurried inside and ran up the stairs. Catching her breath, she stepped out on the third floor and started down the balcony walkway. As Hannah came closer to her door, she stopped abruptly. The keys dropped out of her hand.

She gazed at a padded envelope, balanced between the doorknob and the door frame. She didn't have to guess what was inside the little package.

She knew.

Fourteen

"Well, I made it home in one piece. So you can relax."

"Good," Hannah said, talking into her kitchen phone. "And you didn't see anyone lurking around outside?"

"Not a creature was stirring, honey," Joyce said. "I don't know why you need me to call and report in every night now. It's only eight o'clock. And I'm just a couple of doors down, for Pete's sake."

"It makes me feel better, that's all," Hannah replied.

"Well, phone me tomorrow if something comes up. And honey, again, I'm really sorry about your friend."

"Oh, thank you, Joyce. G'night."

Hannah hung up the phone. She stared at the envelope on the kitchen counter. She hadn't opened it yet.

She checked the front door again to make sure it was locked. She checked the living-room window, too. Then she started down the hall to Guy's room.

He was sitting up in bed, using a crayon to connect the dots in a kids' game book. He was biting down on his lip in deep concentration. His chicken pox looked a little worse today.

"I ought to connect the dots on you," Hannah said, mussing his hair. "Do they itch a lot, honey?"

"Kinda," he murmured, not looking up at her.

"Sorry I couldn't stay home with you today," Hannah said. She felt like the worst mother in the world, leaving her son with a sitter while he was ill. He adored Joyce. But he was sick, and he needed his mom there with him.

"Honey, did you hear me?" she asked, glancing down at the top of his head. "I said I'm sorry I couldn't keep you company today. They needed me at the store."

"It's okay," he said quietly, still not looking up at her.

She stroked his hair. "What do you think that picture is going to be?" she asked.

He studied his rendering. "A nellophant," he muttered.

The telephone rang. Hannah gently patted his shoulder. "Can I see when you're done?"

"Uh-huh," he replied, focused on his work.

With a defeated sigh, Hannah headed for the kitchen. She grabbed the phone on the third ring. "Hello?"

There was silence on the other end.

"Hello?" she repeated.

More silence. Then a click. They'd hung up.

Hannah replaced the receiver on the cradle. She stopped to stare again at the unopened envelope on the kitchen counter.

The phone rang once more, and gave her a start. She snatched up the receiver. "Yes, hello?" she said.

Silence.

"Hello . . ." she said, angrily this time.

"Hannah? Hannah, how's it going?"

She hesitated. His tone was warm and friendly, but she didn't recognize the voice at all. "Fine . . ."

"Great to hear it. How's Guy?"

"He's all right," she answered. "Um, I'm sorry. I—"

"You sound a little strange," he said. "Is everything okay?"

"Um, yeah. I just don't—"

"Well, you probably haven't opened up my present yet," he said. "Because then you'd know things aren't okay at all. Why don't you open it, Hannah?"

A chill swept through her. "Why are you doing this?" she whispered.

"Take a look at the video, Hannah. It's going to happen tonight."

There was a click on the other end of the line.

Hannah hung up the phone, then quickly picked it up again and pressed *-6-9. A recorded voice told her that the number dialed was blocked and could not be reached.

She hung up the phone again, then grabbed the envelope and tore it open. The video fell out on the counter. She remembered Scott reporting a couple of days ago that the store's copy of *Psycho* was missing. But this wasn't one of their videos. The cassette didn't come with a cover, but it had a Blockbuster label on it. It was a movie from the nineties that she still hadn't seen, *Bugsy*.

Her hand shaking, Hannah switched on the TV, then inserted the tape into the VCR. As with the other videos, this was cued to a specific scene.

On the TV screen, Warren Beatty, with his hair slicked back and looking dapper in a thirties-style suit and tie, stood in a darkened room in front of a sofa and a large picture window. He was watching a black-and-white movie of himself on a home projector. He picked up a newspaper and glanced at it.

Hannah flinched at the loud pop and shattering of glass. Beatty's newspaper was suddenly punctured with a bullet hole. Dazed, he looked down at the blood on his chest, and he seemed to realize that he'd been shot. Another shot pierced through that picture window, then another. Beatty recoiled and twisted as he took each bullet.

Hannah quickly grabbed the remote and turned down the volume so Guy wouldn't hear.

The bullets hailed through the splintered front window now, hitting Beatty and several art deco items in the room. He finally sank back on the sofa, bleeding and stunned.

Hannah gasped as a final, fatal shot hit him from behind and passed through his forehead. He lurched forward, then flopped back.

Numb, Hannah switched off the set.

Someone she knew would be executed like that. *Tonight*, he'd said.

Breathless, Hannah went to the window and peered outside. She didn't see anyone below. She pulled the drapes shut, then hurried back to Guy's room.

He'd fallen asleep with the crayon still in his little hand and the game book in his lap. Hannah padded to his window and quickly closed the blinds. She pried the crayon out of Guy's grasp, then set aside the game book. She switched off the nightstand lamp.

Hannah glanced toward his window again. On the third floor, they were probably too far up for anyone to shoot at them from the street. Someone else had been targeted for tonight, someone who had a first-floor apartment or a house with big windows.

Ben.

She remembered his place in that tenement, the bars on the large picture window just slightly above street level. This time of night, if he had the lights on, anyone could see him from outside. He was an easy mark.

She rushed down the hallway to the phone. She hunted through her purse for his number. "Please, God," she whispered, unable to find the scrap of paper upon which it was written. Finally, she dumped the entire contents of her purse on the counter. She saw the piece of paper and snatched it up.

Grabbing the phone, Hannah dialed Ben's number. It rang only once; then his recorded voice came on the line: *"Hi, this is Ben. Leave me a message after the irritating beep. Thanks."*

"Shit," Hannah muttered. She could tell from the way it picked up so fast that he was on another line. She waited for the tone. "Ben?" she said. "As soon as you get this, go to your window and close the drapes. I think someone outside your window might try to shoot you. I'll explain later. This is Hannah. I'll keep trying you."

She hung up.

She couldn't think of anyone except Ben. Joyce's apartment was on the third floor. Seth lived above a garage. Tish's house had bushes all around the first floor, and it was impossible to see inside. Scott's hospital room was on the second floor and had small, narrow windows.

It was Ben. She'd been with him most of yesterday and part of today. They'd been seen together. And as much as she fought it, she had feelings for him. Perhaps her stalker could see that as well. So Ben had to die.

She would wait another couple of minutes, count to one hundred and twenty, then call again. Maybe she'd get the operator to interrupt.

She wondered whom he might be talking to, and if he was standing in front of that window right now.

"I can't come back, at least not for a while," Ben said into the cordless phone. "Don't ask me to."

He sat on the edge of the old, beat-up desk, his back to the big picture window. From the streetlight outside, the vertical burglar bars cast shadows on his living-room wall.

He heard the call-waiting tone, and chose to ignore it. If it was important, they'd leave a message.

"Well, do you have any idea when you'll return home?" she asked.

"No, not really."

"In other words, you're not finished punishing me yet," she said. "Is that it? You know, I go to bed crying every night."

"You were doing that before I left. You were crying for *him,* Jennifer. How do you think that made me feel? It's one reason I decided to leave. You can't expect me to be there and comfort you while you grieve for this Lyle guy."

"I know I hurt you," she replied. "I'm not just crying for Lyle. I've been crying for you, too—and for us."

"Well, I'm glad I figure somewhere in your grieving," he muttered.

A car passed by with its windows open and rap music cranked up to full volume. Ben moved over to the picture window and glanced outside.

"This is really your fault, Ben," she said.

"What are you talking about? I didn't give Lyle his god-damn heart attack. In fact, when his widow told me about you and him, she said he had high cholesterol, problems with his weight, and he smoked—"

"That's not what I meant," Jennifer hissed.

"Christ, if you had to cheat on me, why did you pick this guy? He sounds like a mess—"

"He paid attention to me, and you didn't, goddamn it," she replied, her voice cracking. "You were so busy trying to get ahead at work."

"Do you know how much we owe on the house?" he countered. "Jennifer, I don't give a crap about getting ahead at that place. I merely want to get out of debt. And that means focusing on the job, giving them what they want."

"And do they want you in Seattle on a leave of absence without pay?" she argued. "How's that going to get us out of debt, Ben?"

"You know why I left," he said glumly.

From the window, Ben noticed a man coming up the street. He wore a bulky jacket with the collar turned up and a hood pulled down almost over his eyes. His hands were shoved in the pockets of that jacket.

He heard the call-waiting beep again. "Listen, Jennifer, that's my other line," he said. "I should—"

"It can't be more important than what we're discussing right now," she interrupted. "Can it?"

Outside, the man with the hood stopped. He seemed to stare back at Ben with those shrouded eyes, almost as if he wanted a confrontation. There were guys like that, roaming the streets of this neighborhood, intent on stirring up trouble. Then again, maybe this one was merely looking at the building.

"Ben? Are you listening to me?"

He turned away from the window. "I hear you," he said tiredly. "But I don't know what's left to discuss—unless you want to know about Rae. She's the main reason I came out here, and you haven't even asked about her yet."

"All right, how is Rae?" she asked.

"I think she's dead," he answered soberly. "I'm ninety-nine percent sure someone murdered her." Ben sighed, then glanced over his shoulder—out the window. The hooded man had moved on. The sidewalk was empty.

"I'm sorry, Ben," she whispered. "I truly am. Isn't that all the more reason for coming home? There's nothing you can do for her now."

"The police still show her as missing. I have no actual proof that she's been murdered—"

"Let the police take care of it," she said. "And let me take care of you. We've both lost someone dear to us. Come home, Ben. I know what you're going through. We need each other right now."

"Wait a minute," he said, rubbing his forehead. He began to pace in front of the window. "Are you trying to draw a parallel here? You were screwing this guy behind my back for three months before he dropped dead of a heart attack. I've known Rae half my life. She was my friend."

"She was still in love with you," Jennifer argued.

"You had nothing to be jealous about, and you know it."

"She made you feel important. I was jealous of that. Maybe if you'd made me feel a little important, I wouldn't have needed Lyle."

Ben watched a car slowly pull up the street. He sighed. "Maybe," he granted, pacing again. "Listen, even if I wanted to come home right now, I couldn't. The same thing that happened to Rae is now happening to someone else. And she's all alone. I've got to do what I can to help her."

"I'm all alone, too," Jennifer whispered.

He said nothing.

"Is she pretty?" she asked.

Ben heard another call-waiting beep. At the same time, he noticed the car, a beat-up, red Subaru station wagon, had stopped in front of his building. He sighed. "Yeah, Jennifer, she's very pretty," he grumbled. "I'm hanging up now."

"Ben? I'm really sorry about Rae. I'm sorry about everything. Okay?"

"Thanks," he said. "I'll talk to you in a couple of days. Take care."

He hung up, and the phone immediately started ringing. "Oh, fuck off," he muttered. "Goddamn telemarketers won't give up."

Ben decided to let the machine answer it. While his recorded greeting clicked on, he remained at the window, gazing out at that car. Someone on the passenger side slowly rolled down the window.

"Ben? Are you there?" Hannah asked urgently. "Ben? It rang more than once. You must be off the phone. Please, pick up!"

He reached for the phone on the edge of his desk.

"Ben, listen—"

"I'm listening," he said into the phone. "What's going on?"

"Are you by the front window? Are the drapes open?"

"Yeah. Why?" He moved toward the window. "What's happening? Are you okay?"

"Ben, don't—"

He couldn't see who was in the passenger seat of that old Subaru. But he noticed something pointing at him from the car window.

Hannah heard him on the other end of the line: *"Oh, God, no!"*

"Ben, what's happening?" she cried. "Ben?"

The sound of the first shot made her jump. Hannah heard glass shattering, then another loud pop. There was a sudden thud on his end of the line, and she realized Ben must have dropped the phone. Helplessly, she listened to him cry out. His voice was muffled.

The gunshots came one after another, so close together. Each discharge made Hannah recoil. She clutched the phone to her ear. "Ben?" she cried.

There was another round of gunfire, and glass splintering. A hollow ping resonated, perhaps a bullet hitting one of the bars across his window.

Then silence.

Hannah thought she heard gasping. He sounded like he was dying. "Ben? Are you there?"

In the distance, she could make out some screeching wheels, maybe a car peeling down the street. A woman screamed. It seemed far off, maybe on the sidewalk outside Ben's apartment.

The receiver on the other end of the line knocked against something. Hannah winced. Someone was moving the phone. "Ben? Is that you?"

"Hannah?" he said, his voice raspy. "I guess"—he took a breath—"you were trying to warn me, huh? You saw it coming?"

"Are you okay? Are you hurt?"

"I'll survive," he said, still breathing heavily. "I just got a little cut-up from flying glass. But I'm okay. So th—this was on a video?"

"Yes, *Bugsy.* Warren Beatty's character gets shot several times, standing in front of a picture window in his home."

"Huh, I think saw that movie," Ben muttered. "Yeah."

"I just got the tape less than an hour ago. I was by your place once, looking for you. I—I remembered the front window."

She could only hear his labored breathing on the other end, and far away, the sound of a police siren.

"Ben, are you still there?"

"Yeah, until the cops arrive," he replied. "They'll probably take me to the hospital first, then maybe the station house. I don't know where I'll end up tonight. This place is a wreck."

"You can come over here, Ben," she heard herself say. "Doesn't matter how late. I'll fix up the couch for you."

"Thanks. That would be nice."

Hannah listened to the siren, louder than before. It

sounded like the ambulance or police car was right outside
his place.

"Ben?" She hesitated. "I—I'm in trouble with the police.
It's pretty bad."

"I figured as much," he replied. "Don't worry. I won't say
anything to them." His voice dropped to a whisper. "Listen, they're coming. You take care. I'll see you tonight."

"I'll wait up," Hannah said.

Ben called from the lobby at 11:35, and Hannah buzzed
him in. She quickly checked on Guy to make sure he hadn't
woken up, then stepped out to the walkway balcony. She
waited by the front door.

Ben emerged from the stairwell. Despite a few tiny cuts
on his face, and clothes that were soiled and stained with
blood, he still looked handsome. Tall and lean, Ben ambled
up the walkway, carrying a duffel bag.

Hannah was so grateful to see him alive, she hugged him.
"Thank God you're okay," she whispered.

He returned the hug, patting her on the back almost
paternally.

Hannah gently pulled away. "Listen, I almost forgot to tell
you. My little boy is sick. Did you have the chicken pox
when you were a kid?"

He nodded. "Yeah, I had them. I'm immune."

"Well, come on in," she said. "Would you like some wine?"

"More than anything else right now, I need a shower and
a change of clothes." He hoisted his duffel bag. "Would that
be okay?"

While Ben took his shower, Hannah pulled some sheets
and a blanket out of the linen closet. She had a strange,
schoolgirl thought: *He's just on the other side of the bathroom door, naked, standing in my shower.* She had to remind
herself that he was married, and that she was no schoolgirl.

She made him a grilled-cheese sandwich, which he ate at
the kitchen counter.

Ben reassured her that he hadn't told the police anything. They'd questioned him in the emergency room at the hospital. He'd given them a description of the car, but couldn't offer them much else. The police said the previous tenant in his apartment had been a prominent gang member. As far as the local authorities were concerned, Ben had been the innocent victim of a gang-related drive-by shooting.

"Anyway, you don't have to worry about the police connecting you with what happened tonight," he said, wiping his mouth with a napkin. "If you don't mind my asking, what did you do that got you in trouble with the law? You indicated it was kind of serious."

Hannah was at that sink, washing the griddle. She hesitated before responding. "My husband used to beat me up," she said. "He even put me in the hospital once, for an extended stay. He was from a very rich and powerful family in Wisconsin. There was no way I could have left him and kept my son. So—I withdrew some money from our joint account. I took my son, left Wisconsin, changed my name, and moved here. That detective, Ronald Craig, must have been hired by my husband or his family. Remember, he was from Milwaukee? Anyway, I'm wanted for kidnapping, grand larceny, and I don't know how many other charges. Since—Mr. Craig's demise, I've been living on borrowed time."

Ben didn't say anything for a moment. He moved his plate aside. "It's kind of weird," he finally remarked. "Even though he was probably covering his own tracks, this killer did you a big favor when he absconded with all the paperwork from Craig's investigation."

"Yes. But it's only a matter of days—or hours—before they send in another investigator, maybe even the police." She took his empty plate. "See what I mean, 'borrowed time'?"

"Maybe all you need is a good lawyer," Ben offered.

"My husband and in-laws would buy a better one," Hannah replied. She rinsed off his plate.

"So—what are you going to do? Just keep running?"

"I can't right now, not with Guy sick." She shut off the

water, then dried her hands "But as soon as he's well, we're out of here—that is, if this maniac, the police, or my husband's family don't get to me first."

Hannah put the plate away, then took another sip of wine. "By the way, I spoke with Seth Stroud tonight. He remembered Rae. Apparently, Paul Gulletti was seeing another student before Rae. Her name was Angela Bramford, and she was found strangled on the second-floor deck of the Convention Center."

"What do you suppose that's patterned after?"

Hannah shrugged. "I don't know. But according to Seth, our esteemed professor wasn't even questioned about the murder, which has remained unsolved—big surprise."

"I'd say the case against Paul is piling up," Ben remarked. "You know, when I first got out here, I spent several days following him around—his home, his office at the newspaper, the college. I didn't notice anything unusual." He sat back on the barstool. "Maybe I'll start tailing him again tomorrow. Did Seth have anything else to say?"

Hannah recounted her conversation with Paul's assistant. She and Ben moved to the sofa, each with their glass of wine. It was well past midnight when Ben glanced past her and announced, "We're not alone."

Hannah peered over her shoulder at Guy, standing behind her in his pajamas. "Honey, what are you doing up?" she asked, getting to her feet. "You shouldn't be out of bed."

"I'm thirsty," he replied.

Ben handed her the folded blanket she'd set out for him.

"Thanks," Hannah said, wrapping it around Guy. She felt his forehead, then smiled. "Guy, this is Mr. Podowski. . . ." She shot Ben a look and started to laugh. "But you can call him Ben."

"Hi, Guy," he said. "I'm sorry you're not feeling well."

Hannah retreated to the kitchen to get a glass of water. Guy squinted at him. "Do you have chicken pox too?"

Ben touched one of the little cuts he'd gotten from the flying glass. "No, I was near a window that broke and some glass cut me."

Guy sat down next to him. "Does it hurt? Did you cry?"

"A little. But don't tell anybody. Okay?"

Hannah returned with the glass of water, then handed it to him. "All right, let's get you to the bathroom, then back in bed. It's awfully late."

Guy gulped down some of the water. "Can I sit up with you guys?"

"Well, just a couple of minutes," she said, sinking back on the sofa.

Ben asked Guy what he planned to be for Halloween. Guy wasn't sure if he wanted to be a ghost or a pirate. He started rattling off what each of his friends at Alphabet Soup Day Care planned to be for trick or treat. Hannah sat back and watched the two of them. It felt good to have a man in the apartment. She could almost fool herself into thinking they were a family. She'd never had anything like this—certainly not with Kenneth. She wondered if this kind of quiet intimacy was routine for some families, the type of thing they took for granted.

Hannah had to remind herself once again that Ben was married.

"I hate to be a party pooper," she announced, rubbing Guy's shoulder. "But you belong back in bed, honey. C'mon, we'll make a pit stop at the bathroom first; then I'll tuck you in." Hannah adjusted the blanket around him, then lifted him up. "Say good night to Ben."

"Can he come tuck me in, too?" he asked, yawning.

Hannah threw Ben a smile. "Looks like someone's taken a shine to you."

He stood in the doorway while she put Guy to bed. She made the choo-choo sound to lull him to sleep.

They stepped out of his bedroom together. "I'll get you another blanket," she whispered.

"It's okay," he said, stopping. They were standing so close to each other in the dim hallway. For a moment, neither of them said anything. They could hear Guy's steady breathing in the next room. Ben touched the side of her face "Thanks for all this," he said. Then he hesitated, and stepped back. "I better turn in. I'll make up the couch. You don't have to bother."

Hannah nodded. "All right. See you in the morning. I'll make you breakfast."

Hannah went to bed, but she was too wound up to sleep. The one night in three weeks that she had someone in the apartment to protect her, and she couldn't drift off. She had another little cry about Britt. Reaching for some tissues on her nightstand, she glanced at the alarm clock: 1:20. Only a half hour had passed since she'd said good night to Ben. It seemed longer.

Hannah climbed out of bed, wiped her eyes, and put on a robe. She padded down the hall to the living room, then peeked around the corner at Ben. He was lying on his side, the sheets wrapped around him. He turned toward her. "Hannah?"

"I'm sorry. Did I wake you?"

He sat up, and the sheets fell down past his hairy chest, and bunched around his waist. He scratched his head. His blond hair was tousled. "I wasn't really asleep," he said softly. "You okay?"

Clutching the folds of her robe, Hannah stepped to the edge of the sofa. "Remember you asked me earlier tonight what I planned to do?" she asked, in a hushed tone. "I haven't really had an actual plan since all of this started. Even if we find this killer, I'll still have my problems with the police. Ben, I need to ask you a favor, a big favor."

"Sure. What is it?"

"When we find out who's behind all these killings and we're ready to go to the police, can you go alone? I'll need a head start to move on with Guy. We'll need to begin someplace else—with new identities."

"But don't you think if we went to a lawyer and explained—"

"I can't risk losing my son," she cut in. "When the time comes, can I count on you to help me get away?"

"That's the only option?" he asked.

"Can you think of another?"

He sighed. "If we can't come up with a better plan, I'll help you get away, Hannah. I'll do whatever you want."

"Thanks," she replied. "Good night again, Ben."

Hannah started back down the hall. Just this morning, she'd been wary of him. She still didn't know Ben Podowski very well. But now, she had to trust him. She trusted him with her life, and the life of her son.

Fifteen

"Who the hell is this supposed to be?"

Kenneth Woodley studied the photo. He sat at a small table by one of the floor-to-ceiling windows overlooking Shillshell Bay. At this time of night, the water was black with silver-white ripples. Twinkling lights across the bay marked the start of land again.

Kenneth had heard Ray's Boathouse was one of Seattle's finer restaurants, so he'd arranged to meet his private detective in the bar upstairs. He had a late supper date in the formal dining area downstairs immediately following the meeting. The Sunday-night dinner rush had already peaked, but some muted chatter among lingering customers still competed with the Ella Fitzgerald recording piped through the elegant bar.

Kenneth tossed the photograph on the table. "This damn thing is so blurry and far away, it could be a picture of my wife or the goddamn Prince of Wales for all I can tell. Is this the best you could do?"

"I took it last night with a telephoto lens," explained the private detective, a man named Walt Kirkabee. He was thirty-six, with straight, close-cropped black hair, a goatee, and the solid, husky build of a baseball player.

He offered Kenneth Woodley another photograph. "This guy stayed with her last night," he said. "I took that shot earlier today."

Setting down his martini glass, Kenneth snatched up the

picture. "Looks like a doofus," he muttered. "Have you ID'd him yet?"

"Not yet. He left her place—on foot—around ten this morning, and didn't come back until a couple of hours ago. He was gone all day. But she stayed inside; never stepped outside the apartment."

Kenneth tossed the photograph across the table at him, then sipped his martini. "So—you wasted the whole day waiting outside her place?" he asked, eyebrows raised. "You could have followed this joker around. Maybe he's the guy who wasted your predecessor. Ever think about that?"

"I can't be two places at once," Walt argued. "And Hannah Doyle is the person you hired me to stake out." He leaned back in his chair and sipped his club soda. "You might consider hiring another man to work with me, Mr. Woodley. It's really a two-man job. We could work in shifts, or split up when we had to."

Kenneth was shaking his head. "Christ, you guys are milking me dry as it is. I've already spent enough on this investigation. You guys aren't even positive this *Hannah Doyle* bitch is my estranged wife. All I have to go on is Ron Craig's last report. She fits the description, and has a kid the right age. She calls him Guy. My wife used to call our son 'Guy-Guy.' Maybe it's just a coincidence. Well, I've forked over a lot of money, hoping it's *not* a fucking coincidence. You won't squeeze me for any more. You tell that to your bosses at Great Lakes Investigations, okay, Sherlock?"

Sighing, Walt set another photo down on the table between them. "Take a look at this," he said.

"What is it?" Kenneth asked, squinting at the picture. The shot was slightly out of focus, and appeared to have been blown up several times.

It was a photo of some bushes by a dumpster, but the detective traced an area of the bushes with his finger. "That's a man," he said.

Kenneth realized it was indeed a figure, lurking in the shadows between an alleyway dumpster and some shrubbery.

Walt slapped a similar shot on top of it. In this photo, a dark, phantom shape was skulking behind a tree.

"Someone else is watching her, Mr. Woodley," the detective said. "I haven't gotten a good look at him yet. These pictures are the best I could do. He seems to catch on whenever I've spotted him. It's weird. It's like he knows the camera and how to elude it. I've tried to take his picture several times the last couple of days, but those shots are the best I could do." He set another photo in front of Kenneth. "Check this one out."

Kenneth stared at a grainy, nighttime photograph of a parking lot. He didn't notice anything unusual until the detective pointed to a ghostly image hovering behind a minivan. "That's outside my hotel, Mr. Woodley," Kirkabee said. "He's following me too."

Shaking his head, Kenneth laughed.

"It's not funny. This could be the man who killed Ron Craig."

"Maybe he's working for her," Kenneth said. He raised his martini glass. "That's just what I'm after. We need to implicate her in your buddy's murder. That's why we're not busting in on her and the kid right now. I want the goods on this bitch." He glanced once again at the blurry figure in the photo. "Think this could be the doofus who was screwing her last night?"

Kirkabee shrugged. "I'm not sure. It could be."

Kenneth smirked. "Well, just keep doing what you're doing, and watch your ass. Sounds like he'll be coming to you."

Walt Kirkabee began to collect the photographs. "Ron was reporting directly to you, Mr. Woodley. We—and I mean the agency—we had no information for the police when they came to us about Ron's murder. We had to refer them to you."

Kenneth drained his martini glass. "Yeah? So? Tell me something I don't know."

The detective shrugged. "Well, I was about to ask you that same thing. Is there something we don't know? You told

the police that Ron wasn't having any luck tracking down
your wife and son. But you have me staking out this Hannah Doyle woman, and half the time I'm watching her from
a parking lot where my predecessor was murdered. You
withheld information from the police, Mr. Woodley. Is there
something you're not telling me?"

"I didn't tell the cops about Hannah Doyle because I
wanted to come here and personally nail her ass. You've
been hired to help me do that, Sherlock. I'm paying you top
dollar." Kenneth leaned forward. "If you're too chickenshit
for the job, just say the word and I'll ship your ass back to
Milwaukee and hire a private detective with some balls."

He videotaped the private detective and his client as they
stepped outside Ray's Boathouse restaurant. The client
didn't look too happy. He was talking to the detective, stabbing the air with his finger to make a point. Frowning, the
detective nodded, then retreated toward his car.

At the restaurant entrance, the client pulled out a cell
phone and made a call. Meanwhile, the detective pulled out
of the large parking lot. Some detective. Apparently he had
no idea he was being watched.

Neither did the client, who ducked back inside the restaurant.

He waited patiently in the shadows between a parked RV
and some bushes. This close to the water, the night air was
cool and smelled of fish. He watched people come and go.
Someone else was meeting the client. Smart money was on
the blonde who arrived by taxi forty minutes after he'd made
that cell-phone call.

He was right, of course. An hour after the blonde had
sashayed into the joint, she was stepping out with the client.
She had a passing resemblance to Hannah, sort of a cheap
imitation. Her hair was pinned up in the back. She wore
tight silver pants, heels, and a tiny black blouse that was
open in front to show off some ample cleavage.

Obviously, the client had picked out a high-class hooker for the evening. They waited for the valet to fetch the rented sports car. The tall, brown-haired guy with the big nose was cracking these jokes, and the prostitute was laughing her head off. The client threw a few dollars at the valet; then the two of them climbed into the sleek car.

Without running any yellow lights or making any sudden moves, he followed the sports car a few miles to a marina parking lot.

Leaning outside the window of his car, he photographed the client and his hooker as they climbed out of the sports car. He could still hear the woman's high-pitched laughter as they walked down the dock together.

The client had a medium-sized yacht—two, maybe three, rooms on board—moored at the crowded dock. All was quiet this time of night—except for the girl, who kept talking and laughing as the man helped her on the deck. Then the two of them slipped down below.

After a few minutes, he got out of his car. Video camera in tow, he skulked down the dock, past all the other boats. He approached the yacht and found a perfect spot to hide, behind a big, green-painted equipment box. From there, he had a view into the yacht's oblong, horizontal windows. The client hadn't bothered to pull the little shades closed.

The video camera framed them perfectly through the first window as they sat at the galley table and did some lines of cocaine together. The blonde unbuttoned her blouse, then dabbed a little bit of cocaine on her nipple and had him lick it off. She let out that loud laugh again. The client kissed her neck, and tried to kiss her on the lips, but she pulled away. Apparently she didn't do that with her johns.

The camera caught them moving into the next room, where the man peeled off his shirt. He sat her down on the built-in sofa bed. She seemed to stumble a little, or perhaps she was resisting. It was hard to tell. But their movements were clumsy. She stepped out of her heels, then unfastened the top of her silver pants. He started pulling them off, and she gave him a playful little kick, pushing him away. He grabbed her pants again, and—almost violently—yanked them off her legs. She laughed, and quickly wriggled out of her black panties.

The camera zoomed in, lovingly moving up and down her nude body. The client advanced toward her, and she teasingly pushed him away again with her foot. She reached across the sofa for her bag, then pulled out a condom and waved it at him.

He swatted it out of her hand. She looked stunned for a second, then started to chuckle. But he reeled back and slapped her across the face.

She banged her head against the wall in back of the sofa bed. She seemed dazed. He grabbed her by the hair and pulled her down to the cushions. She let out a shriek. He smacked her across the face once more—this time with the back of his hand.

The camera zoomed in again, catching her startled, horrified expression. He stopped looking through the viewer for a moment to check around him. He was certain others on the water heard her cries. But he didn't see any lights go on inside the boats. No one came topside to look for the source of the screams. From his spot by the equipment box, he was able to keep taping for the next ten minutes.

The client never had intercourse with her. But at one point, when he had his hand on her throat and seemed to be choking the life out of her, he masturbated.

While she got dressed, he brought her some ice for her face, then pulled eight one-hundred-dollar bills from his wallet. The camera zoomed in for a close-up of the money.

The last shot captured that night was of the blonde, the cheap imitation of Hannah, looking shaken and dazed. Despite the ice application, her face was already a bit swollen.

She wobbled a bit as she walked up the dock to a waiting taxi. It was a great last shot before the fade-out.

* * *

Hannah knew she had another long night ahead waiting for sleep to come. The digital clock on her nightstand read 1:49. Ben had probably nodded off already. He was on the sofa again—just down the hall. They'd said good night about forty-five minutes ago, awkwardly shaking hands.

He'd spent the day staking out Paul Gulletti. He'd watched him step out for Sunday brunch with his wife. Then, Paul went to his office at the newspaper. He emerged almost three hours later and went to a Starbucks, where he sat at a cafe table. He was met there by a younger man with long, red hair pulled back in a ponytail. The younger man carried a camera or binoculars in a case that hung from a strap over his shoulder. Paul gave him some money. Ben was too far away to see how much cash was exchanged.

He told Hannah it was the only encounter he'd witnessed today that raised his interest. "Paul could have owed this guy a couple of bucks. I don't know," Ben had admitted. "But those bills could have been hundreds, too. And the red-haired guy carried this camera case. Maybe he's working for Paul. You said some stranger was videotaping you last Thursday night at about the time class started. Maybe this was the guy." He shrugged. "Hell, I don't know. I'm just guessing."

One thing they were both sure about: the video-killer wasn't working alone. Someone else had been driving that Subaru station wagon when shots were fired from the passenger window at Ben's apartment.

They had a long talk while she cooked a spaghetti dinner. They ate at her kitchen counter—by candlelight, no less. But the conversation was far from romantic.

Ben had never been in Paul's office at the college. He asked her if Paul kept video equipment and cassette tapes there.

Nodding, Hannah dabbed her mouth with her napkin. "Paul has all sorts of stuff in that office. Why? What are you thinking?"

"Maybe I can get in there and take a look around," Ben said, reaching for his glass of Merlot. "In the meantime, you're working beside Seth at the store tomorrow, aren't you?"

"Yes. He started there today."

"Keep pumping him about the professor," Ben said. "And watch out for Seth, too. There's something I don't like about that guy."

"Seth?" Hannah said.

"Yeah, him and his roommate."

She laughed. "They're just a couple of kids."

"So were Leopold and Loeb."

"You saw where they live," Hannah pointed out. "Not exactly deluxe accommodations. Whoever is behind these murders has a lot of money and leisure time. The work on that *Goodbar* tape was very professional. High production values. It was made by someone who can afford expensive video equipment and state-of-the-art editing machines. Those two guys couldn't even afford a maid."

"Just the same, I don't trust him," Ben argued, pushing his plate away. "He's suddenly taking this job where he'll be working beside you all day. That bugs me."

Hannah figured maybe Ben was a little jealous—or just protective. Either way, she kind of liked it.

They had another faux "family night." After the candlelit dinner, he read a story to Guy, who was crazy for him. When she and Ben were alone together again, he told her what had happened with his wife.

At around the time Rae Palmer's e-mails to Ben were reporting the first murder, he got a call from a Mrs. Lyle Seidell. Her husband had just dropped dead of a heart attack, and did Ben know that Lyle had been screwing a certain Mrs. Jennifer Podowski for the last three months?

While his wife was grieving for her dead lover, Ben kept hearing from Rae, who begged him to come to Seattle. Ben decided to leave Jennifer alone with her grief. Every tear she shed was a jab to his heart. At the time, his friend seemed more worth rescuing than his marriage.

As far as Hannah was concerned, this Jennifer sounded

like a jerk. But she tried to remain quietly impartial as Ben told his story. Besides, once he found Rae's killer, he planned to go back to Jennifer and work things out.

In the meantime, Hannah was playing house with Ben Podowski. All through the evening she'd had to keep fighting her attraction to him. Lying there, alone in bed, she told herself that she couldn't afford to get involved. She was leaving Seattle herself—very soon.

Small wonder she couldn't sleep.

She wanted a glass of water. Or maybe that was just an excuse, giving herself permission to walk through the living room and check on him. Still, she was thirsty.

Hannah threw back the covers, climbed out of bed, and donned her robe. She felt butterflies in her stomach. The truth was, she wanted something to happen.

Unconsciously fussing with her hair, she tiptoed down the hallway to the living room. She peered around the corner. The couch had been vacated. The sheets were still in a tangle across the sofa cushion. She reached for the end-table lamp; then she looked toward the window and froze.

Ben stood against the wall, by the edge of the curtains. He was shirtless and barefoot, wearing only a pair of jeans he must have put on hastily. The front snap was still open. He shook his head at her, then put a finger to his lips.

Hannah didn't understand at first. Then she saw the silhouette on the other side of the curtains. At the half inch where the drapes didn't quite meet, someone was trying to peek inside.

Hannah gasped and accidentally knocked over the lamp. It fell to the floor with a crash.

The figure outside reeled back from the window, then raced toward the stairwell.

Ben headed out after him. "Stay inside," he told Hannah. "Lock the door." He ran down the balcony walkway, and ducked into the stairwell.

Hannah watched him from the doorway. Then she retreated inside, closed the door, and locked it. Stepping over the broken lamp, she hurried down the hall and checked in on Guy. Miraculously, he was still asleep.

Hannah went back to the living room and opened the curtains. She watched and waited for Ben. With every passing minute, she grew more and more anxious. She couldn't help thinking that Ben had been set up, lured outside for his execution. But she would have gotten a video first, a coming attraction for Ben's death. Then again, maybe all bets were off, now that their last attempt on his life had failed.

Hannah cleaned up the broken lamp, hoping the time would go by faster. It occurred to her that while she was inside waiting for him, Ben could be hurt. She pictured him lying in a pool of blood at the bottom of those cement stairs. She struggled with the idea of going out there and looking for him. But she didn't dare leave Guy alone.

Suddenly, she heard a soft tapping on the door. Hannah glanced out the window. To her utter relief, it was Ben. She flung open the door.

"I lost him," Ben announced, out of breath.

"Are you okay?" she asked.

He nodded.

Hannah embraced him, almost collapsing in his arms. She touched his hairy chest, and felt his heart pounding. Her heart was racing, too.

Ben stoked her hair, then stepped back. "I didn't get a good look at the guy," he said. "I was trying to catch a glimpse of him when you came in."

"I'm sorry," she muttered. "I screwed it up, knocking over the damn lamp."

Ben locked the door again. "He must have used the second floor and taken the back stairs down. I searched everywhere—including the basement. I think he's gone."

Hannah stood near the door. She touched his arm. She was still trembling. "Well, can I—get you anything?"

"No, I'm okay," he said, scratching his head. "I don't think I'll fall asleep again right away, but I might as well give it a try."

"Ben . . ." She hesitated.

"Maybe you ought to try getting some sleep yourself," he suggested. He closed the curtains. "You have work in the morning. I'll be okay out here. You shouldn't stay up. That guy's not coming back." He tried to smile at her. "Nothing more is going to happen tonight, Hannah."

She sighed. "You're right. Nothing is going to happen."

Hannah started back toward her bedroom. She never did get her glass of water.

Sixteen

It was nine-twenty, and only a handful of students still lingered around the third-floor lounge area. The windows on one side had a sweeping view of the Seattle skyline, brightly lit against the cloudy night. Most of the classes were out, and the hallways seemed deserted. Paul Gulletti's Monday evening class had ended at seven-thirty. But he was still in his office—just down the hall.

The alcove where Hannah and Ben were hiding couldn't be seen from the hallway. It was tucked behind a corner, partially concealed by the lounge's vending machines and pay phones. The little niche had room for only a couple of sofa-chairs. Hannah sat in one while Ben stood guard. He peered around the corner, past the vending machines and down the hallway.

For the last two hours, they'd been waiting. Ben had stolen a master key from one the janitors. He'd told her about his discovery of a maintenance-crew lounge and locker room in the basement. This morning, he'd followed one of the night crew janitors down there, then "borrowed" his key ring while he was in the shower. A green plastic doodad around the base of one key set it apart from all the others on the ring. Ben had figured it must be the master. He'd tested it on a few basement doors and it had worked. Ben replaced the key ring before the janitor had finished his shower. Later, the key got him into every office and classroom he'd tried. Ben figured the custodian probably wouldn't realize his master key was missing until tomorrow.

"You're pretty good at following people around, aren't you?" Hannah had said when he'd told her about stealing the key. "I certainly had no idea when you were watching me."

She was a bit irritated with him today. This morning, they'd been eating breakfast together when Joyce had shown up. She pulled Hannah aside. "Wow. He sure is cute," she whispered. "You hold onto him."

But holding onto him was impossible. Hannah had gone off to work feeling horribly depressed. And it wasn't just Ben either. It was everything. She couldn't stop thinking about Britt, and what she might have done to prevent her death. She hated leaving Guy's side while he was sick—and while this maniac was out there. Hell, she hated constantly looking over her shoulder. And as much as she had to, she dreaded having to run away again, starting over in a new city with a new name.

At the video store, her plans to obtain more information from Seth went down the drain. Paul's assistant wasn't working at the store today.

Later, when Ben came by to tell her that he had the key to Paul's office, Hannah insisted on coming with him. Ben had never been in Paul's office. He wouldn't know what to search for. He'd never met Cindy Finkelston, Lester Hall, or Britt. Hannah was the one who would recognize possible souvenirs from those killings.

From the store that afternoon, she'd called Joyce, saying she wouldn't be home until after eight. But now it was nearly nine-thirty, and they hadn't even started searching Paul's office yet.

"So what do you think?" Hannah asked Ben while she dug some change out of her purse. "Did he fall asleep in there, or what? I better call Joyce again." She got to her feet. "Huh. You'd think one of us would own a cell phone."

Ben peeked around the corner. "Coast is clear."

Hannah stepped up to the pay phone and dialed home.

"You're going to loathe me," she said when Joyce answered on the other end. "I'll be another hour—at least. Does that screw you up?"

"Yes, hon, I have a date with Robert Redford tonight. He's picking me up at ten. Ha, don't sweat it. Everything's copacetic here. In fact, want to say good night to my pal here? I'm taking the cordless into his room."

Out of the corner of her eye, Hannah saw Ben urgently signaling to her. She glanced over her shoulder. Paul Gulletti came down the hallway with a folder tucked under his arm.

Hannah swivelled around so her back was to him. She could see his reflection in the darkened window across the lounge. He was coming at her.

"Hi, Mom," she heard Guy say on the other end of the line.

"Hi, honey," she whispered, shrinking away as Paul Gulletti drew closer. "Um, how are you feeling?"

"The chicken pox itches a lot today," he whimpered. He sounded groggy. "Is Ben spending the night?"

"Yes, but—um, you'll be asleep by the time we come home."

Paul passed her, and continued down the corridor to the elevators.

"Why aren't you guys home now?" Guy was asking on the other end of the line. "I want to see Ben."

The elevator arrived for Paul, and he stepped aboard. Meanwhile, Ben gave her a secret wave; then he hurried up the hallway and turned the corner to Paul's office.

"Mom?"

"You'll see Ben in the morning, honey," Hannah said into the phone. "I love you. Now, give the phone back to Joyce, and get some sleep."

In the background, she heard Joyce talking to him. The four students who were in the lounge all left together, slowly moving toward the stairwell. One girl's laughter echoed in the hallway.

"Hi," Joyce said, back on the line. "As you can tell, someone's a little cranky. I think he'll be down for the count after a session with Dr. Seuss."

"Well, I should be home sometime around ten-thirty," Hannah said. "I'm sorry to screw up your whole evening like this."

"I'll see you when I see you. And if you're with that tall drink of water from this morning, please don't rush home on my account."

Hannah let out a sad laugh. "That's not how it is with us. But thanks anyway. See you soon, Joyce."

She hung up the phone, then turned around in time to see Paul Gulletti step out of the elevator. Hannah froze. She wondered why the hell he was back so soon.

They were the only two people in the corridor. Paul started toward her. The closer he got, the more he smirked. "Well, hello, stranger," he said at last. He looked her up and down. "What are you doing here?"

"I wanted to see you," Hannah explained, forcing a smile. "I was just about to leave a message at your office."

"Well, I walked by here only two minutes ago," Paul said. "I didn't see you, Hannah. It's been too long. You know, you missed my last class."

"Yes, I'm—sorry about that." She glanced down the other corridor toward Paul's office. "It's um—one reason I wanted to see you, Paul," she said loudly. "Also I wanted to ask what you thought of the notes I e-mailed. You know, the ones about the blacklist?"

He laughed. "What are you shouting for?"

She shrugged. "Oh, I'm sorry. I have a little of that inner ringing in my ear. It's gone now."

He cocked his head to one side. "Come to my office with me. I forgot something in there earlier. Now, I'm glad I did."

She hesitated, then started walking with him. "So—about the notes, Paul?" she asked, a bit too loudly again.

"I haven't gotten around to them yet." He smiled. "But it doesn't mean you haven't been on my mind, Hannah."

She started talking about the content of her notes, babbling really. All the while, she hoped Ben could hear them approaching.

Paul unlocked the door, stepped inside, and switched on the overhead light. Hannah glanced back at the hallway, half-expecting to see Ben hiding in one of the other doorways. But there was no sign of him.

She walked into the office, where Paul circled around to the other side of his desk. He lifted up a miniature fake Oscar that served as a paperweight, then grabbed a key hidden beneath it and unlocked his desk drawer.

Standing near the door, Hannah took in the office, her eyes darting back and forth. She wondered how Ben could have escaped without so much as a sound.

Paul pulled some reading glasses from the desk drawer, locked it, then returned the key to its place under the ersatz mini-Oscar. He looked up at her and smiled. "You know, standing there in that black sweater with your blond hair, you look like a Hitchcock leading lady."

Hannah rolled her eyes. "I don't think so. But thanks."

"I'm not sure if you look more like Grace Kelly or Eva Marie Saint," he said, slipping the glasses in his breast pocket. "You've got that kind of classic beauty, Hannah. I've always thought so. I was very disappointed last week when you turned down my dinner invitation. Maybe you've reconsidered. Is that what this little visit is about?"

"Sort of," Hannah replied. "I'd like to go out with you, Paul. I just haven't had any time recently. But—" Hannah stopped in mid-sentence.

Something in the tall picture window caught her eye. The sill was a couple of feet off the ground, and Paul had a stack of film books on one end. On the other end, Ben stood motionless behind the folds of the open beige curtain. His back pressed against the glass, he gazed down at her.

She shifted her eyes back to Paul. "Um, I have a sick little boy at home. I—I can't see you this week. Maybe next week?" She let out a nervous laugh. "I guess what I'm saying is I'd like a rain check on that date, if the offer still stands."

Grinning, Paul came toward her. "You bet it does," he whispered. "And I'm holding you to it." He kissed his fingertip, then touched her lips.

Hannah managed to keep smiling. She stole a glance up at Ben again. "Maybe we should go," she said to Paul. "They'll probably be locking up soon."

He took her by the arm and led her out of the office. Paul switched off the light, then closed and locked the door. "Speaking of Hitchcock and his blondes, we're showing *The Birds* in class this Thursday. I hope you're not planning another no-show."

"I'll try to be there," Hannah said, starting down the hall with him. Their footsteps echoed in the vacant corridor. "I, um, haven't seen *The Birds* in a while."

"Remember the scene near the end of the movie, when Tippi Hedren hears the wings flapping somewhere on the second floor of the house? She grabs a flashlight and goes up to the bedroom to investigate. Remember?"

Hannah nodded. "She gets attacked by all those birds."

Paul rang for the elevator. "Do you know what kind of special effects they used for that scene?"

Hannah shook her head. She was having a hard time following his conversation. She wondered how she was going to get rid of Paul. She didn't feel safe alone with him. As the elevator door opened, she balked.

He took her by the arm again, then led her inside. She quickly pressed the button for the first floor. Paul's shoulder rubbed against hers. The elevator door shut.

"They used real ravens and gulls in that scene, Hannah. Two stagehands in thick gloves spent hours and hours hurling birds at Tippi Hedren. It took three days to shoot that scene. The poor girl had a nervous collapse at the end of it."

He slowly maneuvered his body so that he was standing between her and the elevator doors. "What do you think of that, Hannah?"

She shrugged uneasily. "Sounds pretty—harrowing."

"But Tippi was Hitchcock's discovery, don't you see? She

may have suffered, but it was for his artistic vision. How far would you go for the sake of realizing an artistic vision?"

"I don't think I'd go that far," she replied, shaking her head.

The elevator door opened. Hannah brushed past him and ducked out to the corridor. It was as if she hadn't been able to breathe in there. She glanced up and down the hallway.

Except for a janitor wheeling a garbage pail and two students lingering by the main entrance, Hannah didn't see anyone else in the area. She caught a couple of breaths, but she tensed up again when Paul came up to her side.

"That's going to be the topic of discussion after the movie," he said. "How much power should a director have over his leading lady? How much intimidation and control—for the sake of art?"

"Ought to make for a stimulating discussion," Hannah said, with a weak smile.

She remembered Seth talking about how Otto Preminger badgered Jean Seberg during the filming of *Bonjour Tristesse*. He'd made the same point as Paul about a director's right to unlimited power over his actors—especially a leading lady he'd "discovered." She wondered if perhaps Seth had picked up that notion from one of Paul's lectures. Or did they simply think alike? Maybe Ben was right, maybe Paul and Seth were working together, and she was their unwitting leading lady, their *discovery.*

"You seem tense," Paul said, placing his hand on the back of her neck.

"No, I'm all right."

"I give a terrific neck rub, you know. You'd love it."

"I—I better take a rain check on that, too," she said, edging away from him, toward the main doors.

"Well, at least let me give you a lift home," he suggested.

"Actually, I have someone coming to pick me up. But thanks anyway." She pushed the heavy door and stepped outside. The chilly October night air felt good.

Paul came up to her side once more.

"You don't have to wait around," she said. "I'm fine here.

I'll see you in class Thursday. By then, I'll know when we can get together for our dinner date. I'm really looking forward to it, Paul."

His eyes narrowed at her. "Who's coming to pick you up? Is it that Ben Sturges character? I know you've been seeing him."

"How would you know that?" Hannah asked.

"I just know," he replied. "You disappoint me, Hannah."

"Well, don't be disappointed," she said, staring him in the eye. "Because you're wrong about Ben What's-his-name. I barely know him. The person who's picking me up is a friend of my son's baby-sitter. His name is Lars, and he's sixty-seven years old. Any more questions or objections?"

He laughed, then kissed her on the cheek. "You can't fool me. I know you better than you think. Good night, Hannah."

Hannah watched him walk toward the parking lot, then disappear around the corner.

She shuddered, and wiped his kiss from her cheek.

Hannah didn't step back inside the school right away. She waited until Paul drove by in his Toyota. She gave him a little wave, and watched the car continue down the street.

Only then did she duck back inside the college. On her way to the stairwell, she didn't see anyone in the main corridor. Hannah hurried up the stairs to the third floor. Stepping out to the hallway, she discovered someone had switched off most of the overheads. Only a few spotlights at the exits illuminated the way.

She headed down the dark corridor, past the lounge. The lights inside the vending machine cast strange shadows across the deserted study area. Everything seemed so still. But then, out of the corner of her eye, she saw some movement near the window. Hannah stopped.

It took her a moment to realize the phantom motion was merely headlights from passing cars below. Hannah told herself that she was alone here. If someone else was on this floor, she would hear footsteps. Every little sound seemed to reverberate in the empty hallway.

She continued on toward Paul's office. She saw a line of light at the threshold under his door. Hannah tried the knob. Locked. "Ben?" she called softly. "Ben, it's me."

The door opened. "Are you okay?" Ben asked. "Did he make a pass?"

Hannah sighed. "Mostly, he just gave me the creeps." She stepped inside, then quietly closed the door behind her. "I never figured he was capable of murder, but now I'm not so sure. Something he said has me wondering about Seth, too."

Ben nodded. "I told you I didn't trust him."

He moved over to an old wooden file cabinet. The bottom drawer was open. "I've already been through the other drawers," he said, searching the files. "Nothing so far. Ditto the coat closet. But I saw some videos on the shelf. He's labeled each tape *Such and Such a Lecture,* and the date. We should take them back to your place tonight and have a look. I can return them here in the morning."

Hannah walked around the desk.

"I tried there," Ben said, looking up for a moment. "It's locked."

Hannah pulled the key from under the mini-Oscar paperweight, and unlocked the top right-hand drawer. Ben smiled at her. He finished with the file cabinet, then circled around to the desk.

They each took one side of the desk, and looked through the drawers. Hannah found paper clips, old receipts, and loose change in the top drawer. Just junk. The next drawer down held old lecture notes, clippings of his newspaper reviews, and a couple of spiral notebooks. Hannah paged through one of the notebooks. She read the start of an incomplete screenplay he'd written, called *Love in Equinox.* The opening scene was of a couple making love. All the while the man talked about how much he hated his dead father. It was pretty terrible.

"I found his old class lists," Ben announced, shuffling

through some papers. "Names, addresses, phone numbers. Here's Rae. Huh, Angela Bramford is on this page. I wonder if anyone else listed here died from unnatural causes." Grabbing a pen and legal pad from the desktop, Ben started copying down the list.

Hannah went back to flipping through Paul's rough draft of *Love in Equinox*. He must have realized how god-awful it was, because there were only twenty-three pages. Hannah noticed that the young heroine stayed naked through most of it, and there was a scene with her masturbating. "You should read how sleazy this script is," Hannah said. "He—"

Ben held up his hand, then shushed her.

Hannah fell silent, and she listened. Footsteps. Someone was coming down the corridor.

Ben hurried toward the door. He quietly turned the lock and switched off the light. He remained with his back to the wall. They listened to the footsteps becoming louder, closer. Hannah held her breath. She waited until the person outside passed the office. The footsteps grew fainter. Hannah let out a sigh. Ben flicked the lights back on, and he darted back to the desk. "We'd better hurry," he muttered, sitting on the floor.

Hannah checked the next drawer down. She noticed a folder hidden beneath some more clippings of his reviews at the bottom of the drawer. She pulled it out and opened it up.

Several pieces of paper were clipped together. Hannah studied the first page: a montage of slightly grainy photos of a seminude Diane Keaton. The pictures had been taken off a TV set. It was the end scene of *Looking for Mr. Goodbar*. The second page had the stabbing sequence.

"Oh, my God," Hannah murmured.

Paper-clipped to the montage from *Looking for Mr. Goodbar* were three candid photos. The pretty blonde in the pictures seemed unaware that she was being photographed. The snapshots were all taken on the street, most likely at a distance, then blown up.

Hannah passed the batch of photos to Ben. "Is this Rae?" she whispered.

He stared at the snapshots and the stabbing scene from the movie. "Yes, that's Rae," he said, his voice strained. "And that's how he killed her, isn't it?"

"I'm sorry, Ben." Hannah squeezed his arm. Then she glanced down at the next "murder sequence" in the folder.

Again, the first page showed a series of images photographed from a TV screen. This time, Marilyn Monroe was being chased up a stairwell in a dark, austere-looking building. One photo revealed that the location was an institutional bell tower of some sort. On the second page, Marilyn's stalker caught up with her. There was a close-up of Joseph Cotton as he put his hands around her throat. The last shot showed Marilyn, dead on the cement floor.

Attached to the Marilyn death sequence were two photos of a striking redhead in her late twenties. Again, the woman didn't seem aware of anyone taking her picture.

"This must be Angela Bramford," Hannah murmured, giving the photos to Ben. "The pictures of Marilyn are from *Niagara*."

"I don't get the connection," Ben whispered. "Wasn't Angela Bramford found strangled somewhere around the Convention Center?"

"The bells," Hannah whispered. "The Convention Center has bells by the stairway to the second-floor terrace. He strangled her under the bells, like Marilyn in the movie."

Hannah glanced in the folder. Nothing but a blank piece of typing paper.

"Shouldn't he have something about Rae's friend, Joe?" Ben asked. "And the girl, what's her name? The Floating Flower . . ."

"Lily Abrams," Hannah said. She looked in the drawer. There weren't any other folders. "I don't know."

There should have been photographs of those two rude customers, and Ronald Craig, and Britt. Baffled, Hannah gazed down at the class lists that Ben had left on the floor.

Then she stared at the two separate batches of murder montage photos and candids.

"It's only the two women who took his class," she said. "Maybe the others don't matter to him. Maybe he only cares about these two women—the way he now cares about me."

"I don't understand," Ben said.

"First Angela Bramford, then Rae, and now he's working on me. The seduction, the intimidation, pulling the strings and putting them through the paces until the death scene is carried out."

Hannah slipped the photos back in the folder and closed it. "I think I know what he's doing," she whispered. "One after another, he's made each one of us his leading lady."

Seventeen

"Well, hello there, Hannah, you sorry bitch," Kenneth Woodley muttered. He studied the photograph taken the day before by his private detective, Walt Kirkabee. It was clearly *his* Hannah standing outside a store with her tall, blond-haired doofus boyfriend.

"That's in front of the place she works," Kirkabee said. "Emerald City Video, it's called."

Nodding, Kenneth looked up from the photo long enough to grab the plastic coffee pitcher and refill Kirkabee's cup for him. "Nice job," he said.

They shared a corner booth in Denny's, where the bar wasn't yet open, so the waitress wouldn't give him a Bloody Mary. Kenneth had to settle for coffee. Kirkabee was picking at his Grand Slam breakfast.

From the picture, it looked as if Hannah had lightened her hair a bit. She'd lost some weight, too.

"Have you seen the kid yet?" he asked.

Kirkabee shook his head. "Sorry. I've been watching that place for the last four days, and I haven't laid eyes on him. There's a fat old broad who comes and goes every morning and night. I'm guessing she's the baby-sitter."

Kenneth shifted in the booth, then leaned forward, elbows on the table. "It's kind of a cheap-ass apartment complex, isn't it? I mean, it wouldn't be too tough breaking in there and grabbing the kid."

Kirkabee put down his fork; it clanked against his plate. "Hey, I don't do that kind of thing."

"I know, I know, relax." Kenneth chuckled. "I'm just thinking out loud. I mean, if we stole the kid right from under her, she couldn't do a damn thing, could she? Would serve her right."

"So—you want to break into her apartment and abduct your own kid?"

He smiled. "I'm not getting my hands dirty. You don't have to be involved, either. I'll hire a couple of guys to do it—while she's there."

Kirkabee was shaking his head. "Hey, a million things could go wrong. Do you really want to entrust a couple of baby-snatchers-for-hire with the life of your son? You have the law on your side. You'll get him back. Why take stupid chances? Is it really worth the risks involved—just to stick it to your wife?"

Kenneth nodded. "Yeah," he whispered. "It sure as hell is."

"Can I take your coat?" Britt's older sister asked.

"Thank you very much," Hannah said. It was stuffy in the funeral home. Hannah quickly took off her trench coat and handed it to the thin brunette who looked like a conservative, slightly homelier version of Britt.

Hannah started to explain that she was a coworker of Britt's, but the sister was called away.

There were two distinct camps of mourners at Britt's service: her estranged, white-bread, upper-class family; and her current friends, most of whom resembled homeless drug addicts. The family members seemed uncomfortable with the unabashed display of emotions from the pierced-and-tattooed gothic types mingling among them.

"You're Hannah," said a pale, tiny young woman with dyed jet-black hair, gobs of mascara, and a ring pierced through her lower lip. She wore a black hooded sweatshirt and army fatigue pants.

"Hello," Hannah said, managing a smile. She remembered seeing the girl in the store a few times. "How are you holding up?"

The girl embraced her. She stank of cigarette smoke. "Britt was fuckin' crazy about you, Hannah," she said. "You were like—her personal goddess. She thought you were so fuckin' cool. She said you got her through a lot of shit."

"Oh, well, um, thanks a lot," Hannah replied, at a loss for anything else to say.

The girl went to talk to one of her pals. Hannah glanced towards the other side of the room. The closed casket was on display between two potted palms. It was hard to imagine her friend Britt in that mahogany box. Hannah felt such a sadness swell within her that she ached. She pulled a handkerchief from her purse, then ducked back into the cloakroom.

She kept thinking she could have prevented Britt's death. Trying to warn her hadn't been enough. She could have done more. If she'd taken her chances and gone to the police, there wouldn't be a funeral for Britt today.

Tish had given her the day off to attend the service. Hannah didn't plan on going to the cemetery. She was tired and emotionally drained. She'd hardly slept at all last night.

After they'd left the college, she and Ben had returned to her apartment with the stack of videotapes from Paul's coat closet. Bleary-eyed, they watched the videos—mostly at fast-forward speed—until two in the morning. The tapes were indeed film lectures, just as they'd been labeled.

While suffering through those videos, Hannah and Ben wondered about Seth's possible culpability in the murders. Hannah went to bed, resolving to dig deeper with Seth when they worked side by side on Wednesday.

She had another resolve. Nothing was going to happen between Ben Podowski and herself. That evening, she'd caught Ben gazing at her several times. She pretended not to notice the look of longing in his eyes. It didn't mean anything. He was just lonely, discouraged, and far away from home.

Ben had left in the morning to return the lecture tapes to Paul's office. He planned to keep tabs on Paul for the rest of the day.

Walking to the funeral parlor, Hannah had the feeling she was being watched again. She was also struck with a strange thought. What if Ben wasn't really following Paul? He could have been following her. He might have slipped that folder of photos inside Paul's desk drawer last night. He'd had plenty of time to do it. What if he was friends with that man who had been trying to look through her living-room curtains the night before last? Ben had disappeared for over ten minutes, then come back with his story about trying to chase down that elusive prowler. And she'd believed him.

Hannah shook off the notion. Ben couldn't be one of the killers. He'd barely escaped becoming one of the victims. She just wasn't thinking right. Too little sleep.

Perhaps that explained her extra-fragile emotional state at this funeral service. Having a breakdown in the cloakroom, no less.

"Hello, Hannah."

The handkerchief clutched in her hand, Hannah turned around. "Oh, hi, Ned," she replied, clearing her throat.

Ned Reemar stood in the cloakroom doorway. He wore his usual brown shirt with Snoopy over the pocket, jeans, and sneakers. But he'd added an ugly tie to the ensemble. It looked like a clip-on. He carried a windbreaker over his arm.

Wiping her eyes, Hannah edged past him. "I'll get out of your way here," she said. "It's awfully sweet of you to come."

"A lot of freaks attending, aren't there?" he said, hanging up his coat.

And you win the prize, Hannah thought. But she merely shrugged. "It's a diverse group. I didn't know Britt had such a wide range of friends."

"Well, I hate to say it," Ned muttered, smoothing back his greasy hair. "But I used to see her hanging out with some of these weirdos when she wasn't working. Talk about the wrong kind of crowd. I could have told you she'd end up dying young."

Hannah frowned, but didn't say anything.

Ned came up beside her. "How's your son?" he asked. "Gotta be careful with chicken pox. Do you think Scott caught the chicken pox from Guy?"

"No, I—I think they were both exposed to it around the same time," Hannah replied. It was unsettling how Nutty Ned always knew what was happening with everyone in the video store. Still, Hannah managed to smile. "But both patients seem to be doing all right, Ned."

She glanced toward the casket and saw Webb standing near one of the potted palms. Tall and crudely handsome, he had a five o'clock shadow and a perpetual sneer that someone must have once told him was sexy. He wore a leather jacket, jeans, a black shirt, and a bolo tie. With his hands shoved in his pockets, he leaned against the wood-paneled wall and glared at her.

"Hannah, do you know if the store will be carrying any of the old Twentieth Century Fox classics in DVD?" Ned was asking. "There's a whole bunch coming out next week, but they didn't say if the DVDs will be in the original screen ratio from CinemaScope. I was reading about it—"

"Um, Ned. I really don't know," Hannah gently interrupted. "I'm sorry. I'm kind of not in the mood to talk about work-related stuff right now. You understand, don't you?"

He frowned. "Oh, well, okay, sure. See you later."

Hannah watched Ned retreat into the crowd; then he stopped in front of the casket. She watched him touch the coffin, running his hand over the polished wood. Ever so casually, Nutty Ned poked his finger in the crevice between the coffin and its lid. Like a curious child, he must have been wondering if the casket was sealed shut.

Dumbfounded, Hannah stared at him.

Suddenly, someone shoved her, almost knocking her down. Hannah grabbed on to a chair to keep from falling, then swiveled around to see Webb.

"Because of you," Webb growled, "I have the police on my ass. You fucking ratted on me."

Glaring back at him, Hannah caught her breath. "I simply told them Britt was with you last weekend. That's the truth, isn't it? She was with you, wasn't she? Or did you ditch her someplace?"

"I didn't ditch her that night," Webb muttered. "She ditched me."

"Well, good for Britt," Hannah replied, keeping her voice down. "Too bad her timing was off. She should have ditched you ages ago."

"What the fuck are you talking about?" he snarled.

"I'm talking about all the times you beat her, Webb." Hannah shook her head at him. "That poor, sweet girl. At least she won't be getting smacked around and hurt by you anymore, you low-life creep."

He grabbed her arm. "You listen to me, you stupid—"

Hannah wrenched free of him. "Don't you touch me," she hissed. "If you ever lay a goddamn hand on me, I swear I'll have the police down on you so fast, you won't know what hit you."

He grinned defiantly. "Oh, really?"

Hannah suddenly realized people were staring. Her eyes wrestled with his. "You can count on it, you son of a bitch," she said under her breath.

"You're gonna sic the cops on me?" Webb chuckled. "That's a good one. You wouldn't dare. You're in trouble with the police. Britt told me. Hell, you never would've talked to the cops at all if they hadn't tracked you down at the store after Britt OD'd."

Hannah took a step back from him. "What?" she murmured.

He nodded. "Yeah, they told me they came to you. I'll bet you were pissing in your panties, you were so scared." He raised his voice. "What kind of trouble are you in with the police, Hannah? Britt said you must be in some pretty deep shit."

Hannah turned away. She stiffly edged through the crowd to the cloakroom. She couldn't look at anyone. Her heart was pounding, and she felt sick. She hated shrinking away, leaving him with a smirk and the last word.

Hannah fetched her trench coat. She was still nauseous and shaking inside as she left the funeral parlor.

The chilly autumn wind whipped at her as she hurried down the sidewalk. Hannah threw on her coat. She felt something slightly bulky in the left pocket, something that hadn't been there before.

Hannah stopped dead. She shoved her hand in the pocket and felt the plastic box. "Oh, no," she whispered.

She knew what it was.

"Wasn't he one of the doctors on *St. Elsewhere?*" Ben asked.

Gazing at the TV screen in her living room, Hannah nodded. "William Daniels, he was also Dustin Hoffman's father in *The Graduate.*"

They sat by each other on the floor, watching William Daniels and Warren Beatty on the screen. In the scene, Daniels and Beatty were in the galley of a small yacht, discussing a photo that had been taken at the Space Needle. The film was *The Parallax View*, a political thriller from 1974. It had been years since Hannah had seen it. But she had watched this particular scene just a few hours ago. The tape had been set to start there.

The next two minutes of footage was wordless, just Beatty and William Daniels aboard the yacht, with a third man at the wheel. "He's a bodyguard, I think," Hannah explained to Ben.

At a certain point, Beatty moved to one end of the boat; then he watched Daniels and his bodyguard at the stern. The camera pulled back for a long shot of the yacht gliding along the water's choppy surface. Suddenly, the stern and aft sections of the boat exploded, shooting flames, smoke, and debris up in the sky. Beatty dove into the water just as a second blast ripped the boat in half.

"Jesus," Ben murmured. The light from the TV cast shadows across his handsome, chiseled face. He sat on the floor with his long legs in front of him. He wore jeans with a white T-shirt, and was barefoot.

"So someone you know is going to die like this," he murmured. "In a boat explosion?"

Sitting beside him, Hannah took the remote and switched off the TV. "I've been racking my brain for the last couple of hours." She sighed. "I can't think of anyone I know here who owns a yacht."

"Maybe a customer at the store?" Ben asked. "A sailing enthusiast?"

"No one comes to mind. I'm totally clueless." Hannah stood up. "Do you want some wine?"

He smiled up at her. "Yeah, thanks."

Without thinking, she reached down and mussed his hair. As she moved toward the kitchen, she felt a little flushed. It was a silly little gesture. But she'd wanted to touch him. She was so grateful to have Ben at her side. Watching the video wasn't quite as awful this time, because Ben was with her. She didn't have to face it all alone.

She poured them each a glass of Merlot, then returned to the living room. She might have been more comfortable on the sofa. But she wanted to be near him. He looked so unself-consciously sexy—with his bare arms and bare feet. She handed Ben a wineglass, then settled down next to him on the floor.

"Thanks," he said. "Can you think of anyone who might have plans to go sailing this weekend?"

Hannah shrugged. "Nobody. The only person I know who's a big sailing nut is my husband, Kenneth. And he's in Wisconsin."

Ben frowned. "Are you sure? I mean, do you think it's possible he's here in Seattle?"

Automatically, Hannah started to shake her head, but she stopped herself. Of course he was in Seattle. She'd known that sooner or later someone would be coming after Ronald Craig. She just hadn't expected Kenneth. Obviously, he was having her watched. Or maybe he was watching her himself, just waiting to make his move—whatever that might be.

Ben caressed her arm. "Are you okay? You look pale all of a sudden."

"I think you're right," she said. "If Kenneth knew for sure I was here, he couldn't stay away. He's vindictive; I know him. He wouldn't leave it up to the police or some private detective to settle the score."

"And you think he'd take a pleasure cruise while he's here in town?"

Hannah sipped her wine, then nodded. "He couldn't resist."

She stared at the blank, dark TV screen, and imagined Kenneth dying in a boat explosion. For a fleeting moment, she thought about how much easier her life would be if Kenneth were dead.

"So this killer is going after your husband now," Ben remarked. "It's the Ronald Craig situation all over again. Kenneth's private investigators probably spotted your stalker; maybe they've even identified him." Ben sipped his wine. "This video-killer got more than he bargained for when he went after you."

Hannah sighed. "So it's only a question of who'll get to me first: Kenneth, or this maniac. They both want the same thing. They both want to see me die."

"I won't let that happen," Ben whispered. His hand came up behind her neck, beneath her hair. His fingers massaged the taut nerves there.

Hannah let out a grateful little moan, and she started to cry. "This murderer, he'll kill you too if you're in his way. Or maybe he'll kill you because he can see how much I care for you, Ben." She shook her head. "You should just go home to your wife. Every day you stay here with me, you're risking—"

"Shhhh," he whispered. "I'm not leaving you, Hannah."

He pulled her toward him and gently kissed her cheek. It was moist with her tears.

Hannah touched his handsome face, then ran her fingers through his hair. She felt his strong arms around her, and she started to melt inside.

Ben's lips slid over to her open mouth. He kissed her deeply. She tasted the wine on his lips. No one had kissed her like this in years. Her head was swimming. She felt a rush of warmth coursing through her, all the awakened desire. She was actually moaning. It embarrassed her, but she couldn't stifle herself.

Hannah clung to him, and they gently reclined on the floor. She wrapped her legs around his, their bare feet entwining.

He kissed her again, then pulled back to gaze at her. "So beautiful . . ."

She could feel him trembling. She loved the way he kissed her. He was such a handsome, sexy man. And all he wanted to do was protect her and make love to her.

Ben's lips brushed against her neck. Did he have any idea what that was doing to her? Arching her back, Hannah pressed against him. She could feel his erection stirring through his blue jeans. She stroked him, and listened to Ben's breathing become heavier.

He unbuttoned her blouse, kissing each section of exposed flesh. His whisker stubble grated against her skin, a tiny delicious pain.

She ran her hands down his strong back. Hannah found the bottom of his T-shirt and pulled it up to his shoulders. Then her hands roamed down his spine until her fingers wedged under the top of his jeans, beneath his undershorts. The skin at the start of his buttocks was cool and baby-smooth. She longed to be naked with him.

Ben must have been reading her mind, because he drew back from her, then pulled his T-shirt over his head and tossed it aside. She sat up and started to kiss his hairy chest. She glided her tongue against one of his nipples, grazing it with her teeth. Ben shuddered, then suddenly recoiled.

A hand over her mouth, Hannah numbly stared at him. "Oh, God, I—I'm sorry," she said. "Did I hurt you? Was that—too weird?"

Blushing, he shook his head. "No, actually it was—um, pretty hot. But I think we ought to move this into your bedroom. Don't you?"

Hannah nodded. "Yes, I think so," she said, catching her breath. "I think so—very much."

Ben was a wonderful lover; tender, sweet, and passionate. He actually held her afterward. Snug in Ben's arms, Hannah rested her head on his chest and listened to his heartbeat.

And there wasn't a snowball's chance in hell she'd fall asleep like that. After years of solitude, Hannah had become way too accustomed to sleeping alone.

She nodded off for a few moments, but woke up again. Comforting and stimulating as it was in Ben's arms, she eventually wriggled out of his embrace. She waited a few minutes to make sure he hadn't woken. Sleeping, he looked like a little boy.

Hannah carefully crept out of the bed. She adjusted the blinds and peered out her bedroom window. She wondered if Kenneth or one of his bloodhounds was out there somewhere watching the apartment right now. Or was her secret admirer keeping vigil alone tonight? Despite all the evidence against Paul Gulletti, she still felt uncertain about his part in these murders.

What is it that Ben had said? *This video-killer got more than he bargained for when he went after you.* The same could be said about Kenneth—if indeed he was in Seattle. Did he have any idea his life was in danger?

"Wow, what a beautiful thing to wake up to," Ben muttered.

Hannah turned to see him sitting up in bed, giving her a sleepy grin. Blushing, she smiled back at him, then grabbed her blouse off the back of the chair and put it on.

"Oh, rats," he said. "You know, it was like a vision, seeing you there naked with the moonlight coming through the blinds. I'm serious."

She was still blushing. He made her feel so self-conscious.

"You still look pretty damn good," he said. "What are you doing way over there?"

She glanced out the window again. "I was just thinking about my estranged husband." She sighed. "This killer—whoever he is—he might be doing me a big favor by blowing Kenneth to bits."

"Oh, Hannah, no," he whispered. "It would only make things worse for you. The police might think you had something to do with his death. And if we don't try to prevent it from happening, we'd be just as guilty as this killer—"

"Relax," Hannah said, sitting on the end of the bed. She let out a sad laugh. "I really don't want Kenneth dead. I couldn't live with myself if I just sat back and let him get killed. I mean, Good Lord, in a few hours, by the light of day, I'll have a hard enough time trying to rationalize sleeping with a married man. My guilt plate is already full."

Ben leaned over and kissed the side of her cheek. "Jennifer and I are more or less separated, if that's any help."

She shrugged. "I guess it helps—more or less. So what are we going to do to prevent this son of a bitch from getting blown to bits?"

"We'll have to get in touch with him," Ben said. "I know Ronald Craig worked for a place called Great Lakes Investigations. I'll call them, for starters. Do you still have your in-laws' phone number?"

Hannah frowned. "You want to call my in-laws?"

"Yeah, if the detective agency won't help. In fact, I might try your in-laws first. I'll call from a pay phone, of course.

We need to find out if he's here in town and how to get in touch with him."

Hannah was shaking her head. "I don't like this. A call from a Seattle pay phone? They'll know I'm here."

"Well, they probably already know that, Hannah. Don't you think?" He put his arm around her shoulder. "Listen, if we can get in touch with Kenneth—or his private detective, we might be able to straighten some things out, maybe even persuade them to drop the charges."

She rolled her eyes. "Huh, dream on."

"Well, at least we might get a description of our video-killer. They're sure to have seen him." He kissed her again. "I'll figure out how we can do this, Hannah. We'll come up with a plan in the morning. C'mon, let's get back under the covers."

"I want to check on Guy first," she said, kissing his shoulder. She put on her robe and crept out of the bedroom.

When Hannah peeked into Guy's room next door, she could see him curled up in bed, sucking his thumb. But his eyes were open, and he looked back at her.

Hannah sat on the edge of his bed. There were still little abrasions on his face. She felt his forehead. "Can't you sleep, sweetie?"

"I heard Ben talking," Guy said. "Is he awake?"

"Oh, he's just gone back to bed. But you'll see him in the morning." She smoothed back his blond hair.

"Can Ben be my dad?" he asked.

Hannah tried to smile. "I don't think that will happen, honey. But he's our friend, and that's important."

He yawned. "My dad's in heaven, isn't he?"

Hannah hesitated. "Um, yes."

"Joyce says he's watching over us. Is he?"

Hannah kept stroking his head. "Yes, honey," she said, swallowing hard. "Your father is watching us."

Eighteen

They were using the pay phone by the abandoned little grocery store a few blocks from Hannah's apartment, the same pay phone from which she'd called the Green Bay police department a few nights ago.

But this time, Hannah wasn't alone. And the surroundings seemed a lot more innocuous on this crisp, sunny Wednesday morning. Though she wouldn't be talking to anyone, Hannah still had a lot of trepidation about this call.

Ben had stepped out earlier and bought a phone card. He'd been gone most of the morning, then returned with Starbucks coffee and a cinnamon roll for her, as well as a coloring book for Guy.

An hour later, as they'd left her apartment building together, Ben had taken hold of Hannah's hand. She'd told herself it shouldn't matter if anyone saw them, but it did. Someone was watching and judging, maybe even getting a little angry that she was happy with another man. Before they were halfway down the block, Hannah muttered, "Excuse me." Then she causally pulled her hand away to move her windblown hair out of her eyes. She didn't take hold of his hand again.

She felt extra anxious about leaving Guy and Joyce alone—especially today. There was no reason for the increased apprehension on this particular morning. Maybe it was the Catholic schoolgirl in her. She almost expected to be punished for giving in to her desires last night. Whatever the rationale, she dreaded being away from Guy today.

She would be working alongside Seth at the store. It was a chance to talk with him more about Paul Gulletti—and about certain theories on film directors and their leading ladies.

For now, Ben would be doing the talking. Hannah had mixed feelings about this whole venture. Part of her wished she could hear what was said on the other end of the line. Another part of her hated making any kind of contact with her in-laws. The idea of reconnecting with them—even through a third party—made Hannah sick to her stomach.

As Ben punched in the Woodleys' number, then the phone-card code, Hannah stood behind him, wringing her hands. With the receiver to his ear, Ben smiled reassuringly at her. Then, he suddenly looked away. "Yes, hello," he said into the phone. "Is Mr. or Mrs. Woodley there, please?"

Biting her lip, Hannah stared at him.

"They don't know me. This is in regard to their grand-son," Ben said. "I think they'll want to talk to me. . . . Yes, thank you. I'll wait."

He covered the mouthpiece. "I got the maid."

Hannah nodded. "Sylvana. She's very sweet. She—"

Ben turned his back to her. "Yes, Mrs. Woodley, hello," she heard him say. "Yes, that's right. I have information re-garding the whereabouts of your grandson. I need to get in touch with your son, Kenneth, but I can't reach him. Do you have a number I can call?"

Ben paused and shot a look toward Hannah for a moment. "My name wouldn't mean anything to him—or to you. . . . Uh-huh. Well, Mrs. Woodley, I don't have time for a lot of nonsense, either. I need to talk to Kenneth about your grand-son, Kenneth Woodley the Third. I know where the boy is, but I don't know where Kenneth is. So here's what I'm ask-ing you to do, Mrs. Woodley. Do you have paper and pencil handy?"

Ben sighed. "Yes, I can wait—for about fifteen seconds;

then I need to hang up. . . . Oh, really? Well, I could hang up right now. Then you can forget any chance of ever finding your grandson, lady. I'm just trying to help here. . . . Yes, well, I thought so."

He covered the mouthpiece, and frowned at Hannah. "God, what a pain in the ass."

"I had two years of her," Hannah whispered. "And compared to her husband and son, she's Mother Teresa."

"Yes, Mrs. Woodley," he said into the phone. "I'm still here. Tell your son to contact me at this e-mail address. Are you ready? Ralph-at-eight-oh-nine-oh-three-dot-net."

Hannah listened to him repeat and spell it out. She wondered whose e-mail address he was using.

"Tell your son to contact me today," Ben was saying. "Because after tomorrow, he won't be able to get ahold of me at all. Do you understand, Mrs. Woodley? Fine, then. Goodbye, Mrs. Woodley."

Ben hung up the phone and let out a long sigh.

"Where did you get that e-mail address?" Hannah asked. "What if they trace it?"

"Just a second," Ben said, glancing at a scrap of paper with notes scribbled on it. "I want to get this other call out of the way."

Hannah stood by while Ben dialed the second phone number.

"Great Lakes Investigations?" he said. "Yes, I'm calling in regard to one of your detectives, Ronald Craig, now deceased. I need to get in touch with the client who hired him, a Mr. Kenneth Woodley. I believe he's in Seattle at the moment. . . . Hello? Hello? Are you talking to me? Excuse me. . . . No, I can't hold. Let me give you an e-mail address where Mr. Woodley can contact me. . . . No, I'm sorry, I need to hang up soon. Believe me, Mr. Woodley will want to contact me. The e-mail address is— Well, I don't care. Scratch it in your arm if you have to. It's Ralph-at-eight-oh-nine-oh-three-dot-net."

Ben repeated the e-mail address, then hung up without

saying good-bye. "Damn, that was weird," he said. "The receptionist was trying to stall. I could hear someone on the other end whispering at her to keep me talking. They were probably trying to trace the call."

Wiping his forehead, Ben put the scrap of paper away. Then he pulled out his sunglasses and put them on.

"So—whose e-mail address is Ralph-at-eight-oh-nine-oh-three-dot-net?" Hannah asked.

He glanced down at the pavement and shuffled his feet. "Well, I set that up this morning with Jennifer."

Hannah stared at him. "You mean, your wife Jennifer?"

"Yes. She knows computers. I couldn't think of anyone else." He shrugged. "Anyway, I explained the situation to her. She set it up so they can't trace us through the e-mail address. In fact, by tonight, that e-mail address will no longer exist. In the meantime, your husband has a way of contacting us. We have a line of communication, but he won't be able to track us down."

Hannah squinted at him. "When did you do all this?"

"Early this morning, after I stepped out," Ben explained. "I called her from a coffee shop. Jennifer was at work. The East Coast is three hours ahead of us."

Hannah nodded. "Yes, I'm aware of the time difference. What I don't understand is how you could call up your wife and ask her for a favor this morning when you slept with me just last night."

Ben frowned. "Like I told you, she's the only person I know with computer smarts."

"My God," Hannah murmured, shaking her head. "Ben, how can you cheat on her, then turn around and expect her to do you a favor? In fact, you're having her do something for *me,* the woman you just had sex with. Christ, that's even worse. Did you tell her about us?"

"No, Hannah," he sighed. "Though I probably will—eventually."

"Well, I don't understand you. What, is it okay for you to call her now and act like everything is fine, because you evened the score last night? Is that it? She cheated on you, and now that you've had sex with me, everything's copacetic?"

He shook his head. "It's not like that. What happened with us last night has nothing to do with my marriage. Jennifer and I are separated, but we're still talking. We're still trying to work things out."

"Oh, and did you think sleeping with me would help?" Hannah asked pointedly.

"Like I said, last night had nothing to do with my marriage. It was about you and me, Hannah. It was about us."

"Well, how much of an 'us' is there when you're trying to work things out with your wife?"

He sadly shook his head, then shrugged. "I don't know. You're the one who wants a head start running away to another city. My guess is you don't see any future for an 'us.'"

Biting her lip, Hannah took a step back. She couldn't look at him. He was right, of course.

"How's this e-mail thing supposed to work, anyway?" she asked finally. "Do we just wait to hear from Kenneth, or what?"

"Yeah, we wait," Ben said, nodding. "Jennifer will keep checking for a response. I gave her your numbers at work and home. She'll call when Kenneth sends an e-mail."

"Your wife's calling me? What if she asks about—us?"

"Well, she didn't ask me this morning," Ben said. "But if she tries to put you on the spot, tell her to talk to me."

"Let me get this straight," Hannah said. "She's our link in communicating with my vindictive-as-hell husband. And you've given her my work and home phone numbers. What makes you so certain she won't totally screw us here?"

"I trust her," Ben replied.

"You trust her? Wasn't she fucking this guy behind your back for three or four months? And you trust her? Are you nuts?"

He smiled a little. "It might seem that way. But I know Jennifer would never do anything to betray me again."

Hannah frowned. "Yeah, just wait until she figures out about us last night." She glanced at her wristwatch. "I'll be late for work," she muttered. "We'd better get going."

They crossed the street together. Ben took her arm, and Hannah awkwardly pulled away.

He didn't say anything. Neither did she. They both kept walking.

"Hannah, I looked it up in the computer, and I couldn't find anything," Seth said. He was working on the register alongside her. "Maybe you know. I have this lady on hold right now. She was asking for inspirational videos by Mr. T."

"As in *I pity the fool?*" Hannah asked. "That Mr. T?"

"Yeah, believe it or not. She says he has a series of inspirational videos, and she's looking for them. Do you think it's a joke?"

"Or a cry for help," Hannah replied. Then she shrugged. "Either way, we don't carry them."

Hannah watched him handle the woman on the phone with a polite, professional air.

She'd been working with Seth for about three hours now, since he'd started at eleven. So far, Hannah was impressed. He knew movies, and the customers seemed to like him. With his black V-neck, the designer glasses, and his wild hair, he was very avant-garde handsome. Some of the gay clientele clearly noticed, and Hannah watched Seth tactfully dodge a couple of overt passes. "Same thing happened yesterday," he'd muttered to her, after weathering the second flirtatious overture. "Five different guys came on to me. Maybe I ought to wear a sign: I AM STRAIGHT."

"We'll fix you up one," Hannah had offered. "Like one of those vanity plates, I-M-S-T-R-and the number eight."

He had a decent sense of humor, and he seemed to master the job very quickly. Hannah couldn't find anything wrong with him.

Tish was pleased with him too; so she'd told Hannah

when she phoned the store this morning. "Talk about a fast learner," she'd said. "This kid caught on to the layout of the place like you wouldn't believe. I'm serious, he was in the door only two hours on his first day, and already he was telling customers where to find such and such a video."

"Maybe he's been in the store before," Hannah had offered. "And we just didn't notice."

"Well, something about him is a little familiar," Tish had allowed. "Maybe that's it. Whatever, I'm glad you recommended this kid, Han. Unless he suddenly turns out to be a total psycho, he's a keeper."

After hanging up with her manager, Hannah had looked up Stroud, Seth in the computer. She'd figured he might have been a customer at one time. He was in the system; only he'd just opened up a new account two days ago.

Seth chose a video to play in the store: Alfred Hitchcock's *Shadow of a Doubt*. Hannah used the movie as a segue into a line of questioning.

"Hey, speaking of Hitchcock," she said as she Windexed the countertops. "We're seeing *The Birds* in class tomorrow night. I ran into Paul at the college the other night. He mentioned something, and it reminded me of a conversation you and I had earlier."

"Oh, yeah?" Seth replied, checking in returned videos.

"Yes. He said that for discussion period we were going to talk about a director's power over his leading actress, like Hitchcock putting Tippi Hedren through the paces. The courtship, the molding and controlling. It made me think about what you said." Hannah kept wiping off the counters. She peeked up at Seth. "You know, the way Otto Preminger picked on Jean Seberg while making *Bonjour Tristesse*. Svengali and Trilby. Remember that conversation?"

Seth was shaking his head. "Oh, brother. Paul Gulletti doesn't have an original bone in his body. I wrote a paper for him on that subject two years ago. He got it published, practically word for word, in a book of film essays. The SOB put his own name on it. I'd have sued, only the book

hardly made back its printing costs. It had a bunch of contributors, all these egghead film critics. Just didn't seem
worth the hassle of raising a stink with him."

Hannah had stopped working to stare at Seth. "That's
awful."

"Well, that's Paul Gulletti," Seth grunted. "He mentioned
you were writing something on the Hollywood blacklist for
him. Don't be surprised if your work turns up someplace
with his name on it."

"What's this book called, anyway?" Hannah asked. "I'm
interested in reading what you had to say, Seth. Even if Paul
grabbed the credit."

He blushed a little. "Well, thanks. It's called *Darkness,
Light, and Shadows: Essays on Film,* published by one of
those small university presses."

"I'll look it up in the library," Hannah said. She was
telling the truth. She very much wanted to read what Seth
Stroud had to say on the subject of certain film directors and
their obsessions with leading ladies.

Hannah put away the Windex and dust rag. "Paul's kind
of a sleazoid, isn't he?" She leaned on the back counter.
"The other day, when you were telling me about that Angela
woman from his class, the one who was strangled, you
hinted that Paul might have had something to do with it.
Were you serious?"

Seth chuckled. "Not really. He's sleazy, but he doesn't
have the guts to actually kill anyone. Ha, though if he did,
he'd probably copy someone else's murder."

Seth laughed, then smiled at Hannah.

She stared back at him. She tried to laugh too, but she
couldn't.

"Hannah, line one is for you," Seth announced, as they
wound down from a rush. "It's Jennifer Somebody. Says it's
personal."

It was unusual to have a swarm of customers descend on

them at three-thirty, and, of course, the phone had started ringing off the hook at just the same time. But Seth and she had sailed though it without incident. Tish was right; unless Seth turned out to be a total psycho, he was a keeper.

Both Hannah and Seth were just finished up with her last customers. She spotted Nutty Ned approaching the register, smiling at her. "Seth, can you cover for me?" she said, moving around the counter. "I need to take this call in the break room. Hi, Ned." She bypassed him, then called back to Seth. "Give me a shout if it gets crazy again!"

Hannah ducked into the break room, stepped over to the desk, and stared at the blinking light on the telephone. She needed a moment before saying hello to Ben's wife.

She finally picked up the receiver. "Hello, this is Hannah."

"Hi, Hannah. It's Jennifer Dorn calling."

"Dorn?"

"I kept my name," she explained. "It's a bit easier to carry around than Podowski."

Hannah let out a nervous laugh. "I'm sure." She sat down at the desk. "Um, listen, Jennifer, I want to thank you for helping us—or helping me, actually. It's very nice of you to do this for a total stranger."

"Well, Ben asked me," she replied. "Anyway, ten minutes ago, I got an e-mail on that account I set up this morning. It's from W-KIRK-A-BEE-at-G-L-I-dot-web. I did a trace on that, and it's someone named Kirkabee at Great Lakes Investigations in Milwaukee, Wisconsin. But the e-mail was sent from the Pacific Coast, according to the send time."

"Ben was right," Hannah said. "You are good."

"Thanks. Are you ready for the message?"

"Yes."

"It reads: *Who the fuck are you?* and it's signed *K. Woodley*. That's all, short and not-so-sweet. Do you want me to respond?"

Dumbfounded, Hannah was at a loss for a moment.

"Hello?"

"Yes, I'll respond," she said. "Are you ready?"

"Go ahead," Jennifer said.

"Okay, here goes: *Mr. Woodley—Someone else is following her. If you or Mr. Kirkabee—*" Hannah paused. "Is that the name?"

"That's right. Kirkabee, go ahead."

Hannah continued. She could hear the faint clacking of fingers on a keyboard as she dictated. Jennifer was taking it all down. *"If you or Mr. Kirkabee have seen this man, please furnish a description or identification at this address as soon as possible. He is dangerous. Be advised, he may be responsible for the death of Ronald Craig, and could target you next. Avoid sailing or boating. There is a high risk of sabotage to a sailboat or yacht."*

"Is that it?" Jennifer asked.

"Yes, I think so," Hannah replied, with a sigh of relief. Yet she was still gripping the receiver a bit too tightly.

Jennifer read the message back to her. It sounded all right. With the note mentioning both Ronald Craig and the new detective, Kirkabee, by name, at least Kenneth would know to take it seriously.

"No changes? I'm about to send it," Jennifer said.

"Go ahead. Thanks."

"Okay, it's sent, Hannah," she said. "I'll call you when I get a reply. What time will you be home tonight?"

"Around six."

"All right. Is—um," she paused. "Is Ben going to be there?"

"He might be," Hannah answered carefully.

Jennifer didn't say anything.

Hannah let out a skittish laugh. "This sure is awkward, isn't it?"

"Ben asked me to do this for him," Jennifer said. "That's why I'm doing it, Hannah. I want my husband back."

"I understand," Hannah murmured.

"So I'm not asking any questions I don't want to hear the answers to. I'll call you when I get a reply here."

"Thank you, Jennifer," Hannah said.

She heard a click on the other end of the line.

"Darkness, Light, and Shadow: Essays on Film, edited by Brendan Leonard," said the librarian at Seattle's downtown branch. The wiry, middle-aged black man stood behind the counter at his computer terminal. Hannah could see the computer screen reflected in his glasses. "That's checked out right now. Went out today, in fact."

"Today?" Hannah asked. "Does it say what time today?"

He nodded. "About two hours ago; four twenty-three P.M., to be exact." He started typing something. "And I'm sorry, but that's the only copy we have in the whole system. The current due date is November twelfth. Would you like to put it on hold?"

Hannah sighed. "Thanks anyway. You couldn't tell me who checked out the book, could you?"

He shook his head. "I wish I could help you, but I can't."

Hannah worked up a smile. "I understand. Maybe you could help me with something else. Does it say there in your computer when the book was previously checked out?"

With a sigh, the librarian started typing on the keyboard again. "Yes, the book was last checked out on February sixteenth of this year."

"So—it just sat on the shelf for eight months, up until two hours ago?" Hannah said.

"At four twenty-three," the man said, nodding.

"Just a little over an hour after someone told me about the book."

"Funny coincidence," the librarian said. "But then, isn't that the way it always is?"

"It's no coincidence," Hannah murmured.

She thanked the man, then turned away.

* * *

Ben was waiting to walk Joyce home, while Hannah helped her on with her raincoat.

Joyce paused in the doorway and peeked inside her purse. "Oh, my keys . . ." She smiled at Ben. "Could you be a dear and check Guy's room? I think I left them there."

Ben nodded. "No sweat."

Once he started down the hall, Joyce pulled Hannah out to the walkway. "Honey, I don't mean to be a buttinski," she whispered. "And if it's none of my beeswax, just say so. But I don't want to see you get hurt—"

"What is it?" Hannah asked in a hushed tone.

Joyce grimaced. "Oh, Hannah, I hate to tell you, but he's married. His wife called here tonight."

Hannah quickly shook her head. "It's okay, Joyce. I know he's married. He's separated. In fact, I talked with his wife today myself."

"Oh, I see," Joyce replied, her brow wrinkled. "Kind of."

"It's hard to explain," Hannah said, taking hold of her hand. "In fact, it's pretty messed up, but I think it'll work itself out. At least, I hope so."

"All right, honey." She squeezed Hannah's hand. "You're like my own daughter; you should know that. I just don't want to see you get hurt."

Hannah kissed her on the cheek. "Thanks, Joyce."

Ben came from the hallway, empty-handed. "Sorry, no luck . . ."

Joyce pulled her keys from her purse. "Oh, silly me," she announced. "They were here all the time. I must be getting senile. Thanks, handsome. C'mon, walk me home. I'm liable to lose my way."

Hannah watched them leave; then she stared out at the city and the Space Needle. She would have to leave Seattle very soon. *It'll work itself out,* she'd told Joyce. Her packing up and skipping town with Guy was the only way it could work out.

She went to check on him. He was dozing. His chicken pox seemed to be clearing up. Joyce said he was on the mend. All this week, he kept talking about how he wanted to be better in time for Halloween. He would probably be spending the holiday in a motel someplace—away from his friends, and Joyce, whom he adored. He was becoming too fond of Ben as well.

Hannah grabbed a sweater and walked back out to the balcony. She saw Ben emerge from the stairwell. Smiling, he came up to her and kissed her on the mouth.

Hannah carefully pulled back. "I hear Jennifer called tonight," she said. "Joyce told me."

"Yeah," he said, nodding. "In fact, Joyce is worried. While I was walking her home just now, she said I'd better not break your heart."

"She's a little late," Hannah murmured. The chilly night wind kicked up, and she rubbed her arms.

Ben leaned against the railing. "Are you still sore at me for calling Jennifer this morning?"

Hannah shrugged. "Maybe not so sore as I am confused. I don't understand how you can be so—cool about it."

He smiled sadly. "The thing is—staying with you and Guy these past few nights has been pretty terrific. It would be easy to fool myself into thinking we have a future together, Hannah. But we don't. You made that clear to me early on. Anyway, this morning, it hit me—my future is with my wife."

He gazed out at the cityscape, and sighed. "So—I went out this morning, had a cup of coffee, and called her from the pay phone in Starbucks. And I asked for her help. You know, you can't be mad at someone and ask them to help you at the same time. It's impossible."

"That's very nice," was all Hannah could say.

Ben touched her shoulder. "But it doesn't change how I feel about you. For me, last night was wonderful. I realize we have to go in separate directions. But you know something? If I never see you again after tomorrow, I won't ever forget you—or the past few nights with you."

Hannah started to cry. She turned away from him and

clung to the railing. "What did your wife call about tonight?" she asked, her voice strained.

Ben sighed. "She was relaying another message. Kenneth and this private detective, Kirkabee; they've seen your stalker. They even have a couple of photos of him."

She gazed at him. "Really?"

"Well, we still need to find out if Kenneth is on the level. I'm meeting him tomorrow night at Duke's restaurant."

Hannah started shaking her head. "No, you can't. It's probably some kind of trap—"

"Hannah, he's agreed to show me the photos of this stalker. We could put an end to this nightmare. And maybe I can work something out with Kenneth, get him to drop the charges. You won't have to spend the rest of your life on the run—"

"You don't know him," Hannah said. "He'd never give me a break. He's going to take Guy away. He'll follow you back here. He'll break in, and take Guy. I'd have no recourse—"

"Hannah, I'm pretty certain he already knows where you live," Ben said. He motioned with his arm toward the parking lot where Ronald Craig had been mowed down. "Hell, Kenneth or one of his detectives is probably out there right now, watching us. Isn't it crazy? We're communicating through my wife in New York and her e-mail account, while they're right out there. HEY!" Ben yelled, "SEE YOU TOMORROW AT DUKE'S! FIVE-THIRTY!"

"Stop it!" Hannah hissed. She quickly pulled him inside and shut the door. She broke down and wrapped her arms around him. "Oh, everything's so screwed up," she cried. "I don't want to hurt your marriage, but I can't stand losing you, either. Don't take any chances tomorrow. Kenneth might try to hurt you, and whoever is behind these murders—he, well, if anything happened to you, I don't know what I'd do."

Ben kissed her forehead and rocked her back and forth in his arms. "Hush now," he whispered. "It's okay. We'll get these guys before they kill anyone else. Quit worrying about me. Everything's going to work out . . ."

Hannah held onto him. She didn't believe a word. Still, she held onto him.

Nineteen

"Say *cheese!*" Tish called, aiming her Polaroid camera at them.

Seth put his arm around Hannah. She tried not to tense up. *"Cheese,"* they said in unison. The flash went off, blinding her for a moment.

"All right, now I want just Seth in this next one," Tish declared. "Oh, and take off your glasses."

Hannah stepped toward Tish, who handed her the undeveloped photo.

Seth removed his glasses, then smiled self-consciously for the camera. "I still don't understand why we're doing this," he said.

"It's for my personal Rogue's Gallery," Tish replied from behind the Polaroid camera. "I put all the newbies through this. Now, say *cheese.*"

"Havarti," Seth said. Then he blinked as the flash went off.

"Okay, customers in the store," Tish announced. "Back to work." She plucked the first photo out of Hannah's hand, and started for the break room.

Seth put on his glasses and stepped back behind his register.

Hannah followed Tish. "We need to talk about next month's schedule," she said, ducking into the break room after her. Hannah closed the door.

Tish gave her the Polaroid photos. "Okay, so why did I

have to bring in my camera this morning?" she whispered. "What's with the photo session?"

"I'll tell you later," Hannah said. She glanced at the two Polaroid photos. The images were starting to emerge.

"I want you to take a look at these pictures for me," Hannah said.

Scott was sitting up in his hospital bed. His chicken pox seemed to have cleared up—at least on his face. He frowned at her. "Well, that's a fine greeting. No *Hello, how are you, how are your chicken pox?* Just a very brusque *Take a look at these pictures for me.* Sweet."

Hannah figured he couldn't see her smiling behind the surgical mask they'd made her wear along with the disposable smock. Scott was still in isolation. "Mea culpa, mea culpa," she said, stepping up to the foot of his bed. "So—how are you? How are your lousy chicken pox?"

"Well, I must be okay," he said. "Because they're springing me from this joint day after tomorrow. And remember that cute intern I liked? Guess what?"

"He's straight?" Hannah asked.

"No. Gay as a Maypole—and a *resident,* not an intern. We have a dinner date next week. Can you feature that? I'm going to be the wife of a doctor."

"Well, that's fantastic. So—you're not holding out for Nutty Ned?"

"No, Ned's all yours, babe," he replied. "I know you've had your eye on him. So what's going on with you? I haven't talked to you since the day before yesterday—"

"The day after Britt's funeral," Hannah said soberly.

"Yeah," Scott muttered. "Well, we've managed to avoid the obvious. What about this video-killer? Do these pictures have anything to do with him?"

Hannah nodded. "Maybe. This is the teacher's assistant in my film class. He just started working at the store. We had a strange discussion yesterday about an essay he wrote for my film professor. It's kind of hard to explain, but I think he could be involved in these murders somehow. Anyway, this morning I had Tish take these snapshots. I thought you might recognize him from hanging around the store." She pulled the Polaroids out of her purse and started to hand them to him.

"You have to show them to me, Han," Scott said, leaning forward. "I can't handle anything yet."

"Oops, sorry." She walked around to the side of the bed and held up the photos for him to see. "Does he look familiar?"

Scott squinted at both pictures. "Oh, yeah. He used to come into the store a lot. It was a while back—before you started working there. The glasses are new. Is he a pal of yours?"

"I'm not sure. Like I said, he's the new guy at work. He took over for Britt."

"Well, that's gonna suck."

"What do you mean?" Hannah asked.

"It's gonna suck working with him. He's an arrogant SOB, if I remember correctly. The guy had attitude up the wazoo."

"Does the name Seth Stroud ring a bell?"

Scott shook his head. "Nope, that's not it. I mean, if he's who I think he is. This guy went by some other name." He shrugged and sat back against the bed pillows. "Maybe I'm wrong."

"Well, Tish thought he looked familiar, too."

"She always works the day shift. I doubt she would have seen this guy very much. He usually came in at night. He was a real film buff, and snotty about it, too. I remember him taking off on me one afternoon because I mispronounced Akira Kurosawa. Very big deal."

Hannah frowned. "That sounds like Seth."

"Well," Scott said, settling back. "When I knew that SOB, his name wasn't Seth Stroud."

* * *

Ben was late.

They were supposed to meet in the hospital's little court-yard. Hannah had been waiting on a park bench for the last ten minutes.

The notion that she'd never see Scott again hit her hard. Somewhere down the line, she might call him from a pay phone from another city, but that was all she could hope for. This quick visit had been the last time she would ever lay eyes on Scott. What a shame she couldn't even hug her friend good-bye.

Hannah fought off the pangs of premature homesickness. She dug the photos of Seth Stroud out of her purse, and studied them. She wondered why he'd changed his name, and what he was hiding.

She glanced up from the Polaroids to see Ben approaching. He wore a denim shirt, jeans, and a tan jacket. His face was flushed.

"Sorry I'm late," he said, catching his breath. "I practically ran up the hill here." Despite a late-autumn chill in the air, he was perspiring.

"Well, I'm due back at work—two minutes ago," she said, glancing at her wristwatch. "Want to walk back down the hill with me?"

He nodded again. "Fine. Sorry to hold you up. You had a visitor this morning. And I was following him—up until about ten minutes ago."

"A visitor? Where, at my apartment?"

"Gulletti," Ben said, wiping his forehead with the back of his hand. "C'mon. I'll tell you on the way back to the store."

They started down a residential street, past piles of fallen leaves along the sidewalk.

"I followed Gulletti from his house, to Seattle's Best Coffee, to the college," Ben explained as they strolled. "Then, something must have happened, because he suddenly tore-ass out of his office. He tried to hail a cab in front of the college, but without any luck. So he hoofed it to your apartment building. He buzzed, and I guess Joyce gave him the heave-ho. She wouldn't let him up. So he went to the video store. He didn't stay long. I could spot Seth in there through the window. I didn't know what to make of it, but they both seemed surprised to see each other."

"Seth didn't want Paul knowing that he was working there with me," Hannah explained.

"Maybe that's it," Ben said. "Anyway, something weird was going on between them, I could tell. Then Paul went back to the school—and his office. That's where I left him."

"I wonder what Paul wanted," Hannah murmured. "By the way." She dug into her purse, then took out the two Polaroids and handed them to Ben. "Here are the pictures of Seth. Do you have a photo of Paul?"

Studying the photographs while they walked, Ben nodded. "Yeah, the portrait from his review column in the newspaper. This one is cute of you."

Hannah plucked it out of his hand. "You know, the picture of Seth alone should be enough—even without the glasses. I don't want Kenneth seeing any current pictures of me."

"Well, they claim they have photos of your stalker. They probably have photos of you already, Hannah."

"Just the same, I'd rather not *give* them any."

"I understand," Ben said, shoving the photo in his jacket pocket. "I can always draw a pair of glasses on this picture of Seth—if they don't recognize him without the specs." He looked toward the store, just a block away. "You be careful. I hate the idea of you working alongside of Seth Stroud all afternoon."

"If that's his real name," Hannah said.

"What?"

"I'll tell you later," she replied. "Besides, he's probably gone already. He only works half a day today. Paul's class is tonight."

She wrapped her arm around his. "You're the one who needs to be careful. You're taking all the risks this afternoon. I don't trust Kenneth. Just get in and out of there as quickly as possible."

He nodded. "I know, I know. We already went over this last night. Three things: one, I warn him about the boat explosion; two, I get a description of your stalker; and three, I set up a meeting between you and Kenneth for Saturday night."

"By which time, Guy and I will be long gone," Hannah added, staring straight ahead. "At least, I hope."

A Seahawks game was broadcasting over three strategically located TV sets in Duke's Chowderhouse. The Happy Hour crowd in the bar seemed rather sedate, and the restaurant area was just starting to fill up. Through the floor-to-ceiling windows, the sunset cast an amber haze over the Lake Union marina.

Ben sat down at a small table near the window. Hannah didn't have any pictures of her estranged husband, so Ben had no way of recognizing Kenneth Woodley. But Kenneth and his detectives had been watching Hannah for several days. They knew him, they had an advantage. Ben imagined they were staring at him this very moment.

He ordered a Lite beer, and sat there, waiting to be recognized. He glanced over at the different men at the bar. One of them was smirking back at him. He had black hair, a goatee, and wore a tight, gray, long-sleeve T-shirt that showed off his brawny physique. Ben wondered if this was Kenneth, or the detective, or maybe just some gay guy who found him attractive.

Ben looked away, toward one of the TVs. His beer arrived and he paid for it. After the waitress left, he glanced again at Mr. Tight T-shirt, who was still staring at him.

Ben turned away again. Gazing out the window, he sipped his beer.

"Mind if I join you?"

Ben glanced up at the Tight T-shirt Man. "Actually, I'm waiting for someone."

The man chuckled, then slid into the chair across from Ben. He sipped his martini, then sat back. "Maybe you're waiting for me, buddy." He glanced out the window. "You know, for somebody who's so full of gloom and doom about sailboats, it's pretty weird you agreed to meet here."

Ben looked at all the boats docked just outside the restaurant. "It was your suggestion. I've never been here before. Are you Kirkabee?"

The man with the goatee smiled. "I might be. Who are you?"

"Who I am doesn't matter," Ben said.

"That's true. You don't matter to me at all."

Ben gave him an ironic smile. Someone sat down in the chair directly behind him, and Ben inched forward. "Okay," he said, keeping his voice down. "I want to explain my warning in that e-mail. There's someone else following her, and he's responsible for several murders—including the hit-and-run of your pal Ronald Craig. This killer likes to give my friend videos illustrating how he plans to murder his next victims—and it's always someone she knows. In the last video, there was an explosion aboard a yacht."

The man shook his head and chuckled. "Pretty incredible."

"Before Ronald Craig was killed, my friend received a video showing someone repeatedly mowed down by a car."

The man stopped smiling. "Yeah?"

Ben nodded. "In your response to my e-mail, you said you've seen this stalker. You said you have surveillance photos of him."

"That's right."

"Well, maybe we can identify him. He murdered Ronald Craig. I'd think you'd want to see this killer brought to justice."

The man stared at Ben, and his smile returned. "Funny. Bringing someone to justice is exactly why I'm here. Speaking for my client, most fathers don't appreciate having their sons stolen out from under them."

"We can get to that in a minute," Ben said. "For now, I'd like to see these photos you have of the stalker."

"Why?" the man asked. "You already know who this *stalker-killer* is. And so do I." He sat back. "You can cut the bullshit. We both know—it's you."

Hannah went through the last of the kitchen drawers. She'd managed to fill two tall trash bags with junk. One drawer had been full of finger paintings and art projects Guy had made at Alphabet Soup Day Care. She didn't want to part with them. At the same time, someone planning to skip town couldn't afford to be sentimental.

She'd sent Joyce home. Guy was feeling better. He sat in bed, playing with an Etch A Sketch that Ben had brought for him earlier today.

The doctor had told her the recovery time for chicken pox was ten to fourteen days. By Saturday, it would be ten days. She didn't want to take chances with Guy's health. But they couldn't risk staying on any longer. They had to leave Saturday. They'd take a cab out of town, stay in a cheap motel, then catch a bus or train heading south, maybe Phoenix, Tucson, or San Diego.

Hannah worked the bottom drawer back in its opening, then glanced at her wristwatch. Nearly six. If all was going smoothly, Ben was wrapping up the meeting with Kenneth right now. But, she knew from experience, things never went smoothly with Kenneth.

She opened the cupboard, and took out a canister of bread crumbs and a packet of elbow macaroni. She was baking a macaroni and cheese souffle tonight, one of Guy's favorites. She'd let him put on his robe and socks, and eat at the kitchen counter; his first meal out of bed in over a week.

The intercom buzzer went off, startling her. It was too soon for Ben to be here already.

Hannah hesitated before picking up the intercom phone. It buzzed again, then again. Whoever was outside must have started leaning on the button, because the buzzer droned continuously.

"Mom?" Guy called from his bedroom.

"It's all right, honey," she called back. "I've got it!"

She snatched up the intercom phone. "Yes? Hello?"

"Hannah? It's Paul," he said anxiously. "Paul Gulletti. I need to see you. Could you buzz me in? It's important."

"Well, I—ah, have people here, friends of mine," she said. "I'll meet you out on the balcony. All right? Come up the stairwell to the third floor."

Hannah pressed the entry button, then hung up the phone. She stepped back into the kitchen. Opening the top kitchen drawer, she pulled out a small steak knife and carefully slipped it into the back pocket of her jeans. She untucked her pullover to cover up the knife handle. Then she grabbed the cordless phone, stepped outside, and closed the door.

Paul came from the stairwell with an envelope in his hand. The customarily laid-back, confident professor now seemed rattled. He was out of breath from running up the three flights. As he came toward her, Hannah instinctively backed away.

"Don't you have class in fifteen minutes?" she asked.

He nodded. "Yeah. I'm double-parked outside. You want a ride there?"

She shook her head. "No, I—as I told you, I have company." She showed him the phone in her hand. "Plus, I'm expecting an important phone call. So—now really isn't a good time, Paul."

"Hannah, listen. I came here because I'm worried about you. I think someone might want to—hurt you."

"Who?" she asked, stealing a glance toward her neighbor's window. No one seemed to be home.

"I don't know," Paul replied. "Someone broke into my office last night, or maybe early this morning. They left these photos of you on my desk."

Paul pulled three black-and-white photographs out of the envelope. Hannah tucked the phone under her arm and studied the pictures. They were shots taken without her knowledge. It was unsettling to view her stalker's handiwork. In two of the photos, she was in front of the store; the third caught her stepping out the lobby door of her apartment building.

"This has happened twice before," she heard Paul say. "Both times with students of mine, women I—women with whom I'd become involved."

Hannah gazed up at him. Paul shrugged. "The first girl was an artist I was seeing named Angela Bramford. Not long after we broke up, I found two photos of Angela on my desk at the college. A couple of days later, someone slipped an envelope under my office door. It had a series of snapshots taken off a television. . . ."

Hannah didn't interrupt him as he described the photos of Marilyn Monroe's death scene from *Niagara*.

"The day after I got those pictures, Angela was strangled. Her body was found near one of the entrances to the Convention Center, beneath three big bells. . . ."

Paul then told her about Rae Palmer, and the next group of candid portraits he'd received. If he was the killer, he was giving away an awful lot.

"The day after I found the pictures of Rae in the pocket of my jacket—hell, I still don't know how they got in there—another envelope was slid under my office door. Seth was with me at the time. I remember having to wait until he left. In the envelope was this horrible murder sequence from *Looking for Mr. Goodbar*."

"What happened to Rae Palmer?" Hannah asked, though she already knew the answer.

Paul frowned. "I have no idea. She disappeared without a trace. But I'm pretty convinced she died like Diane Keaton's character in *Goodbar*. God knows what happened to the body."

"Why haven't you called the police?"

He sighed. "Hannah, I'm a married man. I'm also a professor. I have a newspaper column. I've had books published. I'm a respected man. . . ."

That's not entirely true, Hannah wanted to say. *I don't*

respect you. But she kept her mouth shut and continued to study him. She wanted to see if he was lying.

"When I found those photos of you this morning, it scared the hell out of me. I'm worried about you, Hannah. I've been running around like a crazy man today. I tried to get ahold of you earlier. I stopped by here—and the store. I'm pretty sure someone was following me."

Hannah said nothing. Apparently, Paul had felt Ben's presence.

"Listen," he said. "Do whatever you have to do; buy a gun, or leave town, or get police protection. I'd go to the police myself, but I can't get involved in this. I have a marriage and a reputation to protect."

Hannah bit her lip. She couldn't very well criticize his reluctance to go to the police. "You don't have any idea who might be behind these murders?" she asked finally. "None at all?"

Paul shrugged.

"Well, what about Seth?" Hannah asked. "He knew both victims. He knows me. And he knows movies. He'd have access to your office, too."

"But he was in my office when the *Goodbar* photos were slipped under the door."

"So? His roommate probably delivered the pictures. They're probably working together on this."

"What roommate? Seth doesn't have a roommate."

"Yes, he does," Hannah argued. "I've met him."

Paul frowned. "That's news to me. I was sure Seth lived alone."

Hannah glanced at her wristwatch, then tucked the photos in her back pocket. She felt the knife there. "You'll be late for class," she said. "Could you do me a favor? Can you get me a copy of that book you helped write, *Darkness, Light, and Shadow?* I want to read your essay. Seth claims he wrote it."

Paul put on an indignant look and started to shake his

head. "Seth merely contributed a few notes," he said, with an uneasy laugh. "That's *my* essay. I wrote it."

Hannah studied him. For the first time tonight, she could see he was lying. Did that mean all the rest of it was the truth?

"Could you just get me a copy of that book as soon as possible?" she heard herself say.

"Is there anything else you want?" he asked. "Isn't there anything I can do?"

"Yes, let me know when you get the next series of photos," Hannah steadily replied. "I'd like to know how I'm supposed to die."

"What the hell are you talking about?" Ben asked.

The man with the goatee took another sip of his martini. "We know it's you out there, watching her every move—and watching us. And when you're not doing that, you're doing *her*. You're fucking her, aren't you? Don't you ever sleep? She's got you jumping through hoops, doesn't she, buddy?"

Ben shook his head. "Listen, you're way off base." He glanced around at the other people in the bar, then lowered his voice. "I'm no murderer. Hell, I contacted you and set up this meeting to *warn* you. I'm trying to prevent another murder from happening."

"Seems more like a threat than a warning," the man retorted.

"Have you actually seen this guy?" Ben asked. "You said you have surveillance photos of him. Well, let's see them. Show me some pictures of *me* stalking her."

The man with the goatee just shook his head.

"He still hasn't denied that he's fucking her."

Ben turned in his chair to stare at the man seated behind him. With his thin face, prominent nose, and receding wavy hair, the man's looks were borderline ugly. He wore a sweater that looked expensive and imported. He gave Ben a cocky grin.

"You're Kenneth Woodley," Ben murmured.

Kenneth got up and brought his chair to their table. He dropped a few photographs in front of Ben, then took his martini and sat down. "Well, you're not quite as stupid as you look," he told Ben. "Though you misspelled *rendezvous* in your last e-mail, doofus."

Ben looked at the photos. They were all taken at night. In each one, there was a phantomlike figure that couldn't be identified. The pictures reminded him of those photos Kennedy assassination experts showed of the grassy knoll, with blurred objects that could be killers lurking in the bushes.

"This isn't me in these pictures," Ben muttered. He reached into his pocket, then pulled out the Polaroid of Seth—along with Paul's photo from his review column. "Here. Do either of these guys look familiar?"

Kenneth glanced at the photos for a moment, then shoved them across the table to his private detective friend.

"The younger guy just started working with her at the video store," Kirkabee explained. "The other one I don't know about."

"So tell me the truth," Ben said. "Have you ever gotten a good look at this stalker?"

Kenneth smirked. "No, you've managed to elude us until now."

"Goddamn it," Ben hissed. "I'm not the guy."

"I don't scare easily," Kenneth went on. "The only reason I responded to your threatening e-mails was mere curiosity—"

"That wasn't a threat," Ben cut in. "It was a warning that—"

"I wanted to meet you and see just how far that sorry bitch has sunk," Kenneth continued. "Nice arrangement, huh? She spreads her legs for you, and you do her talking for her. I was going to say you do her *killing* for her, but now that I've met you, I don't think you have the balls or the smarts to pull off a good hit. She probably hired someone else to mow down Ron Craig, didn't she?"

"Jesus Christ," Ben muttered. "You're delusional. Haven't you listened to a word I'm saying?"

Kenneth nodded to his private detective, then got to his feet. Kirkabee gathered up the photographs.

"You're the one who's going to listen to me," Kenneth whispered, leaning over the table. "Next time you fuck that bitch, it'll be a conjugal visit in a federal penitentiary. So long, doofus."

The two men headed for the front door. Ben threw a few dollars on the table, then hurried out after them. A gust of cold night air hit him. The restaurant was right on the water. Kenneth and the private investigator were walking ahead, winding toward the parking garage on the land side.

"Are you actually going to press charges against her?" Ben called out. He caught up with them. "Do you want it coming out in court that you beat the hell out of that woman? She ran away to protect herself—and her son."

Kenneth whispered something to Kirkabee. They stopped and turned to look at him in front of the garage entrance.

"No jury would convict her," Ben continued. "There are hospital records. She's got scars. I've seen them. Listen, she's willing to meet with you on Saturday and talk this out. You'll have a chance to see your son—"

"Shut him up," Kenneth muttered to his private investigator.

All at once, Kirkabee slammed his fist across Ben's jaw.

Ben reeled back against the garage wall. The searing pain rushed over his face. He was blinded, and for a moment all he saw was white. But he heard Kenneth say *"I'll see my son tonight. As for Hannah, she might just chalk up another stay in the hospital."*

Ben felt someone step behind him and grab his arms with a talonlike grip. Still blinded by the sucker punch, he tried to struggle. He had just started to see again when Kenneth Woodley came into focus. He slapped Ben across the face with the back of his hand. Then he stepped forward and shoved his knee up into Ben's groin.

"Let him go," he grumbled.

Ben collapsed to the pavement. He couldn't breathe. Lying on his side, he curled up in a fetal position. He watched Kenneth Woodley and his detective friend heading back toward the water, down to the marina.

He realized one of the boats docked outside the restaurant was theirs.

Ben finally caught a breath, and then another. Lifting his head from the pavement, he felt something warm trickling down his face. He realized his mouth and nose were bleeding. He pulled himself up and staggered a few feet until the dizziness overpowered him. He grabbed onto a post and tried to focus on Kenneth Woodley and the private investigator.

They were on the deck of a yacht, with Woodley at the helm, barking orders at Kirkabee. They started to move away from the dock.

"NO! DON'T!" Ben yelled.

Frustrated and helpless, Ben watched the boat arc around the restaurant toward the open water.

He backtracked toward the garage and ran through the parking lot near the marina. He tried to follow the course of Kenneth's yacht as it glided across the silver-black water. He figured they must have been headed for another dock off Lake Union.

Ben didn't try to call to them. They were too far away. But he could still see Kenneth at the wheel and Kirkabee sitting near him, pulling at the rope lines. Ben could see the white and blue sail starting to ascend against the dark horizon.

Then he saw the flash, the first spark.

The explosion seemed to light up the sky. Flames and debris shot fifty feet in the air. Smoke plumes belched from the center of the yacht.

Ben's ears rang from the loud detonation, yet he thought

he heard a bloodcurdling scream. He saw someone aboard what was left of that yacht, and the man was on fire. It might have been Kenneth. Ben wasn't certain. That burning, flailing figure was like a ghost amid the flames.

A second blast ripped through the boat, tearing the scorched, sinking vessel into pieces—along with its two passengers.

Twenty

Hannah hadn't expected to cry.

But after Ben had called from a gas station and told her about the boat explosion, she hung up the phone and burst into tears. She kept wondering why she was crying over the death of someone who had made her so miserable for so many years. Kenneth was a son of a bitch, but she hadn't wanted him to die.

Maybe she was crying for herself—for the poor, stupid waitress/actress who had just lost her father, and who had fallen for a cocky, charming man she'd known was all wrong for her. She'd had such great hopes back then, such potential. Perhaps Hannah was finally allowing herself to mourn for that young woman, and everything Kenneth Woodley had done to her. Whatever the reason, she wept for almost an hour, stepping out to the balcony much of the time so Guy wouldn't hear.

Ben came back around eight o'clock. Hannah gasped at the sight of him. One side of his handsome face was swollen, and his shirt was splattered with blood.

While he was washing up, Hannah went into Guy's room and told him that Ben had fallen off a bicycle. That didn't stop Guy from cringing—then crying—when he saw Ben's battered face a few minutes later. Ben stayed with him a while and managed to calm him down.

Hannah retreated to the kitchen, where she warmed up some of her macaroni and cheese souffle. She also loaded

two Ziploc bags full of ice; one for Ben's face, and the other
to assuage the pain from a strike below the belt. Typical
Kenneth.

"He's sleeping," Ben announced, coming from the hallway. He winced a bit as he sat down at the counter.

"Here," Hannah said, handing him the impromptu ice
bags. "One's for your face, and the other one's for your—
whatevers."

"My whatevers thank you," Ben said, putting one ice bag
between his legs, then holding the other to his jaw. "I tried
that choo-choo-train routine with Guy, the one you do to
help him fall asleep. And it worked. He's really sweet, Hannah. Rest assured, there's none of his dad in him."

Hannah removed a saucepan from the burner. "I have
vegetables steaming," she said. "They need a few more minutes. I'll get lost, go clean the bathroom or something. Why
don't you call your wife?"

"Did Jennifer call here?"

"No," Hannah said. "But you should call her. She helped
you set up that meeting. She knows it was dangerous. She's
probably worried."

"You don't mind?" he asked.

She took the cordless phone out of its cradle and handed
it to him. "Call her."

Hannah headed down the hallway. She went into Guy's
room and tidied up while he slept. She could hear Ben talking on the phone, but tried not to listen. In a strange way, she
was glad he hadn't thought to call his wife. It gave her a
chance to be noble. After playing house with Ben Podowski
for the last two nights, this was a good reality check for both
of them.

Still, a couple of minutes later, as she tossed some things
in the bathroom hamper, Hannah couldn't help catching part
of his conversation with Jennifer.

"No, I can't," Ben was saying. "Not for few more days. It
could even be a few more weeks. . . . No, she's leaving town
very soon, but I need to stay. I'm involved in this now. . . . I'll

know more later. Either way, I can't leave, honey. . . . Well, I know, but I'm not going anywhere until I find out who's responsible for Rae. . . . I'll talk to you tomorrow, okay? Get some sleep, honey. Thanks again—for everything."

Hannah felt a little tug at her heart. She'd wanted a reality check, but hearing him call Jennifer "honey" was a little too real.

Clearing her throat, Hannah started up the hallway. She turned the corner in time to see Ben put down the cordless phone.

"You were right," he sighed. "Jennifer said she was freaking out over this meeting. She was hoping I'd call."

Hannah walked around to the other side of the counter. "It's nice to have someone to worry about you at times," she said, serving up his dinner. She set the plate in front of him. "Think you can chew without it hurting?"

"I'll give it a try," he said, putting aside the ice bag and picking up his fork. "Thanks, Hannah. This looks great."

She poured each of them a glass of wine. "After all the phoning and e-mailing back and forth, now there's this boat explosion. They're going to think I arranged it." Hannah sighed. "How much time do you think we have before the police are banging on that door?"

"There wasn't much left of the boat," Ben said, frowning. "It might take a few hours to connect the yacht to Kenneth—and then to Kirkabee. Chances are pretty good Kirkabee already gave his agency your name and address, Hannah." He took a sip of wine. "My guess is we might be okay here tonight. But you'd be pushing your luck to stay on any longer than noon tomorrow."

"God," she murmured. "Everything's closing in at the same time." Hannah reached on top of the refrigerator, where she'd stashed the photos Paul Gulletti had given her. She set them near Ben's plate. "I think these pictures mean he's very close to killing me."

Ben studied the pictures.

"Paul came by tonight and delivered those," Hannah said. "He found them on his desk this morning—"

"You let him in while you were alone here with Guy?" Ben asked. "Hannah, you shouldn't have taken a chance like that—"

"I don't think it's Paul," she cut in. "He told me about the photos we found in his desk. Someone has been leaving those pictures for him in weird places—under his office door, in his coat pocket. It's a pattern. First come the candid shots of the girl; then, a day or two later, the pictures from a movie murder. And after that, it happens for real—to the girl in the candids."

"So why didn't he call the police?" Ben asked.

"He's married, Ben. He's afraid. He was involved with the first two victims."

"So you think it's Seth?"

She frowned. "I want to read this essay he wrote for Paul. Maybe I can figure out his way of thinking. I have a hunch the other murders—those two rude customers, Ronald Craig and Britt, Kenneth and the other private detective, even the attempt on your life—I have a feeling those people were killed as part of some weird manipulative game he was playing with me."

"I don't understand," Ben said, putting the ice pack on his cheek again.

"I think the explanation might be in this essay Seth wrote and Paul ripped off. It's in a book called *Darkness, Light, and Shadow*. Paul said he'd try to get me a copy."

"I don't think you'll have time for that, Hannah. You need to leave here tomorrow."

Hannah started to refill his wineglass.

Ben shook his head. "No more for me, thanks," he said. "In fact, I could use some coffee—if you don't mind making it. I need to step out again."

"Where are you going?"

He glanced at his wristwatch. "There's still another hour of class. Seth won't be home for a while. His roommate could be out, too. This might be a good time to take a look at that garage apartment of his. Maybe Seth has a copy of the book you're talking about."

Ben lowered the ice bag from his face. "And I'd also like to check out his collection of home videos."

He stopped to catch his breath as he stood in front of the Tudor estate on Aloha Street. Ben started down the long driveway toward the garage. He could see his breath in the cold night air. Most of the trees surrounding the estate had lost their leaves already, and the old mansion seemed rather sinister against the indigo sky. There was a light in one of the upstairs windows, but it didn't look like anybody was home. It was so deathly quiet, he could hear the wind whistling through those naked trees.

All at once, a dog started barking. Ben froze for a moment. He glanced over at the main house. A light went on over the front door, and Ben quickly ducked into some bushes at the side of the driveway. The dog's incessant yelping continued.

Ben waited, and watched the front of the house. After a couple of minutes, the dog finally shut up. Ben crept out of the bushes, but then two cars—one after another—sped down Aloha Street. He almost jumped back into the shrubbery, yet his feet stayed rooted on the pavement.

Ben made his way down the driveway, hovering close to the bushes. He studied the darkened windows on the side of the house. He kept expecting to see a figure standing in one of them—or perhaps a curtain moving. But he didn't notice anything.

In the mansion's shadow, the garage area was dark. Ben glanced over his shoulder at the back of the house. He saw lights in three of the upstairs windows, but no sign of life.

He grabbed hold of the stairway bannister on the side of the garage. "Shit," he muttered. Small wonder Seth didn't break his neck going up and down the rickety stairs in the dark.

Each step squeaked as Ben made his way toward the landing at the apartment's entry. It was too much to hope for an unlocked door, but he tried it anyway. No luck. Pulling his credit card from his wallet, he worked it around the lock area. He thought a burglar alarm might go off at any moment, but apparently Seth and his roommate felt they had nothing worth stealing.

Ben gave up and put his Visa back in his wallet. He stopped to stare at a window about three feet from the other side of the landing's bannister. It had been left open a crack.

He moved over to the edge of the landing, then threw one leg over the railing. The bannister let out a loud creak. As Ben tried to grab at the windowsill, he felt the railing give way beneath him. He quickly pulled back and braced against the door.

Another car sped by on Aloha Street, and for a moment its headlights swept across the driveway, down toward the garage.

Shaken, Ben didn't move. He peered back at the house again. It occurred to him that they were probably used to a certain amount of noise back here. Two single men in their twenties lived in this garage apartment. The two roommates probably came and went at all hours. How many times had they locked themselves out? Or did they have an extra key someplace?

Ben reached up for the ledge above the doorway, patting the length of it. Nothing. And there wasn't a key under the doormat. Frowning, Ben glanced down the stairs. By the bottom step was a flowerpot with a dead plant in it.

He crept down the creaky stairs. Each squeak underfoot seemed amplified in the still night. He finally reached the bottom of the stairs. He moved aside the heavy flowerpot, and found a key.

Skulking back up the steps, Ben prayed the key would open Seth's door.

It worked.

The apartment was warm, and a bit smelly—like a poorly

vented locker room: sweat, testosterone, and dirty clothes.
Closing the door behind him, Ben waited for a minute for
his eyes to adjust to the darkness.

He stood in the living room. A newspaper was strewn on
one end of the Salvation Army sofa, and a couple of beer
cans littered the coffee table, along with copies of *Premiere*
magazine and *Entertainment Weekly*.

Ben saw a stack of videos by the TV. He checked the boxes.
Six videos had Emerald City Video labels on them, and two
of these were porn movies. There were store-bought, slightly
beat-up copies of *Goodfellas* and *Apocalypse Now*. Three unlabeled videos rounded out his collection.

Peering out the window, Ben checked the house and the
driveway. He decided to take a chance, and switched on one
of the living-room lamps. He had stay low now; he couldn't
afford to be seen in the window. He switched on the TV and
turned the volume to mute.

Popping the first unlabeled video into the VCR, Ben wasn't
sure what he'd see; perhaps some surveillance of Hannah, or
maybe Rae's death, or even someone else's murder.

What Ben saw was an old *Seinfeld* rerun. He pressed fast-
forward, then stopped in several places on the tape. All he
came up with were a couple of other old sitcoms and part of
a *Saturday Night Live*.

Ben found more of the same with the other two unlabeled
tapes. He spent over a half hour reviewing them. But he
didn't just watch the TV. He also checked the brick-and-
board bookshelf for more videos and the book Hannah had
wanted. No luck. He unearthed an envelope full of photos,
but none of Hannah or Rae; no surveillance shots. They
were snapshots of Seth and his roommate—on a hike with
some other guys, and at the beach with a cute girl who
seemed to be the roommate's girlfriend. Ben also searched
the front hall closet and kitchen cabinets, but he didn't find
anything.

Switching off the television, he went into the bedroom.
There was only one bed for the two of them. Ben didn't

think they were gay. The porn tapes from the store indicated that the two roommates weren't lovers. And if there was any room for doubt, when Ben checked under the bed, he uncovered several *Playboy* and *Hustler* magazines. He figured one of the guys must sleep on the sofa.

He glanced at the clock on the nightstand. It was past ten-twenty. Seth might be home at any minute.

Still, Ben kept looking—in the dresser drawers, the closet, and the built-in linen cabinet in the bathroom. If Seth Stroud had a secret collection of videos, camera equipment, and photographs, they weren't here in this apartment.

Ben switched off the overhead in the bathroom, then returned to the living room. All at once, a beam of light swept through the windows. Ben heard a car.

He quickly ducked down. He could hear loose gravel and pebbles crunching under tires as the car came up the drive. His heart racing, he stayed crouched near the floor. There was no other way out, except for those stairs. He'd break his neck if he tried to climb out the bedroom window.

The dog started barking again.

Ben could hear muted music on the car radio, some oldies station; then the engine stopped purring. The headlights died. A car door clicked open. Then another door.

"Well, I don't want to walk him," a woman was saying. The car door shut. "Besides, Kaiser will only do a number two for you, honey."

"Yeah, I bring out the best in him," the husband replied. Another door shut. "You don't suppose Phoebe or Chad walked him, do you?"

"Huh, dream on . . ."

Their voices faded as they walked up the driveway toward the house.

Ben let out a sigh. He wanted to get out of there before Seth or his roommate came back. But now he had to wait for that man to walk his dog and return home. Maybe then they'd turn off the front light.

With a shaky hand, Ben reached up and switched off the

lamp in the living room. He would wait on the floor, in the dark. He'd already searched the place. He wasn't going to find anything. He had a feeling they were wrong about Seth Stroud.

Hannah was in her bedroom, packing a second suitcase. She planned to leave tomorrow morning.

She'd called Dr. Donnellan, explaining there was a family emergency in Portland. And did he think—after nine days, and no residual fever or symptoms—that Guy was all right to travel? He'd given a cautionary okay for the commute, so long as Guy was kept comfortable, warm, and as isolated as possible. Hannah had decided to take a cab down to Tacoma. She'd lay low in a cheap hotel for a couple of days. Then they'd take a train to Portland or Eugene, maybe even further south. Guy liked trains.

The intercom buzzed. Ben had been gone for over ninety minutes, and she hoped it was him. She wasn't expecting anyone else—unless the police worked even faster than she and Ben had figured.

Hannah grabbed the intercom phone. "Yes, hello?"

"Hi, it's Paul. I brought that film book you wanted. Can I come up?"

Hannah hesitated. "Ah, sure. Just a sec." She pressed the entry button, then hung up the phone. Retrieving the small knife from the kitchen drawer, Hannah hid it in her back pocket again. She unlocked the door, stepped outside, and closed the door behind her.

Paul came from the stairwell. He looked more relaxed this time around, and even had a confident stride to his walk as he approached her. Hannah noticed the book in his hand.

"Do you still have company?" he asked, handing her the book.

She nodded. "Yes. Thanks for bringing this, Paul."

"I missed you in class tonight," he said. "You know who else wasn't there? That Ben What's-his-name."

She shrugged. "Well, thanks again, Paul." She reached for the door.

He stepped toward her, then glanced in the window. "Could I come in for a drink? I'd like to meet these friends of yours."

Hannah wrinkled her nose. "Now's not a good time."

He smiled. "You don't really have people over, do you?"

Hannah hesitated.

"Are you afraid of me, Hannah?" He smiled. "I just want to help you." He reached over and touched her face.

She backed against the door. "Paul, I do have someone here right now. He's—um, spending the night."

He frowned. "Is it that Ben character?"

"That's really none of your business," she said quietly. "Anyway, thank you for the book—"

"Hannah, I wouldn't trust him if I were you—"

"I'm all right," she said, cutting him off. "Okay, Paul? Good night."

Shaking his head, he turned and started for the stairwell.

Hannah ducked back inside, and locked the door. She slipped the knife out of her back pocket and set it on the kitchen counter. She glanced at the book's cover. *Darkness, Light, and Shadow: Essays on Film* was emblazoned across a series of celluloid strips. Hannah anxiously flipped through the book until she found the piece Paul had stolen from Seth. It was on page 216: *Objects of Obsession: Directors and Their Leading Ladies, Essay by Paul Gulletti.*

Hannah began reading:

> *In Alfred Hitchcock's masterpiece,* Vertigo, *Scottie Ferguson's (James Stewart) unquenchable obsession for the blond, enigmatic Madeleine (Kim Novak) leads to a Kafkaesque courtship, ultimately realized in Madeleine's apparent suicide, her resurrection through a surrogate—the shop girl, Judy (Novak again)—and finally Judy's death. It is one of Hitchcock's most personal films, and a parallel to the director's own obsession with certain leading ladies.*

Hitchcock is unquestionably not alone in this phenomenon. Observe, among others, Chaplin, Von Sternberg, Bunuel, Preminger, and Polanski in their personal as well as cinematic relationships with particular actresses, especially those whom they have discovered, groomed, and introduced in their films. Master puppeteers pulling the strings on their beautiful marionettes, these master directors . . .

Hannah shook her head and sighed. "God, what a snooze." Somewhere, amid the heavy-handed writing and paragraph-long sentences, was a possible explanation for what was happening to her. She read on, and found something in the fifth paragraph:

Just as Marilyn Monroe was known to "make love to the camera," the greatest directors use their camera to make love to their leading ladies. They are the voyeurs, guardians, and manipulators of these screen goddesses. Often, they became executioners as well, killing off the objects of their obsession in their movies. . . .

Hannah grabbed a piece of paper and scribbled down the words *voyeur . . . guardian . . . manipulator . . . executioner.*

Those were the roles her secret admirer had taken on with her. He made love to her with his camera. And that camera would be focused on her when he carried out her execution.

Hannah started reading again. But the intercom buzzed once more, catching her off guard. She put down the book. Without thinking, Hannah grabbed the intercom phone. "Ben?"

"Hannah, it's me again, Paul," he said urgently. "Let me in."

"What?"

"It's important! C'mon, buzz me up."

"Paul, I told you—"

"Hannah, please," he said. "Something just happened,

and I need to talk with you *now.* We can meet out on the balcony again. I don't care. Just buzz me in, goddamn it."

"All right," she said. Against all her better judgment, Hannah pressed the entry button. She ran down the hall to Guy's room to make sure he was asleep. Then she hurried back toward the door, stopping for a moment to grab the knife off the counter. She concealed it in her back pocket again.

Paul was already halfway down the balcony walkway when she stepped outside. He was frazzled, and breathing hard. Hannah noticed he had some photos in his hand.

"What's going on?" she whispered. "You know, my neighbors just called to complain about us talking out here—"

"I don't give a shit," he said, interrupting her lie. He showed her the photos. His hand was shaking. "I found these in my car just now."

Hannah numbly stared at the pictures, two high-quality photocopies on card-stock paper: a series of shots off a TV screen, about forty smaller images in sequential order showing Janet Leigh being stabbed in the *Psycho* shower. Hannah remembered Scott telling her early last week that the store copy of *Psycho* had been stolen.

"I think he's out there now," she heard Paul say. "I locked my car earlier. I don't know how he got in. I was only up here talking with you for—what, a couple of minutes?" Paul glanced down toward the parking lot. "I'll bet you anything he's watching us."

Hannah was gazing at one of the small photos: Janet Leigh wincing as she tried to fight off her attacker, the knife just a blur in front of her.

"You realize what this means?" Paul asked, pointing to the photos. "Once he gives me a photo of the movie murder, it's not long before . . ." He trailed off.

"Before I end up dying just like this," Hannah murmured. "But no one will know—except maybe the girl after me. He'll videotape my murder in the shower, then make sure his next leading lady sees it."

"What are you talking about?" Paul asked, snapping Hannah out of her stupor. "What girl? Whose leading lady?"

"I'm talking about the next girl you'll be screwing around with, Paul," she replied, frowning at him. "Your next 'favorite student,' my replacement. Can't you see the pattern? These are women you've been involved with—or, in my case, a woman you wanted. We've all become his leading ladies, his victims, *Objects of Obsession*."

He shook his head. "Hannah, I've had nothing to do with any of this—"

"No, you just keep moving on to the next one," Hannah said. "And you don't look back. If no one found out, it didn't happen, right?"

He was still shaking his head. "I don't understand what you're talking about. But listen, if you don't want to go to the police, maybe you should pack up and get out of town, go stay with some old friends, someplace where you know you'll be safe."

She backed toward the door. "Thanks, Paul. You can go now."

"Hannah, please—"

Ducking inside, she closed the door on him, then locked it.

Her back to the door, Hannah suddenly realized that she was stepping right into her killer's trap. Tomorrow she would leave Seattle a fugitive, and stay the night in a cheap roadside motel.

It was just what Janet Leigh had done in *Psycho*.

Crouched down at the foot of the stairs, Ben put Seth's key back under the flowerpot. He had watched the owner of the house, a stocky man with red hair, return from walking the dog. Now, only two of the windows were lit up in the big house. It was almost eleven o'clock.

Ben started up the driveway, past the car, a Dodge Caravan. He glanced over his shoulder toward the garage, and stopped. He wondered if the family let Seth store anything in their garage. They didn't seem to use it for parking their car.

Skulking back toward garage, Ben found the side door, and tried the handle. It wasn't locked. He stepped into the dark two-car garage. It was crammed with so much junk there was no room for a car. A dim shaft of light came from a window on the opposite wall. Ben could make out silhouettes of bicycles, a lawnmower, rakes, brooms, a broken chair on top of a table, old lawn furniture. But he couldn't see anything else.

Ben noticed the light switch by the door. There was no window along the wall where he stood. No one from the house would know the garage light was on. He decided to take a chance, and flicked on the switch.

All at once, he heard a click, then a loud mechanical humming noise. The light went on, and the garage door started to yawn open.

"Jesus," Ben murmured, flicking the switch again. The gears shifted noisily. The light from the garage had already spread out to the driveway. But the descending door started to block it out again.

Ben knew he would have to make a run for it. He quickly glanced around the garage while the light was still on, taking everything in before it became dark again. He saw an old kiddie pool, more lawn equipment, old cans of paint stacked up; but no file cabinets or mysterious boxes—nothing where somebody might be storing some secret videotapes or photographs. No one would leave expensive video equipment in such a dusty, unkempt place.

The garage light went out.

Ben opened the door a crack and peered back at the house. No change: the same two windows with lights on. Everything was quiet again.

Slowly he opened the door and stepped outside. In the distance, he could hear a siren. He crept around to the front of the garage. Looking up at the house again, Ben noticed someone at one of the windows. He ducked behind the car.

The wail of the police siren grew louder, closer.

Ben carefully peered above the hood of the Dodge Caravan. He could still see someone in the window. It was the stocky, red-haired man, and he seemed to be looking out toward the garage. He finally turned away, then disappeared from view.

Staying low, Ben darted from behind the car to the bushes at the side of the driveway. It sounded as if the police car or fire truck was coming up Aloha Street. He glanced back to see if he could escape into the neighboring yard. A tall chain-link fence divided the properties.

The siren was deafening now. The trees and houses along Aloha were bathed by a swirling red strobe. He held his breath as the squad car sped past the old Tudor mansion, then continued up the block.

He waited another minute. Staying close to the tall shrubs at the side of the driveway, Ben hurried to the street. Then he started back toward Hannah's.

She hadn't quite fallen asleep, but she felt herself drifting off. Hannah was lying on the sofa with her head resting on Ben's lap. He'd covered her with a blanket. From his breathing, just a decibel away from snoring, she guessed he'd nodded off an hour ago. They were both still dressed. It might have been more comfortable in her bed, but she didn't feel right about that. At the same time, she needed to be with him. Perhaps they were meant to be uncomfortable tonight, a reminder that he was going back to his wife, and in a few hours she would be leaving town.

Ben had been upset with her for letting Paul come by a second and third time tonight. Having found no evidence whatsoever in Seth's apartment, Ben was now convinced that Paul was the killer.

Perhaps he was right. Though Seth claimed to have written the essay, it was Paul's name on the piece.

The article kept focusing on the director's courtship-by-camera with the objects of his obsession. Once again, the author mentioned four stages to this type of fixation, with the director as voyeur, protector, manipulator, and finally, executioner.

Ben had said it was a bit far-fetched to assume someone would commit a series of murders based on some theory about film directors.

"What about Charles Manson basing mass murder on the Beatles song 'Helter Skelter'?" Hannah had pointed out.

Ben had been worried about her going off alone tomorrow, repeating all of Janet Leigh's movements in *Psycho*. He'd mentioned possibly accompanying her—or at least following her to make certain she was safe.

Hannah wondered whether or not it would be easier for the three of them to "disappear" together. Part of her felt the need to end things with Ben now, and just move on. She and Guy had already become too attached to him. She was used to being alone—even when it was scary.

Hannah listened to Ben's breathing. There was a comfort to that sound, and she felt herself drifting off.

Suddenly, a loud banging jolted her awake. Startled, Ben nearly knocked her off the sofa.

"My God, what's happening?" Hannah whispered. It took them both a moment to realize someone was pounding on the door.

All at once, Guy let out a shriek.

Hannah bolted off the couch and ran down the hall to his room. She flicked on the light switch.

Guy was sitting up in bed. He'd already thrown back the covers. He was still screaming.

Hannah ran to him, and took him in her arms. Hugging her son, she anxiously glanced around the room.

The pounding outside had stopped.

"What happened, honey? Are you okay?" she asked, trying to get her breath.

Guy pressed his face against her stomach. "A lion was chasing me," he cried, the words muffled.

Hannah heard the locks clicking on the front door. "Ben?" she called nervously.

"I'm just checking things out," he answered.

Her hand trembling, Hannah stroked Guy's hair. "You just had a bad dream, honey. That's all." She waited until she heard the front door close, the locks clicking once more. "Ben?" she called again.

A moment later, he appeared in Guy's doorway. He held up a videocassette in his hand, the label turned in her direction. "They left this," he whispered. "It's *Vertigo.*"

It was another forty-five minutes before Guy was asleep once again. Hannah had taken his temperature: 98.5. Ben had read him some Dr. Suess. Then Hannah had fallen back on her standard choo-choo routine to lull him to dreamland.

Hannah switched off the light in Guy's room. Ben picked up the *Vertigo* tape, which he'd left on the floor in the hall, outside Guy's door.

"I don't understand," he whispered. "Didn't you tell me that Gulletti showed you the shower scene from *Psycho?* Why is he giving us a tape of *Vertigo?* "

Hannah shrugged. "Maybe he showed me those pictures to throw me off. I don't know." Hannah switched on a light in the living room. "That essay in the film book kept mentioning *Vertigo* again and again. Maybe this is his way of making a point to me about something."

Ben frowned. "It was weird, him pounding on the door like that. It's as if he wants us to see this now—right away."

"He did something like this before when he tried to kill you. You know, the *Bugsy* reenactment? He even phoned to tell me it was about to happen." Hannah took the video from him. "This has that same kind of urgency to it. I think this murder will happen very soon. And I've seen *Vertigo*. Someone will die in a fall."

Hannah put the *Vertigo* cassette in her VCR. The tape was cued to start with James Stewart chasing Kim Novak up the stairs of a church bell tower.

Hannah knew the movie, and she knew the scene. Stewart wouldn't make it to the top; he couldn't save her. And the object of his obsession would plunge to her death.

Twenty-one

"I know you sometimes go to church before you come over here," Hannah was saying into the phone. "I was just wondering if you were planning to do that this morning."

"Oh, I don't think so, honey," Joyce replied. "My, you're calling awfully early. You're up with the roosters. Is everything okay there?"

"Well, actually, I'm a little worried. I got a strange phone call. I'd feel a lot better if you didn't go out this morning. Let Ben come over and walk you back here, okay?"

"Good Lord, Hannah," she sighed. "I'll be safe for a half a block in broad daylight."

"So—humor me, okay?"

Hannah couldn't think of any women friends besides Joyce or Tish who might have been tagged for Kim Novak's *Vertigo* death. At the same time, both Tish and Joyce were heavyset women, and she couldn't quite imagine anyone successfully dragging either one of them up a church tower staircase with a hundred-plus steps.

"All right, I'll stay put," Joyce agreed. "I didn't have a lot of social plans set before seven-thirty this morning anyway. Tell Dreamboat Ben I'll be here—waiting for him."

After Hannah hung up, Ben asked if she really needed Joyce to baby-sit today. "Aren't you leaving in about two and a half hours?"

"Oh, I forgot." Hannah rubbed her forehead. Then she

poured herself another cup of coffee. "Force of habit. Well, I want Guy to say good-bye to her anyway."

"A lot of good-byes this morning," Ben remarked.

He'd tried to talk Hannah into letting him go with her. But Hannah's mind had been made up. She and Guy were traveling by themselves. They needed to cut all ties and disappear.

Nevertheless, Ben had made her promise to contact him tonight and let him know that she and Guy were okay. She could call or leave a message for him at the Best Western Executive Inn, where he'd made reservations for the evening.

They watched the local six A.M. news for an update on Kenneth's death. It was the fifth featured news story. *"Police investigators are still baffled over the cause of a yacht explosion last night on Lake Union,"* the pretty anchorwoman announced. In a box behind her, Seattle police were shown on a tugboat, raking in bits of floating debris. *"So far, investigators have recovered the remains of two passengers who were aboard the yacht. The boat was a twenty-nine-foot Sloop rented from a Westlake marina chartering company. According to KING-Five News sources, police are very close to identifying the victims. But the cause of the blast is still a mystery. Stay with us for continuing coverage. . . ."*

Hannah was leaving town just in time. If all went well, by this afternoon she would be in another city, checked into a hotel under a different name. She might even persuade Guy to take a nap, and catch a little shut-eye herself.

Guy woke up at seven-fifteen. He had no fever, and not even a remnant of chicken pox on him. He was brushing his teeth when Ben left to pick up Joyce.

Hannah stood in the bathroom doorway and watched him on his tiptoes at the sink. He wore a plaid robe over his pajamas.

"Honey, we're going on a trip today," she said, folding her arms. "It'll be fun, kind of an adventure."

"Is Ben coming too?" Guy asked, his mouth full of Colgate.

"No, honey. Ben has to stay here and work. It'll just be you and me."

Hannah watched him overfill the bathroom tumbler with water and rinse out his mouth. Some of it got down the front of his robe and on the bathroom floor. Hannah took a hand towel and wiped him off. "Now, we'll be in a taxicab for a while today," she explained, crouched down in front of him. "So I want you to tell me if you're feeling tired or sick or anything. Okay?"

He rubbed his eye. "Okay, Mom."

"Joyce is coming over in a couple of minutes, and I think you're well enough to give her a big hug. Make it a great big one, because you won't be seeing her for a while."

Guy was still in his pajamas and robe, sitting at the kitchen counter and eating his Capt'n Crunch, when Ben returned with Joyce. She made a fuss over the fact that Guy was out of bed and looking well again. Then she noticed the suitcases in the hallway. "What's this?" she asked. "Is somebody going on a trip?"

"C'mon, Guy," Ben cut in. "I'll help you get dressed."

Hannah waited until Ben took Guy back into his room. "Actually, Guy and I are taking off for a couple of weeks," she explained, pouring herself more coffee. "Some friends of mine in Yakima wanted us to come visit—"

"Well, do you think it's okay for him to travel, honey?" Joyce asked, setting her purse on the counter.

"The doctor said Guy should be all right as long as he takes it easy. What do you think, Joyce? I mean, you've had kids with chicken pox. He looks pretty healthy now, doesn't he?"

"I suppose he'll be okay," she muttered, obviously confused. "Isn't this all rather sudden?"

"Yeah, it's been crazy," Hannah said, walking around the counter. She retrieved a large box she'd loaded and set beside the suitcases in the hallway. "I was cleaning all night. I do that before taking a trip. Anyway, I want you to have these things, sort of a thank-you for working overtime this week." Hannah placed the box on the sofa.

Mystified, Joyce started to shift through the items, which included, among other things, a quilted blanket she adored and always pulled out on cold nights, a framed photo of Guy, Hannah's tea kettle, and a Waterford vase she clearly coveted.

"I can't take any of this," Joyce said, her eyes welling up. "Honey, I've told you before, this is Waterford. It's worth at least three hundred dollars."

"And I've told you, I got the vase for twenty at a flea market. I know you like it, Joyce. Make me happy and take it, okay?"

"Oh, I couldn't, I just couldn't."

"Well, force yourself," Hannah said, setting the vase back in the box.

Joyce stopped to glance around the living room. "Where are all the family pictures?" she asked.

"Oh, I—put them away," Hannah answered. "I didn't want them to get sun-faded."

Joyce studied her for a moment with her sharp, old eyes. "You're not coming back, are you?" she whispered. "You're on the run again. You have to move on."

Hannah numbly stared back at her. "What—what are you talking about?"

Joyce smiled sadly. "I've been taking care of Guy for nearly two years, honey. I pretty much had it figured out the first week. You're in some kind of trouble, aren't you?"

Hannah couldn't say anything.

Joyce put a hand on her cheek. "It's none of my business what it's about. I know you couldn't have done anything really bad." Her eyes were tearing up again, and she let out a sad laugh. "Y'know, I've always been afraid you'd suddenly have to leave—for whatever reason. Oh, shoot. This sure crept up on me pretty fast. Well, I'm glad you gave me a chance to say good-bye, sweetie."

Hannah didn't try to deny it or argue with her. She just hugged Joyce, and whispered, "I'll miss you."

Ben and Guy reemerged from the bedroom. Guy was dressed in jeans and a rugby shirt. He didn't seem to understand why Joyce was crying. But at Hannah's urging, he gave her a hug and a kiss.

Carrying the box of keepsakes, Ben left with Joyce to escort her home.

Hannah switched on the TV for Guy. Then she retreated down the hallway to the bathroom. She closed the door, sat down on the edge of the tub, and cried.

The three of them took a cab to the bank. Hannah had a little over fourteen hundred saved up. She didn't expect to run into any trouble closing the account, but the teller had to check with the manager about something. Hannah waited, and nervously tapped her fingers on the countertop.

Ben was supposed to stay in the taxi with Guy. But after a minute, the two of them walked in and went up to one of the other teller windows. Holding Ben's hand, Guy waved excitedly at her. Smiling, Hannah waved back at him. The two of them looked like father and son.

She continued to wait, and began to wonder why it was taking so long. Had they discovered that her driver's license was a fake? It had never stopped them before. Then again, she'd never emptied out an account with them before. What if they were calling the police on her?

Finally, the teller returned to her window. He made her sign something to close the account, then counted out her money.

Ben finished up at his window a minute later, and they started back to the parking lot, where the taxi was waiting for them. Guy was happy because the teller had given him a lollipop.

"Well, I'm set for the week now," Ben said, as they started toward the taxi. "How much did you get?"

"Fourteen hundred and change," Hannah murmured. She rolled her eyes. "Kind of kills my plans to spend tonight in a suite at the Four Seasons."

Later, as the taxi turned down her block, Hannah almost expected to see police cars in front of her apartment building. But there were none.

Ben paid the driver and asked him to wait. He carried Guy piggyback up the three flights of stairs. Guy ran inside ahead of them. Ben stopped her in the doorway. "Don't forget," he whispered, taking hold of her arm. "I really need you to call and let me know you're okay."

She nodded. "I will, I promise."

He reached into his pocket and pulled out a wad of bills. "Here," he said, handing it to her. "It's two thousand. I wish it were more. And don't give me a goddamn argument, because you and I both know you need it."

Hannah took the money and slipped it into her purse. She let out a cry and tried to turn it into a laugh. "Why couldn't I have met you five years ago?" she said, her voice cracking.

"Because I was busy getting married," he said.

"So was I," Hannah whispered. Then she kissed him.

For a moment, they held each other in the doorway. Hannah didn't want to let go.

"The taxicab's waiting," Ben said, finally.

Guy came from his room. "Ben, do the ex-a-sketch with me!" he cried.

"Well, why don't you get started on a picture, then show me?" he said, stepping into the apartment. "You and your mom have to leave pretty soon."

Guy perched on the sofa, set the Etch A Sketch on his lap, and furiously started working the dials.

Hannah took one long, last look at the living room, and she fought the tightness in her throat.

"If you leave a message at the Best Western for me," Ben whispered, "don't forget to give the name you're registering under at your hotel. If you think someone's been following you, I'll come out there and stay with you and Guy; whatever we need to do."

Hannah just kept nodding.

"I'll be following Gulletti again today," Ben said as he moved the suitcases near the door. "He's probably camped out at Starbucks right now. That's his Friday morning routine. I'll know if he starts to follow you."

The phone rang. Hannah wasn't about to pick up.

"Guy, honey," she spoke over her own greeting. "We have a long drive ahead. So why don't you go tinkle? Even if you don't have to, give it a try."

Too wrapped up in his Etch A Sketch, Guy wasn't listening.

And Hannah wasn't listening to the answering machine—until she recognized Tish's voice.

"Are you there?" Tish was saying. *"Han, it's kind of an emergency. I can't believe this is happening—"*

Hannah stood frozen for a moment. She imagined her video-killer making good his *Vertigo* threat, using Tish as his Kim Novak.

She snatched up the phone. "Tish? Are you okay?"

"I've had better mornings. Listen, Han, I don't know what's going on, but we lost Seth this morning."

"He quit?"

"No, honey," Tish said. "I mean, we lost him. He's dead."

"What?" she whispered.

"He didn't show up for work this morning," Tish continued. "So I called his place, and got a cop. When I explained who I was, he told me what had happened. He wanted to know if I could help them out with next of kin. It looks like Seth killed himself."

"My God," Hannah murmured. "How did it happen?" She already knew, yet she heard herself asking.

"He broke into that church a few blocks up the hill from here. It happened early this morning. He went up into the bell tower, then jumped." Tish sighed. "Christ on a crutch, what's going on with this store's employees lately? First

Scott gets sick, then Britt dies, and now this new kid—it's crazy." She paused. "Hannah, are you still there?"

"Yes," she replied, in a stupor. "I—I'm here," she managed to say.

"Okay," Tish said. "Well, call me heartless, but I need you to fill in for him today. I know, it's awful of me to ask, and you're not supposed to come in until eleven. But I'm here alone with a stack of new videos and DVDs I have to catalogue. There's no one else. You'd really be saving my ass, Han."

"Um, I'm sorry, I can't," Hannah said. "In fact, I was about to call you. I can't come in at all today. Guy's sick, and his baby-sitter just phoned. I have to stay put."

"Oh, no," Tish groaned. "I wish I were in hell with my back broken. Well, I hope Guy feels better. Try to get another sitter, and come in if you can—even for just a little bit. Oh, crap. I have people lining up. Gotta go."

Hannah heard a click on the other end of the line.

"What was that?" Ben asked. "Did something happen?"

She turned to Guy. "Honey, were you listening to me? I want you put down the Etch A Sketch and go to the bathroom. Now!"

Guy scowled at her. Setting aside his game, he hopped off the sofa and stomped down the hall. He slammed shut the bathroom door.

Hannah rubbed her forehead. "Seth is dead," she whispered. "Just like *Vertigo*. It happened early this morning at that church near where he lived. They seem to think it was a suicide. . . ."

She relayed to Ben everything Tish had told her. "So—ah, the cops are in his apartment right now?" he finally asked.

Hannah nodded. "They were there when Tish called a while ago."

He ran a hand through his hair. "Maybe they have a lead. I'll go see what I can find out. Seth's roommate could be there. He might know something." Ben glanced at his wristwatch. "It's nine-thirty. Do you want to stick around for another forty-five minutes? I might come up with something concrete. I understand if you want to hightail it out of here. It's your call."

Hannah bit her lip. "All right," she said finally. "You go on. I'll stay a little while longer."

The taxi that had been waiting for Hannah was now letting Ben out at the big Tudor house on Aloha Street. Ben had expected to find a couple of police cars parked in the long driveway. There were six of them. Dozens of onlookers stood in front of the mansion, many of them craning their necks to get a peek at the garage. Ben couldn't imagine an apparent suicide attracting so much attention. Seth hadn't even died on the premises.

Ben wondered about the roommate. Was he dead too?

He threaded his way through the crowd. "Do you know what happened?" he asked one young woman, who looked like a college student.

She shrugged. "This guy offed himself or something."

Ben felt someone nudge him. He turned to face an overweight, middle-aged man with copper-colored hair and a hint of eye makeup. He had a miniature schnauzer on a leash. "The young man who lived above the garage there killed himself this morning," he whispered. "He jumped from the tower of that church up the block, you know, Sacred Heart?"

Ben nodded.

Touching his arm, the man looked Ben up and down. "But that's only part of it," he said. "Looks like he video-taped a bunch of people, then murdered them."

Ben frowned at him. "What?"

The chubby man nodded conspiratorially. "I hear he kept photos and videotapes of his victims, women mostly. The police found it all in the garage apartment back there—

along with some video equipment and God knows what else. Can you imagine? Right here in our neighborhood?"

"No, I—I can't believe it," Ben murmured.

"Do you live around here?" the man asked.

"Excuse me," Ben said. He made his way toward the mouth of the driveway, where a husky, mustached patrolman kept the people back. The cop was talking to a stocky man with red hair. Ben recognized him from last night. He owned the Tudor house.

"Did something happen to Seth Stroud?" he asked loudly.

The cop turned to frown at him. "Who are you?"

A few other people were looking at him, too. "Um, my name's Jack Stiles," he lied. "I'm in Seth's film class at the community college."

The man with the red hair squinted at him. "Film class?"

Ben nodded. "Yeah, he's a teaching assistant for a film class over at the community college."

"Well, that's news to me," replied the owner of the Tudor house. "Seth worked at Bourm's Lock and Key on Fifteenth." He turned to the cop. "I don't understand this. One of you guys said this morning that his boss from the *video store* called him. Something's screwed up here. I was his landlord. I know how he made a living."

"What about his roommate?" Ben asked. "Have you talked with him?"

"What roommate?" the man said. "You must have the wrong guy."

Bewildered, Ben stared at him. None of it made sense. He'd searched every inch of that garage apartment just last night, and hadn't found a thing. And now it seemed Seth Stroud was two different people.

The cop took hold of his arm. "Listen, Mister—ah—Stiles," he said. "I need you to stick around. One of our detectives will want a statement."

Ben quickly shook his head, then took a step back. "Hey, you know, you're right. I must have the wrong guy."

"Just the same, I need you to stay put, Mr. Stiles—"

"Oh, that's okay," Ben said, giving him a curtailed wave. Turning away, he weaved through the crowd. All the while, he thought someone might grab him. He finally broke free from the swarm of people and walked at a brisk clip. He kept expecting to hear a police whistle or someone yelling at him to stop.

Ducking into an alley, he cut through someone's yard, then ran several blocks. Ben looked over his shoulder. No one was following him; at least, he didn't see anybody. He spotted a pay phone in the window of a coffeehouse, and hurried inside.

Catching his breath, he dug into his pocket for change. No quarters. There was a line at the counter. He stepped up to the front. "Could I just get change?" he asked.

"End of the line, bub," the skinny young man at the espresso machine said, barely glancing up.

Ben pulled a five-dollar bill out of his wallet. "Look, five bucks," he said, still out of breath. "I'm exchanging this for two quarters." He dropped the bill in the tip jar, then took out two quarters.

"That's pretty cool," the young man said, nodding.

Ben hurried to the phone, put in his money, and dialed Hannah's number. While the phone rang, he glanced out the coffeehouse window. A cop car came down the block. Ben stepped away from the window. He heard Hannah's machine click on, and her recorded greeting. As he waited for the beep, he watched the squad car continue down the street.

"Hannah, are you there?" he asked. "Can you pick up?"

There was another click. "Ben? Where are you?"

"In a coffeeshop not far from you."

"Well, that narrows it down to about fifteen places. Did you find out anything more about Seth?"

"Something's really screwy here, Hannah. Apparently, the cops found video equipment, tapes, and photographs—all linking Seth to several murders."

"Which murders? You mean Britt—and Rae and—"

"I wasn't able to find out for sure," Ben replied. "But it

looks that way. The thing is, none of that stuff was in the apartment when I searched it last night. Somebody set this up. And according to Seth's landlord, he worked in a lock and key place. The guy didn't know anything about the film classes or the video store."

"That's ridiculous," Hannah said. "Tish just talked to one of the police there this morning—"

"I know, I know," he said. "They mentioned that. I guess it threw them for a loop."

"What about the roommate?" Hannah asked.

"According to the landlord, Seth Stroud lived alone."

"Then who was that guy we talked to at Seth's apartment?"

"That's what I'd like to know. Do you remember his name?"

"Oh, just a sec. Um, Something Kidd . . . Michael . . . no . . ."

"Richard," Ben said. "That's it, Richard Kidd. Hold on." Cradling the receiver against his ear with his shoulder, Ben pulled the phone directory out of a little nook below the pay phone. He quickly paged through it. "I'm looking him up right now. Here we go, *Kidd . . . Randall, Robert, Roy . . .* shit, nothing."

Ben heard a click on her end of the line. "Are you still there?" he asked.

"Yeah, it's my call-waiting," she said. "I don't know if I should take it. Oh, what the hell. Hang on. I'll be right back."

Guy was mesmerized in front of *Sesame Street*, and sitting too close to the TV. Four suitcases and a box of toys sat by the front door. And Hannah stood at the kitchen counter, the cordless phone in her hand. She pressed the call waiting button. "Um, hello?" she said warily.

"Hannah, it's Tish again." She sounded anxious and rushed. "I hate to keep bugging you when you have a sick child at home. Any luck in getting another sitter?"

"Oh, Tish, I'm sorry, no," she said, picking up the *Vertigo* cassette, then frowning at it.

"Well, I wouldn't call, but I'll have to close the store if you can't come in. They want me at the East Precinct to answer a bunch of asinine questions. I'm supposed to be there *now.*"

"What kind of questions?" Hannah set the video back on the counter.

"Oh, seems they don't think Seth was really working at this store. Right. Hello? He opened a new account his first day here. Same address, same phone number, same birthday, and the same social security number on his W-2 form. What more do they want? I think they may ask me to identify the body, and believe you me, I ain't up for that. God, listen to me. I'm awful. The poor guy's dead. It'll hit me tonight and I'll have a total breakdown. Anyway, Han, I just thought I'd try you again. Any chance you can get a neighbor to come over and look after Guy—just for a couple of hours?"

"I'm sorry, Tish. I really can't."

"Well, on the off chance you get away, you have your key to the store, don't you?"

"Yeah, but I honestly don't think I can do it, Tish."

"Okay. Just thought I'd try. Take care, Han."

"Bye," Hannah said. She pressed the flash button. "Ben, are you there?"

"Yeah, what took so long?"

"My boss at the video store. She's frazzled."

"Well, have her join the club. I still can't figure out what's going on. We were both there when Richard Kidd told us he was Seth's roommate. Did Seth confirm that to you?"

"Yes. I remember him saying later *My roommate told me you came by,* or words to that effect."

"So how come no one else knows he had a roommate?" Ben said. "It's like Seth Stroud was two different guys."

Hannah stared at the *Vertigo* tape on the counter.

"Are you there?" Ben asked.

"Two different Seth Strouds," she said. "You know, in *Vertigo*, Kim Novak's character was pretending to be someone else for the first half of the movie."

"What are you talking about?"

"She was pretending to be a woman named Madeleine," Hannah explained. "And when she jumped from the church tower, it was faked. The real Madeleine was thrown from the tower instead, and Kim's character just went back to being her old self—until Jimmy Stewart rediscovered her."

"Hannah, I still don't understand. It's been a while since I saw that movie."

"I'll explain later. I have a feeling Richard Kidd is behind all this. And he might be in our customer files at the video store. If so, his address would be in the computer at work. Listen. How far are you from store?"

"A few blocks," Ben said.

"Meet me out front," Hannah said. "Guy and I are leaving right now. We'll see you in five minutes."

"Take a cab," Ben advised. "I'd feel better knowing you have someone with you. Besides, you can bring my duffel bag."

"Will do," she replied.

"See you soon," he said. "Be careful, Hannah."

Twenty-two

TEMPORARILY CLOSED DUE TO EMERGENCY
We'll Reopen by 2:30 Today (Friday)
Sorry About the Inconvenience

Tish had left the sign on Emerald City Video's door. The lights were switched off inside, and the door was locked.

Hannah had brought her key. She paid the cab driver and asked him to wait. Guy jumped out of the taxi and ran to hug Ben.

Hannah pulled out her key and unlocked the door. "C'mon, hurry up, guys," she urged, stepping inside. "I need to turn off the alarm."

She locked the door behind them, then made a beeline for the break room, and punched in the alarm deactivating code.

With the cold, gloomy, overcast morning, not much light came through the store window. Hannah switched on one set of lights in the store—over the children's section. She planted Guy in front of the shelf of kids' videos. "Okay, you know the drill, honey," she told him. "Look all you want, but don't make a mess." She pointed to the break room. "Ben and I will be right over there. Okay?"

"Can we watch *Monsters, Inc.*, Mom?" he asked.

"Only for the fifteenth time? I don't think so, Guy. Not tonight." She felt his forehead, then mussed his hair and hurried to the break room.

Tish had left the computer on. Sitting at the desk, Hannah

began to type. She pulled up the customer file. Ben looked over her shoulder.

She typed in *Kidd, Richard.* What came up was the closest name to it: Kidman, Andrew.

"Oh, shit," she muttered. "He's not in here."

"Back it up," Ben suggested. "See if there's another person with the last name Kidd."

Hannah scrolled back to the previous customer: *Kidd, Matthew . . . Kidd, Lawrence . . . Kidd, Laura . . . Kidd, Eustace (Richard).*

"That's him," Hannah said. The birth date listed made Eustace Richard Kidd twenty-five. Hannah clicked on the Related Customer icon to see if he had anyone else on his account: *Stroud, Seth.*

"Bingo," Ben muttered, grabbing a piece of paper and pen from the desktop. "What's the address listed?"

"1313 East Republican Street," Hannah read from the screen. "It's not far from Seth's place."

Hannah clicked into his rental history file. "It's all here," she said. "Angela's the first victim we know of, right? Seth said she was Paul's summer fling last year. She was killed in late August; strangled under the bells at the Convention Center, like Marilyn Monroe in *Niagara*. Look at the rental dates. He checked it out twice."

Hannah pointed to the listing:

NIAGARA-V0901-Rented: 8/8/01 Rtrn: 8/11/01
NIAGARA-V0901-Rented: 8/20/01 Rtrn: 8/22/01

"Guy, are you okay out there?" Hannah called, while scrolling down the alphabet.

"Can we watch *Charlie Brown Great Pumpkin?*" he yelled back.

"It's *It's the Great Pumpkin, Charlie Brown*," Hannah corrected him. "Not tonight, honey." On the screen, she pointed to another rental listing:

*ON THE WATERFRONT-V1122-Rented: 7/14/02
Rtrn: 7/16/02*

"That's a week or two before Rae's boyfriend fell off the roof," Ben said. "Like Eva Marie Saint's brother in *On the Waterfront.*"

"They were boning up on how to do it like the movie," Hannah remarked. She scrolled to the S's:

*STRANGERS ON A TRAIN-V0205-Rented: 6/7/02
Rtrn: 6/9/02
STRANGERS ON A TRAIN-V0205-Rented: 6/11/02
Rtrn: 6/13/02*

"That's before they killed the woman in Rae's office. Lily, the one who was strangled on that island near the Arboretum."

"The Floating Flower," Ben murmured. "What about *Looking for Mr. Goodbar?*"

Shaking her head, Hannah scrolled back to the L's. "I don't think so, no. It's not here. I must have already been targeted as Rae's successor by then. They probably didn't want to take any chances renting it here."

"You keep saying *they.* You mean Richard and Seth?"

She nodded. "Didn't we pretty much establish that two people have been behind all these killings? You said one was driving and another was shooting at you the other evening. Right?"

Ben scratched his head. "So—the theory is, for one reason or another, Richard turned on Seth and killed him last night. Or are you saying maybe Seth really isn't dead?"

Hannah cleared the computer screen. "No, I think Seth is dead, all right. The real Seth Stroud. We only met him once."

Hannah turned around in the chair to face him. "It's why Seth's fall from the bell tower copied *Vertigo.* I started to tell you on the phone. Kim Novak's character was pretending to be Madeleine during the first half of the movie. Jimmy

Stewart was led to believe she'd killed herself by jumping from the church tower. But it wasn't a suicide. It was the real Madeleine's murder."

He nodded. "I remember. But what does it have to do with—"

"The *Vertigo* clip we saw was a fake suicide," Hannah interrupted. "The woman Kim Novak pretended to be was murdered. Last night, the real Seth Stroud was murdered. The person we've known as Seth was just pretending to be him."

"What makes you so sure?" Ben asked.

"The film clip. He's never misled me before."

"So—you're saying the person who has been calling himself Seth Stroud is really—"

"Richard Kidd," she said, handing him the scrap of paper with Richard Kidd's address written on it. "He was friends with Seth Stroud. We know that. Remember when you and I went to the garage apartment, looking for Seth?"

"Sure, yeah. Of course,"

"When that young man answered the door, at first glance, I thought he was Seth, because they looked so much alike. Remember before he said anything, we asked if Seth Stroud lived there?"

Ben nodded.

"His response was something like 'What do you want to see him about?' "

"And we told him we were in Seth's film class," Ben finished for her. "Then he said he was Seth's roommate, Richard Kidd." Ben gave her a wary, sidelong glance. "You think he was lying?"

"Yeah." Hannah got to her feet. "I think *he* was Seth Stroud. He was the one killed last night. He lived alone in that garage apartment, and worked at a lock and key store. That must have come in handy when he and Richard Kidd broke into several of their victims' homes."

Ben frowned at her. "But why would they switch identities?"

She shrugged. "I don't know. Maybe part of some game. They were into playing games, manipulating people."

"I don't understand how Richard Kidd could be employed at the community college—and here at the video store—under the name Seth Stroud. What about his Social Security number, his paychecks, his bank account?"

Hannah sighed. "I don't know, maybe he's independently wealthy, and doesn't need the money. We know he used his friend's Social Security number. Maybe he gave his paychecks to the real Seth—for the use of his name. I said it before. This killer must own some pretty expensive, sophisticated equipment to have put together that *Goodbar* video. Hell, those glasses Seth—or rather, *Richard*—wears are designer, at least a cool thousand. He dresses pretty nicely for a part-time teacher's assistant and video-store clerk."

Shaking his head, Ben folded his arms. "I still don't understand why they switched identities."

Hannah shrugged. "Well, maybe it wasn't a total switch. When we met the real Seth Stroud, we put him on the spot. My guess is he only lied that one time about who he was—when we came knocking on his door. Maybe Richard Kidd borrowed Seth's name and identity for certain things—and certain reasons."

"Well, what reasons?" Ben pressed.

"I don't know, dammit!" Hannah said, exasperated. "I'm trying to make sense of this too, same as you."

"Mom, you said *dammit!*" Guy called from the next room.

Hannah let out a weak laugh. "Um, sorry, honey!" she called back. She gazed at Ben. "I keep thinking of something you said a couple of days ago. You said this killer ended up with more than he bargained for when he started stalking me. He got in over his head, killing a couple of private detectives. Things are closing in on him. He had to cut all his ties and move on. I certainly know how that feels. He's kind of like me in that sense." She shook her head. "It's weird to find I have something in common with a serial killer. Anyway, maybe that's why he killed his friend. He must have—"

A sudden pounding on the store's glass door cut her off.

"Mom!" Guy yelled.

Hannah and Ben hurried out of the break room. She ran to Guy and hugged him. Glancing over at the video store door, she saw the cab driver. "It's okay, honey," she assured Guy, with a skittish laugh. "It's just our cab driver. He thought we'd forgotten about him."

Ben was signaling to the driver, holding up two fingers. "Two more minutes!" he yelled to the man on the other side of the glass.

The driver waved back at him, then ambled back his taxi.

Guy had left a pile of videos on the floor. Hannah started returning them to the shelf. Ben crouched down to help. "So—you think Richard—um, *took care* of his friend; then he went to the garage apartment with enough evidence so it would appear the late Seth Stroud was—alone—responsible for these—*unfortunate incidents?*"

She gave a cautious glance at Guy, who wasn't picking up on any of their conversation.

"Can we watch this one tonight?" he whispered, handing her a copy of *Aladdin*.

"Not tonight, sweetie." She nodded at Ben. "Yes. I think he got into that apartment after you."

"But if he was so hot on covering his tracks and moving on, why did he give himself away to you with the *Vertigo* tape? He must have known you'd figure it out."

"I think he *wanted* me to figure it out," Hannah said, frowning. "He wants me to know he's still around. My guess is—he's not finished with me."

"All the more reason I should stay with you today," Ben said, straightening up.

Hannah shook her head. "No, Ben. It would just prolong everything. You said so yourself. There are too many unanswered questions. I can't afford to stick around and find those answers. But you can."

Frowning, Ben pulled the piece of scrap paper out of his pocket and glanced at it. "1313 East Republican," he said. "That's only a few blocks from here, isn't it?"

She nodded. "Why don't you two guys step outside so I can set the alarm again? C'mon, Guy."

As they walked to the door, Ben whispered to her. "I'll stick around and watch you go. If someone starts following the cab, I'll call from a pay phone and leave a message for you at home. Check your answering machine when you swing by to pick up your bags."

Hannah nodded. "Thanks, Ben."

He and Guy ducked outside. Hannah locked the door, ran back and set the alarm, then quickly retraced her steps to the door again. Once outside, she locked the door behind her.

Ben had already taken his duffel bag out of the taxi, and Guy sat in the back, waiting. Ben stood in the light, drizzling rain, holding the taxi door open for her. She stopped for a moment and stared at his handsome, chiseled face, still bruised, shiny with raindrops. He smiled sadly at her. "When you get where you're going, don't forget to call me at the Best Western. Okay?"

She nodded and took hold of his arm. "Thanks, Ben," she whispered. "Thanks for everything."

"I'm never going to see you again, am I?" he asked.

Her heart ached. Hannah threw her arms around him.

Ben kissed her on the lips. She clung to him fiercely, but then forced herself to break away. "Take care," she said, her voice cracking. She jumped into the backseat of the cab.

Ben closed the door.

Hannah pulled Guy closer to her. She glanced through the rain-beaded window to see Ben's face again, but the taxi pulled away. She didn't get a last look at him.

"Why are you crying, Mom?" Guy asked.

Hannah had hoped he wouldn't notice. They'd been driving for five blocks, and he hadn't uttered a word. She didn't want to tell him that they wouldn't be seeing Ben again. If Guy knew, he'd be crying too.

"I'm just feeling sad, honey," Hannah said, wiping her eyes. "Some people cry when they're about to go on a trip. I'm one of them. I'll be okay in a little while."

As the taxi approached her street, Hannah glanced out the rear window. She didn't notice anyone following them. Then again, she didn't know what type of car to look for.

The cab turned down her block. Hannah let out a gasp. "Um, keep going, please," she said to the driver.

A police car was parked in front of her apartment building. "Isn't this your address?" the cabby asked.

"Yes, but keep driving, please," Hannah said.

As they passed her building, Hannah saw one cop step out of the squad car while his partner remained behind the wheel. Hannah glanced over her shoulder to watch the policeman step toward the front door.

"Turn left up ahead, please," she told the driver. Hannah had him take another left, then pull into the parking lot of a condominium behind her building. Fishing her keys and some money from her purse, she gave the driver twenty dollars. "Keep the meter running, please," she said. "We'll be back down. I promise it won't take as long as the last time."

"Fine with me," he replied. "It's your money, lady."

Hannah took Guy's hand, and they walked up some steps to a little walkway at the side of the condominium. "Now, honey, for the next few minutes, I need you to be quiet and do exactly what I say, all right?"

"'Kay," he said, holding out his free hand to catch the light raindrops.

Hannah opened a swinging gate in the fence that divided the properties; then she and Guy stepped up to the back door of her building.

Inside the dark stairwell, they climbed up the cement stairs. Guy was stomping. "You have to be very quiet, honey," Hannah whispered, squeezing his hand. "We don't want anyone to hear us."

" 'Kay," he said, slowly taking each step on his tiptoes.

"All right," Hannah whispered. She hoisted him up in her arms. He was close to forty pounds, and the stairs were hard and steep. But Hannah was so scared she didn't realize how much of a struggle it was carrying him until she stopped at the door to the third-floor balcony. She put Guy down, then leaned against the door frame. She tried to get a breath.

"Mom?" Guy said, his voice echoing in the stairwell.

"Shhhh." Hannah shook her head at him.

"Why are we stopping here?" he whispered.

"Just a second, okay?" Hannah opened the door a crack, and peeked out to a small alcove. No one. Taking Guy's hand, she stepped outside, then peered around the corner down the long balcony walkway. Again, she didn't see anyone.

At a brisk clip, Hannah headed toward her door, dragging Guy the whole way. He had to run to keep up with her. "I'm sorry, honey," she said under her breath. "I need you to stick by me."

With her hand shaking, it took Hannah a moment to unlock her door. She pulled Guy inside, then closed the door behind him. "Good boy," she muttered.

The intercom buzzed—twice. Hannah knew it was the police. She stared at the four suitcases and shook her head. She could maybe manage three, tops.

"Honey, pick two toys you can carry back to the taxi," she told Guy. "They'll have to last you a couple of days."

She could hear the intercom next door. They were going for her neighbors now.

Guy started rummaging through the box of toys. Hannah checked her answering machine. The message light was blinking. She played back her messages, cutting short each old one until she came to Tish's call this morning. She skipped that one too, and listened to the next.

"Hi, it's me," Ben said hurriedly. *"Keep your eye out for a burgundy-colored Volvo. It pulled out of the lot across the way after your cab drove off. I couldn't tell if it was following you or not. Call and leave me a message as soon as*

*you get where you're going. I'm on my way to Richard
Kidd's place. I love you, Hannah."*

Then he hung up.

She felt a little pang in her gut as she erased the message.
She didn't want the police to hear it.

"C'mon, Guy," she announced. He'd picked out his new
Etch A Sketch and a toy fire engine. Hannah slipped them
in a bag. "Now, hold on to these and don't drop them. You
have to keep up with me, and I can't hold your hand. How
are you feeling?"

"Fine," he muttered, looking a bit scared.

Hannah smiled bravely and touched his cheek.

She decided to leave behind a suitcase full of clothes.
There was enough for them to wear in the other three suitcases. One of the bags had a shoulder strap, and the other
two had wheels and pull handles.

Hannah opened the door an inch, glanced up and down
the balcony, then nudged Guy outside. "The back stairs,
honey," she whispered. "Same way we came up."

Taking giant steps on his tiptoes, Guy swayed back and
forth as he moved toward the rear stairwell. Tussling with
her purse and three bags, Hannah followed him. The wheels
on her suitcases made a loud, scraping noise on the cement
walkway.

Hannah heard a siren in the distance, and she wondered
if it had something to do with her. She wasn't really certain
the squad car parked outside was for her, either. Still, she
hurried toward the back stairs. At the end of the balcony, she
headed into the stairwell. She heard voices—behind her,
outside. She put her finger to her lips and stared at Guy.

He nodded, and put his finger to his lips.

Hannah took a step back and peeked around the corner.
One of the cops and a man in a raincoat were coming from
the other stairwell—with the building manager. Hannah was
too far away to hear what they were saying. But the three
of them headed toward her door. The manager was bran-

dishing a large key ring. The three men stopped at her door. The one wearing the trench coat knocked.

Hannah ducked back into the stairwell. Lugging the three heavy suitcases, she straggled half a flight behind Guy as they fled down the stairs. The suitcases weighed her down, throwing off her balance. After the first flight, the bag handles pinched and tore at her palms. Her arms ached. The valise with the strap seemed to be dislocating her shoulder. She teetered down another flight, certain at any minute she'd hear the stairwell door up on the third floor open. For all she knew, someone could now be posted outside the back exit, and she'd bump right into him.

"Guy, please," she gasped. "Hold the . . . door open . . ."

She watched him push at the door, and a dim patch of light filled the dark alcove at the bottom of the stairs. Her lungs burning, Hannah made it down the last few steps. Guy was braced against the open door. She didn't see anyone outside, and she wondered if they were hiding.

The cold air felt invigorating. The rain had stopped—for the time being. Hannah set down her luggage and readjusted the shoulder strap on the one bag. "Thanks, sweetie," she said to Guy, between breaths. "You're—you're being so good. Just a short—little walk to the cab. Come on. . . ."

She couldn't pull the suitcases. The wheels made too much noise on the pavement. Her arms felt numb. The palms of her hands were raw. But Hannah hauled the suitcases along the narrow walk and down the steps. Guy ran ahead of her.

The cab driver popped open his trunk, then stepped out of the taxi to help her with the bags. Hannah kept thanking him between gasps for air. She prodded Guy into the backseat, then practically collapsed in after him.

The cab driver climbed behind the wheel. Hannah straightened up, and thought to glance around for a burgundy Volvo that could be idling nearby.

"Just to let you know," the driver said. "We've driven one-point-eight miles, and so far, this ride has cost you fifty-one bucks. Minus the twenty you gave me, of course. Where to now?"

Hannah didn't see a burgundy Volvo in the vicinity.

"Pacific Place downtown, please," she said. There was a hotel practically across the street from the chic shopping center. She could catch another cab there. She couldn't let this driver take them to their destination for the night. The police could track him down too easily.

He started to pull out of the lot. "I think someone might be trying to follow me," Hannah said. "I want to lose this guy. Can you help me?"

"Yes, ma'am," he said, with a glance at her in the rearview mirror.

"Thank you." She sat back, then gave Guy's shoulder a squeeze.

Twenty-three

Ben found 1313 East Republican Street just a few blocks uphill from the video store. The little two-story cedar cottage was at the end of four houses in a row just like it. They were squeezed close together on one lot. Ben figured it took some big bucks to live in one of those cozy, individual homes. He remembered what Hannah had said about Richard Kidd possibly being independently wealthy.

From across the street, Ben studied the house. He stepped back into a narrow alley beside a tall, brick apartment building. The weather had taken another turn, and it was drizzling again. He took cover under a carport canopy, and hid behind some recycling bins.

Ben wasn't sure if anyone was home across the way. He wasn't even sure if Richard Kidd still lived there.

After several minutes, he noticed a mail carrier on his route, working his way up the block. Ben glanced at the front door to 1313 East Republican Street. The mailbox was outside.

Ben stashed his duffel bag in the cement stairwell leading to a basement door of the apartment building. The stairs and threshold area were covered with leaves. He piled a few on top of his bag until it was completely hidden.

Emerging from the stairwell, he checked his wristwatch: 11:10. Hannah and Guy were probably well on their way by now.

On the other side of the road, the mail carrier made his deliveries to the four cedar cottages. Ben waited for a few more minutes until the mailman moved further up the street. Then Ben darted across the way to the front stoop of number 1313.

He dug the envelopes out of the mailbox: junk mail and a bill from a place called VideoTronics. All of the letters were addressed to *Richard Kidd* and *E. Richard Kidd.*

Ben put the mail back in the box. He didn't think anyone was home, but he rang the bell anyway just to be certain. A minute passed, and he rang again. No answer.

Glancing over his shoulder, Ben tried the door. Locked. He pulled out his credit card and slid it in the doorjamb. He tried again and again, but he couldn't trip the lock.

He heard a car coming, and he quickly backed away from the door. He crept around to the side of the house, looking for a way in. Continuing on to the backyard, he peeked in the living room window, then gave it a tug. Locked. He tried the back door; also locked. Ben skulked around to the other side of the house, then stopped. The neighbor's identical cedar cottage was only about twenty feet away. Ben didn't see anyone in the other residence. There were no lights on, despite the dreary overcast sky.

He glanced back at Richard Kidd's house and spotted an open window on the first floor, but it was out of reach.

Ben grabbed an empty garbage can from around back and hauled it to the side of the house. Turning it over, he set the tall, heavy-duty aluminum bin under the open window. He stole a glimpse toward the sidewalk and street. He didn't see anyone, so he climbed on top of the garbage can. It was wobbly, and slippery from the rain. He grabbed ahold of the windowsill.

Checking over his shoulder, Ben suddenly froze.

A middle-aged man stood at the window of the house next door. He was facing Ben. He didn't move.

For a moment, it seemed like a standoff. Ben wasn't sure if he should make a run for it or not. Once the neighbor called the police, it would take less than five minutes for a patrol car to arrive. There was no time to search the house. There was barely enough time to get away now.

The man remained in the window, his face expressionless. Ben stared back at him, totally perplexed. Finally, he gave the man a tentative wave. No response. After a minute, the man wandered away from the window.

Ben watched him inside the dim house. With the overcast skies, he should have had at least one light on. The man moved to a clock on the wall and put his hand on the dial, touching the hour and minute hands.

"He's blind, stupid," Ben muttered to himself.

Sighing, he turned and raised the window higher. His hands were shaking. He glanced around one more time. With the coast clear, he hoisted himself up, then climbed through the opening.

Catching his breath, Ben realized he was in the pantry of Richard Kidd's small, modern kitchen. On the counter, he saw something that looked like a small transistor radio. A tiny green light was blinking on it face.

He heard a strange series of clicks in the next room. He figured he must have set off some kind of motion detector or alarm device.

Ben hurried into the living room for the source of the mechanical noise. On the floor, tilted against the wall by the front door, he saw another little device with a flickering green light. But the clicking sound wasn't coming from there.

It came from the VCR beneath the television set. Lights were blinking on and off. It was on some kind of timer.

Ben wasn't sure whether or not he should cut his losses and get out before the police arrived. If an alarm had gone off, it was a silent one. But wouldn't the police or security company phone before responding in person?

Still undecided, he stood in the middle of the living room, which was decorated with black leather furniture and chrome-and-glass tables. Very cold and sleek. Ben noticed two big boxes by the foot of the stairs. He knelt down and looked through them. He recognized several books that had been at Seth's place last night. He also discovered the same envelope with photos of Seth and Richard together—on their group hike, and on the beach with that girl. Richard had removed these things from the garage apartment last night.

In one box, Ben found a wad of paycheck stubs from the community college. Hannah was right. Richard had been giving his paychecks to Seth Stroud.

Ben opened one of the books, a high school yearbook from Missoula, Montana. He looked up Stroud, Seth, and on page 37, he saw a graduation photo of the young man he'd met only once. His hair was longer, and he had one of those teenage-boy wispy mustaches, but it was the same man Ben had seen at the garage apartment.

E. Richard Kidd was on page 33. The glasses were different, and he had some baby fat on his face, but it was Paul Gulletti's assistant, all right.

Ben found a photo of them together on page 59. Posed behind a table with a movie projector on it, they looked slightly nerdy with their six cohorts in the Film and Video Club.

At the beginning of the yearbook, Ben unearthed an old, yellowed clipping from a Missoula newspaper. The small headline read: "LOCAL HIGH SCHOOL STUDENT PREMIERES SHORT FILM AT GRAND CITIPLEX THEATERS." The article had a photo of the young Richard Kidd without his glasses. He looked a bit pompous. The caption said: *"Richard Kidd, 18, wrote and directed* Sticks and Bones, *a twenty-minute experimental short subject, which was a finalist in the National Film Scholarship contest."*

Ben stared at the picture and wondered when Richard Kidd had started borrowing Seth Stroud's name. He didn't understand why Richard lived and received mail at this address, but took his friend's identity to work. With his background in film, it didn't make sense that he claimed to be someone else at the community college.

Ben kept looking through the two boxes, uncovering more books, two shirts, a bag of marijuana, a camera, and junk mail from the college. Ben also unearthed an address book. Richard Kidd's name was in it, along with his address, phone number, and cell phone. Ben copied down both phone numbers.

He wondered how they worked out the phones. He checked Richard's answering machine on the glass-top end table by the leather sofa. Ben played back the recorded greeting: *"Can't come to the phone. You know what to do after the beep."* Short and sweet. He didn't mention his name.

Ben imagined Seth's greeting was just as anonymous. He couldn't call to find out. The garage apartment was probably still packed with policemen.

Looking out the front window, he didn't see anything unusual; no cops creeping up to the house. Perhaps those small transistor devices weren't part of an alarm system after all.

He glanced over at the VCR again. It was counting down from twenty-two minutes. He'd never seen a VCR with a timer like that. It was strange how the machine had clicked on a moment after he'd climbed inside that window. Was it a coincidence? Or did those little transistors have something to do with it?

The telephone rang. Ben felt himself jump a bit. He waited until the answering machine came on with that anonymous greeting. The caller hung up.

Ben went back to work, quickly rummaging through a cabinet in the living room. Finding nothing of interest, he decided to try upstairs.

As he started up toward the second floor, the VCR counter read nineteen minutes.

Hannah peeked at the meter on the dashboard: sixty-one bucks so far. They were on Interstate 5, about thirty miles south of Seattle. Most of the way, Guy had been quiet, mesmerized by the taxi ride. Since she didn't have a car, he rarely rode in one. This was a real adventure for him. Hannah had pointed out landmarks they passed: Safeco Field with its retractable roof, Boeing Field, and Sea-Tac Airport. She'd felt Guy's forehead a couple of times, and checked his complexion. He seemed fine.

The cab driver was an East Indian man who said very little. He had the radio on, easy-listening stuff. He'd picked up her and Guy at the hotel across from Pacific Place. She'd told the driver to take them to Tacoma.

They were almost there. Hannah could already see the Tacoma Dome up ahead. Looking for hotel signs, she barely noticed the easy-listening station had switched over to the local news. But then she heard the announcer say something about a boat explosion on Lake Union.

Hannah leaned forward and listened intently.

"The victims of that blast have now been identified as a thirty-six-year-old Wisconsin businessman, Kenneth Woodley, and a private detective, also from Wisconsin, forty-year-old Walter Kirkabee. Both men were in Seattle searching for Woodley's estranged wife, who abducted their son two years ago. Police are seeking the woman for questioning. In other news, a fraternity prank at the University of Washington went awry late last night when two seniors . . ."

Hannah sat back and gazed out the window. It was strange. Guy had just heard his father's name on the radio, but he didn't know it. If this morning's visit from the police had left any room for doubt, now it was official. They were looking for her. They were announcing it on the radio, for God's sake.

She saw a roadside sign for Amtrak at an upcoming exit. There were also signs for restaurants and motels: a Best Western, a Travelodge, and two more places.

Hannah leaned forward again. "Could you get off at the next exit, please?" she asked.

She decided that the Sleepy Bear Motel looked clean—and cheap enough. The sign out front showed a yawning bear wearing a nightcap and sitting in bed. *"It Feels 'Just Right!'"* was the slogan above the blinking Vacancy sign. The motel was a sprawling two-story stucco with outside access to each room. Hannah noticed several fast-food places within walking distance.

There was also a train yard nearby. She could see the tracks on the other side of the parking lot's chain-link fence. One advantage; they could probably walk to the Amtrak station.

The taxi driver unloaded their bags from the trunk. He even helped Hannah carry them into the lobby. The place smelled of coffee and had floor-to-ceiling windows on two sides. There were also a lot of teddy bears. There was teddy bear-patterned wallpaper, a teddy bear calendar, a bookcase full of teddy bears behind the registration desk, teddy bear crochet pillows on the sofa and easy chairs, and porcelain teddy bear lamps.

Guy was fascinated with the place. Hannah paid the driver. She noticed the same easy-listening type of music playing on a radio behind the registration desk. She wondered if the motel clerk had just heard the same news report.

A middle-aged woman emerged from a back room on the other side of the counter. She had short brown frizzy hair and a kelly-green polyester skirt with a polka-dot blouse. She had a slightly desperate smile on her face. "Hi, there!" she chirped. "Do you need a room?"

Hannah stepped up to the desk. "Yes, please."

"If you could fill out our little form, it would be wonderful." The woman handed Hannah a pen, and put a card in front of her.

She borrowed Ben's alias for the registration form: *Ann Sturges & son, 129 Joyce Avenue, Yakima, WA 98409.* She'd improvised the address, and purposely made the phone number undecipherable.

"I'm a little concerned about the noise from the railroad yard," Hannah said, while filling out the form. "If you can give us a room that's kind of quiet, I'd appreciate it."

"Two beds?" she asked, typing on her computer keyboard. "One for Mamma Bear and one for Baby Bear?"

Hannah glanced up at her, a smile frozen on her face.

"Um, yes. I—I'll be paying in cash, and we're staying two nights—maybe three."

"Well, it's lovely to have you," the woman replied.

"Thank you," Hannah said, handing her back the pen. She glanced out past the rain-beaded window at the parking area. She noticed an old burgundy-colored Volvo in the lot. Had it been there before? Was it the same car Ben had warned her about?

She couldn't tell if anyone was in the front seat. The windshield was too dark. Hannah kept staring at the car. Then she saw the wipers sweep across the windshield for a beat.

A chill rushed through her. She grabbed Guy's hand and pulled him closer. She turned her back on the car. The desk clerk was saying something, but Hannah didn't really hear her. She remembered one of Rae's e-mails. In it, she'd said her stalker drove a "wine-colored" Volvo.

Hannah didn't know what to do. She couldn't grab a taxi and go to some other motel. He'd simply follow her. She couldn't call the police, either. She thought of Ben. But he probably hadn't even checked into his hotel yet.

She stole a glance over her shoulder at the old Volvo again. He wouldn't be just watching her tonight. His *Psycho* scenario was all set: the roadside motel, the rain, a woman fugitive, a cleansing shower. He'd have to use force to get her in the shower. Hannah imagined being stripped and dragged into a tub. What would he do to Guy?

"Ma'am?" the desk clerk said. She was holding out a room key. "I have you and the little one in Room 220. It's very quiet."

"Do you have two rooms that are adjoining?" Hannah asked.

The woman frowned at her. "Well, yes, on the first floor," she said. "I can't promise they're as quiet as—"

"That's fine, thank you," Hannah said, stealing another look over her shoulder. "I—I want two rooms, with the inside door between."

"Alrighty," the woman murmured. She started typing on her computer keyboard again.

When the desk clerk gave her the keys to Rooms 111 and 112, Hannah quickly stashed one in her purse. She slung the tote strap over her shoulder and pulled the other two suitcases on their wheels. Guy insisted on helping. With one hand beside hers on the strap, he grunted and huffed and puffed.

As they moved across the shiny wet parking lot, Hannah spied the burgundy Volvo out of the corner of her eye. She could see someone in the front seat now. He sat behind the steering wheel. But his face was in the shadows.

They reached Room 112, and stepped inside. Hannah switched on the lights, then closed the door behind them. Guy caught his breath, then fell down on the brown shag-carpeted floor as if passing out.

"Honey, that floor's probably filthy," Hannah said, gazing at the room. There was a TV, and two full-size beds with comforters of a brown, gold, and beige paisley design. They matched the drapes. The headboards and other furnishings were of dark-stained wood in a Mediterranean design. Sixties chic. Framed pictures of pussy willows and birds were screwed to the wall above the beds.

Hannah unlocked the door between the rooms, then opened it. There was a second door, which could only be opened from the other side. Neither of the doors had knobs on the inside.

"Guy, please, get off the floor," Hannah said. "C'mon. We have to take another trip back to the lobby."

Hannah and Guy reemerged from the hotel room. She switched off the lights and shut the door. They started back to the lobby, lugging the suitcases again.

"Why couldn't we stay?" Guy asked.

"That room isn't very clean," Hannah announced loudly. She was shaking her head. "We need to switch to another room."

When they returned to the lobby with all their luggage,

the desk clerk gazed at Hannah with concern. "Is there something wrong, ma'am?"

Hannah shook her head again, and set her room key on the counter. "No, not at all," she said. "I just wanted to know if you can recommend a nearby restaurant."

"Oh," the woman smiled. "Well, from the way you came in here, I got the impression there might be something wrong with the room."

That was the exact impression Hannah wanted to create—for Richard Kidd.

"No, the room's fine," Hannah said. "It's terrific."

"But Mom, you said—"

Hannah shot Guy a look that shut him up.

The desk clerk praised the fare at the Yankee Diner down the block. Hannah thanked her, and made a show of taking the room key from the countertop. Then she grabbed her bags again.

"Ma'am, if you don't mind me asking," the woman said. "Why did you—um, bring your luggage back here with you?"

Hannah waved the room key at her. "Oh, no reason. Thanks again."

She ignored the woman's baffled look, then stashed the key in her purse. She eyed the man in the burgundy car again. He seemed to be watching her every move.

With a semblance of help from Guy, Hannah hauled the suitcases to Room 111, right beside the room she'd just "rejected." She pulled the key out of her purse, and unlocked the door.

Once inside, she switched on the lights, then closed the door behind her. Guy ran to the bed and began bouncing on it. The room was identical to 112—right down to the paisley brown bedspread and curtains.

Hannah hoisted one of the suitcases up on the bed and opened it. She found the first-aid kit she'd packed. She pulled out a roll of white adhesive tape.

She went to the door to the neighboring unit, unlocked

and opened it. The room next door was dark, just as she'd left it.

"Cool!" Guy said. "A secret passage!" He started to run into the other room, but Hannah stopped him.

"Guy, honey, you can't go in there," she said. "Not until I say so, okay? I'm playing a game with someone, and I don't want him to know we have a connecting room. We may have to hide in here—but not until I say so. All right? Do you understand?"

With a sigh of resignation, he nodded.

Hannah taped up the lock catch to the door.

"What game are we playing?" Guy asked. "Hide-and-seek?"

"Sort of," Hannah replied, flattening out the tape.

"Who are we playing with?"

"You don't know him, honey," she said nervously. "I hope you never do. Listen, I want you to lie down for a while. You need to take it easy. I'll get you a glass of water in a minute."

She ducked into the dark room next door. Through a crack in the closed curtains, she saw the figure alone in the car, still parked in the lot. The rain had started up again.

Without moving the curtain, she made sure the window was locked. There was an aluminum bar that kept the window from sliding open. It reminded her of the broom handle she'd sawed down for the front window in their Seattle apartment.

"Mom?" Guy cried from the next room.

"I'll be right there, honey," Hannah called softly to him.

"When do we start playing the game?" she heard him ask.

"Very soon," Hannah replied.

She dead-bolted the outside door, then started back to her son in the connecting room.

Richard Kidd must have been in a sentimental mood last night—or early this morning. On the floor near his unmade bed was a scrapbook with a sleek steel cover. Some drug paraphernalia and a glass that smelled of scotch were on the nightstand. The room had all black-lacquer furniture, with a silver-gray bedspread. Above the headboard was a huge, framed poster from the movie *Peeping Tom*.

Sitting on the bed, Ben opened the album. He glanced at photos of Richard Kidd as a little boy, with bangs and Coke-bottle glasses. In one snapshot, he posed with his Polaroid camera. A laser-printed caption beneath the photo read: *"The beginning of a great career."*

There were several Polaroids of a German shepherd, captioned: *"Misty—1988."* Ben turned the page, and cringed at three photos of the same dog, lying on the ground with its head chopped off.

"Jesus," he muttered.

Ben forced himself to go on. He grimaced at a series of grisly photos showing the bloody, butchered corpses of teenage boys. It took Ben a moment to realize that many of the victims were the same boy. He looked like Seth Stroud, and he was smiling in a couple of shots. They were faked death scenes. Some of the corpses were even played by the young Richard Kidd.

Richard's habit of stalking women must have developed in high school. He'd taken several shots of a pretty young blonde apparently unaware of someone photographing her. The style of these candids was consistent with his later photos of Angela Bramford, Rae, and Hannah.

Richard had saved the same Missoula newspaper article about his short film premiering as an added feature at a chain of local theaters. There were snapshots of him at the opening, along with an old ticket stub.

Ben paged through pictures of Richard at Berkeley. He'd collected letters from movie companies and amateur film contests, all rejections. Seth got in the last word with his captions beside these letters, everything from *"They Can't See Genius"* to *"I Will Persevere."*

While Ben browsed through the album, he listened to make sure no one was outside. The clock ticking on Richard

Kidd's nightstand seemed especially loud, like a metronome.

He noticed—for the first time—above the bed's headboard and below the *Peeping Tom* poster, there were a few speckles. At first, Ben thought they were shadows of raindrops on the big picture window across the room. But Ben leaned closer. It looked like traces of red wine had splashed on the white wall. Someone must have tried to wipe off the stains, but the little dark red spots had sunk in; a permanent remembrance of some wild night.

Wild indeed. On the dresser across from the bed, Ben noticed several cameras. He wondered if Richard Kidd had taken pictures in here for another kind of scrapbook.

Ben went back to the album on his lap. He glanced at a letter from the West Coast Film Institute, informing Richard Kidd that his thirty-minute short, *Sue Aside,* had won first prize in their student film contest. Richard's caption read: *"A Genius Is Discovered."*

"You don't mind yourself at all, do you, Dickie," Ben muttered.

There were articles about *Sue Aside,* scheduled to show at a number of film festivals. Richard had saved preliminary reviews, praising the short movie as *kinky, disturbing,* and *a masterpiece in black comedy.*

From what Ben read, the movie was about a young woman who, after several comic, failed attempts at suicide, finally gets it right by hanging herself from a cord of blinking Christmas lights. Some stills from the movie had made their way into the scrapbook. The film's star was an attractive, edgy-looking, dark-eyed brunette.

Richard had kept solicitous letters from film companies, agents, and independent producers. Apparently, he was very hot stuff.

Ben wondered why Richard wasn't now a famous film director. What had happened to the young movie maverick? The answer came a few pages later, in a *Los Angeles Time* news clipping with the headline:

FILM SHORT, SUE ASIDE,
PULLED FROM RELEASE
*Amateur Director Filmed Actress's
Death on Movie Set*

Heather Stuart, the twenty-two-year-old star of Richard Kidd's breakthrough masterpiece, had, in fact, slowly strangled to death on those cords of blinking Christmas lights. Her panic and struggle, recorded on film, were real. Her strange facial contortions, which brought titters from some viewers, weren't an act.

Richard Kidd gave conflicting accounts of the incident. In one article, he said Heather must have hung herself for real after they'd finished the film that night. In another version, he claimed Heather had wanted to commit suicide, and asked him to film it.

The West Coast Film Institute denounced *Sue Aside,* and revoked Richard Kidd's award. And in a printed response to one editorial suggesting he be charged with manslaughter, Richard Kidd said he should be entitled to *artistic immunity.*

Another editorial predicted Hollywood agents and production companies would be falling all over themselves to snare the notorious Richard Kidd for their projects. But still another editorial maintained that selling popcorn in a movie theater would be the closest Richard Kidd would ever come to working again in the film industry.

Ben couldn't find any evidence in the scrapbook indicating an investigation or trial. But the next few pages held letters of rejection from agents, film companies, and studios. Richard Kidd captioned these with phrases like *"Believe in yourself"* and *"You Have a Vision; They are Blind."*

Richard's address on the letters changed from San Francisco to Seattle. But his luck remained the same. Numerous rejections to applications for film contests, grants, and college teaching-assistant programs seemed to attest to Richard Kidd's undesirability.

But there was a letter to a Seth Stroud on Aloha Street,

dated January 27, 2001, complimenting him on the experimental videos he'd sent, *Sticks and Bones* and *Dead Center.* The gentleman writing back to Seth Stroud was interested in meeting him. He planned on making his own independent film, and wanted Seth's participation. The note was signed by Paul Gulletti.

Under the letter, Richard had the caption *"A New Beginning."*

Ben sighed. Ironically, that was the last page of Richard Kidd's scrapbook. It was also the last of Richard Kidd, filmmaker. He'd borrowed his friend's name in order to work in the movies. Too bad he'd hung his hopes on Paul Gulletti, whose big talk about making an independent film would probably never amount to anything.

But Richard certainly got his revenge on Paul; torturing his mentor by stealing his women, then letting him know when and how he was going to kill them.

Ben figured there had to be another scrapbook somewhere, one with Angela Bramford, Rae, and all the others. Hannah too, of course. Perhaps the second volume was in Seth Stroud's garage apartment, now tagged as police evidence against suicide victim Seth Stroud.

Ben glanced at the ticking clock on the nightstand: almost a quarter to twelve. He wondered where Hannah and Guy were right now.

Downstairs, on the VCR in Seth's living room, the digital counter switched from eleven to ten minutes.

Through the rain-beaded windshield and across the parking lot, Richard Kidd watched her open the curtains. He reached for his video camera.

But Hannah wouldn't quite come into focus. The light wasn't strong enough in the hotel room, and he kept getting a reflection of the parking lot in her window. There wasn't much to photograph anyway. She was unpacking a few things while the kid sat up in bed, watching TV.

He wasn't sure how far Hannah intended to run. But this hotel was as far as she would ever get.

Like his prey, Richard had also packed this morning. In addition to clothes, he'd brought along some essentials: spare cameras and film, skeleton keys from Seth's job, and a gun, among other things.

He knew the police might be looking for him soon. His friend, Seth, was a loose end with dozens of loose ends connected to him. He'd had to go. But even after planting all that evidence in Seth's apartment and removing everything of his own, Richard figured in his haste something might have gotten past him.

He was prepared for the possibility of never returning to Seattle. He had also prepared for the possibility of the police invading his home. They would find a lot of evidence there, certainly enough to put him away for life.

He'd fixed it so none of that evidence would ever leave his house. It wouldn't happen right away. He had a timer set for twenty-eight minutes after motion detectors picked up activity. By that time, his house would be full of cops.

Dead men and women, all of them.

Too bad he wouldn't be there to film it.

But he had a far more important scene to realize today, here at this crummy hotel. He'd been preparing for this for some time now. The wait would soon be over.

Richard Kidd gazed at Hannah in the window, and he smiled.

The timer on the VCR in Richard Kidd's living room was counting down from nine minutes.

Upstairs, Ben discovered Richard's large walk-in closet, which had been converted into an office with a built-in desk, state-of-the-art video equipment, a TV-VCR, and a library of homemade tapes. There must have been a hundred of them, all labeled. Ben noticed about a dozen tagged *Video Store,* with various dates. He also saw one called *On the*

Yacht, from earlier in the week. He wondered if it showed Richard and Seth planting the bomb on Kenneth Woodley's boat. Which one of them was the explosives expert?

Ben popped the tape into the VCR and switched on the TV. He recognized Kenneth Woodley. He was with a cheap-looking blonde below the deck of that doomed yacht. They were doing lines of cocaine together. He started undressing her. Then, suddenly, he hit her—again and again. Her screams came over the soundtrack. Ben winced at each brutal blow. He saw what Hannah had endured while married to the son of a bitch.

He couldn't fathom how Richard Kidd just sat back and videotaped Kenneth beating the hell out of that poor woman. Then again, this was a killer, a voyeur who had kept the cameras rolling while his star strangled to death in *Sue Aside.*

What was going on in the galley of that yacht bordered on rape. Ben couldn't watch anymore. He stopped the VCR and ejected the video.

Among the cassette boxes on the shelf, one labeled *Goodbar, Raw Footage* caught his eye. Ben glanced at his watch. Almost ten to twelve. He didn't want to linger there much longer. But he needed to make certain he had enough evidence for the police. Then they could come in and turn the place upside down.

Ben inserted the *Goodbar, Raw Footage* tape into the VCR. He found himself staring at a shot of the bed in the very next room. But the *Peeping Tom* poster was gone. His old girlfriend, Rae, and Richard Kidd wandered into the picture, then sat down on the bed. It broke Ben's heart to see her again, looking so pretty and vulnerable.

What she and Richard Kidd were saying to one another was garbled. Ben experimented with the volume, but with no luck. Apparently, the mike wasn't within range. Another thing was apparent: Rae didn't know she was being videotaped. She laughed at a joke Richard made, then kissed him. They fell back on the bed, and their faces were no longer in the picture. The two entwined bodies could have belonged to any horny couple. Ben impatiently hit the fast-forward button. After a moment, Richard shifted her around in the bed. He obviously knew where the camera was, and wanted Rae's face in the frame. He climbed on top of her and started to unbutton her blouse. Then he reached for something beside the bed.

Ben slowed the tape to normal speed, and watched as Richard recreated the *Goodbar* scene with a strobe light. Rae looked uncomfortable. She was saying something, but the words were indecipherable. Amid the staccato, flickering image of those two people on that bed in the next room, Ben noticed Richard pull a knife from under the mattress. All at once, he started stabbing Rae in the chest.

Ben felt sick as he watched his old girlfriend struggle with this maniac. Then she stopped struggling.

Richard climbed off the bed, leaving her to lie there, lifeless. Her dead eyes gazed at the ceiling. Bloodstains bloomed on the white bedsheets tangled around her.

Ben could see some of the blood splattered on the headboard and wall. He realized those weren't wine stains he'd noticed earlier. He'd been looking at Rae's blood.

Ben swallowed hard, then wiped the tears from his eyes. He was about to eject the tape, but accidentally hit the fast-forward button again.

In rapid, sputtering motion, Richard switched off his strobe light. Then his friend Seth Stroud wandered into the bedroom. The two of them started to strip the bed, leaving Rae's semi-nude corpse in the middle.

Ben slowed the tape to normal speed again. He could see a shiny plastic lining beneath those bloody bedsheets. Seth said something that he alone thought was funny. He was laughing as they peeled the plastic sheet off the mattress. They bundled Rae and the blood-soaked linens inside the tarp-like sheet.

Seth started moving toward the camera. "Lighten up," he muttered as he came into range of the microphone. "I'm the one who should be in a shitty mood. I spent the better part of my night digging a fucking hole for her in that ravine near the cemetery. You owe me big-time. I'm gonna—"

Seth switched off the camera. Ben stared at the snowy static for a moment.

He remembered a ravine near the cemetery where Bruce and Brandon Lee were buried. Hannah had pointed it out.

He quickly ejected the video.

He wouldn't let this particular cassette out of his sight until he handed it over to the police. It answered all questions as to what had happened to his friend, Rae Palmer. The content of the tape sickened him. But it ended a month-long search.

Ben could hear the clock ticking in Richard's bedroom. He glanced at a wastebasket near the desk, and spotted a plastic bag. He loaded the video inside. He figured he should go. He now had what he'd come a long way to find. Getting to his feet, he took one last look at the video library. He wondered about a video labeled *Hannah* and another, *Vertigo Revisited.*

He inserted *Vertigo Revisited* into the VCR.

"COULD YOU PUT DOWN THE FUCKING CAMERA FOR A MINUTE, MAN?" Seth said.

It was startlingly loud. Ben had forgotten he'd tinkered with the sound in the *Goodbar* video. He grabbed the remote and lowered the volume.

On the screen, the picture was so dark and murky, Seth could barely be seen walking up a continual flight of stairs. He seemed to be inside a tower. He was addressing the camera, apparently held by Richard Kidd.

"You're getting on my nerves with that thing," Seth went on, sneering at the camera. "I mean it. Why are you taping now anyway?"

"It's a test shoot, dum-dum," Richard responded, a disembodied voice behind the camera. "We have to get it right for tomorrow night when we take Hannah up here. We'll need a higher-exposure film, that's for sure."

"Yeah, the lighting here sucks." Seth sighed, forging up the staircase. "Plus we'll have to drag her ass up here. This is gonna take a helluva lot of work tomorrow."

The handheld camera was a little unsteady keeping up with him. "You know the one we should have filmed dying?" Seth continued, a bit out of breath. "That bitch we threw out of the apartment-building window. Perfect light, and lots of room to move around."

"I told you already," Richard replied. "I only videotaped her for surveillance. The death scenes are exclusively for my leading ladies. The others don't matter."

"You and your goddamn leading ladies," Seth groaned, shaking his head at the camera. "You hold onto those tapes of them like an old miser. I helped make them too, you know. Hell, who's the one who went in that video store time after time wearing a wire so you could hear what was going on with your precious Hannah? If it weren't for me and that wire, you never would've heard those two customers bitching at her. And those were two of our best kills. I put a lot of hours on each one of your mini-masterpieces. Least you could do is loan them out to me once in a while. I'm sentimental too, you know."

"I'd will them to you, Seth," Richard said. "Only, we both know you'll die first."

"Always cheers me up whenever you say that," Seth muttered.

"Anyway, the tapes will probably go up in smoke. No one else is getting them. In fact, I've had the place rigged in case the cops ever start gathering evidence."

Seth laughed. "Shit, no. You mean like in the boat? With a timer and a delay?"

Ben wasn't sure he'd heard him right. He stopped the tape, then backed it up again. For a moment, while the tape rewound, he could hear the clock ticking in the bedroom.

He was about to stop the tape again. But all of a sudden, he heard someone downstairs. *"She had me show her how to rig it to a door—with a little delay. . . ."*

Ben froze for a moment. He realized the voice downstairs was someone on TV.

He ran through the bedroom and stopped at the top of the stairs. He could see the living-room television. It had come on by itself. Mickey Rourke was talking to William Hurt.

"Does any of this mean anything to you?" Rourke was asking.

Ben knew the movie: *Body Heat.* They were talking about Kathleen Turner's character, plotting to kill Hurt in a boathouse with a delayed explosive device.

For a second, Ben couldn't move.

. . . the tapes will go up in smoke . . .

. . . I already have the place rigged . . .

Does any of this mean anything to you?

Suddenly, Ben bolted back toward the bedroom closet. The video was still rewinding in the VCR. On the television screen, Richard was moving backward down the church-tower steps at an impossibly rapid pace.

Ben ejected the tape, then swiped up a couple of the videos on the desk and stashed them in the plastic bag. He raced past the bed where Rae had been slain, grabbed one of the small cameras from the dresser top, and headed for the large picture window.

There was no time to think about what he was doing. Ben had to get out of the house. He hurled the camera at the window, punching a hole through the center and splintering the glass. Ben covered his face and neck the best he could, then dove through the opening.

For a second, he didn't feel anything. He was aware of falling, and he heard the window breaking and popping. Everything else was a blur. He was working on pure adrenaline. Survival instincts.

At that same moment, an explosion tore through the tiny house.

The force of it shattered windows in a couple of neighboring homes. The people who saw the blast would describe the flames, and the black, billowing smoke. They said the ground shook. Sparks and debris shot hundreds of feet through the air.

They said no one could have survived it.

Twenty-four

"Has Ben Podowski checked in yet?" she asked, glancing at her wristwatch. It was five-twenty.

"No, ma'am, not yet," the Best Western operator told her on the other end of the line. "But we're expecting him."

"Do you know if he called in for his messages? He said he might."

"Is this Ann Sturges?" the operator asked.

"Um, yes," Hannah said. She looked over at Guy under the covers. He stirred a little in his sleep. He'd been napping since four-fifteen.

"We still have you on the message board, Ms. Sturges. So he hasn't called in yet, no. Can he still reach you at the Sleepy Bear Motel in Tacoma at 360-555-0916?"

"Yes, thanks."

"We'll make sure he gets the message when he checks in or calls."

"Thank you. Good-bye." Hannah hung up the phone. Something had happened to Ben; otherwise he would have called her. She prayed he was all right, but Hannah had a horrible feeling her prayers were too late. She'd left the first message for him over four hours ago.

In that time, she and Guy had had Chinese food delivered for lunch; they'd watched cartoons on the TV; Hannah had called Ben's hotel two more times; the rain had let up; and that lone, shadowy figure hadn't moved from the front seat of the burgundy Volvo.

Hannah wandered to the window. She could see her reflection in the darkened glass. She knew he could see her, too. He was still out there in the parking lot. He was probably waiting for her to take a shower.

Hannah wanted him to know she was settling in for the night, so she'd kept the curtains open. What he didn't know was that they had a connecting room, an escape route, their own panic room—with a phone.

She glanced down at the aluminum bar in the window groove, a security device meant to keep the window from sliding open too far. She furtively lifted the bar from between the grooves along the windowsill. Then she let it drop on the floor, near her feet.

Hannah walked away from the window and sat down on the bed across from Guy. Peeking up at her from his pillow, he rubbed his eyes and yawned. "Hi, Mom," he muttered.

She felt his forehead. He didn't seem to be running a fever at all. "Honey, remember how I said earlier that we were going to play a game?"

He nodded. "We were gonna play after lunch, but you said no."

Hannah stroked his hair. "That's right. But we're starting the game now. It's a very serious game, Guy. I need you to do exactly what I tell you. Do you understand?"

The brat climbed out of bed. He was in his T-shirt and underpants. He said something to his mother, then retreated into the bathroom.

With his camera, Richard Kidd zoomed in on Hannah Doyle as she unbuttoned her blouse. The light was better now, no reflection on the window. She was in focus. She had her shirt open, with a bra underneath. She pulled a robe out of the closet.

Richard didn't expect it, but he felt himself getting hard. He watched Hannah tie back her blond hair in a ponytail.

The brat emerged from the bathroom and scurried back into the bed.

Hannah said something to him; then she stepped into the bathroom. Richard put down the camera for a moment. He reached into the bag on the floor of the passenger side.

He found the butcher's knife he'd brought along specifically for tonight. He'd wrapped it up in a towel. The blade was eight inches long. He kept the knife hidden in the towel as he stepped out of his car. He glanced again at the window to Room 111.

Hannah came out of the bathroom, still wearing her robe. She had a shampoo bottle in her hand.

Richard stood by the car with the door open. He watched her say something to the brat. The kid yanked up the comforter, covering his face. She pulled it down to speak to him, but he only tugged the comforter back up again, huddling beneath it.

Hannah turned down the lights. It was so dim in there, Richard didn't think the place would photograph well. But he'd have good, strong light in the bathroom, and that was where it really mattered.

He'd have to cheat a little, of course. Holding a camera and wielding the knife would be difficult. Later, he'd videotape a few shadowy shots of himself raising the knife and plunging it downward. Then he'd splice those shots into footage of the actual murder.

He watched his leading lady saunter over to the window and close the curtains.

He tucked the swaddled knife under his arm. After retrieving his video camera from the front seat, he shut the car door.

He headed for Room 111, where Hannah Doyle would give her final performance.

"Oh, Guy, you're being so good," Hannah whispered, quickly leading him into the connecting room. She was carrying his clothes, shoes, and jacket. She sat him on the floor, between the two beds. "Now, I want you to get dressed. Then stay down here, and be very quiet. Stay there until I say it's okay. Understand, sweetheart?"

Wide-eyed, he nodded.

Hannah kissed the top of his head. She threw off her robe. She was still dressed underneath it. Buttoning up her blouse, she went to the window and peeked through the slit between the curtains. She could see Richard Kidd skulking toward Room 111. She'd been right about him and the *Vertigo* murder. The teacher's assistant she'd known as Seth Stroud was indeed someone else, and he wasn't really dead.

Richard Kidd neared the row of rooms. Hannah could see he had a video camera in his hand and a towel tucked under one arm.

Grabbing a pillow from the bed, Hannah hurried back to the other room. She shoved the pillow under the sheets of the bed Guy had just vacated, then pulled the comforter back up. It looked like there was a small body in the bed. Hannah rolled her eyes and hoped he'd fall for it.

She swiped the aluminum bar off the floor by the window. Breathlessly, she ran into the bathroom and turned on the shower, full blast. She closed the curtain, then darted out of the bathroom, shutting the door behind her.

On her way to the connecting room, Hannah paused. She noticed a shadow on the window curtains, the silhouette of someone creeping up to the door. Past the muffled roar of the shower, she could hear him rattling the doorknob and fiddling with the lock.

Hannah ducked into the connecting room. She checked the adhesive tape over the lock. Still secure. There was no knob on the inside, so she gave the door a quick tug. It shut, but not quite all the way.

"All right now, honey," she whispered. "Be very quiet."

" 'Kay, Mom," Guy answered in a loud whisper.

Clutching the aluminum bar in her hand, Hannah leaned

close to the door. She heard some clicking. He was still working on the lock next door.

Richard Kidd managed to unlock the motel room door with his dead friend's skeleton key. Seth had always been the expert at breaking and entering. But Richard had picked up a few of his tricks.

Quietly, he opened the door. He didn't want her brat interfering. He'd planned on slitting the kid's throat very quickly, then moving on to Mommy in the shower.

But the kid appeared to be asleep again already. The covers were still pulled over his head from their game of peekaboo earlier. He didn't stir.

Richard closed the door behind him. He decided to leave the little shit alone until afterward. He liked the idea of killing Hannah with a clean knife. And he needed to catch her while she was still in the shower. Stopping to do away with the son might screw that up.

As he crept toward the bathroom, Richard could hear the shower water churning. He glanced back toward the beds. The kid hadn't moved at all, just a lump under the covers.

Clutching the knife handle, Richard shook off the small towel, and tucked the blade back under his arm. He switched on the video camera and put it up to his face. He reached for the bathroom door with his free hand.

For a fleeting moment, he missed his friend. How much easier it might have been with one man filming, and another stabbing. But he only needed one hand to work the knife. And he'd become accustomed to operating a camera while running, driving, and conducting all sorts of activities. He was up for the challenge.

Richard filmed the door opening. A bright light swept across the dim bedroom, and steam fogged up the lens for a moment.

The bathroom came into focus: white tiles, beige wallpaper. The shower curtain was white plastic, not the semi-transparent kind. He couldn't see her on the other side. But he could imagine.

She was naked, of course. She probably had her eyes closed. She couldn't hear him. And she certainly couldn't hear the quiet, mechanical humming noise from his video camera.

Gazing at that closed shower curtain, he felt a little giddy and nervous. It wasn't just the steam that was making him sweat. Richard filmed his hand slowly reaching for the curtain.

Suddenly, his movements became accelerated. His adrenaline was pumping. He yanked the curtain open, then quickly pulled the knife from under his other arm. Richard was looking through his camera as he raised the butcher's knife. He wanted to capture her screams on videotape.

But the shower was empty.

Another heavy wave of vapor clouded his camera lens.

"What the hell?" Richard Kidd muttered angrily. He lowered the camera and the knife, then turned toward the open door.

He didn't expect to see Hannah. He barely had time to realize she was there. All at once, she slammed the aluminum bar over his head.

Richard Kidd howled in pain. The video camera fell out of his hands and broke on the tiled floor. The butcher's knife flew into the tub. Though stunned, Richard remained on his feet. Blood oozed from the gash on his forehead.

Hannah hit him again, knocking his glasses off. He stumbled back, almost falling into the tub. He accidentally knocked the shower head askew. The hot water doused both of them.

"Fucking bitch!" Richard growled, enraged. He managed to regain his footing.

The steam from the shower set off the smoke detector in the next room. The beeping noise echoed in the brightly lit white bathroom.

Hannah tried to strike him again with the aluminum rod. But Richard Kidd reeled back and hit her across the face.

Hannah's feet slipped from under her. She fell back on the slick, tiled floor, bumping her head on the side of the tub.

Catching his breath, Richard Kidd stared at her. Without his glasses, it took a moment for him to focus. She'd been knocked unconscious. The shower spray was pelting her. Hannah's blond hair was matted down. The blood coming from her mouth looked like pink drool that the pulsating water waved away. It stained the front of her blouse.

The knife was still in the tub.

Richard glanced at the mirror above the sink, then wiped the fogged glass. He had two gashes on his forehead, seeping blood.

"Goddamn you," he muttered. He gave Hannah's leg a fierce kick. Then he kicked his broken video camera. It slid across the wet floor. He picked up his designer glasses. Both lenses were cracked.

The smoke alarm continued to beep at an obnoxious, high pitch.

Grabbing a washcloth from the sink, Richard held it to his bleeding forehead. Again, he stared at the butcher's knife in the tub.

She'd ruined his death scene. All those weeks of planning and preparing, and she'd fucked it all up. Killing her now was too easy. She was semiconscious at best. She'd barely even feel it. That wouldn't do. He wanted her to suffer.

He wanted Hannah to regain consciousness. And then she would wake up to a nightmare.

Hannah tasted blood in her mouth. Soaked and shivering, she lay in a puddle of cold water on the bathroom floor. When she sat up, her head started to throb.

She'd lost some time. But she didn't know how much. A few moments? An hour? The shower wasn't running anymore. The smoke detector was no longer beeping. Hannah squinted up at the ceiling in the next room. The alarm device had been smashed. She noticed blood smears on the bathroom door, and a bloodstained washcloth on the floor just beyond the bathroom threshold. She glanced around for the butcher's knife, but didn't see it.

Suddenly, she heard a door slam in the next unit.

"Guy," she whispered, panic-stricken. She got to her feet, and nearly collapsed again. The floor was so slippery. Her leg ached something awful. Had he kicked her?

Hannah hobbled out of the bathroom. Tracking water on the brown shag carpet, she hurried to the door connecting to Room 112. It was locked.

"Guy?" she called, pounding on the door. Tears stung her eyes. "Guy, are you in there?"

No response.

Hannah ran out the other door. It was cold outside, and she was soaked to the bone. But she hardly noticed.

She banged on Room 112. The door creaked open. "Guy, are you in here?" she cried, stepping inside the dark room. She checked between the beds, then under them.

The lamp on the nightstand table had been knocked over. There was blood on the white shade.

Hannah bolted back outside. She spotted the old burgundy Volvo in the lot. Richard hadn't driven away with him.

She had hoped to use that car to get away. After knocking Richard Kidd unconscious, she would have phoned the police and reported a man attacking a woman in Room 111 of the Sleepy Bear Motel. Then she would have taken his car and driven off with her son.

But now Richard Kidd had her little boy.

Hannah gazed around the parking lot. She was shaking. Tears streamed down her face. She had to remind herself to breathe.

She heard Guy scream, but for only a couple of seconds. He was drowned out by the sound of a train whistle. Still, she knew it was Guy. She knew his voice.

Hannah ran to the side of the motel. Beyond some shrubbery and a barbed-wire fence was the railroad switching yard. She stared at the rows of freight cars lined up on the tracks. The yard was well lit. Rain puddles had formed in the shallow, rocky gullies between the tracks. The place smelled of oil and freshly cut wood. A couple of the trains were moving.

Hannah saw an opening in the fence, then wove through the bushes. She passed a couple of old empty boxcars on the first track line. Her leg began to hurt more as she forged over the coarse rocks and gravel around the tracks. A cold wind cut through her, and she shuddered.

She heard another scream, much closer this time. Hannah found an opening between a tanker and a flatcar stacked with lumber. Down the next line of tracks, she saw them.

Richard was hauling Guy toward a moving train on the next track. He paused for a moment, then glanced back at Hannah and smiled. Blood from the cuts on his forehead streaked down his face.

Guy was shrieking and struggling in his arms.

"Let him go!" Hannah screamed. She hurried toward them. Up ahead, a train rounded a curve in the tracks. For moment, the locomotive's front light blinded her. The loud horn muted the sound of Guy's screams.

Past the glaring light, Hannah caught sight of them again. Richard was loading Guy into an empty boxcar of an idle train. He climbed aboard after Guy.

Hannah started running after them, sidestepping around wooden ties and rails. She tripped on a lockbox, and toppled forward onto the rocky gravel. It hurt like hell. She knew she'd scraped her hands and knees. She knew she was bleeding. But there was no time to stop and look.

Pulling herself up, Hannah felt a loose spike on the ground. She hid it in the waistband along the back of her jeans. Once again, she staggered toward the train. She heard its air brakes hissing, and the engine starting up.

Out of breath, Hannah hobbled toward the open boxcar.

Then she stopped dead.

Richard Kidd was standing inside the freight car, holding a butcher's knife to Guy's throat. Silent, with tears running down his cheeks, Guy looked utterly terrified. His little body was shaking. The front of his jacket had been smeared with blood. It took Hannah a moment to realize that the blood was Richard Kidd's.

He was grinning at her. She'd never seen him without his trademark glasses. She didn't realize how cold his eyes could be. With his face covered in blood, he appeared almost demonic.

"Let him go," Hannah gasped. "I'll do anything you say."

Richard Kidd merely snickered. "Come and get him."

Hannah hesitated, then boosted herself up into the car. Putting weight on her bad leg, she nearly fell backward onto the rock piling and the next set of rails. She grabbed hold of the boxcar's sliding door. "Please," she said, catching her breath. "Please, it's me you want—"

Another blast from a locomotive drowned her out. As much as Hannah pleaded, she knew he couldn't hear her. And she knew it didn't matter what she said. He was still going to kill her little boy.

With the knife tip, Richard Kidd traced a thin line of blood along Guy's neck. Guy didn't register any sign of pain. But he was still trembling.

"What do you want from me?" Hannah screamed.

"I wanted you to be my leading lady, Hannah," he yelled over the churning, noisy din of the train yard. He took the knife away from Guy's throat for a moment, only to wipe the blood out of his eyes with the back of his hand. "I was pulling all the strings for you," he went on, the blade against Guy's neck once again. "I was watching over you, Hannah, protecting you. I have hours and hours of screen-test footage shot of you. What a fucking waste. You could have been my leading lady. But you're just as bad as those other bitches who came before you." He shook his head at her. "At last when it didn't work out with them, I got to film their

death scenes. They were sacrificed for my art. At least I had
something to show for my efforts with them. But you, Hannah, you've left me with nothing."

"I'll make it up to you, Seth," she said. "I mean *Richard*.
I'll do whatever you want. I'm sorry."

He glared at her. "You think you're very clever," he retorted. "You don't know what sorry is yet."

He dragged Guy over to the other side of the huge, open
door. He glanced back at a train approaching in the distance.
Holding Guy under the chin, Richard pushed him toward
the opening. "Ever see anyone thrown in front of a moving
train before?" he asked.

Guy shrieked.

"Please, no . . ." Hannah begged. Poised on the other side
of the door, she reached back for the railroad spike tucked
in the waistband of her jeans. The train was coming closer,
picking up speed. The sound of its grinding engine grew
louder.

Richard laughed. Again, he took the knife away from
Guy's throat so he could wipe the blood out of his eyes.

Just then, the car gave a jolt that shook all three of them.
Suddenly, they were moving.

Guy broke away from him. At the same moment, Hannah
lunged at Richard, stabbing him in the shoulder with the rail
spike. He dropped his knife and howled in pain.

The deafening noise from the train wheels and engine
drowned out his cries. The boxcar rocked and quaked as it
picked up speed.

Grabbed hold of the sliding door, Richard managed to
stay on his feet. He pulled the spike from his shoulder.
Blood leaked down his jacket.

Crouched near the floor on the other side of the opening,
Hannah pulled Guy behind her. Richard was breathing hard
as he came at them. He shook his head and said something.
But she couldn't hear what it was.

The car took another jolt. Richard lost his balance. Red

ing toward the edge of the open door, he clawed at Hannah and managed to grab hold of her sleeve.

But she clung to a latch on the door.

His arms flailing, Richard fell out of the boxcar—into the path of the oncoming train.

There was a loud blast from the engine. The brakes screeched. Hannah pulled Guy toward her, shielding his face. She turned away as well. She didn't want to see Richard Kidd mangled and crushed under the locomotive.

Watching people die had been something he liked. But not her, and not her little boy.

Curling up against the wall of the boxcar, Hannah held onto Guy. Wind swept through the open door. They were both shivering. "It's okay, honey," she assured him. "We're both all right."

" 'Kay," he said in a small voice.

She felt him nodding against her shoulder.

Hannah patted him on the back. "It was just like a nightmare, sweetie," she said, over the churning locomotive. "But we're safe now. Everything's all right."

He stopped crying. Hannah rocked him in her arms. "Listen to the choo-choo train, Guy," she whispered. "Listen to the train. . . ."

Epilogue

The nightmare wasn't over for Hannah.

Guy was taken from her. She spent the night at a women's holding center at the King County jail. At least they gave her a private cell.

Another small solace, Guy got to stay with Joyce—and not in some children's shelter.

Hannah had called her from the emergency room o Tacoma General, near the rail yard. Joyce had made it to the hospital by cab five minutes before the Seattle detective showed up. Guy had been released into her care.

Hannah, who had severe bruises on her leg and face, ha been taken back to Seattle—in handcuffs.

On Saturday afternoon, Jennifer Dorn Podowski wa making arrangements for her husband. She handled every thing on-line and on the phone. She'd instructed the Seattl Medical Examiner's office to have the remains flown t New York after the autopsy. The body would be buried in cemetery not far from their home in Croton-on-Hudson.

Ben said it was the least they could do for Rae. She ha no family.

That Saturday morning, police had searched a ravine i north Capital Hill, and they'd found her remains, wrappe in a plastic sheet buried in a shallow grave. They kne where to look, thanks to Ben.

He'd spent Friday night in Harbor View Hospital, where doctors reset his broken left arm, then put it in a cast. They also sewed seventeen stitches in that same shoulder. There were dozens of other cuts and abrasions from the broken glass, and some second-degree burns from the explosion.

The police detectives who questioned Ben in his hospital bed said he was lucky to be alive.

Another bit of luck; they'd found two videotapes in a plastic bag hidden under his torn, seared shirt. He'd given the tapes to the cop who had discovered him. Bloody, charred, covered with dirt and debris, he'd been wandering near the recycling bins of the apartment building across the street from Richard Kidd's residence—or what was left of it. The cop had written on his report that Ben Podowski had appeared dazed and incoherent.

But Ben had known exactly what he was doing at the time.

The first tape had Seth Stroud ascending the church tower, talking to his friend with the camera. Between the two of them, they made references to the boat explosion, a plot to kill Hannah Doyle, and Richard Kidd's booby-trapped house.

If that wasn't enough to shed light on their culpability in this killing spree, the second video showed Richard stabbing Rae Palmer, and Seth Stroud helping dispose of the body.

While detectives in the East Precinct were viewing the tapes and becoming more interested in the whereabouts of Hannah Doyle, their colleagues were interviewing Ben Podowski in Harbor View Hospital's emergency ward. The doctor on duty didn't appreciate the constant police presence while sewing up his patient.

Ben kept asking to use the phone. He wanted to call the Best Western Executive Inn. He had to find out if Hannah had left a message, and make sure she was all right. But the police kept telling him that if he needed to phone anyone, they'd make the call for him. The doctor finally had to knock Ben out with a sedative, because he wouldn't sit still.

Kevin O'Brien

He woke up at seven o'clock that night, in a hospital bed. He was covered with bandages and salve for his burns. A nurse was there. And a couple of detectives were waiting to talk with him. Ben's first words were: "Is Hannah okay? Hannah Doyle?"

"Yes, we have her in custody," one of the detectives answered.

They questioned him for the next two and a half hours. At Ben's suggestion, the police interviewed Paul Gulletti about the man calling himself Seth Stroud, and about Paul's relationships with a couple of the murder victims.

Detectives also spoke with several students in Paul's class. Most of them misidentified photos of the real Seth Stroud, claiming he was the teacher's assistant. Tish at the video store also had trouble differentiating photos of the two men.

The pair of killers had indeed looked very much alike. If not for Ben and Hannah, perhaps Richard Kidd might have gotten away with murdering his friend—as well as so many others.

On Saturday morning, Ben's wife faxed the police hard copies of Rae Palmer's e-mails. The documents linked the rooftop "suicide" of Joe Blankenship and Lily Abrams's death with the others. They would finally put the Floating Flower case to rest.

Richard Kidd had been living quite well off a monthly allowance from his late father's trust fund. His mother in Missoula, Montana, refused to believe the awful stories the police were telling about her son.

The murders made national news by Saturday morning. The media couldn't help comparing Richard Kidd and Seth Stroud to their kill-for-kicks predecessors, Leopold and Loeb.

By Saturday afternoon, CNN was showing a clip from Richard Kidd's film short *Sue Aside*. A video and DVD company was already trying to acquire distribution rights to

Sue Aside as well as Richard's other student films, *Dead Center and Sticks and Bones*.

According to news reports, Hannah Doyle, the killers' most recent prey, was unavailable for comment. She was being held by Seattle police as a "person of interest" in several investigations unrelated to the murders.

Ben desperately wanted to talk with her, but the police weren't allowing Hannah any incoming calls.

When he was released from the hospital at three-thirty Saturday afternoon, Ben took a taxi to Emerald City Video. He'd had one of the nurses buy him some new clothes at the Gap: black pants, a crisp white shirt, and a fall jacket. But with his arm in a cast and three small bandages on his face, Ben still looked pretty beat-up as he hobbled into the video store.

The place was a mob scene.

"We had a TV news crew in here a couple of hours ago," Scott told him. "Plus we have all these morbid nutcases coming in. They're not even renting. They're just poking around, being major pains in the ass. I'm not supposed to be working today. I just got out of the hospital. You too, I guess, huh?"

Threading through the crowd, Ben and Scott ducked into the employee break room. "I'm only putting in a couple of hours to help Tish out, because I'm such a saint—or such a sap," Scott explained, shutting the door behind him. "You look like you need to sit down more than I do," he said, pulling out the chair. "Take a load off."

"Thanks," Ben said, sitting down. His painkillers were wearing off.

"So have you heard anything about Hannah?" Scott asked anxiously.

"No, I was hoping you could tell me something. I tried phoning Guy's baby-sitter, Joyce, but I wasn't getting an answer."

"She came by earlier," Scott said. "I guess Hannah's in-laws flew in this morning. They're staying at the Four

Seasons. They were smart enough to have Joyce bring Guy over there. Joyce said they sent a limo for them. Then the limo drove her back. Anyway, Guy's with his grandparents now. Joyce said he started crying when she left."

"Oh, God," Ben whispered. "The poor kid."

"Hannah's in-laws sent someone over here, too," Scott said, folding his arms and leaning against the door. "I think he was a detective working for their attorneys. I don't know. He talked with Tish mostly. He was asking about Hannah's tax records, and any forms she might have signed."

"What for?" Ben murmured.

"I think Hannah's in-laws are going after her with both barrels. This guy mentioned something about Hannah committing fraud against the government—in addition to kidnapping, theft, and forgery charges." Scott shook his head, and his eyes teared up. "Looks like they're really sticking it to our girl."

Ben frowned. "I don't get it," he said. "You'd think they'd want to sweep it all under the rug, and pay her to keep quiet. Don't they know why she took Guy and left? Do they have any clue that their son was an abusive asshole?"

"Apparently not," Scott replied, shrugging.

Ben glanced up at the tiny TV-VCR on the shelf above the desk. "Hey, Scott?"

"Yeah?"

He nodded at the little television. "Do you think I could borrow that for the afternoon?"

The small TV had a carrying handle on the top, and didn't weigh much at all. Still, Ben took a taxi from the video store to 1313 East Republican Street, only a few blocks away.

Richard Kidd's bungalow was now a burnt-out shell, cordoned off with yellow police tape. The front yard was littered with rubble and debris. A patrol car was parked in front, and a couple of curiosity-seekers stood on the sidewalk, trying to get a better look at the place.

Ben had the cab drop him off, then wait up the block. He headed for the apartment building across the street from the blast site. He walked under the canopy, past the recycling bins, then down the basement stairwell. He found his duffel bag, still buried under a pile of leaves at the bottom of those cement steps.

The cop who had found him wandering around there yesterday had said Ben appeared disoriented. But Ben had known what he was doing.

Taking the duffel bag, he hobbled back to the waiting cab. Ben thanked the driver for waiting. He put his bag on the seat, beside the portable TV.

"Can you take me to the Four Seasons Hotel, please?" he asked.

Answering the door to Suite 619 was a well-groomed, thirty-year-old man in a three-piece suit. He could have been a lawyer, a bodyguard, or someone who worked for a funeral parlor. He didn't introduce himself to Ben. He just looked him up and down, and asked, "Are you Ben Podowski?"

Standing at the threshold with a portable TV-VCR tucked under his one good arm and holding onto his duffel bag, Ben nodded.

"Mrs. Woodley will give you five minutes, that's all," the man said stiffly.

Ben followed him into the living room, where Mrs. Woodley sat on a sofa. The elegantly appointed room offered a sweeping view of Puget Sound. She had the television on mute, and in front of her was a fancy tea set and a plate of fruit and cookies that she'd been picking at.

With her frosty gaze, stiff mink-colored hair, and the pink suit, Mrs. Woodley looked like a First Lady—minus the people skills. She sipped her tea, and nodded at Ben.

Though he had a cast on one arm and was struggling with

the little TV and his bag, Mrs. Woodley didn't ask her lackey in the three-piece suit to lend him a hand.

"I was hoping to talk Mr. Woodley," Ben said, setting down his bag.

"Mr. Woodley is terribly busy," she said. "And so am I. Now, what is it you wanted to see me about?"

"How's Guy doing?" Ben asked. "Is he okay?"

"Little Ken is napping right now," Mrs. Woodley replied. "And he can't be disturbed."

Ben glanced down around the baseboards for an outlet. "Well, tell him that Ben said 'hi.' We got to be good friends in the last few days." He propped the TV on a desk by the window, then plugged it in.

"You have about three and a half more minutes," the man in the business suit announced. His arms folded, he stood behind the couch where the woman sat.

Ben glanced at Mrs. Woodley, then rolled his eyes toward the man. "Does he have to be here?"

"Yes," she said. "And he's quite right. I have other appointments."

"Then I'll get to the point," Ben said, standing between Mrs. Woodley and the TV. "I was hoping to persuade you and Mr. Woodley to drop any charges you were planning to file against your daughter-in-law."

Mrs. Woodley sipped her tea and said nothing.

"In fact, I thought you might want to help her out," Ben continued. "Maybe even get some of your high-powered attorneys to clear her of any other charges like fraud or forgery or whatever. And with all your money, I thought you'd want to help her out financially, too."

Hannah's mother-in-law glanced over her shoulder at the man.

"I think you've taken up enough of Mrs. Woodley's time," he said with a stony gaze at Ben.

"If she's put on trial, it's going to come out why she took the baby and left," Ben said. "You're aware that your son beat her, aren't you?"

Putting down her cup of tea, she squirmed a little on the sofa.

"Even if you drop the kidnapping charges, and she went on trial for fraud or something else, she'll still have to explain why she did what she did. It'll still come out that your late son was an abuser—in every sense of the word."

Ben unzipped the duffel bag, and within a moment, the man was right behind him. "It's just a video," Ben explained, showing him the cassette.

"Hannah doesn't know I'm here, Mrs. Woodley. In fact, she doesn't even know this video exists." He switched on to the little TV-VCR. "No one knows this exists except the three of us. The man who made it is dead. He was one of the young men who killed your son."

Her brow wrinkled, Mrs. Woodley frowned at him.

"I really don't want to show this to you," Ben said. "But I'll show it to the world if you insist on prosecuting Hannah. Anyone who sees it would have a good idea of what Hannah had to put up with. It explains why she took her baby and left."

Ben inserted the video and pressed "Play."

The image on the screen was dark and grainy. The footage had been filmed at night, through the window of a yacht. There were a man and a woman seated in the galley below deck. They were snorting lines of cocaine.

"It'll get pretty awful in a few minutes," Ben warned.

Hannah's mother-in-law leaned forward and numbly gazed at the image on the little TV.

"Do you recognize your son, Mrs. Woodley?" Ben asked.

At the memorial service for Kenneth Woodley II, Guy stood between his mother and grandmother. Each one held onto his hand, and occasionally Guy swung their arms back and forth.

The service was held in a park overlooking Lake Michigan. It was a gloomy day, and everyone was bundled up in coats and jackets. Hannah noticed several of Mrs. Woodley's country-club friends in their fur coats.

A minister read some prayers, and one of Mr. Woodley's golf buddies reminisced about his godson, Kenneth Junior.

Guy was understandably confused. He'd been told his father had died in a car accident a long time ago. And now everyone was saying he'd been killed in a boat explosion just two weeks before.

"I thought he was dead," Hannah ended up telling her son. "But I was wrong. Your father was alive, and he was in Seattle looking for us when he died."

The explanation seemed the best temporary answer to all his questions. She couldn't very well tell him that his father wasn't a good man, when everyone at this memorial service was extolling Kenneth's virtues. She would tell him the truth in a few years when he was old enough to understand.

If Guy was a bit baffled, so was she. The Woodleys gave no reason for suddenly wanting to help her in Seattle. They posted bond for her, and their attorneys worked overtime, smoothing things over and making deals so Hannah wouldn't face any criminal charges.

The Woodleys made some deals, too. They wanted to see their grandson at least twice a year, and they wanted Hannah to attend the memorial service for Kenneth. "I realize you had your reasons for taking Little Ken and running away," Mrs. Woodley had told her. "But I don't think it's necessary you share those reasons with anyone else. I see no point in treading on anyone's grave, do you?"

Hannah had agreed to cooperate. In a strange way, she felt it was important that Guy remember this memorial service for his father.

She had told her in-laws that she and Guy would be leaving after the service. That morning, they'd presented her with a car. It was Hannah's third automobile from the Woodleys. This one was a Saturn that Kenneth had never used. They'd already had the papers transferred to her name.

The memorial service was mercifully brief. A brunch a

the country club followed. Hannah used Guy being tired as an excuse to leave early.

A valet brought her new, secondhand car around to the front entrance while the two Mrs. Woodleys and Guy waited. Hannah loaded Guy into the backseat. He was already asleep by the time she got behind the wheel and buckled her seat belt.

"Do you have any idea where you'll be going?" Mrs. Woodley asked, leaning toward the car window.

Hannah shrugged. "Maybe Chicago. I'd like to look up some old friends. Then we'll probably end up back in Seattle."

"What about your friend, the Polish gentleman?"

Hannah squinted at her for a moment. "You mean Ben Podowski?"

Mrs. Woodley nodded. "Will you be visiting him?"

Hannah turned away. She felt herself tearing up a bit, and she didn't want to cry in front of her mother-in-law.

She'd never gotten a chance to see Ben. He'd left Seattle soon after her release. What with the police, the Woodleys, all the lawyers, and reporters, there had been no time to say good-bye.

Since then, they'd had a couple of brief, awkward phone conversations. Hannah couldn't get over the feeling that his wife was always within earshot. She figured she'd have to settle for e-mailing him on occasion, as his friend Rae had.

"I don't think I'll be seeing Mr. Podowski," Hannah told her mother-in-law.

"Well, if you talk to him," Mrs. Woodley said, "be sure to tell him how we've treated you. Make sure he knows we've held up our end of the bargain."

Hannah squinted at her. "What bargain? What are you talking about?"

Mrs. Woodley stared back at her through the window. "He didn't tell you about meeting with me at the hotel in Seattle?"

"Ben visited you?" Hannah murmured.

Mrs. Woodley shot a look at Guy sleeping in the back. Her voice dropped to a whisper. "You mean, you don't know anything about that horrible video?"

Hannah sighed. "Mrs. Woodley—*Mom*," she said. "I've seen a lot of horrible videos in the last few weeks. Which video are you talking about?"

His directions made finding the place easy.

The house was a modest two-story tan brick with green shutters and a chimney. Mr. and Mrs. Podowski lived on a quiet street in the quaint town of Croton, an hour away from New York City on the Metro North line.

Ben came to the door with his wife, Jennifer, right behind him.

Guy was thrilled to see Ben again. As he ran up and hugged him, Hannah kept having to remind Guy to be careful of Ben's cast.

"What happened to your face?" Guy asked him.

"I was trying to be like Indiana Jones," Ben explained. "I jumped through a window and a house blew up. Good thing you didn't see me a couple of weeks ago. I look a lot better now."

He smiled at Hannah, and she felt a little flutter in her heart. Even with his face slightly bruised, Ben's smile still did something to her.

It was awkward with his wife there. Ben introduced them. Jennifer was pretty, with auburn hair and pale green eyes. She wore khakis and a white tailored shirt. She smelled nice, too.

By comparison, Hannah thought she looked like a slob in her jeans and pullover. She'd been driving most of the morning. She felt a bit better after freshening up in their bathroom.

Jennifer served lunch: homemade split-pea soup and a spread of deli meats, cheeses, and bread. Sitting around the table, they chatted politely over their lunch. Hannah did most of the talking, sticking to the neutral topic of her and

Guy's travel plans. She hoped to be back in Seattle in time for Thanksgiving. She and Guy had put a lot of miles on that secondhand Saturn. "And Guy, what's your favorite new expression?" she asked.

He put down his glass of milk and looked at her inquisitively.

"Are . . . we . . ." Hannah prompted him.

"ARE WE THERE YET?" Guy cried out, delighted to get a laugh.

After lunch, Guy napped in the guest room. Jennifer started washing the dishes.

Ben said something about a family of deer that often came up to the house from the forest beyond their backyard. "I want to show Hannah around outside, honey," he said. "Maybe Bambi will pay us a visit."

Outside, it was cold and they could see their breath. Ben apologized for all the leaves on the lawn. The cast put a crimp in his yard work.

Huddled in her jacket, Hannah knew this was probably their only chance to talk by themselves. She figured Ben knew it too, as did his wife.

"So—how are things with you and Jennifer?" she asked, picking up a leaf from the ground. "She seems really nice, Ben."

He glanced at the forest and nodded. "Things are good, Hannah. I think we'll be okay. We're even talking about having a baby."

"Oh, well, that's great," she said. "It really is."

He smiled at her, and she wanted so much to hold him.

But Ben merely patted her arm. "I'm really glad you and Guy came here. Means a lot to me."

"Ben, I—I know about your visit to my mother-in-law back in Seattle. She told me about the tape with Kenneth eating up that girl."

"I hope I did all right," he said.

"All right?" She let out a sad laugh. "If you hadn't done that I—I don't know what would have happened to Guy and me. I'd probably still be in jail right now. You gave me my freedom again. I don't have to hide anymore. Guy and I can go anyplace we want. I'm no longer scared. And I owe that to you, Ben. Thank you."

He shrugged. "Oh, it was nothing."

"It was everything," she whispered. "I'll never forget what you did for me—and Guy."

His eyes teared up. "Well, I'll never forget you, Hannah."

She hugged him. Hannah knew his wife was probably watching from the kitchen window, but she hugged him anyway, holding him one last time.

An hour later, as they said good-bye in front of the house, it was Guy's turn to hug Ben. He threw his arms around Jennifer, too, and kissed her cheek. Hannah thanked them both, then helped Guy into the car.

Before climbing behind the wheel, she glanced back over the roof of the car and waved at Ben and his wife.

Jennifer was huddled behind him in the doorway, shivering and rubbing her arms from the cold. Ben waved back at Hannah. He smiled wistfully at her.

She felt her heart flutter again. Hannah had tears in her eyes as she ducked inside the car. "Seat belt fastened, honey?" she asked Guy, while buckling herself up.

"Yeah," he said. "Where are we going now, Mom?"

She wiped her eyes dry, then started up the engine. "We can go wherever we want, honey," she said, with a triumphant smile. "Anywhere we want."

"Let's go home, Mom," Guy said.

Hannah nodded. "I think that's a swell idea."

Filmography

The following is a guide to a few of the movies mentioned in this book. These films helped inspire this novel, and I pay homage to the following movies and their creators. If you want to see what my characters were talking about, check out these titles at your local video store. And be nice to the clerk.

ALL FALL DOWN (1962) Director: John Frankenheimer; Screenplay: William Inge, from the novel by James Leo Herlihy. Cast: Eva Marie Saint, Warren Beatty, Karl Malden. Available in VHS from M-G-M home video.

THE BIRDS (1963) Director: Alfred Hitchcock; Screenplay: Evan Hunter, from the short story by Daphne du Maurier. Cast: Tippi Hedren, Rod Taylor, Jessica Tandy, Suzanne Pleshette. Available in DVD and VHS from Universal Home Video.

BODY HEAT (1981) Director: Lawrence Kasdan; Screenplay: Lawrence Kasdan. Cast: William Hurt, Kathleen Turner, Richard Crenna, Mickey Rourke. Available on DVD and VHS from Warner Brothers Home Video.

BONJOUR TRISTESSE (1958) Director: Otto Preminger; Screenplay: Arthur Laurents, from the novel by Francoise Sagan. Cast: Deborah Kerr, David Niven, Jean Seberg. Currently not available for purchase on home video.

BUGSY (1991) Director: Barry Levinson; Screenplay:
James Toback, from the book by Dean Jennings, "We Only
Kill Each Other: The Life and Bad Times of Bugsy Siegel."
Cast: Warren Beatty and Annette Benning. Available on
DVD and VHS from Paramount Home Video.

CASINO (1995) Director: Martin Scorsese; Screenplay:
Nicholas Pileggi and Martin Scorsese, from the book by
Nicholas Pileggi. Cast: Robert de Niro, Sharon Stone, Joe
Pesci. Available on DVD and VHS from Universal Home
Video.

THE GODFATHER (1972) Director: Francis Ford Cop-
pola; Screenplay: Francis Ford Coppola and Mario Puzo,
from the novel by Mario Puzo. Cast: Marlon Brando, Al
Pacino, Diane Keaton, Alex Rocco (as the victim, Moe
Greene). Available on DVD and VHS from Paramount
Home Video.

LOOKING FOR MR. GOODBAR (1977) Director:
Richard Brooks; Screenplay: Richard Brooks, from the
novel by Judith Rossner. Cast: Diane Keaton, Tuesday Weld,
Richard Gere, Tom Berenger. Available on VHS from Paramount Home Video.

NIAGARA (1953) Director: Henry Hathaway; Screenplay:
Charles Brackett and Richard L. Breen, from a story by
Walter Reisch. Cast: Marilyn Monroe, Joseph Cotton, Jean
Peters. Available on DVD and VHS from 20th Century Fox
Home Video.

ON THE WATERFRONT (1954) Director: Elia Kazan;
Screenplay: Budd Schulberg, from a series of articles by
Malcolm Johnson. Cast: Marlon Brando, Eva Marie Saint,
Karl Malden, Available on DVD and VHS from Columbia
Home Video.

THE PARALLAX VIEW (1974) Director: Alan Pakula; Screenplay by David Giler, Lorenzo Semple, Jr., and Robert Towne (uncredited), from the novel by Loren Singer. Cast: Warren Beatty, Paula Prentiss, William Daniels. Available on DVD and VHS from Paramount Home Video.

PSYCHO (1960) Director: Alfred Hitchcock; Screenplay: Joseph Stefano, from the novel by Robert Bloch. Cast: Anthony Perkins, Janet Leigh, Vera Miles, John Gavin. Available on DVD and VHS from Universal Home Video.

ROSEMARY'S BABY (1968) Director: Roman Polanski; Screenplay: Roman Polanski, from the novel by Ira Levin. Cast: Mia Farrow, John Cassavetes, Ruth Gordon, Angela Dorian (also known as Victoria Vetri, as the victim, Terry Gionoffrio). Available on DVD and VHS from Paramount Home Video.

SHADOW OF A DOUBT (1943) Director: Alfred Hitchcock; Screenplay: Thornton Wilder, Alma Reville, and Sally Benson, from a story by Gordon McDonnell. Cast: Teresa Wright and Joseph Cotton. Available in DVD and VHS from Universal Home Video.

STRANGERS ON A TRAIN (1951) Director: Alfred Hitchcock; Screenplay: Raymond Chandler and Czenzi Ormende, from the novel by Patricia Highsmith. Cast: Farley Granger, Robert Walker, Laura Elliot (as the victim, Mariam Haines). Available on DVD and VHS from Warner Brothers Home Video.

VERTIGO (1958) Director: Alfred Hitchcock; Screenplay: Alec Coppel and Samuel Taylor, from the novel by Pierre Boileau and Thomas Narcejac. Cast: James Stewart, Kim Novak. Available on DVD and VHS from Universal Home Video.

WAIT UNTIL DARK (1967) Director: Terence Young; Screenplay: Robert and Jane-Howard Carrington, from the play by Frederick Knott. Cast: Audrey Hepburn, Alan Arkin, Richard Crenna, Jack Westen (as the victim, Carlino). Available on VHS from Warner Brothers Home Video.

Feel the Seduction of Pinnacle Horror

When Darkness Falls
Grab One of These
Pinnacle Horrors